Dora Russell

A Hidden Chain

Dora Russell

A Hidden Chain

ISBN/EAN: 9783741186820

Manufactured in Europe, USA, Canada, Australia, Japa

Cover: Foto ©Andreas Hilbeck / pixelio.de

Manufactured and distributed by brebook publishing software
(www.brebook.com)

Dora Russell

A Hidden Chain

ALPHA LIBRARY.

A Hidden Chain

By

Dora Russell.

Chicago and New York:
Rand, McNally & Company,
Publishers.

A HIDDEN CHAIN.

CHAPTER I.

COMING OF AGE.

"Well, Jeanie, and are you satisfied?"

"Oh! Kilmore, satisfied! I am more than satisfied; I am proud—so proud."

The speakers were a pair standing arm in arm on the green and wide-spreading sward of Kilmore Park, just as the soft August twilight began to steal around. The man was tall, middle-aged, somewhat rough-featured, but the expression of his face was dignified and kindly; while the woman was still in her lovely prime. She looked up at him as she spoke, and her eyes were shining with joy and love.

"He did not speak badly," said the man, smiling.

"He spoke beautifully, and he looked so handsome, Kilmore—like a young king."

"Well, my dear, as kings as a rule are not particularly handsome that is hardly a compliment—but the lad did very well."

They were talking of their only son, whose coming of age had just been celebrated by a banquet given to all the tenants of the great properties to which he was the heir. He was a lucky young man, seemingly, this Arthur Victor, Lord Clair, whose father and mother, the Earl and Countess of Kilmore, were thinking and speaking of with such tender pride. Lucky in his birth, in his good looks, and in all the future prospects of his life. And to-day he had been told this; he had realized perhaps for the first time as he stood the hero of the hour—bowing his thanks for all the good wishes showered on him, that he had his full share of the gifts which all men prize. The thought had flushed his face and brightened his eyes, and loosened his tongue, and he had returned thanks, after his health had been drunk, in such well-chosen, graceful words, that no wonder his mother's heart beat high with pride, and the Earl himself was not unmoved.

Lord Kilmore's own up-rearing had not been as his son's. Born the younger son of a younger son, he had been told early in life that he had his own way to make in the world, which way, as we all know, is not smoothly paved. Educated as a barrister, he had struggled on until his thirty-fifth year, when a sudden change came in his fortunes.

His uncle, the sixth Earl of Kilmore, a penurious old man of past seventy, who had taken very little notice of his brief-less nephew, and considered that "Arthur had not got on as he should," was after a short illness called upon to leave his wealth and his honors behind him. He was succeeded by his son, who was as reckless in his expenditure as his father had been careful. But an extraordinary fate in less than a month after his father's death overtook the young seventh Earl of Kilmore. He died of blood-poisoning, said to have been contracted by sleeping in a room newly painted. By this time the briefless barrister's father, who had been a country parson, also was dead, and to his own extreme surprise news came to the Temple which in a moment changed the poor barrister's whole career. He was the next heir to his cousin, the young Earl, who had died unmarried, and thus became eighth Earl of Kilmore, a rich man, with the bitter experiences of his poor and struggling youth stored usefully in his heart.

Among his troubles had been a hopeless, but strong attachment to the beautiful young daughter of a distin-guished judge. He had never spoken of love to Janet Gower, but none the less he had loved her, and this love had been silently and secretly returned. When he became Earl of Kilmore, and his great good fortune was known, the judge congratulated him, and invited him to dinner. But Lord Kilmore forgave the judge his former neglect and all other things. He married his Janet, and on the day of their son's coming of age had been married to her for twenty-three years. There was a little grave in the village church-yard of Kilmore, where their first-born slept, but this early loss and sorrow had but drawn closer the hearts of the husband and wife, and their second son, Arthur Victor, Lord Clair, was everything that their hearts desired.

"There is only one wish I have now," said Lady Kilmore, as they still strolled arm in arm through the fast darkening Park, listening smilingly to the strains of the band proceeding from a large tent where dancing had now commenced; "that Clair would think of Annette."

"My dear little woman, let these things alone," answered the Earl, laying his hand affectionately on his wife's; "Annette is a nice girl, and a pretty girl, and moreover is your niece; but unless Clair really fancies her, it is no use trying to put it into his head."

"I wonder if he is dancing the first dance with her?"

"Very likely; but dancing the first dance with her does not mean marrying her, you know. Take my advice, Jeanie, don't lead Annette to think of Clair, until he thinks of her; it might only end in unhappiness for the poor girl, and I am sure you would not like that?"

"No, indeed," said Lady Kilmore, quickly, and then she gave a little wistful sigh.

"And now, my dear," continued the Earl, "I think it is quite time that a man of my age should retire off the damp grass. Let us go in, Jeanie; Clair and Annette will tell us how the dance goes off, and," he added with a smile, "you can inquire then how many times they danced with each other."

Lady Kilmore smiled also, and together the husband and wife left the Park and entered the great mansion standing in its midst, each thinking still of the young heir, who at the present moment was enjoying himself to his heart's content.

For we may be sure that his good looks and his neat and well-chosen words had not been lost on several pretty maidens, who had formed part of the guests at the banquet. All the farmers' wives and daughters had been invited as well as themselves, to assemble to do honor to the coming of age of Lord Clair. One of the largest tenants was a certain Mr. Dighton, who farmed the land adjoining the Park, and lived in the pretty house standing on the green and fertile hillside, at whose foot gurgled the river Ayre over its pebbly bed.

There was a young Dighton, a keen sportsman and fisherman, and this Dick Dighton was on fairly intimate terms with Lord Clair. They fished together, and had known each other from boyhood, and Clair also knew more slightly the rest of the farmer's family. These consisted of a comely wife, and yet more comely daughter. All the Dightons were present both at the banquet and the ball, and Clair honored Mrs. Dighton by asking her to dance the first dance.

But the rosy-cheeked portly dame, who was sitting with her husband on one side and her daughter and another girl on the other, and her son standing in front, wisely but proudly shook her head.

"No, my lord," she said, "my dancing days are over; you must choose one of the young ones."

Upon hearing this speech of her mother's, Annie Dighton, who was really a pretty girl, blushed, cast down her blue eyes, and moved uneasily in her seat.

"Well, if you won't, Mrs. Dighton," answered the young lord, good-naturedly, "perhaps Miss Dighton will allow me to dance the first dance with her?"

Annie Dighton blushed more deeply still, but Mrs. Dighton replied promptly for her daughter.

"Annie will only be too proud, my lord," she said. "Get up, Annie, and dance with his lordship."

Upon this Annie rose smiling and fair, and timidly raised her eyes and looked at her future partner.

Another pair of eyes, but not timid ones, were at this moment also looking at the young lord with a grave, inquiring glance. These eyes, dark, languid, and beautiful, belonged to the other girl who was sitting at Mrs. Dighton's side, and whose remarkable personal appearance had already attracted the notice of Lord Clair. He looked at her again as Annie Dighton rose, but the girl neither blushed nor shrank from his admiring glance.

"Dighton," said Clair, as Annie took his arm, "come, get a partner, and you can be our vis-a-vis."

Upon this Dick Dighton, who was a heavily-built, rather good-looking young man, advanced somewhat loutishly to the dark-eyed girl by his mother's side.

"Miss Moore, will you dance with me?" he said.

"Yes, Mr. Richard," answered Miss Moore, with a half smile, and then she also rose.

"Let us go to the head of the tent," said Clair, "and I will make up a set there. Excuse me a moment, Miss Dighton, until I see about getting the others to dance, and tell the band to begin."

The young lord hurried away as he spoke, and ordered the band to commence to play, and busied himself about getting up the different sets for the first quadrille.

It was by his wish entirely that this dance had been got up, Lord and Lady Kilmore having allowed him to manage it all his own way. He had ordered and arranged the decorations of the tent, fixed the music—in fact, managed it all, assisted only by his cousin, Annette Gower.

And the whole thing was well done. It was a tenants' ball, but one or two young men of his own class were also present. But it was intended for the farmers' wives and daughters, and Clair was very anxious that everyone should enjoy themselves.

Thus he went round the tent getting up sets of dancers, and as he did so the three young people standing before Mr. and Mrs. Dighton were all watching his movements.

"What do you think of him when you see him near, Eva?" whispered Annie Dighton to the dark-eyed girl.

"He is pleasant looking," she answered.

"Oh! I think he is so handsome," continued Annie with enthusiasm. She was in fact so delighted and excited at the idea that she was going to dance the first dance with the young lord, that she could think of nothing else. Mrs. Dighton also felt very proud, and glanced around at her neighbors with a beaming face. She was pleased that they should see the honor which "her Annie" was about to receive; and in his somewhat thick-headed way her substantial husband also shared this feeling.

"John," she whispered in his ear, "do you see Mrs. Richards staring at our girls? My! they will be jealous about Lord Clair dancing first with our Annie."

John grunted his assent, but being a man of few words said nothing.

"Annie is the prettiest girl in the room by far," continued Mrs. Dighton.

"Bar Miss Moore," quoth John.

"Indeed, John, I don't think you need run down your own children like that. Miss Moore isn't bad looking, but look at Annie's color."

"Ask Dick's opinion," said John, with a grin.

But further discussion on the respective attractions of

really the two prettiest girls in the tent were cut short by Lord Clair's return.

"Now, Miss Dighton, I am ready at last," he said with a smile, offering his arm to Annie Dighton, who delightedly accepted it. "Come, Dighton, let us take our places!"

Upon this Dick Dighton offered his arm to Miss Moore also, and these two followed Lord Clair and Annie Dighton to the head of the tent, and dancing speedily commenced.

"Who is the young lady your brother is dancing with, Miss Dighton?" was the first question that Clair addressed to his pretty partner.

"Oh, that is Eva Moore," answered Annie, smiling. "She was at school with me, you know, two years ago, at South Kensington; at least I was at school," she added, "and Eva was a parlor boarder at the same time, and that's how I got to know her. Dick thinks her awfully handsome; do you?"

"Yes, she is handsome," answered Lord Clair.

"Yes, most people think her very handsome; she is staying with us, and she likes being in the country, and I hope she will stay a little longer. The way she came to stay was she wrote to me that she was traveling past here, and should like to see me again. I knew her very well at school, and we have often written to each other since. How I knew her so well was we used to sing together at school; she has a beautiful voice."

As the rustic little maiden chattered on in this artless fashion, to the delight of her mother, whose maternal eyes never left her, and who was inwardly congratulating herself on "how well Annie was getting on with his lordship," Clair's eyes again and again rested on the beautiful face opposite to him. It was of singular regularity, pale, dark-eyed and dark-haired, and with marked and delicate brows. She was tall, slender and graceful, and about her expression there was a certain indifference, a certain languor, as though she cared very little about what she was doing, and certainly did not care for the look of eager admiration on the face of her partner, young Dighton.

"Annie seems to be making up to the young lord at a fine rate," presently remarked young Dighton.

"Is she?" answered Miss Moore, with just a little touch of weariness in her tone.

Annie herself was perfectly delighted with the success of her dance and her conversation, and even after it was over and Lord Clair was conveying her back to her mother's side, when he said as they approached Mrs. Dighton:

"Will you introduce me to your friend, Miss Dighton?" Annie was still quite charmed.

"Yes, to be sure," she answered, and accordingly she presented Clair to Eva Moore.

"Eva, this is Lord Clair," she said, and as she spoke Eva bowed her head coldly and gracefully.

"Will you dance with me the next dance; it is a waltz?" said Clair.

Eva again simply bowed her head, and accepted the arm of the young lord as indifferently as she had accepted Dick Dighton's. But a moment or two later as they were dancing together a delicate flush rose to her fair cheeks, and her shining eyes grew less languid. She waltzed most gracefully, and Clair grew quite enthusiastic about her dancing.

"Pardon me," he said, in his frank, bright way, "but I little thought I should find such a partner as you this evening."

Eva Moore smiled.

"Why?" she asked.

"You dance so beautifully; you are so different—to everyone else."

Again Eva smiled. They were standing to take breath now, and Clair's admiration for his beautiful partner was increasing every moment.

"You will dance with me again?" he said, eagerly, drawing out his programme. "May I have the fourth and the sixth, and any more you will give me?"

"I must not monopolize you."

"I wish you would," answered Clair, smiling. "Well, at all events I will write your name down for the fourth and the sixth."

She did not refuse; it seemed rather to amuse her the young lord's sudden and eager admiration. She declined to dance except with him during the rest of the evening. She sat calmly by Mrs. Dighton's side, who began to fidget and feel uncomfortable when Lord Clair came a third time for her charge.

"I have been so impatient for this dance," he whispered as he led her away.

Eva made no response to this. She danced with him as gracefully and as calmly as she had done the first time, and then presently when they paused, she looked up with her dark eyes in his face.

"Who is that girl sitting there?" she said. "The little girl with small features?"

"Oh, that's my cousin, Annette Gower," answered Clair with a smile, and a somewhat conscious look. "I should have asked her to dance before—you make me forget everything, Miss Moore."

"I thought she was someone different to the rest," replied Miss Moore, calmly, "and I saw her looking at us while we were dancing."

The pretty, dark, small-featured face that Eva Moore had remarked on had been growing paler and paler during the last hour, as Annette Gower had noticed the evident devotion of her cousin to the beautiful stranger. Clair had indeed forgotten all about his cousin Annette until Eva had recalled her to his mind. But after the dance was over he went up to her.

"How are you enjoying yourself, Annette?" he said, kindly. "The flooring is splendid for dancing, isn't it? Will you dance with me the next dance? I have been so much engaged I haven't had time to ask you before."

The small, pretty face of his cousin flushed painfully as Clair thus addressed her.

"I have seen you dancing a great deal," she answered in a peculiarly sweet-toned voice.

"Oh, I must, you know; but come along, Annette, let us have a turn together now."

She rose and danced with him, and presently asked him the name of his former dark-eyed partner.

"Who is that handsome girl you have danced several times with, Clair?" she said.

"Oh, that is a Miss Moore, a stranger here, who is staying with the Dightons at Holly Hill; she waltzes splendidly, and seems a pleasant girl."

"She is very handsome."

"Yes, she's got wonderful eyes, hasn't she? Miss Dighton's rather pretty, too."

"But in a very different style."

"Yes, the typical fair milk-maid, isn't she? But come, let us take another turn or I shall think you have turned lazy."

So the cousins completed their dance together, and by

and by Mrs. Dighton saw with a beating heart Lord Clair once more approaching her little family group.

"He will surely ask Annie this time," thought the fond mother.

Annie, who had been dancing a good deal with their nearest country neighbors, and who was now sitting without a partner, hoped so too, and looked rather anxiously in Lord Clair's face as he drew near them.

But no; he went straight up to Eva Moore and said a few words in a low tone that Annie could not hear, and Eva at once rose and laid her hand lightly on his arm, and the two passed down the tent together.

Dick Dighton scowled when he saw this, and Mrs. Dighton could not suppress a sigh.

"His lordship is dancing a great deal with Miss Moore, Dick," she said, somewhat uneasily.

"A great deal too much," answered Dick, sullenly. "I say, mother, aren't you getting tired of this? I think it's quite time we were back home."

"I am getting a little tired, dear," answered Mrs. Dighton, meekly.

"Then I'll see about the trap. Annie, you had better not dance any more; we are going away directly."

In the meanwhile the two who were the real cause of this early home-going of the Dighton family had walked down the tent together, and when they came to the open entrance Clair suddenly perceived and pointed out the shining August moon overhead.

"Look what a splendid night it is, Miss Moore," he said. "Suppose we don't dance this time, but go out and breathe a little fresh air in the Park?"

"It would be refreshing, wouldn't it?" answered Eva. "The tent has got rather warm."

"Come, then; but you are not afraid of taking cold, are you?"

"Oh, no; I shall knot my handkerchief over my head."

She suited her action to her words, and tied her delicate little lace handkerchief under her dainty chin. Then, still arm in arm, they went into the moonlit Park, crossing the dewy grass until they came to one of the side paths, and there Eva suddenly stopped and looked around at the lovely silvered sylvan scene.

"How beautiful!" she exclaimed, stretching out her arms,

and drawing a long breath as though to inhale the fragrance of the night. "Can't you imagine the fairies holding their revels here, Lord Clair?"

Clair laughed a low, soft laugh.

"What music do they dance their reels to, I wonder, Miss Moore?" he said.

"To the sough of the wind through the trees, to the gurgle of the stream," she answered in a semi-theatrical tone. "Hark! don't you hear it—the sound of falling water?"

"That is the Ayre; the river runs past the end of the Park, you know."

"Listen—I hear it so plainly," went on Eva Moore, and she raised her head as she spoke, and the moonlight shone full on her beautiful face, on which Clair's eyes were fixed. "Ah—it is lovely here," she continued; "like a dream."

"I shall never forget to-night," said Clair in a low, almost passionate tone.

His voice and manner instantly changed her mood.

"Oh, yes, you will," she said, lightly.

"I am sure I will not," answered Clair.

But any further conversation between them was now interrupted. A sound of footsteps was heard, and a minute later the tall, rather slouching figure of Dick Dighton emerged into the moonlight.

"I have come to seek you, Miss Moore," he said somewhat roughly, as he approached them; "father and mother are waiting for you to go; they are in the trap already."

"What, so soon, Dighton?" exclaimed Clair. "Oh, you mustn't go yet."

"Yes, my lord, we must; so, Miss Moore, if you'll take my arm I'll take you to the trap."

"Nay, I must see Miss Moore safely back into Mrs. Dighton's charge," said Lord Clair, drawing Eva's arm through his, and thus he led her to where the family equipage of the Dightons was standing at the back of the tent ready to start.

Stout, comely Mrs. Dighton was already seated in the dog cart by her husband's side, and Annie Dighton was on the back seat. Mrs. Dighton felt unhappy in her mind, for she "didn't like young girls wandering about with gentlemen at this time o' night," she had confided to her husband. Therefore, when the three—Eva, Clair, and Dick Dighton—approached the dog-cart they were received in silence.

But Clair's pleasant, courteous manner soon made it all
right.

"I am sorry you are going so soon, Mrs. Dighton," he
said, "and thank you so much for coming. Good night;"
and then he shook hands with them all, and last with Eva
Moore.

CHAPTER II.

FIRE.

Clair returned to the tent after the Dightons' departure,
but somehow he had lost his interest in the dancing. And
presently he whispered to the agent of the property, who
was present, a pleasant-looking, middle-aged man, that he
wished he would take his place.

"Mr. Jepson, will you kindly see after everyone and keep
up the dancing," he said; "for I notice my cousin, Miss
Gower, looks rather tired, and I think I had better take her
home."

"I will do my best, my lord," answered Mr. Jepson, smilingly.

"That's all right, then; I'll just go away quietly. You
see it's been rather a long day."

"Certainly; but a most successful one, my lord."

The young lord just nodded his head pleasantly at the
implied compliment, and then went up to the bench on
which his cousin, Annette Gower, was seated.

"Annette, you look most awfully tired," he said, "so I
am going to take you home."

Annette rose quietly and took her cousin's arm, and they
left the tent together, and speedily found themselves at the
entrance of Kilmore Hall.

"Where is Lady Kilmore?" asked Clair of one of the
servants as they went in.

"Her ladyship is in the small drawing room, my lord,"
answered the footman.

"Come along, then, Annette, and let us tell her all about
the dance," said Clair, and Annette Gower followed him,

without speaking, up the wide staircase to a room fitted up with wonderful luxury and taste.

It was Lady Kilmore's favorite room, and opened by folding doors into the large drawing room beyond. But these were nearly always kept closed, and the smaller room had an entrance from the front corridor of its own. A little ante-room led to this, which, with his light, quick step, Clair soon crossed and then found himself in the presence of his father and mother.

They both looked up with a smile to greet him. Lord Kilmore was sitting in a divan chair reading the newspapers by the light of a shaded lamp near him; and Lady Kilmore, also in an easy chair, was reading a novel by the table which held the lamp.

"Well, Clair, and how has the dance gone off?" she asked, laying down her book.

"Oh, splendidly, mother; it was the greatest fun," he answered.

"And you enjoyed yourself?" went on Lady Kilmore, smilingly.

"Immensely! I asked the portly Mrs. Dighton for the first dance, but she handed me over to her daughter, and so Miss Dighton had the honor of opening the ball."

"And you, Annette," said Lady Kilmore, looking at her niece, who was standing a little behind Clair, "did you enjoy yourself, too?"

"Oh, yes, very much," replied the sweet-voiced Annette, but the instant Lady Kilmore heard her tone she knew all was not well with the girl.

"Well, my dears, I told Gregson to have dinner ready for you when you came in, so I think you had better go and get it now."

"I should rather have some tea, please, Aunt Jeanie," said Annette.

"Very well, dear, I will ring for it; and you, Clair?"

"Oh, I am going to have some dinner," answered Clair with a laugh; and a few moments later he left the room and Lady Kilmore's eyes followed him as he turned to go.

"How happy he looks," she said, addressing her husband.

"He is at a happy age," replied Lord Kilmore, with a good-natured little shrug.

Clair felt not only happy, but excited. After he had dined he went back to the small drawing room beside his

father and mother, and chatted on brightly until they
retired for the night. Annette Gower had said she was
tired, and had gone to bed early; and Clair, though he
talked about the dance, made no allusion to his principal
partner.

Then after his father and mother had left him he went up
to his smoking room, which was situated in one of the
wings of the house. He lit a cigarette, opened the window,
and leaned out, looking vaguely at the moonlight flooding
the grounds and the Park beyond. He scarcely knew how
long he leaned there. A white-robed vision seemed to be
floating before him, and a pair of dark, lustrous, languid
eyes shining into his.

Far away in the moonlight he could see the green hill,
which had suddenly become of intense interest to him; the
green hill on which stood Mr. Dighton's house, and where
at this moment he pictured to himself the beautiful girl
he had danced with, sleeping and smiling in her dreams.

Her image presented itself so vividly to his mind that
it seemed almost like reality.

"What a fool I am!" he cried, presently, starting up and
beginning to pace the room. Up and down he went in his
unrest, and then returned to the window; returned to gaze
at the moonlit distance; at the haze which was rising from
the low lands, and enveloping in white and misty shadows
the higher grounds.

Suddenly through this mist a red glow shone. Clair
looked at this curiously, and wondered what it could be.
Presently it was reflected against the sky and then a moment
or two later, as Clair gazed, a flame shot up through the
red glow, and he realized it was a fire. A fire at Holly Hill!
An exclamation burst from his lips, and then he quickly
hurried from the room. As he ran swiftly down the staircase he encountered one of the footmen putting out the
lights.

"There is a fire broken out at Holly Hill, I believe," he
said to the man. "I am going to see; give the alarm and tell
some of the men to follow me, as we may be able to give
some help."

"Yes, my lord," answered the man, and then Clair hurried on.

They were locking up for the night in the hall as he passed
through it, and in a few hasty words Clair told the news,

and then went out into the night. It was past twelve o'clock now, and the fire was distinctly visible outside. The red glow had become brighter, and as Clair ran down the avenue now and again a flame darted forth, each moment with increasing brilliancy.

Clair knew every inch of the road and went by the river path, which was the nearest, and as he approached the homestead on Holly Hill he saw that the whole building appeared to be on fire. Dense masses of smoke were rising, lit by the lurid light of the flames, and he heard voices calling, and saw dusky figures running hither and thither.

In another moment he had reached the garden gate in front of the house, and in the garden he perceived an affrighted group of several women.

A moment later he was among them, and Annie Dighton recognized him. She was clinging to her mother, but when she saw Clair she ran toward him.

"Oh! Lord Clair!" she cried in a voice broken with tears, "isn't this dreadful! Eva Moore is still in the house and we cannot get to her! Dick has tried twice and is terribly burned, poor fellow, with trying—he is lying there—but the staircase is on fire. Oh! what shall we do?" And the poor girl wrung her hands in despair.

"Which is her room?" asked Clair, hoarsely and briefly.

"That—there, look!" said Annie, eagerly seizing him by the arm and pointing to a room in the second story of the house. "She's been at the window, poor thing, and called for help, but what—what can we do?"

"Is there no ladder? I will go up," said Clair, looking around.

Then half a dozen voices called out there was a ladder, but it would not nearly reach the second story.

"Bring a cart!" cried Clair, "that will help with the height, and for the rest I think I can scramble up."

The farm servants ran to obey the young lord, who in the meantime had called for and obtained a rope, which he fastened round his waist.

"If she is in her senses," he said to Annie Dighton, who was following him, "I can throw the rope to her, and then scramble in at the window if she has strength to hold it tight. Ah! there she is at the window—she sees us, and here comes the cart."

Not a moment was now lost; the cart was drawn up

to the burning house by willing hands, and the one ladder available apparently was placed in it and erected. It did not yet nearly reach the story where the woman's form was to be seen bending eagerly out of the open window, but still the cart, of course, raised it considerably.

"Now hold the ladder steadily and fast," said Clair to two of the young farm servants who had brought the cart round, and were now in it after raising the ladder. "Remember the lady's life depends on you."

And as he said this he also sprang into the cart, and the next moment commenced ascending the ladder with swift, sure footsteps.

It was a terrible moment, for when he reached the topmost rung many feet still parted him from the window from which bent the white face of Eva Moore. But Clair was wonderfully calm.

"I will throw you the rope, Miss Moore," he called; "try to catch it and fasten it to some heavy piece of furniture, and I will scramble up by it, and then I can let you down to the ladder."

"If you throw it, I will try," answered Eva Moore's voice, which was distinctly heard even amid the roar and the crackle of the flames.

Then Clair threw the rope up which he had bound round his waist and Eva bent eagerly forward with bare outstretched arms to catch it, but missed it by a hair's breadth.

"We must try again," cried Clair.

Again he threw it up, and again the poor girl failed to seize the one frail chance to save her life. But Clair was still calm.

"Try once more," he said, and this time she caught the rope, and a ringing cheer from below at once told this.

"Now fasten it securely around something," called Clair.

"I can hold it," answered Eva; "there is no time to be lost. The room is on fire!"

And this actually was so. Flames were licking the door with their fierce tongues, and the heat and smoke was terrible. But with an extraordinary effort of courage and calmness Eva Moore rolled the rope which she held round one of her white arms and held fast by the window frame.

"It is steady now," she said; "can you struggle up by it?"

Clair was young, lithe and active, and with the aid of the

rope he scrambled up to the open window, and there Eva
Moore caught him by the arm and helped him in.

"Thank God! I hope I can save you now," said Clair,
breathlessly.

She did not speak; she slightly shuddered, for the strain
upon her arm during Clair's ascent had been terrible.

"Come, you must not lose courage now," he said, taking
her hand.

Again she shuddered and glanced back at the flaming
door.

"It is only a chance," she faltered, "but you have risked
your life for mine, Lord Clair."

CHAPTER III.

SUNNY BROW.

Even in this hour of extreme danger these words of Eva
Moore's sent a thrill through the young lord's heart.

"I would risk a hundred lives," he answered; "but we
have not a moment to lose. See, let me wrap you in this."

And as he spoke he caught a woolen rug from the bed,
which was not yet alight, and put it round Eva's form, who
was just as she had started from her sleep, when she had
been awakened by the smell of fire, which had burned the
staircase leading to her room before doing any great damage to the rest of the house.

Thus the other inmates had escaped, though only with
their lives, and on learning that Eva Moore was confined
in her room Dick Dighton had made two desperate efforts
to rescue her by ascending the burning staircase; and during the second of these efforts the staircase had fallen in,
and young Dighton had been dangerously injured.

He was lying in the garden helpless, covered with a
blanket, when Clair arrived on the scene, and had watched
with the rest the young man's gallant attempt to save the
imprisoned girl. So far Clair had succeeded; he at all
events had reached her, but whether he could save her yet
remained a matter of painful doubt. But he kept his pres-

ence of mind, and after wrapping the rug around Eva proceeded to fasten the rope he had brought with him tightly around her waist.

"It is the one chance," he said, quickly and decidedly; "You can't reach the ladder without it. I will lower you down by it, and you must try not to be afraid, and when once you reach the ladder you are safe."

"And you?" asked Eva, in a trembling voice.

"We must think of you first; after you are all right some of the fellows will throw me the rope up again, and I can swing myself down to the ladder by it. Come, Miss Moore, take courage; mount on the window sill, and I will steadily lower you down by the rope until your feet rest on the ladder."

Then again he tried the rope fastened round Eva's slender waist, to see that it was quite safely secured.

"It is all right," he said. "Now let me help you out of the window; it will only be a few moments, and then you will be safe."

Eva looked from the window and shuddered, but she saw it was the one chance. More men were in the cart below, now, and one young fellow had partly ascended the ladder so as to assist the lady in reaching it after her perilous descent.

"That is right," cried Clair, from the window, to the young man on the ladder; "come up as high as you can, and take hold of the lady as soon as she nears the ladder and guide her to it. Now, Miss Moore, take courage; do not be afraid."

He raised her as he spoke, and with the rope firmly twisted round his own arm, and securely attached to her, he gently let her down from the window, and for a moment or two she dangled in mid-air.

Those below in the cart and the garden held their breath, and Eva clung with frantic hands to the rope, and closed her eyes in her great terror. But it did not last long; the young man on the ladder soon caught her bare white feet, and guided them to the topmost rung. Then he held her fast, and Eva began to descend the ladder assisted by the young man who was behind her. But when she was half way down she suddenly stopped. The rope round her waist had slightly jerked and this recalled her mind from her own peril to that of her preserver's.

"Unfasten the rope round me now," she said to the young man who was holding her. "We must leave it with Lord Clair; it is his only chance; the room is on fire and he must escape at once."

The man hesitated a moment, but he saw the truth of what Eva Moore had said, and so stood still, and contrived to unfasten the rope round Eva's waist, calling up at the same time to Lord Clair to hold it fast.

"The lady is safe now, sir," he said. "I've undone the rope, and you must let yourself down by it."

Thus the rope was left in Clair's hands, who, however, watched Eva Moore safely in the cart below before he thought of his own peril. Then he turned and looked round for some heavy piece of furniture to which to attach the rope so as to swing himself down by it. Half blinded by the smoke and heat he fastened it to the small brass bed where Eva had been sleeping when she awoke to her danger. This bed he dragged nearer the window, and then looking out saw that the young man who had helped Eva was again ascending the ladder in the cart.

"She's safe on the ground, sir," he called up. "Now swing yourself down and I'll catch hold of you."

Clair promptly followed this advice. He was brave and daring, but to feel yourself hanging in the air, with considerable doubt as to whether the little brass bedstead would stand the strain of the rope was not a pleasant experience; and he certainly felt a thrill of pleasure when he felt his legs grasped by the stalwart hands of the young man on the ladder. Then he knew he was all right, and did not need the cheers from below to tell him so. In a few moments more he was in the cart, and the next had leaped to the ground.

There his hand was grasped first by the farmer, Mr. Dighton, who had tears in his honest eyes.

"God bless you, my lord," he said, "for what you have done in saving the poor lass; why, you had more sense than any of us."

"I am very happy to have been of some use, Mr. Dighton," said Clair, heartily returning the farmer's hand-shake; and then he looked round for Eva Moore, and as he did so a shrouded figure advanced toward him.

"Thank you for my life, Lord Clair," said Eva's voice, and for a moment she placed her hand in his.

"I am but too happy——" he faltered, but the next moment both his hands were seized, one by Mrs. Dighton and the other by her daughter Annie.

"Oh, my lord!" cried Mrs. Dighton, tearfully, "I don't know how to thank you—you know my poor Dick tried—he failed, poor fellow, but that wasn't his fault, and now but for you this poor girl would have been burned alive!"

"I shall never forget it! It was noble," sobbed Annie, and then she turned and kissed again Eva Moore's pale face.

But Eva said nothing more. She stood wrapped in the rug that Clair had placed round her in the burning room, and amid all the exclamations and the tears, she only was silent, and her eyes were dry.

"Well, thank God, the horses and the cows are safe, poor beasts," ejaculated the farmer, who had found time to look after his live stock.

"But oh! to think of all my things!" wept Mrs. Dighton. "My lord, the most of the furniture—the beds and that, were my mother's, and to think that they are all gone! And we had just re-covered the drawing-room chairs; and my gowns and my velvet mantle—oh, I have nothing left!"

"Come, mother, you have the children, and no lives are lost," said the sturdy farmer, laying his hand consolingly on his wife's broad shoulder.

"Yes, that's true, John," answered poor Mrs. Dighton, drying her eyes; "but still to lose everything—all the linen, and I had such a good stock; and—and there's poor Dick!"

And again Mrs. Dighton wept aloud.

"Where is your son?" asked Clair, kindly. "I hope he's not seriously hurt."

"He's—lying propped up against the arbor," sobbed Mrs. Dighton. "We've sent for Dr. Davidson, and one of the cottagers gave me a blanket to cover him."

"I will go and speak to him," said Clair, and accordingly he went in the direction of the arbor, which was at one side of the garden. He found young Dighton propped up as his mother said against the trellis work of the arbor.

"I am sorry you are hurt, Dighton," said Clair, bending down and addressing the prostrate young man. "I hope you are not suffering much pain?"

A half groan broke from Dick Dighton's lips.

"I'm burned a good deal I'm afraid," he answered; "but —you saved Miss Moore?"

"I helped at least; but you did far more than I did. But you mustn't lie here, Dighton. Ah, I see one of our people over there, and I'll send him back to the Hall for a carriage, and the sooner you get there the better. My father and mother will, I am sure, be most happy to give you all shelter."

"It is very kind of you, my lord."

"Not at all; I will send the servant for the carriage and then come back to you."

And as he spoke Clair beckoned to the servant from the Hall and gave him directions.

"Tell the coachman to send two close carriages," he said; then he went back to where Mrs. Dighton and Annie and Eva were standing.

But the group had now received several additions. These consisted of the wife and two daughters of a neighboring farmer who having heard of the Dightons' misfortunes had come to offer them shelter and assistance. It was the very Mrs. Richards of Sunny Brow whom Mrs. Dighton had thought was jealous of Annie at the dance who had now come on this neighborly mission.

"You must just all come home with us, Mrs. Dighton," she was urging as Clair approached the group, "and I and the girls will do the best we can for you. You must take pot-luck."

"Thank you kindly," wept poor Mrs. Dighton, "but there's so many of us."

"Never mind; you'll have a roof over your heads at Sunny Brow anyhow."

At this moment Clair spoke.

"Forgive me interrupting you," he said, "but I have just been telling your son, Mrs. Dighton, that I am sure if you will take shelter at the Hall my father and mother will be very much pleased."

"Oh! I could not think of intruding, my lord," answered Mrs. Dighton; "here is Mrs. Richards kind enough to offer to give us shelter for the night."

"At all events let your son come with me. He will need a good deal of care, and I have ordered two carriages to come from the Hall, one for him and the other I hope you will use."

"Indeed, you're most good, my lord, more than good," said Mrs. Dighton, much pleased. "As I've been telling Mrs. Richards, I'm sure I do not know how to thank you."

"It was so brave!" murmured one of the Miss Richards.

"So noble!" whispered the other.

"Heroic!" sighed Annie Dighton.

But no word came from the shrouded figure on which Clair's eyes were fixed.

Clair smiled and bowed in answer to the compliments of the other young ladies, but as he did so a new excitement arose.

This was at the late arrival of the fire-engine that had been sent for to the nearest town. The horses came galloping up the hill to the house; the men in brass helmets on the engine shouting their orders, and water from the river was soon brought to bear upon the burning house. Mrs. Dighton's hopes rose as she saw the effect of the excellent supply of water.

"It mayn't have reached the linen-press," she said, hopefully.

"Are you cold? You are not frightened now, when you were so brave before," Clair took the opportunity of saying in a low tone to Eva Moore when everyone else was looking at the fire-engine and the firemen.

"I am a little cold," she answered, and again she slightly shivered, which faint movement Clair had noticed before. But the truth was that her arm round which she had wrapped the rope to help Clair into the window of the burning room was paining her severely. The delicate white flesh had been absolutely cut in places by the rough hemp.

"The carriages will be here directly and then you will get shelter and rest," went on Clair. "I hope Mrs. Dighton will consent for you all to go to the Hall."

"You are very kind, Lord Clair."

One of the Miss Richards looked round, and seeing the young lord talking to Miss Moore, made a step backwards and joined in the conversation. She remarked on the utility of fire-engines, and the utility of firemen. She had never spoken to Lord Clair before, and she was very glad now to have the opportunity of doing so. Thus as far as she could she made herself very agreeable.

It never struck her that Clair would have much preferred to talk to Eva alone. And presently her sister joined them, and she was equally talkative. They were dark, sensible-looking, but not pretty girls, with a fair amount of brains. Their mother, who was an excellent manager of a household, now bustled up.

"Well, my dears," she said, "Mrs. Dighton and I have settled it all. Dr. Davidson is here and poor Dick Dighton is worse than we thought. So, my lord," and she addressed Clair, "the doctor thinks that as you so kindly offered to take him in that he had better be taken to the Hall, as, of course, at Sunny Brow we shall be very short of room."

"That is much the best plan, and I shall see about it at once," answered Clair. "And Miss Dighton and Miss Moore had better come too."

"No, my lord, Mrs. Dighton and I think not," said Mrs. Richards in her decided way. "You see Mrs. Dighton does not like to be separated from poor Dick when he is so bad, so if your lordship and her ladyship will give her house-room also for a day or so, I will take charge of the girls. My girls, I know, will not mind a pinch to help neighbors, and we'll be very glad to have them at Sunny Brow."

Thus it was settled. Poor Dick Dighton's arm was found to be broken by the doctor, besides the severe burns he was suffering from, therefore he, Mrs. Dighton and the doctor started together in one of the carriages which had arrived from the Hall.

In the other Mrs. Richards, her two daughters, Annie Dighton, and Eva Moore, were conveyed to Sunny Brow, which was the neighboring farm to Holly Hill, the river Ayre dividing the lands.

Clair handed in the party for Sunny Brow, took off his cap and bade them good-night. He then drove on the box-seat of the other carriage to the Hall, where the party were expected, as the news of the fire at Holly Hill had now reached the ears of Lord and Lady Kilmore, who had been aroused by the unusual stir in the house, and had rung their bell to inquire the cause.

Then they heard of the fire, and Clair's ascent into the burning house, and Lady Kilmore rose tremblingly, and when Clair and the others arrived from Holly Hill, his mother was up waiting to receive him. He ran up-stairs when he heard this, and Lady Kilmore, pale, excited, and frightened clasped him in her arms.

"Clair!" she cried, "my dear, dear Clair, how could you run such a dreadful risk?"

"There wasn't much risk, mother," he answered, as he affectionately kissed her; "but who has been telling you anything?"

"James brought word that you had risked your life to save someone. Oh, my dear, fancy if anything had happened to you!"

"That's all right; but, mother, something very bad did happen to young Dighton, and I have brought him and his mother here and the doctor, as there was no place to put him at Holly Hill, and I knew you would take him in."

"Of course, dearest. Ring up the housekeeper if she is not up, and tell her to prepare rooms and beds for them, and do everything to make them comfortable. Is the young man much hurt?"

"Badly burned and his arm broken, poor fellow. But I must go and see after him. I am sorry they disturbed you, mother."

"My darling!" she whispered, and again she laid her soft smooth cheek against his. Then Clair hurried away and had an interview with the housekeeper and saw that everything was done to make his unexpected guests comfortable for the night.

Mrs. Dighton had a room next her son's; and the doctor, after attending to his patient, was accommodated with a bedroom.

In the meanwhile at Sunny Brow the Richards family were doing their best also for their neighbors. Jane and Fanny Richards gave up their room to Annie Dighton and Eva Moore and retired to an attic where they spent this first night without any grumbling or complaining as to the lack of their usual comforts. But it is astonishing how soon poor human nature misses these and grudges them to others. We do kindly and generous things very often on the spur of the moment which we afterwards repent of. It is when the shoe pinches that we dislike wearing it.

The Misses Richards found in the morning that everything they wanted was down-stairs in their usual bedroom. It was inconvenient to say the least of it, and Fanny remarked to Jane:

"It's really an awful bother having those girls there."

"Well, we'll just have to do as best we can. I suppose they won't stay long," answered Jane.

Nevertheless at breakfast time they were both very agreeable to their young guests, and at Annie Dighton's request lent some necessary garments to Eva Moore, whose whole wardrobe was lost. They also lent her a pretty white morning gown, and when breakfast was over took her over the place, which was an old-fashioned picturesque farm-house, the porch in front being covered with roses and jasmine. Annie Dighton felt anxious about her brother Dick, and wondered if her father or mother would come to tell her how he was going on. But Mr. Dighton, who had remained at Holly Hill during the night looking after his property, was too busy, and Mrs. Dighton was unable to leave her son.

But about twelve o'clock, while Annie and Eva were still strolling amid the old-fashioned garden and admiring the old-fashioned flowers, a visitor appeared at the gate, which was no other than Lord Clair.

"Oh! Eva, here is Lord Clair," said Annie in a low fluttering tone, laying her hand on Eva's arm.

Eva winced, for her arm was still very tender where the rope had hurt it.

"Oh! I'm so sorry. I forgot about your arm, dear," cried Annie, repentantly.

"It's no matter," smiled Eva, and the smile still lingered on her face when she held out her hand to welcome Lord Clair.

"Good morning," he said, taking off his cap and bowing his good-looking head; "I am very happy to see that you are well enough to be out this morning."

She was bare-headed, standing in the sunlight with her pure cream-like skin, and her dark shining eyes raised to the young lord's face.

"Oh, but I don't think she is very well, Lord Clair," said Annie, whose blushes were bathing the blooming face for which her mother had so great an admiration. "Her arm is awfully hurt."

"Your arm hurt?" asked Clair, quickly. "How is that?"

A soft wave of color rose to Eva's face.

"It was chafed by the rope, that is all," she answered.

"By the rope?" repeated Clair. "How did it touch your arm? It was round your waist."

"It was before," said Eva; "but do not let us speak of it, I want to forget it."

"I shall never forget it," answered Clair, earnestly.

"Nor I. But let us talk of something else," and Eva turned away her head as if the subject was painful.

"And Dick, Lord Clair?" asked Annie. "How is he?"

"I have seen him this morning, and he is doing fairly well, and is fairly cheerful; but he had a restless night. Dr. Davidson stayed at the Hall all night, you know, and saw your brother, of course, this morning. He thinks your brother will be all right presently, but it will take a little time."

"Poor Dick!" sighed Annie.

"Your mother sent her love, and will come and see you when she can; but had you not better go to the Hall to see her?"

"You are very good; but I hardly like," blushed Annie.

"Why not? If you and Miss Moore will go now I will escort you there?" went on Clair.

Eva gave a low laugh.

"Annie must go alone," she said, "for I am in the unhappy condition of having nothing to wear."

"You do not mean to say—"

"Everything I have on is borrowed; when you came I was just going to write to town for an outfit, and when it arrives I must leave Sunny Brow, for it must be very inconvenient to Mrs. Richards and her daughters to have a stranger like me here."

"Oh, no, Eva, I am sure it is not," said Annie.

"My dear, I know the world a little better than you do. You are an old friend of the Richards, but to have me thrown on their hands without rhyme or reason, except neighborly charity, is a very different thing. So as soon as ever I receive my garments from town I will go."

"I wonder if all our things are really burnt?" said Annie, a little wistfully.

"Suppose we go across to Holly Hill and see," answered Clair, quickly. "I hope you have not lost everything, Miss Moore, but at all events we had better learn."

"Well, I should like to know, certainly," smiled Eva; "I had one or two rings I should not like to lose, but the same reason that I told you of before, Lord Clair, prevents my going—I have no hat!"

"Oh, either Jane or Fannie Richards will lend you one I am sure," said Annie, eagerly; "I'll run in and ask them if you like."

"Will you? That's a good girl; and a little handkerchief or scarf to knot round my neck if you can get one."

"I'll go at once, Eva;" and as she spoke Annie Dighton hurried away toward the house, and left Eva Moore and Clair standing together in the sunny garden.

He felt embarrassed, but after a moment's silence Eva raised her dark eyes and looked in his face.

"It is very pleasant and peaceful here, isn't it?" she said.

"Oh, yes—about your arm, Miss Moore? Was it hurt when you helped me into the window?"

"Yes. I had not time to tie the rope to anything, so I wrapped it round my arm, and, of course, the strain—oh, don't look so horrified, it was a stupid thing to do."

"And it was I who hurt you—I—"

"Please do not worry about it; the pain is nearly gone," interrupted Eva. "See, it is nothing dreadful," and as she spoke she pushed back the sleeve of her white gown and bared an arm lovely alike in form and coloring, except where the cruel rope had marred its beauty.

Clair gave an exclamation of horror when he saw the marks.

"How dreadful! I did this, and you never cried out or uttered a word," he said, taking hold of her slender wrist.

Again Eva laughed her low, rather peculiar laugh.

"I have borne worse pain than that without a cry," she said. "But," she added, and she pulled down her sleeve as she spoke, "here comes Annie with the hat, so let us drop the arm."

CHAPTER IV.

ACROSS THE RIVER.

Annie Dighton returned not only with a large, coquettish-looking hat, but a long black lace scarf, which Eva rolled round her white throat, and which admirably became her. Then she put on the hat.

"Now am I presentable to walk abroad?" she said, looking smilingly first at Annie and then at Clair.

"You look awfully well in the hat," cried Annie.

Clair said nothing, but his gray eyes expressed much more than many words.

"She is lovely, she is perfect," he was thinking, and perhaps Eva guessed something of his thoughts, for she turned away.

"Come, let us go," she said. "I wonder," she continued, stooping down and gathering a crimson carnation from one of the borders by which they were standing, "if I might steal a flower?"

She plucked it and placed it in the folds of the black lace round her throat, asking Annie for a pin to fasten it there.

"Do you like flowers?" asked Clair, eagerly.

"No, I don't like them," she answered, smiling, "I love them."

"May I bring you some then?" said Clair.

"Never ask a woman that if you wish her to refuse, Lord Clair."

"But I do not wish her to refuse," he answered, smilingly also. "Have I permission then?"

"Yes; but we are wasting our time. Come, Annie, let us go and see if the flames have spared any of our belongings. Which way do we turn after we leave here?"

"We go straight down the hill through the corn fields until we come to the bridge across the Ayre," said Clair. "Were you ever in this part of the country before, Miss Moore?"

"Never."

"And you like country life?"

"For a change, yes; we all like change don't you think?"

"Not in everything, surely?"

"Yes, I believe in everything," said Eva, throwing back her head with a little laugh; "in dress, in love, in scenery, in friends—I hope I am not shocking you, Lord Clair?"

"Yes, I am very much shocked, only I am sure you do not mean what you say?"

"How can you tell?" asked Eva, looking at him straight.

"Because I judge by—your appearance."

"Oh! but appearances are very deceitful."

By this time they had reached the garden gate, which Clair opened, and from thence proceeded to a narrow walk by the side of the farmer's corn fields, in which the ripe and yellow grain stood bound in sheaves ready to be garnered. It was a bright and cheery day, the blue sky flecked with white clouds, and a light fresh wind blowing from the east. It stirred the yellow sheaves; it blew in the faces of the three young people descending the corn-clad hill, at the foot of which the river Ayre swept on sparkling in the sun. A one-arched stone bridge spanned the stream, on the parapet of which a rustic fisherman was seated rod in hand, who, however, hastily decamped at the sight of the young lord, as the water was preserved.

"There is one of those rascally poachers," said Clair, as the fisherman hastily disappeared at the other end of the bridge. "Are you fond of fishing, Miss Moore?"

"I never tried."

"I am very fond of it," said Annie Dighton, who felt herself being somewhat neglected.

"We must teach Miss Moore to fish, Miss Dighton," answered Clair.

"Where, when and how?" asked Eva with a laugh.

"To-day, to-morrow, any time," retorted Clair, also with a laugh.

Eva shook her head.

"No, it will be useless," she said; "my stay here will be very brief, and after that—"

"Where do you go?" asked Clair, eagerly.

"I can scarcely tell you; I wander about, hither and thither."

"But you have a settled home?"

"I live mostly in town; but I have no settled home."

Clair felt he could ask no more questions, but he was very much disappointed at the answers he had received. Miss Moore had certainly given him no encouragement regarding her future plans; but with a certain fitful coquettishness of her nature after walking on a few steps in silence Eva Moore suddenly stopped when just about the middle of the arch of the bridge, and leaned against the moss-grown parapet, fixing her dark eyes on the deep, gurgling stream below.

"I like the sound of the water," she said; "do you remember we talked of it last evening, Lord Clair, before—"

"Yes, before your great danger," answered Clair, now also leaning his arms on the parapet by her side.

"Before you saved my life," said Eva in a low tone, still with her eyes fixed on the water.

Clair did not speak for a moment or two. The river ran on; the wind eddied around the green hill opposite, on which stood the blackened homestead of Holly Hill, and Annie Dighton was looking over the opposite side of the parapet of the bridge; and a strong wave of feeling, an emotion he could not subdue, suddenly swept through the young man's heart.

"You say I saved your life," he said, "and yet—"

"Yes," answered Eva, still without raising her head as he paused.

"And yet just now you spoke as if you did not wish to see me again?"

"I did not mean that," said Eva, without lifting her eyes from the gurgling water; "I meant that in all likelihood we shall never meet again after I go from here."

"But why? If I knew where you were we should certainly meet."

Then Eva did look round, and fixed her wonderful eyes on the young lord's face.

"You think so to-day," she said, smiling; "we had a romantic first meeting. I am indebted to you for what most people think a great boon—life. The scene is pretty, and you are young! In a month you will have forgotten my existence!"

"You are perfectly and utterly mistaken. I shall never forget your existence—nor you—nor the circumstances when I was happy enough to be of use to you; and therefore I wish—"

"To carry on an acquaintance that can do you no good? Remember, I warn you!" And again she smiled.

"For good or evil then, I take the risk," said Clair, ardently. "Will you promise when you go from here to let me know where I shall see you again?"

For a moment Eva did not speak. Her lustrous eyes fell; her white dark fringed eyelids drooped, she gave a little quivering sigh.

"Will you promise?" urged Clair.

"Yes," she answered, and then she turned and looked at Annie Dighton.

"Annie!" she cried. "Come, let us go on; we are wasting the time."

"You have made me very happy," whispered Lord Clair, which remark Eva however entirely ignored.

But as they walked up the hill toward the homestead she talked brightly, almost gaily. Annie Dighton felt, on the other hand, rather depressed. She was not a clever girl, but she had sense enough to see that Lord Clair took no notice of her, except from politeness, while he so evidently admired Eva Moore.

"And I introduced them," reflected Annie, and she repressed a sigh.

At length they reached the homestead, and stood in front of the blackened house. The fire was now entirely extinguished, but some of the firemen and one or two rural policemen were engaged in removing the debris. The roof had fallen in at the part of the house where Eva Moore's room had been situated, and when she saw this she gave a little shudder.

Then she looked at Lord Clair, and their eyes met. They were both thinking "a few minutes later!" and involuntarily he bent nearer to her.

"Thank God!" he murmured.

"That you were in time?" said Eva, as if she read his thoughts.

"Yes."

But at this moment their presence was perceived by Mr. Dighton, the farmer, who had spent the night at Holly Hill, sleeping for a short time in one of the laborer's cottages. Now he was busy looking after the welfare of his live stock, which had mercifully been all saved.

But when he saw Lord Clair, his daughter and Eva Moore standing at the garden gate, he hurried out of his fold-yard to meet them.

"Well, my lord, after all it's not so bad as it might have been," he said, heartily shaking the hand Clair held out to greet him. "And how are you, my dears?"

And he kissed his daughter and shook Eva's hand.

"We have come to see if the flames have left us anything to put on, Mr. Dighton," said Eva, smiling.

The farmer looked round at the house and shook his head.

"It's a bad business for you, my dear, I'm afraid," he said. "You see the roof fell in over your room, and but for you, my lord—"

"Of course everything is gone then?" interrupted Eva, hastily, as the farmer paused.

"All your dresses and fal-lals and the chairs and everything are clean gone; but one of the firemen picked up this ring among the rubbish." And the farmer produced a diamond ring, the gold of which was somewhat blackened, from his pocket. "Is it yours? There's a name engraved inside—Eva Temple, I think it is."

A sudden flush rose on Eva's creamlike skin.

"It's mine," she said, quickly, taking the ring from Mr. Dighton's hand. "Thank you, Mr. Dighton."

"Was Temple your mother's name then?" asked the farmer.

For a moment she hesitated; then without looking up she replied in a monosyllable:

"Yes," she said, and Lord Clair wondered why she blushed so deeply at her mother's name.

CHAPTER V.

A POSIE.

"Temple! Oh! that's a pretty name," exclaimed Annie Dighton, who had also noticed with surprise the deep and sudden blush which had spread over Eva's face.

"Do you think so?" she answered, coldly, and she put the ring in the pocket of her dress as she spoke, and turned away.

And during the rest of their stay at the homestead she was very silent. Mr. Dighton would not allow them to go very near or enter the parts of the house that were comparatively uninjured, as he said it was unsafe, until the whole building had been properly examined. Therefore they gained nothing by their visit except the diamond ring, which seemed to have had a strangely depressing influence on Eva Moore. Presently the farmer pulled out his great silver watch and said it was getting on to one o'clock."

"Oh! Eva, and the Richards dine at one!" cried Annie; "we must really be going."

"I am quite ready to go," answered Eva. "Good-bye, Lord Clair," and she held out her hand.

"Oh, I shall see you back part of the way to Sunny Brow," he answered.

"But it is out of your way."

"Not at all. I shall escort you across the bridge at all events."

So they bade the farmer good-bye, and went down the green hill together, but Eva's spirits were not so bright as when they had ascended it. And at the bridge she stopped and again bade Lord Clair good-bye.

"We must make haste," she said, "or we shall get into the bad graces of Mrs. Richards if her mutton is over-roasted."

"Oh! Eva," smiled Annie, deprecatingly, a little shocked that such a speech should have been made before Lord Clair.

But Clair laughed and lingered, and at last said:

"When shall I see you again?"

Eva gave her shoulders a little shrug.

"We must leave it to fate," she said.

"No, fate is too fickle," answered Clair, smiling. "Will you two young ladies walk down here this afternoon and meet me at the bridge?"

"What do you say, Annie?" asked Eva, looking at her companion. "It will be something to do."

"I shall be very pleased," smiled Annie.

"Shall we bring the Miss Richards too?" asked Eva, a little archly.

Again Clair laughed.

"I shall leave that to your judgment," he said. "But you will come, and I shall not forget the flowers."

"Now you may be sure we will come," said Eva, smiling; and then with a little nod she turned away, and Clair stood on the bridge and watched the two girls go up the hill to Sunny Brow through the fields of waving corn.

"He is very nice; he is very attentive, isn't he, Eva?" said Annie, excitedly.

"He wants something to amuse him in the country, I suppose," replied Eva.

"Oh! it can't be that; they keep lots of company at the Hall, and Lord Clair goes away a good deal too. I—think he admires you, Eva."

Annie made this admission half-unwillingly and Eva answered carelessly:

"He is at the age, my dear, when young men admire everyone they come near. But look, there is one of the Miss Richards watching for us; I am afraid we must be late."

They were about a quarter of an hour late, and the Richards family felt injured. They had seen them leave the garden with Lord Clair, and on the whole they were inclined to think such a proceeding was scarcely desirable. And now, as they approached her, Jane Richards was forced privately to admit that she had never seen her own hat look so well as on this beautiful girl.

Perhaps this knowledge made Miss Richards feel unamiable, for her smile was certainly rather a sour one when Eva Moore addressed her pleasantly.

"Thank you so much for lending me a hat and scarf, Miss Richards, or was it your sister?" she said.

"No, they are mine," answered Jane Richards. "So you have been for a walk with the young lord?"

"Yes, we went to see if the fire had left us any of our possessions; but no, at least as far as regards poor me," said Eva.

"Except the diamond ring, Eva," suggested Annie.

"Oh, yes."

"We are waiting dinner," remarked Jane Richards.

"Are you? I am very sorry; I will just leave the hat in the hall and then we are ready," said Eva, taking off the hat as she spoke, and as they together entered the house, she laid it perhaps rather carelessly on the hall table.

Now the hat was Jane Richards' best one, and the two girls had not over much money to spend on finery. Therefore she lifted the hat after Eva had laid it down.

"I will take it upstairs," she said with reproach in her voice.

And as she ran up the stairs Mrs. Richards appeared at the dining-room door also with reproach in her voice.

"Come, young ladies," she said, "Mr. Richards is waiting dinner, and he has no spare time to waste even to keep high company."

"We are very sorry we are late, Mrs. Richards, but we have been to Holly Hill," answered Eva.

"Humph; we saw you go out with the young lord. However, sit down. I am afraid the mutton is over-roasted, and it is one of our prime southdowns."

This was actually the case. In honor of her two young guests Mrs. Richards had cooked the leg of mutton which had been hanging in the larder in preparation for the Sunday family dinner. And now these two young guests had caused it to be over-roasted by not being in time for dinner!

Mr. Richards, a farmer not unlike the type of Mr. Dighton, was actually seated at table brandishing his knife and fork when they entered the dining-room, with impatience on his brow. The commencement of the meal was therefore somewhat trying, but gradually, under the influence of the excellent home-brewed beer, the family thawed. Mrs. Richards was curious to hear what the fire at Holly Hill had spared, and the Miss Richards what the young lord had said.

"He's a fine-looking young gentleman," remarked Mrs. Richards. "I suppose the next holiday making we'll have at the Hall will be for his wedding."

"Is he going to marry anyone?" asked Eva Moore, calmly.

"He's sure to marry some great lady soon," replied Mrs. Richards, sagely. "He'll be vastly wealthy, as well as being an earl when his father dies. I have heard some speak of his cousin, Miss Gower, as his future partner; but she's not up to his mark either in looks or anything else, to my thinking."

"She is the little dark-eyed, small-featured girl that was at the dance. I thought her rather pretty," replied Eva.

In the meanwhile, as the family at Sunny Brow were thus discussing his future prospects, Clair was walking towards the Hall thinking of Eva Moore. He had only met her yesterday, but that meeting seemed suddenly to have changed his whole being. He had been a light-hearted, high-spirited young man before this, ready enough to admire a pretty girl when he saw one, and perhaps even to tell her so; but there was something about Eva, something in the gleam of her lustrous eyes, in her grace and beauty that had completely fascinated him.

"And I saved her life," he thought, excitedly; "that gives me some sort of claim, and yet she would hardly promise to let me know where she is going when she leaves here. But I like her pride; and she will let me know, and I shall see her wherever it is."

Again and again such thoughts as these passed through his heart as he walked toward the Hall. Then he entered the richly wooded park which one day would be all his, where the deer stole through the thickets, and where the pheasants rose on their burnished wings. A beautiful home this Kilmore Hall, old and stately, which had come so unexpectedly into the possession of the present earl. And the young heir looked around as he went on dreaming still fondly of this sudden love which had sprung up in his heart in a single night. He saw her mentally again before him standing in the old-fashioned garden as he had seen her in the morning in her borrowed white gown, and with the sun shining on her beautiful face. A great gift for good or evil is such loveliness as Eva Moore's. He had told her he would take the risks of the good and evil, and he meant to keep his word.

Suddenly in one of the side paths he encountered his father and mother, and Lord Kilmore, who had not seen him since the fire the night before at Holly Hill, stopped smilingly.

"Well, Clair," he said, "so I understand you have been acting the knight-errant, and rescuing distressed damsels from the flames?"

Clair laughed, and a blush spread over his clear brown skin.

"I dare say you have heard a very exaggerated story, father," he said.

"By Mrs. Dighton's account your gallantry could not be exaggerated," continued the earl, still smiling. "That worthy lady has just been telling your mother and myself that you went up on a rope into a window and brought down a young lady in her night-dress in your arms! Really, Clair, I don't know whether it was quite the correct thing to do."

Again Clair laughed at his father's raillery.

"It was very brave but very rash," said Lady Kilmore. "If I had been there I should not have allowed my boy to run such a risk for all the young ladies in the world!"

"Now, Jeanie, don't throw cold water on your son's exploit. Clair, may we ask if the fair damsel was handsome or plain?"

"That depends on taste, father."

"I perceive by your answer to which decision your taste

inclines. Well, it's a most romantic beginning to an acquaintance, which I should suggest might be a little dangerous to go on with. What do you say, Jeanie?"

"What nonsense, Kilmore," said Lady Kilmore, smiling at her husband. "Turn with us a little way, Clair, and then we will all walk home together to lunch."

So Lord Clair turned with his father and mother, and Lord Kilmore was interested in hearing about the amount of damage done to his property at Holly Hill.

"I must send Jepson over in the morning," he said. "Poor Mrs. Dighton seems in a terrible way about her belongings. That young Dighton's badly hurt I hear?"

"Yes, but the doctor thinks he'll pull through all right," answered Clair.

"That's well. Ah, here comes Annette," for at this moment Annette Gower emerged from beneath some trees, where she had been sitting reading, or pretending to read, for she had a book in her hand. "Well, my dear," went on Lord Kilmore addressing her as she approached him, "you see we are out enjoying the air this fine morning."

"Yes," smiled Annette, and then she glanced shyly at Clair.

"Come with us also, dear," said Lady Kilmore. "We are going for a little walk, and then going in to lunch together."

"Yes, Aunt Jeanie," and so the four walked on abreast until the path narrowed, and then Lord and Lady Kilmore advanced a few steps in front and the two young people followed behind.

"You did not tell me at breakfast about your adventure last night, Clair," said Annette Gower, again looking shyly at Clair.

"It was not worth telling," answered Clair.

"Oh! but I hear it was. I went with a message to poor Mrs. Dighton, from Aunt Jeanie, and she said you acted most bravely. It was the handsome girl you danced with in the tent, wasn't it?"

"Yes, Miss Moore; the staircase up to her room had somehow got on fire, and the poor girl was in danger of her life."

"And you saved her life, Clair?" said Annette, with a faint ring of uneasiness in her voice.

"I helped at least; but there were a lot of other fellows about."

"And is the house quite burned down?"

"It is not habitable at present at least."

"Then where are the others—this girl and Miss Dighton
—as only Mrs. Dighton and her son came here?"

"They went to some neighbors across the river; one of
the other tenants."

"And this Miss Moore was not hurt?"

"Yes, her arm was hurt by the rope. It was a terrible
position for a woman to be in; she had to hang in mid-air
by the rope for a few seconds."

"Oh! how dreadful!"

"But she was quite brave and calm; wonderfully calm."

"And she is a friend of Miss Dighton's?"

"Yes, though I do not know how she came to be; but
they were at school together."

"She looks older than Miss Dighton."

"She is quite young; but she has more manner and is
altogether different. Look at that hare scudding over there,
Annette. I could have knocked him neatly over if I had
had a gun."

"I am very glad you have not then. I never can imagine
what pleasure men can have in killing things."

"And a good many women too, my dear."

"Yes, I know; but I don't like hunting women or sport-
ing women of any kind. It always seems so horribly cruel
to see a poor animal chased to its death."

"Then you mustn't marry into some shires, Annette, or
you will give great offense."

Annette Gower's delicate little brown face winced at this
allusion to her marriage.

"Aunt Jeanie does not like hunting women either," she
said after a little pause.

"She was not brought up amongst them, you see, but
in a legal atmosphere like yours, Annette, one's rearing
makes all the difference."

"Oh, yes, I know that; but I like country life."

"So does mother; but they have turned, so we had better
turn too. It's a jolly day, isn't it, Annette, and makes one
feel so happy?"

"Yes, it's a lovely day," replied the girl, but her voice
had not the joyous ring of her cousin Clair's.

They all returned to the house together, and at luncheon

Lady Kilmore asked her son if he were going anywhere during the afternoon.

Clair was conscious that his color rose beneath his mother's gentle gaze.

"Yes, mother, I've got an engagement this afternoon," he answered.

"Oh, well, it's no matter, dear, but I thought if you had nothing to do that you perhaps might drive over with Annette and myself to call on the Stanleys; but we can put it off to another day if you are engaged," said Lady Kilmore.

"Oh, go without me."

"But I should like you to go; they are such old friends, and you have not seen them since you came of age."

Clair gave a good-natured little shrug of his broad shoulders.

"I see you want me to be a very good boy, mother," he said.

"Of course I want you to be a good boy, so some day soon you must go to Dene House with me."

"All right; and now I think I'll go and have a look at the horses. So good-bye, mother, for the present; good-bye, Annette." And with a little nod to each of the ladies Clair rose from the table and left the room.

He was going to keep his appointment with Eva Moore on the bridge over the Ayre, but before he did so he meant to get the flowers he had promised to take her. He, however, did go to the stables for five minutes, and rather disgusted the head groom by his brief visit there.

Then he went in at one of the garden gates and crossed to the conservatories. Lady Kilmore was a passionate lover of flowers, and her green-houses contained all the rarest and most beautiful specimens she could procure. She was famous for roses, and Clair soon found himself amidst a perfect mass of fragrant blossoms. He cut the finest he could find in spite of the disapproving glances of one of the upper gardeners, and then just when he had gathered a most splendid collection he unexpectedly encountered his cousin, Annette Gower.

She gave a little start when she saw him with his hands full of flowers, and then grew very pale, while Clair, it must be admitted, grew very red.

"You see I'm gathering a posie," he said.

"Yes, I see," answered Annette, in a faltering voice.

"They are for Miss Moore, the pretty girl you admired at the dance," went on Clare in a slightly bravado tone, as though he were determined not to be ashamed of what he was doing. "She is fond of flowers, so I promised her some."

"Yes," again said Annette, and she did not look in her cousin's face.

"I must have a string or something to tie them together. I wonder where I can get any?"

"There is generally bass and twine on the shelves."

"Thanks; there is some bass I see over there," and as he spoke Clair crossed the conservatory and returned with a parcel of bass in his hand. "Will you hold the flowers, Annette, until I tie them together?" he continued.

Annette put out her trembling hand and took the flowers, but in her agitation or nervousness when Clair was tying the string she dropped several of them.

"Oh! you stupid little girl," cried Clair, good-naturedly, and then he stooped and picked them up, throwing away those, however, that he thought had been in the least injured by their fall.

"It's quite a swell affair, isn't it?" he said as he finally took the flowers from his cousin's hand. "Thanks, Annette, for holding them; and now what are you going to do?"

"I only came for some flowers for Aunt Jeanie."

"Then I shall go with my posie; I shall not be long away."

Annette made no answer, but as Clair turned and walked down the conservatory and disappeared through the first door he came upon, she sank down on a seat near her, and a deep and weary sigh escaped her lips.

The poor girl sat there long and her heart felt very cold and sad within her. Unconsciously she had learned to love her cousin Clair; to love him for his good looks and his brightness and kindness of disposition. She had been constantly thrown with him during the last two years, as Lady Kilmore earnestly, if secretly, desired that Clair should make her his wife. And Annette Gower had perhaps understood this wish of her aunt's heart, to which her own so fully responded.

Clair was frank and friendly with her always, sometimes even affectionate, but it was with a cousinly affection. But it is astonishing to what small things love will cling. Annette had dwelt on kindly looks and kindly words, which in truth meant nothing. It was not indeed until she saw him with Eva Moore at the dance in the tent, and noted the eager expression of admiration in his face, that she began to understand that she had never roused any of the deeper feelings of her cousin's heart.

"And he saved her life, and now he is taking her flowers," thought Annette with a bitter heart moan. It seemed to her at this moment as if her life were wrecked; as if she no longer cared to live. It was a bright day, but everything had suddenly turned dark and desolate to her.

"I am nothing to him," she told herself as she walked back with languid weary steps to the Hall; "he never gives me even a thought."

CHAPTER VI.

THE FALLEN FLOWER.

When Clair, carrying his flowers, came in sight of the stone bridge over the river Ayre, he instantly perceived that two girls were sitting on the parapet. He perceived also as he approached nearer that one of these girls—Eva Moore —wore no hat, but merely had a black lace scarf wrapped round her head. He saw this before she turned round and smilingly recognized him. Then he advanced on to the bridge, but Eva did not rise to meet him, though Annie Dighton did.

"What beautiful flowers!" cried Eva.

"Will you please me by accepting them?" he answered, placing the fragrant blossoms in her hand.

She put down her face to inhale their fragrance.

"Oh! thank you so much," she murmured, with her rosy lips hidden by the flowers.

"They are beautiful," said Annie Dighton, a little primly; "do they come from the conservatories at the Hall?"

"Yes; my mother goes in for flowers, you know, and is always looking out for new kinds."

"I do not wonder at her taste," said Eva Moore, lifting

her cream-tinted face from the blossoms. "Ah!" she added, smilingly, "I see you are looking at my headgear. Well, you must know that Miss Jane Richards so evidently grudged me the use of her hat that I disdained to ask her for it again, and we got into trouble, too, didn't we, Annie, over the roast mutton?"

Annie smiled and blushed.

"We were late," she said.

"And the prime southdown was over-roasted! Oh! I am so enchanted with the flowers; we hoped you would not forget them, Lord Clair; but I own I had my doubts on the subject." And Eva laughed and showed her small, white, even teeth.

"I am sure you had no doubts," answered Clair, ardently, with his eyes fixed on her face.

"I had, indeed. For one thing it requires a certain amount of moral courage for a man to carry a big bouquet of flowers, with no doubt the admiring eyes of some members of his household fixed on him."

"I assure you I was not at all ashamed of carrying them," answered Clair, and he thought with inward satisfaction at this moment that he had had the courage to tell Annette Gower for whom he intended the flowers.

"Well, at all events we have got them!" laughed Eva. "Now we must divide them equally. Annie must have half. Will you untie the string, Lord Clair, while I hold them?"

"I will do anything you tell me," he answered.

"Rash young man! Remember I am an unreasonable woman. There, that is splendid, and now I must begin to divide them. One for Annie, one for me—it must be a fair count out!"

She looked so lovely as she sat there on the bridge with the black lace wrapped round her comely head and throat, and the roses lying on her knee, that no wonder the young lord's heart beat tumultuously.

"May I sit beside you?" he asked.

"One for Annie, one for me," went on Eva, dividing the flowers into two separate bunches. "What did you say, Lord Clair? May you sit beside me? Yes, of course."

He vaulted on the parapet and sat admiring Eva's delicate profile.

"May I say something that you will perhaps think rude?" asked Clair.

"Please do not say anything rude; I feel happy, and wish to continue to feel happy, and a rude speech might disturb my mental equanimity."

"It is only I think you should always wear a lace scarf over your head and not a hat, it becomes you so splendidly."

"That's a compliment, and like every woman and man I like them, only I don't believe in them much."

"You may believe in this one; were I a painter I should paint you just as you are sitting now."

"Would you? Don't you think a rose would improve me?" And she raised a lovely crimson one to her head as she spoke. "Just fastened in there?"

"That looks exquisite!" cried Clair, in genuine admiration.

"Give me a hair-pin, and fasten it in then, Annie," said Eva.

And as Annie complied with her request she looked smilingly in Clair's face.

"And so you should like to make a picture of me?" she asked.

"I shall always have one now," he answered in a low tone; "I shall always see you as I see you now."

Eva laughed, and then went on dividing the flowers, still with the rose fixed in her shining hair.

"There," she said, "that's an equal division. Wait till I tie them together, Annie, for we must divide the bass too, unless you should like one to wear in your dress?"

"May I have this one?" asked Annie, raising a beautiful rose.

"My dear, that bunch is your own property. Now I shall tie the others together, and then I shall tie my own."

She tied Annie's flowers together and gave them into her hand, and then commenced to gather up her own.

"Will you do me a great favor?" asked Clair.

"With the greatest pleasure."

"Give me a flower for a button-hole then."

"Which will you have?"

"A rose like yours," answered Clair.

She picked one out and held it toward him, and Clair eagerly took it.

"Thank you," he said. "Now tell it never to fade, as I shall always keep it."

"How romantic you are," laughed Eva,

"You make me romantic; you look like a heroine in a romance."

Eva's countenance changed, and a cloud passed over it.

"Romances are not always pleasant," she said. "Come, Lord Clair," and she sprang lightly from the parapet of the bridge, "shall we stroll along the side of the river a little way?"

"I shall be delighted," answered Clair.

So they left the bridge and wandered along the margin of the gurgling Ayre for nearly an hour; Eva talking brightly most of the while, though sometimes a shadow seemed to cross her face. But there was no shadow on Clair's, nor in his heart.

He was happy; he was in the first flush of an hitherto unknown joy—the joy that comes crowned with flowers—though ere long their brightness may fade. The subtle feeling that thrills our breasts with its magic touch had glided into his. This fair woman by his side had opened a new world for him. He was a youth no longer, but a man with the feelings, passions, and tenderness that only a woman can awake. And the river gurgled on, and the birds sang in the boughs, but there was sweeter music still in the heart of Clair.

"We shall get into another row!" suddenly cried Eva.

"What for? You half startled me," Clair answered.

"The tea will be getting cold at Sunny Brow; I feel convinced it is five o'clock," answered Eva, in tones of mock alarm.

"Oh, what matter is the tea," said Clair, looking at his watch, which he hastily returned to his pocket.

"Lord Clair, let me see your watch. You know it is five o'clock?"

"No, it is not," laughed Clair.

"It is past five then? I see guilt written in your face. Do let me see the watch."

So Clair was forced to produce his watch, and the indicator of time pointed to half-past five.

"We will get cold tea and cold looks," said Eva. "Let us go back at once, Lord Clair, and you must leave us when we reach the bridge."

"That is very unkind. Let me see you to Sunny Brow."

"No. Mrs. Grundy, in the three-fold shape of Mrs. Richards and her two daughters, would feel herself affronted.

She would feel it her duty to remonstrate; and now, when I think of it, I think I had better take the rose from my hair before I approach Mrs. Grundy's residence."

"Let me do that," asked Clair, eagerly.

Eva bent her shapely head for him to unfasten the rose, which Clair did with trembling fingers. Then he placed it beside the other in his coat, and neither he nor Eva made any comment on this act.

But when they reached the bridge Eva stopped.

"Now good-bye," she said, offering her hand.

"Must it really be good-bye? But only for to-day?" said Clair reluctantly. "When and where shall I see you to-morrow?"

Eva looked at Annie smilingly.

"Dare we promise, do you think?" she said.

"I do not know," answered Annie, casting down her eyes.

"Well, if we are not forcibly prevented—but we may be—shall we say to-morrow here at three?" said Eva, now looking at Clair.

"Oh! do not be prevented!" cried Clair, eagerly. "I shall be here at three o'clock, and wait until you come."

"Even till midnight!" laughed Eva. "Good-bye then, we will try not to keep you waiting so long."

She nodded, smiled and turned away, and Clair stood watching her until she disappeared. Then he walked down the river path again, which he had so lately trod with her, recalling her looks and words, dwelling on them, his heart full of his new joy.

Suddenly he put his hand to his breast and took from his coat the rose Eva had worn in her hair. He pressed his lips passionately to it, and as he did so the crimson petals fell apart and fluttered to the wet and marshy ground at his feet. Clair stooped down and raised them one by one, but he felt exceedingly discomforted. He had meant always to keep this rose, and now it lay broken and soiled with the stains of the damp earth, that nothing could ever remove.

Was it an omen? If so, the young lord heeded it not, but went blindly to his fate!

CHAPTER VII.

A CHANGE OF OPINION.

The family at Sunny Brow had seen with much disapproval Eva Moore leave the house with only the lace scarf wrapped round her head.

"She's actually going out of the garden gate with it on," cried Jane Richards, looking from the dining-room window, and forgetting that she had made no further offer of her hat to Eva. "I declare it doesn't look respectable, mother, going about the country like that; I wonder who she is?"

"Mrs. Dighton says she was at school with Annie Dighton," said Mrs. Richards. "She is far older, I am certain, than Annie Dighton; Annie is only nineteen, this girl, I am sure, is three or four and twenty," answered Jane.

"She looks to me like a play-actress," remarked Fannie Richards, "with that lace thing wrapped round her head, and she gives herself no end of airs."

"I believe she thinks no one good enough for her," scoffed Jane, "and without a rag to her back too."

"Well, she couldn't help that, Jane," said Mrs. Richards; "but I believe she thinks herself quite a great lady, perhaps because the young lord danced with her so often."

Now no doubt there was some slight truth underlying these comments. Unconsciously to herself perhaps Eva Moore looked smilingly down on the Richards and their belongings. The homely service at the table, the still more homely minds and manners of the family struck her partly with amusement and partly with satire. And though the Richards might be homely they had their wits about them. She was always most pleasant, yet they saw she was unused to such people as themselves and their ways.

Mr. Dighton was a richer man than Mr. Richards, and things in the house were conducted differently at Holly Hill to those at Sunny Brow, especially since Annie Dighton had returned from her London school. Mrs. Richards and her two daughters were really hard-working women, and all credit was due to them for being so. But they were a great contrast naturally to the refined beautiful girl who accidentally had become their guest. And they were jealous of this

4

difference. They did not like to see their coarse red hands beside Eva Moore's white slender ones; and were conscious that their manners lacked the refinement of hers. Therefore, their tongues were bitter against her, and they felt the inconvenience of her presence at Sunny Brow increasing.

And their wrath grew greater when neither she nor Annie Dighton returned to the house for many hours in the afternoon, after Eva had committed the offense of going out with only a lace scarf round her head.

"I've no doubt she's hanging about to see if she can catch a glimpse of the young lord," said Jane, who was the bitterest of the three, on account of her best hat not being treated with proper respect.

"Just as if he would ever look at her," answered Fannie, "except just to amuse himself."

"She's conceit enough for anything," continued Jane.

But their further remarks were stopped by the appearance of Mr. Dighton, of Holly Hill, opening the garden gate and approaching the house.

"Here's Mr. Dighton; I wonder what he'll say when he hears that the girls are wandering about the country no one knows where," said Jane; and then she went and opened the house door for the farmer.

"Well, Mr. Dighton, how are you?" she said, holding out her hand. "Come in; Annie and Miss Moore are out somewhere, and we've seen nothing of them for hours."

"I came to see them," answered Mr. Dighton, wiping his red brow with his red handkerchief, "and to thank you kindly for taking them in."

"Oh, I'm sure they are very welcome, Mr. Dighton; Annie especially," replied Jane.

"Well, you see, I've been to see my missis at the Hall this afternoon, and poor Dick, and the wife and I have been laying our heads together, and we've made up our minds that the best thing for us to do is to take a house for a bit at Eastcliff. You see, Miss Jane, Holly Hill will have to be mostly rebuilt, and that will take a goodish time, and then we can't let the girls trouble you much longer, and the missis feels that though they do everything for her at the Hall, and for Dick, that is kind, still it's an intrusion like, and so we've fixed for me to take the girls over with me to-morrow to Eastcliff, and take a house there, and Annie and Miss Moore can go at once, and the wife and Dick follow as soon as the poor lad is well enough to travel."

"Oh, I'm sure, Mr. Dighton, we'll be very glad for them to stay on here," said Jane. A sort of revulsion indeed took place in her mind immediately she heard their young guests were about to leave them. "Annie, I am sure, would be welcome to stay any time—you see we have known her so long."

"Thank you kindly, Miss Jane, but all the same I think it's a good job that Miss Moore happened to be with Annie just now, because Annie could hardly have gone by herself to Eastcliff, but the two of them can go very well. You and Miss Fannie here must go down on a visit to them."

Jane smiled and her brown skin flushed with pleasure.

"Thank you, Mr. Dighton, that would be so nice," she said. "I always say a sniff of the sea does one a world of good at this time o' year. Oh, here they come," for at this moment Eva Moore and Annie Dighton appeared in the garden, and a moment or two later entered the room.

Annie ran up to her father and kissed him and the farmer held out his hand and shook Eva's heartily.

"Well, my handsome lass," he said, looking at her admiringly, "you don't look a bit the worse for all you've gone through. And I've been telling Miss Jane and Miss Fannie here what we've planned for you both."

Upon which Mr. Dighton proceeded to explain the scheme of going to Eastcliff on the following day, and taking Annie and Eva with him to seek a house.

"If we start in the twelve train," proceeded the farmer, "we'll be there at two, and have the afternoon to look about us, and it will be a nice outing for you both."

Eva looked at Annie with a comical little smile.

"To-morrow, do you say, Mr. Dighton?" she said.

"Yes, my dear, we'd better see about the house at once, and as I've been saying to Miss Jane here it's a good job you are staying with Annie, as you'll be such nice company for each other at Eastcliff, and I'll run over and see you whenever I can."

"I will stay with Annie until Mrs. Dighton can come," answered Eva, "and then I must go."

"Nonsense, nonsense," said the genial farmer, "you must stay till you're tired of us. Dick, poor fellow, would be in

a fine way if he thought he would not see you when he gets
to Eastcliff. And Miss Jane and Miss Fannie must come
down and see you too."

"Oh! that will be very nice," said Annie; "I hope you
will both come?"

"Only too pleased," answered Jane, who had quite recovered her good temper. "Well, Mr. Dighton, you'll stay to
tea with us?"

"I wouldn't mind a cup and a chat with your father. Well,
Annie, your mother sent her best love, and she hopes you
have not been giving Mrs. Richards any bother you could
help?"

"I hope not, father," answered Annie, smiling. "But Eva,"
she added, "don't you think we ought to make ourselves
tidy for tea?"

"I was just going to suggest doing so," answered Eva,
and as the two girls were leaving the room Mrs. Richards
appeared at the doorway.

"So you've got back," she said, "and where have you got
all the grand flowers that are lying on the hall table?"

"That's a secret," laughed Eva, "we have each been presented with a beautiful bouquet."

"Humph!" ejaculated Mrs. Richards, somewhat suspi-
ciously; but at this moment she caught sight of Mr. Dighton
and went forward with outstretched hand.

"Glad to see you, Mr. Dighton," she said, "and my good
man will be glad to see you also; he was just saying he
would go over to see you in the morning."

"Thank you kindly, Mrs. Richards, and for being so kind
to the two girls too."

"Mother," said Jane Richards eagerly, for she was now
afraid Mrs. Richards might give expression to some of the
family feeling in regard to Eva Moore, "Mr. Dighton is
going to take a house at Eastcliff for Annie and Miss Moore,
and he has asked us to go down and see them there. Isn't
it kind!"

"Oh, indeed that's very nice," replied Mrs. Richards, who
was quick, and quite understood her daughter's hint. "But
there's no hurry, Mr. Dighton; the girls are very welcome
here, if they can put up with our ways."

"Thank you kindly, Mrs. Richards, but we've about settled it, and Miss Moore and Annie will be good company

for each other till the wife and Dick go down to them. Miss Moore's a fine handsome lass, isn't she, Mrs. Richards?"

"Yes, she's well-favored. The young lord came here yesterday."

"That was but natural after he had saved her life, poor lass," replied the farmer. "He's a fine fellow, the young lord, not a bit of pride or nonsense about him."

"He seems pleasant spoken," answered Mrs. Richards, and then the conversation drifted to other matters.

In the meanwhile the two girls, Eva and Annie, had gone to their room, carrying their flowers with them, and as soon as they got there Annie said:

"Eva, what shall we do?"

"You mean about our cavalier?" answered Eva, smiling. "Well, we mustn't keep him sitting on the bridge till midnight, so I'll write him a note and tell him we are going tomorrow with your father to Eastcliff, so we can't keep our tryst."

"Oh! Eva, write to Lord Clair!"

"Why not, my dear? Have we not taken flowers from Lord Clair? Have we not walked with him, so why not write to him?"

"But writing seems different; we might have met him out walking by accident."

"But we didn't, you know," laughed Eva. "Yes, after tea I shall sit down and write him a note, and you and I can propose to see your father a little way on his walk home, and then we can post the note. Wasn't it fun about the old lady and the flowers? I mean to wear some at tea and make them all jealous."

Accordingly Eva adorned herself with two lovely roses on her shoulder and two in her waistband, and she insisted on Annie wearing some too.

"I'm afraid they'll guess who gave them to us?" said Annie, half timidly.

"What matter if they do, it will only make them more jealous," answered Eva. "Come, let us go down, and don't let them say we have spoiled the tea."

They went downstairs accordingly, and everyone at once began admiring their flowers.

"Oh! what lovely roses! Wherever did you get them?" cried Jane Richards.

"They are splendid," said Fannie, "I did not think that there were any such grown on the country side."

"You must guess where we got them," answered Eva, gaily.

"I've seen some such at the Hall," said Mr. Dighton. "Ay, I'll guess, the young lord has taken you to see the greenhouses, and given you them? Am I right now?"

Eva shook her head.

"No, we have not been at the Hall," she said.

"Then it beats me, I'll give it up," answered Mr. Dighton with a laugh.

"They were brought to us," continued Eva.

"Brought to you? Oh! you must tell us who brought them," said Jane Richards. "Did you get them from one of the gardeners at the Hall?"

"Do you mean stolen goods?" laughed Eva. "No, Lord Clair brought them for us; wasn't it kind?"

"Lord Clair!" echoed Jane.

"Yes, Lord Clair himself. He asked us if we were fond of flowers, and when we said we were he offered to bring us some, and he did."

"You are highly honored," said Fannie Richards, spitefully.

"Yes, aren't we?" answered Eva, provokingly.

"It's just like the fine young fellow," remarked Mr. Dighton, his mouth full of buttered toast. "He's an open-handed generous young chap, and will make a fine landlord some of these days, not that the old lord is a bad one!"

Mrs. Richards and her daughters said nothing more. They secretly disapproved of Eva and Annie's conduct, but with the prospect of a visit to Eastcliff in view they did not express their opinion. They began talking of other things, and then presently, when tea was over, Mr. Dighton rose and said he must go.

"Can you wait a few minutes?" asked Eva, "and then Annie and I will see you part of the way home, but I have got a few lines to write before we go that I want posted."

"I'll wait with pleasure, my dear," answered the farmer.

Upon this Eva ran upstairs and wrote a few lines to Lord Clair.

"Dear Lord Clair—Annie Dighton and I are going to-morrow to Eastcliff with Mr. Dighton, to choose a house there, so we shall be unable to meet you as we promised. But the day after, if it is convenient to you, I should like to see you to thank you once more for what you did for me, and as I shall not return here from Eastcliff, I wish to bid you good-bye. Will three o'clock suit you, the day after to-morrow, on the bridge?

"Yours sincerely,
"Eva Moore."

Just as Eva was finishing this note a rap came to the room door, and Jane Richards entered it carrying a hat in her hand.

"Oh! Miss Moore, I have brought you the hat," she said, "as you are going out with Mr. Dighton, and I'm so sorry you did not get it in the afternoon."

"Thanks very much," smiled Eva; "but the lace scarf did splendidly in the afternoon, though I am afraid it would not be quite enough protection for the evening. However, I wrote to my banker yesterday to send me a new check-book, and I shall get it to-morrow, and I am sure Mr. Dighton will cash a check for me, and Annie tells me there are some rather good shops at Eastcliff, so I shall be able to buy a hat and some necessaries, and you must let me bring you a hat too, in return for the hat you are so kindly lending me."

"Oh, there is no need for that, Miss Moore. I am sure you are very welcome to it," said Jane, much impressed. "But I am stopping you finishing your letter; but is there anything else you want?"

"Nothing, thanks," answered Eva, and as Jane Richards disappeared she finished and directed her letter to Lord Clair and then went down with it in her hand to the parlor, and a few minutes later she, the farmer, and Annie, were on their way to the postoffice.

And scarcely were they gone when the following conversation took place between the Richards family regarding Eva:

"After all she must be a lady, I think," said Jane Richards, "for she's written to her banker for a new check-book, she says, and she'll get it to-morrow, and will ask Mr. Dighton to cash a check for her, and she is going to buy a hat and other things at Eastcliff, and she said she would buy me one too, as she had the loan of mine, so that is very kind of her."

"If it isn't all moonshine," answered Fannie Richards.

"I don't think it is; she spoke as if she really had money. However we'll see to-morrow, and Mr. Dighton seems to think a great deal of her anyhow, and it will be nice to go down and see them at Eastcliff; they were both very kind and pleasant about that."

CHAPTER VIII.

EASTCLIFF.

Right on the sea marge, built actually on the beetling crags, at the foot of which the waves beat and toss, or lap softly in the summer-time, stands the ancient village of East-cliff. But these wind-swept, time-worn dwellings only now form a very small part of the place. Of late years there have sprung up streets and houses erected further inland, and Eastcliff has grown into a little town, famous for its health-giving breezes, and for the romantic beauty of its coast.

It is situated about fifteen miles from the railway station nearest Holly Hill, therefore the farmer and the two pretty girls in his charge arrived at the village in good time, and first Mr. Dighton, with proverbial hospitality, took Eva and Annie to the principal inn of the place and ordered an excellent lunch. Then, refreshed, and exhilarated by the sea air, they started on a house-seeking expedition, and after some little trouble procured one.

It was a moderate-sized house with a garden at the back, and sandy green hills stretching beyond. It was detached, and the landlady was very glad to get all her rooms let at once, and promised to do her best to make the young ladies comfortable.

She was a widow, of course, but a widow who took her loss, and her life generally, cheerfully. She was named Appleyard, and her cheeks had the fixed, rosy coloring of some American pippins.

Appleyard had hurried his departure from her home, and perhaps her love, by his too strong affection for the company of a neighboring publican. And Mrs. Appleyard, having let lodgings before he went to keep herself and him, went on letting them, and prospered a great deal better after he was gone. Therefore, she positively refused to take another "man," as she called husbands generally.

"My man," she was wont to say, "had his good qualities and his bad qualities, and when he wasn't in liquor he was as kind a husband as could be. But then he was nearly always in liquor, and then the worst of him came out."

With such experience no wonder she resisted the attentions of more than one admirer, who doubtless were attracted by her rosy cheeks and her comfortable home. She had been about ten years a widow, Appleyard having passed away when she was thirty-five, and by that time she had had quite enough of marriage.

Altogether Mr. Dighton and the girls were pleased with her appearance, and a bargain was soon struck, and Sea View House taken for the next three months.

After this was settled Eva went to make her proposed purchases at the shops, as her new check-book had arrived all right in the morning, and Mr. Dighton had cashed her a substantial check. So she bought right and left, and returned to Sunny Brow laden with parcels and bonnet-boxes.

She bought a hat for herself, and the very best one she could find for Jane Richards. She also purchased a black silk mantle for Mrs. Richards, and some pretty trifle for Fannie. She certainly handsomely remunerated the family for her brief stay at Sunny Brow, and the family accordingly were very much pleased with her and her gifts. It had been settled with Mrs. Appleyard that Eva and Annie were to go to Sea View House on the second day following their first visit there. Thus on their return in the evening to Sunny Brow the two girls had only one day more to stay there.

Annie had agreed with her father to go over to the Hall to see her mother the next morning, but Eva declined to accompany her there. Mr. Dighton therefore had promised to call for his daughter, and when these arrangements were explained to the Richards they all expressed great regret that their visitors were leaving them so soon.

"You've hardly come till you're going," said Jane.

"I'm afraid you can't have been comfortable," apologized Fannie.

It was very funny the change of front that the check-book and a few presents had brought about. Human nature generally is so constructed that we cannot help respecting those better off than ourselves. The pinch of poverty is so hard to bear that those who have felt its grip all really envy the well-to-do. The Richards were not absolutely poor, but they had anxieties and frequently troubles about money. Therefore, a girl who could spend some twenty or thirty pounds in one day's shopping suddenly became a person of consequence in their eyes. They became respectful to her and wished that they had always been so. But Eva Moore treated their new manners with the same smiling indifference with which she had regarded their old. They were nothing to her, only she chose to pay for the hospitality she had received, and she had certainly done so.

And the next morning brought Lord Clair's answer to her note, which Eva tossed to Annie with a little laugh after she had read it.

"Read that," she said, and Annie read as follows:

"My dear Miss Moore:—I thank you very much for your note, and I am very, very sorry not to be able to see you to-day, and need not tell you that to-morrow I shall only be too delighted to do so. I shall be on the bridge at three o'clock, and I hope to meet you there, and trust you will not hurry away. I am very sorry you are leaving Sunny Brow; but happily Eastcliff is not far away, and I hope I shall be permitted to see you there.

"And with kind regards to yourself and Miss Dighton,
"I remain, yours very sincerely,
"Clair."

. "Oh, Eva!" said Annie, after she had read this letter, "fancy if he comes to Eastcliff!"

"Well, my dear, it will not kill us if he does," replied Eva, calmly, going on arranging her long, beautiful hair, for Clair's letter had been brought up to their bedroom before they were down in the morning. "It will help to amuse us."

"But—I am afraid people will talk."

"If they do it will help to amuse them," replied Eva, a little scornfully. "I cannot refuse to see Lord Clair when I owe my life to him."

"Certainly there is that."

"It is supposed to be a sort of obligation, not that life is worth much—still to die as I should have died—"

And Eva gave a little shudder.

"Oh, Eva, don't talk of it," said Annie, and she went towards Eva and kissed her cheek. "Certainly we all owe the young lord so much that we never can repay it."

"My dear, don't call him the young lord, like the respected Richards family, as if there were only one young lord in the world! Call him Lord Clair; I am sure the name is pretty enough."

"Yes, it is very pretty," said Annie, meekly. She also had been impressed by the money which Eva Moore scattered so freely about, and also by the attentions of Lord Clair to her friend. For the first time she began wondering who she could be. Eva never spoke of her family or friends, except the school friends, whom they both mutually knew. They had met, as we know, at Annie's London school, where Eva had been a parlor boarder, and only took lessons in singing. She—Eva—had taken a kind of fancy to "the pretty rustic," as she called Annie Dighton, and the two had corresponded after Annie returned to Holly Hill. There had been a sort of promise between them when they parted that "some day" Eva should visit Annie at her home. The "some day," as we know, had come, and was fated to bring great changes in two lives.

"I shall not be sorry, shall you?" said Eva, presently, putting some finishing touches to her dress, "to see the last of Sunny Brow?"

"Oh, the Richards are very kind, but of course—"

"Oh, yes, of course!" answered Eva, with a laugh. "Come, my dear, are you ready? Let us descend."

The two girls went down together, and the Richards family did everything they could to make themselves pleasant. Then Mr. Dighton came for Annie, and Eva again refused to accompany her to the Hall.

"Give your mother my love," she said, "and tell your brother I am very pleased indeed to hear he is going on so well."

So Annie and Mr. Dighton left, and Eva, after walking in the garden awhile, accompanied by Jane Richards, retired to her own room to write letters, she said, but really to escape from the society of the family. She remained there till

Annie returned, looking very pretty, and flushed, and excited.

"Oh, Eva, I have seen the young lord!" she began.

"Lord Clair," corrected Eva.

"Yes, Lord Clair. Just as father and I were coming away from the Hall we met him with Jepson, the agent, and Mr. Jepson stopped to speak to father about the repairs at Holly Hill, and the young lord—at least Lord Clair—walked on with me. And he was so nice; he is coming to meet us this afternoon, and he said he hoped he might come to Eastcliff."

"And what did you say?"

"Oh, I said we should be very pleased; and I told him all about the house, and what fun we meant to have on the sands, and the young lord—oh, I can't help calling him that —but he said we must go out boating with him, and he was just as nice as anyone could be."

"We must make him useful."

"Mother asked if we had seen him and I said yes, but I did not tell her anything about him coming to Eastcliff; and Dick is much better, but he looks very ill, poor fellow; he asked lots of questions about you, and seemed very pleased when I gave him your message."

At this moment Jane Richards rapped at the room door to tell them that dinner was waiting if they were ready for it. And in honor of their departing guests the family had prepared quite a feast for them to partake of. Mrs. Richards had sacrificed two of her best fowls, with a huge tongue placed on the dish between them, while a boiled leg of mutton smoked at the other end of the board. Then there were custards and fruit pies, and only pleasant words and looks. They (the Richards) were in fact so pressing in their attentions that Eva and Annie found the greatest difficulty in getting rid of their company so as to be able to keep their appointment with Lord Clair.

At last it dawned on Jane Richards' imagination that for some reason or other they wished to go out for a walk by themselves. She therefore gave her sister a hint, and Eva and Annie were free to do as they pleased.

They accordingly started off through the cornfields, and when they neared the bridge over the Ayre they saw Clair sitting on the parapet waiting for them. He was smoking a cigarette, but he flung this into the stream as he rose to meet them.

"I was so afraid you were not coming," he said.

"We did our best to come before, but we could not get away," answered Eva.

"It was very good of you to come at all."

Eva laughed.

"Don't be flattered," she said, "when I tell you we prefer your society to that of Mrs. and the Misses Richards."

Clair laughed also at this sally.

"Well, from whatever motive you have come—without any disrespect to Mrs. or the Misses Richards—I am very glad that you have done so. And now tell me about East-cliff. Are you really going to-morrow?"

"We really and truly are. Mr. Dighton will take us down and then leave Annie and me to take care of ourselves until Mrs. Dighton and her son join us."

"And I may come and see you?" asked Clair, with his gray eyes fixed on Eva's face.

"Yes," she answered, smiling, "you may come and see us. What I saw of Eastcliff I liked, but I suppose you have been there?"

"Never since I was a little boy when my mother took me after I had whooping-cough or some other childish illness. But I am told the place is quite changed since then; it was only a village at that time."

"Oh, there are quite grand streets and shops now—witness my hat!"

"Did you really buy that there?"

"I really did; it's not exactly what I should desire; still—it's not bad."

"I don't understand about millinery, but I know what you look in it."

"Charming, of course. That's what you are bound to say," answered Eva, gaily.

"I should not say it unless I thought it."

Eva made a little smiling bow.

"And if you go to-morrow to Eastcliff, how soon may I come to see you?" asked Clair after a moment's silence.

"What do you say, Annie? To-morrow the dust of the journey will be on us, and our tempers may be ruffled with wrangling with our landlady. Oh, we shall leave it to your-self, Lord Clair. Come when you feel inclined."

"I know how soon that would be," he answered.

The three young people were all at that moment leaning against the stone parapet of the bridge, and as Clair was speaking they perceived a horseman approaching it by the roadway which led to it. Annie Dighton and Clair both recognized him; it was Mr. Jepson, Lord Kilmore's agent, and Annie's pink cheeks grew pinker as he drew near.

He rode on and speedily reached the bridge, and when he came to where Clair and the two girls were standing he drew rein and raised his hat. He was a good-looking man, gentlemanly and middle-aged, and a smile crossed his face when he saw who were Clair's companions.

"Good morning, my lord," he said; "good morning, Miss Dighton; it's a fine day, isn't it?" And as he spoke his eyes were fixed on Eva's face.

"Yes, very, Mr. Jepson," answered Clair with just a touch of haughtiness in his tone, for he noticed the direction of Mr. Jepson's glance.

"And is this the young lady," continued Mr. Jepson, still looking at Eva, "who had such a narrow escape, I am told, at the fire at Holly Hill?"

Then Eva raised her large dark eyes and looked steadily at the agent.

"Yes," she said, quietly, "Lord Clair saved my life."

Again Mr. Jepson raised his hat.

"Lord Clair was only too happy, I am sure," he said, "to be able to render you so great a service."

"I was indeed too happy," said Lord Clair, quickly.

"You have made us all envy you, my lord," continued Mr. Jepson, smiling, and then he wished them good morning, and once more touching his hat he rode on and proceeded to the Hall.

He had been in the service of Lord Kilmore for many years and held a good position in the county, being highly esteemed by the earl and also by many of the neighboring gentlemen. He was shown into the library when he reached the Hall, where Lord Kilmore was sitting, who held out his hand cordially to him as he entered the room.

"Well, Jepson," he said, "have you got the estimates of the repairs at Holly Hill?"

"Yes, my lord," he answered. "I have the estimates here, but I am sorry to say the repairs will cost a lot of money, for in some parts the house is completely gutted."

"Still they will have to be done."

"Yes. And as he spoke he laid the estimates on the table before Lord Kilmore, who took them up and began looking them over.

"I have just seen the heroine of the fire," continued Mr. Jepson, quietly. "She was with Lord Clair on the bridge as I came along."

"With Lord Clair!" exclaimed Lord Kilmore, dropping the estimates and looking up hastily.

"Yes, she and that pretty little Miss Dighton and Lord Clair were together on the bridge. She is certainly a beautiful girl, this Miss Moore, and I stopped a moment or two so that I might see her."

"Still—she is scarcely a fit acquaintance for Clair," said Lord Kilmore, after a slight pause.

"That is what I thought, and therefore I conceived it to be my duty to mention to you that I had seen them together."

Lord Kilmore was silent a moment or two, and then he gave a little shrug.

"A young man's passing fancy, I suppose," he said. "The girl is handsome and he saved her life, and I have no doubt she makes the most of the obligation. About these estimates, Jepson?"

He changed the conversation, and did not again allude to Clair during the agent's visit. But no sooner had he gone than he rose and went to seek his wife, whom he found in the inner drawing-room.

She looked up as he went in, and smiled sweetly.

"Well, dear?" she said.

Lord Kilmore went up and stood beside her.

"Jepson has just been here, Jeanie, and he told me that he had seen Clair on the bridge with that girl he saved at the fire. To say the least of it, it is very injudicious."

Lady Kilmore's delicate complexion flushed.

"With that girl?" she repeated, uneasily.

"Yes; and Jepson says she is a very handsome girl. I think you had better speak to him; it would never do for him to get into any scrape of that kind, and of course anything serious is out of the question."

"Yes, of course; but, Kilmore, a girl like that! Clair would never look at her nor speak to her except just out of kindness because he saved her life."

"My dear, Clair is young, and by Jepson's account the

girl is beautiful, and the very fact that he saved her life may attract him to her. I think you had better say something to him, as you have great influence with him."

"I hope it will never be needed in such a case. Kilmore, fancy my boy—I do not believe he has ever spoken more than five words to her."

The earl shrugged his shoulders; he had not quite as much faith in Clair as his adoring mother.

CHAPTER IX.

"YOU MAY COME."

Nevertheless, though she affected to have, and indeed had, such firm belief in her son, her husband's words made Lady Kilmore somewhat uneasy. What she would have felt had she beheld Clair at the moment his father was talking of him could not easily be told. She was a woman with too fine an intuitive knowledge of his nature, if she had seen him lingering on the river bridge by the side of Eva Moore, not to have understood something of the feelings of his heart.

As it was, she contented herself by wishing that her son's adventure during the fire at Holly Hill had never occurred.

"Of course, the girl is naturally grateful to him," she told herself. "Who would not be, but then dear Clair should not forget that he is young and good looking, and that the poor girl's gratitude might lead her to like him too well, and thus bring unhappiness to herself. But no, she would never be so foolish, and Clair, I am sure, will never forget what is due to his position as his father's son."

Still Lady Kilmore listened rather anxiously for the sound of Clair's footsteps. He nearly always came straight to her rooms when he returned to the house, but the summer afternoon waned, and the dusk of the evening gathered round, and yet she heard or saw nothing of him.

In truth, Clair was too much excited after he parted with Eva Moore to go and talk quietly with his mother. He had gone for a sharp country ride with a feeling of boyish exhilaration and happiness in his heart. All the long summer afternoon he had been with Eva; all through the sunny hours he had looked on her beautiful face, and talked of other meetings and coming days.

"I have taken quite a longing for a stiff sea breeze," he said, switching the tall reeds that grew in the water with his stick.

"Since when?" smiled Eva.

"Well, since yesterday," answered Clair, with a little laugh.

"And I have taken a longing for some of those big yellow buttercups," said Eva, pointing to some growing close to the roadside. "Will you get me some?"

Clair needed no second bidding. He went to get the buttercups, and when he returned he found Eva seated on the trunk of a fallen tree with her hat in her hand and the sunlight glinting on her bright hair.

"Thanks so much," she said, looking up smiling as he approached her, and holding out her hand for the water flowers. "I want them to decorate my hat."

"You will spoil your hat, Eva; they are wet," cried Annie Dighton.

"What matter; or I can shake them. You were talking about the sea, Lord Clair, when my erratic fancy was attracted by the buttercups. Yes," she went on, fastening the flowers in her hat as she was speaking. "I love the sea, but its sound often makes me feel sad. If I am very disagreeable, or shall I call it pensive, when you come to Eastcliff you must excuse me."

"I shall only be too happy to be with you whatever you are."

"Don't be too sure. I can be very unpleasant at times. But I don't think anyone has a right to be so, mind. I think all troubles and sorrows should be buried deep right down in our own hearts."

"I think it would be happier to share them," answered Clair.

"Some can never be shared," said Eva, and then with sudden impatience she pulled the buttercups from her hat and flung them on the ground.

"I am only spoiling it," she said, rising and shaking her hat, and then placing it on her head, and as she did so Clair stooped down and picked up some of the buttercups.

"May I have one for a buttonhole?" he asked.

"If you will condescend to wear so humble a flower. But they are really pretty, and it's a shame to waste them, so I'll wear some too."

Again she took the flowers from his hand and placed some of them in the scarf round her throat. Then she proposed that they should walk through the meadows that skirted the riverside. Suddenly she stopped before a mighty oak that had stood in its place a hundred years and more, with its golden-green leaves rustling in the sunshine and the breeze.

"Fancy all the dead people that have stood under the shelter of this big tree," she said, looking up at the quivering foliage. "All the lovers who have courted here, and likely got to hate each other, or at least got tired of each other after the great tree had budded and leafed a few more years. There is something awful in the placid indifference of inanimate things to us animate ones. They don't know what a blessing it would be not to feel."

"I am sure you do not feel that," said Clair, ardently.

"Don't I, Lord Clair? I assure you I do, though; I would rather be a tree than a woman any day."

"Oh, Eva!" said Annie Dighton, with a laugh.

"I'm not joking; I'm in earnest," went on Eva. "Fancy putting on a pretty new green dress every springtime, without any trouble or milliner's bills. Fancy getting handsomer every year instead of uglier, and going on growing and growing while the children who played and the pretty maidens who wooed under my branched arms turned old and gray. Now wouldn't it be nice, Lord Clair?"

"I should rather live a few years of great joy than vegetate for a thousand," he answered.

"Now I should like to vegetate," said Eva, waywardly. "Great joy is mostly paid for, Lord Clair, by great pain, and it's not worth the cost!"

"Oh, yes, it is—it must be. Even to have been happy once is worth bearing anything for!"

Eva shook her head as Clair spoke. His gray eyes were fixed on her face, his clear brown skin was flushed with ardor. He was thinking how gladly he would bear anything to be a few years happy with Eva. And perhaps she understood something of her young lover's feelings, for she sighed softly.

"There," she said presently, "we have talked nonsense

enough. We ought to be thinking of going back to Sunny Brow, Annie."

"Oh, surely not yet?" said Clair.

But Eva would not be persuaded. And so the three retraced their steps along the riverside, and when they reached the bridge Eva stopped and held out her hand to Clair.

"Good-bye, Lord Clair," she said.

"May I come the day after to-morrow to Eastcliff?" he asked, still holding her hand.

"If you like; but something may come in the way."

"Nothing shall come in the way if you give me permission."

"All right; you may come."

And Eva laughed, and thus they parted; the two girls returning to Sunny Brow and Clair going for a long ride, only returning to the Hall in time to dress for dinner.

Both his father and mother looked at him when he entered the inner drawing-room before that meal was announced. No one else was present but his cousin, Annette Gower, who also glanced at him shyly.

"What a long while you have been out, Clair," said his mother, with a slight ring of anxiety in her voice.

"Yes, all the afternoon," he answered, brightly. "I had a walk, and then a long ride cross country."

"Oh, you've had a long ride, have you?" said Lady Kilmore in a relieved tone, and she glanced at her husband.

"Jepson told me he saw you," remarked the earl, dryly, and a faint flush rose to Clair's face as his father spoke.

"Yes, I saw him on the bridge," said Clair, in a tone of affected carelessness; "and he was riding an uncommonly good horse."

"He's a good horseman and good judge of horseflesh," replied the earl, and nothing further was said on the subject, and the family went down to dinner. Clair seemed in the highest spirits, and talked and laughed during the whole meal.

Then when they all returned to the inner drawing-room, which was their usual custom when no visitors were present, Clair went and sat by the side of his mother on a couch, and she softly put her hand in his.

"Will you go with us to-morrow, my dear," she said, "to call on the Stanleys?"

"I shall be very pleased, mother," he answered, to her great relief.

Then she quite made up her mind not to speak to him on the subject of "that girl."

"It was folly even to talk or think of it," she told herself, and the evening passed very quietly and happily away.

The earl was not in very good health, and as a rule they lived the simplest of lives. Annette Gower sang and played, and Lady Kilmore also sang in a cultivated voice of extraordinary sweetness, though not much power. But her husband listened to her so well pleased that he called her to his side after her song was ended and took her hand and looked up in her face affectionately.

"You sing as well as you did twenty-four years ago, Jeanie," he said, smiling.

A tender look stole into Lady Kilmore's eyes, and a soft flush to her fair cheeks.

"Thank you, my dear," she answered, and she stood there with her hand in her husband's, both thinking of the old days of their young love.

In the meanwhile Clair was turning over Annette's music, and leaning on the piano talking to her. He liked her, and Annette's dark eyes grew brighter when he was near. She had never spoken to her aunt of that scene in the conservatory, when Clair had told her that the flowers he had gathered were for Eva Moore. But she had not forgotten it, and she knew he admired Miss Moore as he had never admired her.

"But the girl will go away," hope whispered, as Clair leaned on the piano talking to her in his bright, kindly fashion. And Lady Kilmore, glancing round, saw the flush on Annette's pretty dark face, and smiled well pleased.

Presently she crossed over to them, and they planned together the visits they would pay on the following afternoon, and Clair agreed to everything they proposed.

"It will be so nice to have you with us, dear," said Lady Kilmore, with her hand on his shoulder.

"I am afraid Clair will think it a great bore to pay two visits in one afternoon," smiled Annette, looking at her cousin.

"Not when I'm with you, my dear, and mother," he answered, kindly, and the poor girl repeated these words to her heart again and again during the night that followed.

But Clair was repeating other words and recalling other smiles. He was thinking, "Only one day and I shall see her again—only one day"—the day on which Annette Gower was building her foolish hopes; the day she was looking forward to was the same that Clair was wishing would quickly speed away!

CHAPTER X.

A FALL.

And the day came and went, and Annette felt very happy driving through the still green country lanes with Clair opposite to her. He had gone to pay these visits to please his mother, and he was too kind-hearted not to do his best to make the hours pass pleasantly. He laughed and chatted, but it must be admitted felt decidedly pleased when on their return they neared the Hall.

It was late, and the bright August moon had risen and was shedding its fair beams on the hedge-rows and the trees. Annette felt excited, and the peaceful beauty all around stirred strange emotions in her breast. But Clair felt rather tired, and thought the drive had been decidedly long.

"However, the day is nearly over," he reflected, well pleased, as they drove up the avenue and came in sight of the stately outlines of the Hall. Lady Kilmore also was tired, but Annette Gower wished they had miles and miles further to go.

In these different frames of mind they entered the house, and the evening passed as usual, except that Clair said, before he bade his mother good-night, on her proposing some other excursion:

"No, mother, I can't go with you to-morrow. I'm going away for the day."

"For the whole day, dear?" asked Lady Kilmore, rather surprised.

"Yes, for the whole day; I'm going down to have a look at the sea."

"At the sea, Clair! Where are you going, then?"

"To Eastcliff. They say it's grown a wonderful place

now. Do you remember when we went there when I was a little boy?"

"Yes, I remember, Clair," replied Lady Kilmore, somewhat slowly. And when her son had left the room for the night she was still thinking of this brief conversation.

"It's an odd freak of Clair's going to Eastcliff to-morrow, isn't it, Kilmore?" she said to her husband.

"I have just been thinking so, Jeanie," he answered. "Ten to one he is going on a day's excursion with the beauty he rescued at the fire at Holly Hill."

"Oh, Kilmore!"

"My dear, young men will be young men, and Clair is young and impulsive. But it will be a great pity, as I told you before, if he gets entangled in any such folly."

Lady Kilmore did not speak, but she felt uneasy. Clair had gone to bed, and she therefore had no opportunity of asking him any further questions. And the next morning when she went down to breakfast she heard from Annette Gower that he was already gone.

"How early for him to start," said Lady Kilmore.

"Yes," answered Annette, and she began moving about the room restlessly, and Lady Kilmore noticed she scarcely swallowed anything during the meal that followed.

But the morning did not pass without Lady Kilmore's uneasiness about Clair being greatly increased.

During the days which Mrs. Dighton and Richard Dighton had been at the Hall, Mrs. Dighton had always, by her own request, had her meals served in the room with her son. But Lady Kilmore, with the kindly courtesy of her nature, had gone each morning to inquire after the invalid and say some pleasant, hospitable words to Mrs. Dighton, who was highly flattered, but very uncomfortable during these visits. As usual, therefore, about eleven o'clock, Lady Kilmore proceeded to the wing of the house where Mrs. Dighton and Richard were located. And having rapped at the door of the small sitting-room which had been given up to Mrs. Dighton's use, Lady Kilmore speedily found herself in the presence of the farmer's wife.

"And how is your son this morning, Mrs. Dighton?" asked Lady Kilmore, pleasantly.

"Oh, thank your ladyship kindly," answered Mrs. Dighton with her best curtsey, "I think Dick's going on all right, and I hope in a day or two I'll be able to get him away to

Eastcliff, for I'm sure I'm ashamed of intruding any longer on your ladyship's kindness."

"To Eastcliff?" repeated Lady Kilmore, with a quick throb in her heart.

"Yes, my lady; my husband has taken a house there until the repairs are done at Holly Hill, and my daughter and her friend, Miss Moore—the young lady that your ladyship's son so bravely saved at the fire—went there yesterday."

Lady Kilmore could not speak for a moment. The fact passed through her mind with vivid distinctness that Clair had actually gone the very day after she went to see this girl at Eastcliff, and this thought was a very startling one.

"I expect the sea air will quite set Dick up," continued Mrs. Dighton, on receiving no reply from Lady Kilmore. "You see poor Dick got his hurts in trying to save Miss Moore too, though he wasn't so fortunate as your son, Lord Clair. But he did his best, poor fellow, and he's very anxious to get to Eastcliff now when Miss Moore's there; not that he's anxious to leave the Hall, my lady," and again Mrs. Dighton curtsied, "for I am sure nothing can exceed the kindness and attention he's received here; but the truth is," and Mrs. Dighton's comely face grew more comely with a pleasant smile, "that poor Dick's very sweet in that quarter, and thinks there's not such another as Miss Moore."

"And—have you known this young lady long?" asked Lady Kilmore.

"No, my lady, I haven't, but my Annie has known her these two years and more. Annie met her at the school in South Kensington where we sent Annie for a year to finish, and Miss Moore was there too at the time, though not a scholar, but a parlor boarder. I think she's a good bit older than our Annie, who's just gone nineteen, but anyhow my Dick seems very far gone."

And Mrs. Dighton gave a little laugh.

"And the young lady—does she—?" hesitated Lady Kilmore.

"That I can't say, my lady. She's a queer kind o' girl to my mind, so cold and haughty, and not like a young thing a bit. She's stand-offish like, and talks worldly, but all the same she takes with the men-folk. Why, even my old man," and Mrs. Dighton gave her genial laugh, "thinks no end of her, and took her and our Annie down to Eastcliff two days ago to give them an outing, and Miss Moore, it seems, has a good lot of money, and bought no end of things."

"And she is handsome?"

"Oh, some think a vast of her looks, but I like a little bit more color. However, she takes our Dick's fancy for sure, and fancy's the great thing, you know, my lady."

"Yes," said Lady Kilmore, slowly. And then after a moment's silence she roused herself. "Have you everything you require, Mrs. Dighton? Be sure you ask the housekeeper for everything you want."

"Thank you kindly, my lady, there's nothing we lack for," replied Mrs. Dighton.

Then, after a few more words, Lady Kilmore went away, and with a very anxious face proceeded to her husband's bedroom, who had not yet risen, but was reading the newspapers in bed, with his double glasses fixed on his somewhat prominent nose. He looked up from his paper as his wife approached him, and saw at once something was disturbing her.

"Well, Jeanie, what's the matter?" he asked, kindly.

"Oh, Kilmore, it's about Clair," she answered. "I fear you are right. I should have spoken to him—about that girl."

"What's the matter now?"

"I have just been talking to Mrs. Dighton, and it seems that they have taken a house at Eastcliff until the repairs are done at Holly Hill, and this Miss Moore and Miss Dighton are at Eastcliff now—and—"

"Clair went to-day. Well, this begins to look serious."

"It's most foolish, almost wrong of him, I think," said Lady Kilmore, anxiously; "wrong to the girl, who may take all sorts of foolish ideas into her head. I will point this out to him; he had better go abroad; don't you think so, Kilmore?"

"My dear, I don't think you need distress yourself particularly. It's foolish of Clair running after the girl; but it's her pretty face, I suppose, and the romantic notion that he saved her life. You had better speak to him quietly. I wouldn't say too much, and he's a sensible young fellow enough and I dare say will listen to reason."

"I will speak to him," answered Lady Kilmore, and then

after a little further conversation she left her husband, to spend, however, a very anxious day thinking of her son.

Clair in the meanwhile was spending a very happy one. He arrived at Eastcliff about twelve o'clock and soon found his way to Sea View Villa, and when he inquired for Miss Dighton and Miss Moore he was told by a shiny-faced young woman that the ladies were out.

"Have you any idea which way they went?" asked Clair.

The young woman vanished on this question being put to her, and a few moments later Mrs. Appleyard, the mistress of the house, appeared, looking as rosy and fresh as sea breezes could make her.

She curtsied when she saw the good-looking young man standing at her door and approached him.

"Jane says you are inquiring for the young ladies, sir," she said. "They went out about a quarter of an hour since and left a message that if anyone called they would be down on the sands."

"Oh, thank you; then I can easily find them," answered Clair. "Good morning."

"Who may I say called, sir?" inquired Mrs. Appleyard as Clair was turning away.

"Lord Clair," he replied, to Mrs. Appleyard's great surprise.

"Lord Clair," she repeated to her handmaiden, who was standing behind her; "but he can't be a real lord, not one of the nobles. Oh, I see now; his Christian name must be Lord. Dear me, he quite took my breath away."

Clair, having received the information he required, proceeded direct to the sands, smiling to himself as he went, for he remembered the road so well, though he had never seen the place since he was a little boy. But it had impressed itself on his memory because at Eastcliff he had for the first time beheld the sea. There it lay now before him, the great blue-green mass of water sparkling in the morning sun. The sands, wide, and as a rule smooth, were in parts ribbed with the action of the tide and dotted with little groups of children and their nurse-maids. Above towered the tall cliffs, crowned with the ancient village, while the new town lay at the back, further inland.

Altogether the place looked bright and sunny, but Clair as he walked on began to scan each group, and looked eagerly around, hoping to see the slender, graceful form of Eva Moore.

At last, seated on a rocky promontory that jutted out into the sea, near the end of the sands, he perceived two girls with white sunshades, the outlines of whose figures seemed to him to have some resemblance to Eva Moore and Annie Dighton.

Acting on this belief he commenced to cross the slippery rocks, over which the sea washed each tide, in the direction of the two girls. With his eyes fixed on them he was not careful enough of his footing, and suddenly stepping on a piece of tasseled brown seaweed, he slipped and fell forward, and came down—rather an awkward fall—in one of the crevices of the rocks.

As he did this one of the girls rose with a little cry and came towards him. It was Eva Moore, and in a moment or two she was beside him, holding out her hand to assist him out of his anything but pleasant position.

"Are you hurt?" she said. "These rocks are so frightfully slippery I am always afraid to cross them."

"Oh, no, I am all right," answered Clair, looking up with a smile to her as she stood on the rock above him. "Thank you for coming to help me. It was awfully stupid of me to slip."

He sprang out of his crevice as best he could as he spoke, and joined Eva, conscious, however, that he had sprained his right foot by the severe pain he felt in it. But he scarcely thought of this as he stood by Eva's side. The sea air and perhaps the excitement of seeing him fall had tinted her cream-like complexion with the color of a wild rose. Never had she seemed so beautiful in Clair's eyes as she did at this moment, and she looked bright also and animated.

"The sea suits you," he said; "it has not made you sad or—"

"Disagreeable!" laughed Eva. "I see you came prepared for the worst."

"No, no; I did not. I knew you would like the sea."

"I like to hear the gurgle of the waves among the rocks; it is so mysterious; and the sea flowers in some of the crevices here are lovely. But here comes Annie. Take care, Annie, and do not emulate the tragedy of Lord Clair."

Annie came towards them smilingly, but carefully. Then she shook hands with Clair.

"Your brother is going on all right, Miss Dighton," he said; "I saw him yesterday."

"Thank you. I hope you are no worse with your fall," replied Annie.

"I'm afraid I've sprained my foot a bit, but it's nothing."

"Is it painful?" asked Eva. "Let us sit down here for a little while, and perhaps the wrench will go off."

They all sat down, therefore, on the rock on which they were standing, with their faces to the sea. There was a light wind and a blue sky, flecked here and there with scudding clouds, and on the waves before them a white sea gull floated, while another hovered overhead.

"I like to watch them," said Eva, looking up, "and hear their weird cries."

"I don't think people should be allowed to shoot them, do you?" asked Annie.

"Not even for ladies' hats!" said Lord Clair, smiling.

"No, I hate to see their wings in hats; the wings meant to ride upon the storm and float upon the waves!" cried Eva. "There! isn't that quite poetical? You must have inspired me, Lord Clair."

"I wish I could," he answered, looking at her.

"It's the sea air, I suppose," said Eva; "but all sorts of funny ideas come into my head since we have been here. I have been speculating this morning on the nature of mermaids."

"Very mischievous, I should think," smiled Clair.

"As to the captivation of mariners? Well, of course, from a masculine view that is mischievous—to snare them down into the deep sea."

"To their destruction."

"But why need they go?"

"Perhaps they can't help themselves," answered Clair, with a laugh.

"Oh, yes, they could if they never looked at the mermaids or any other dangerous maids."

"You give advice which I cannot follow."

"Then I will not throw any more away. How is your foot now? Has the pain gone off?"

"I had forgotten all about it, thinking of the dangers of mermaids."

"In that case, Annie, I suggest that we should think of returning to Sea View House. We ordered lunch at half-past one, and by the time we get there it will be ready. You will lunch with us, won't you, Lord Clair?"

"I shall only be too happy."

"Let us be going, then," and Eva sprang lightly up.

But when Clair tried to follow her example he was painfully reminded of the fact that he had sprained his foot. He, however, bore it manfully, but could not help limping slightly, which Eva observing she held out her hand to help him over the rocks.

"I believe your foot is worse than you will allow," she said. "What a pity it is. Let me help you."

She held out her hand frankly to him, but Clair took it with tingling fingers. The slight pressure of this girlish hand filled his whole being with emotion. He could not speak, though Eva went prattling on, and when she turned round and looked in his face, wondering at his silence, she saw he had grown quite pale.

"Are we going too fast for you?" she asked.

"Not at all," answered Clair. "It is very good of you to help me on my way."

Then when they reached the level sands Eva drew her hand gently from his.

"Now you don't want any help, do you?" she said.

Clair did not speak. His foot was now really extremely painful, and by the time they reached Sea View House he was completely lame.

"We must get our landlady, Mrs. Appleyard, to bathe it for you," said Eva, "and you must rest it all the afternoon. This is a misfortune!"

"I am so sorry to give so much trouble."

"I am so sorry to see you in so much pain. There, take my arm. It's a pull up the hill here, and I am sure that you cannot manage it alone."

Clair put his trembling hand through the slender arm offered to him, and the sense of pain died away in that touch.

Annie Dighton ran on to ring the door bell of Sea View House, and Eva and Clair went on slowly, arm in arm, after her.

"How can I ever repay you for your kindness?" said Clair, in a low tone.

"There can be no question of obligation between us," answered Eva. "I do not forget—though I never speak of it —what I owe you."

"To hear you speak of it fills my very soul with joy."

"Why? We both know it. You saved me from a terrible death, and as long as I live—" and Eva suddenly paused.

"Say it gives me some claim—ever so little—on your heart," said Clair, eagerly, bending closer to her, and unconsciously pressing the white, soft arm his hand rested on.

"Hush, hush, we must not talk nonsense," she answered, quickly. "Here come Annie and Mrs. Appleyard, and they will help you too. This gentleman has had an accident, Mrs. Appleyard," she went on, addressing the rosy landlady. "He has sprained his foot. Do you think you could bathe it for him?"

"Oh, yes, miss; certainly. It's the gentleman who called, I think—Mr. Lord Clair?"

Neither Eva nor Clair could suppress a smile at this new title.

But Mrs. Appleyard was a handy woman, and speedily Clair was laid on the parlor couch, and his boot taken off, and his foot, which was considerably swollen, bathed. Eva and Annie went up to their bedroom during this operation, and when Eva got there she sat down and sighed softly.

"Poor fellow!" she said.

"Yes. Isn't it a pity?" answered Annie.

"It is, but we must make the best of it," said Eva, starting up again. "What a blessing we ordered a good lunch, but I had a presentiment he would come to-day."

The lunch certainly was a good one, and did Mrs. Appleyard and her handmaiden every credit, but the guest did not eat much. He was too much excited, and his gray eyes scarcely left Eva's face. He also was suffering a good deal of pain; so much so that after lunch was over Eva proposed he should see a doctor.

"Do you think it is necessary?" asked Clair.

"Well, sprains are rather bad things, you know," answered Eva, going up to the couch on which he was lying and standing near him. "Or will you try to go to sleep, and Annie and I will go upstairs and keep everything quiet?"

"I could not sleep," answered Clair, looking with a smile. "I am going to be awfully selfish. Will you stay with me a little while? Or is it keeping you indoors?"

"Of course we will stay with you. I will read to you if you like?" said Eva.

"I should like.   But I'm afraid I shall not be able to travel back to Kilmore to-night, so I must take up my quarters at one of the hotels; and I must telegraph to my mother to tell her so, or the dear woman will be uneasy."

They settled it thus. Clair sent his telegram to Lady Kilmore, and Eva began reading little bits from the newspapers, and then flung them away and talked to Clair. It was not a dull afternoon in spite of the sprain, and when Annie Dighton left the room for a short while Clair was going to rise from his couch, but Eva would not allow him.

"No," she said, going towards him; "you must lie still."

He caught her hand as she spoke, and pressed his lips ardently on it.

"Do you know how glad I am that I fell?" he said.

"You must not make foolish speeches," replied Eva, trying to pull her hand away.

"But it is not folly; it is truth. I should rather have fallen ten thousand times than not spent this afternoon with you."

"What nonsense!" cried Eva. But at this moment Annie Dighton returned, and Clair sank back on his couch and the little scene ended.

In the meanwhile, however, Clair's telegram was speeding on its way to Kilmore, and reached the Hall about five o'clock, and was at once taken to Lady Kilmore.

She opened it, read it, and started to her feet with a sudden exclamation.

"What is the matter, Aunt Jeanie?" asked Annette Gower, who was sitting in the room.

"Clair has had an accident—" began Lady Kilmore.

"An accident! Clair?" cried Annette, also starting to her feet, and in an instant so deadly pale did she become that her aunt feared she was about to faint.

"It is not serious; he has sprained his foot," went on Lady Kilmore in trembling tones. "Are you ill, Annette?"

"It is nothing," answered the poor girl, huskily, and for a moment or two everything grew dark around her.

Lady Kilmore went up to her and put her arm round her and led her to a couch, her own heart sinking within her as she did so.

And after a little while Annette revived and drew a long, quivering sigh.

"It was the heat made me feel rather faint," she said.

"Yes, dear; lie down while I take Clair's telegram to his father," answered Lady Kilmore, gently. "Clair slipped on the rocks, it seems, and he is going to stay all night at Eastcliff, but he says it is not serious."

"Yes, Aunt Jeanie."

Then Lady Kilmore propped up Annette's head with a cushion, and having done so left the room with hasty steps, carrying Clair's telegram with her. She went straight to the library, where she found her husband.

"Kilmore, I have had a telegram from Clair," she began, half breathlessly. "He has had an accident on the rocks, and has sprained his foot, and he is not coming home to-night—and that girl is there—I must go to him at once."

CHAPTER XI.

A MOTHER'S ADVICE.

Lord Kilmore looked up with an annoyed expression on his face as his wife made this somewhat startling announcement, and held out his hand for the telegram.

"What fools young men are," he said. And after he had read the telegram he looked more annoyed still. "It was absurd of Clair to go to Eastcliff," he added.

"I did not think he would have done such a thing," replied Lady Kilmore, almost tearfully. "And this accident, of course—"

"Will form a grand opportunity for the young lady. Yes, Jeanie, I think you had better go, and bring him back with you."

"To-day? What about the trains?" asked Lady Kilmore, eagerly.

"You need not be in such hot haste as that. Go to-morrow, and I should go with you but for this confounded gout."

"My dear, you are not well enough to go. I will take Annette—and yet—"

"You had better take Annette, and she will be a companion for you. I will look out the trains, and I should certainly not leave Clair behind you there."

"Oh, no, of course not; I will stay with him until he returns with me; and I will speak to him—this acquaintance must not go on a day longer, Kilmore."

"If you can prevent it. And after all there may be nothing in it; a youth's fancy for a pretty face."

"Still I feel uneasy. Oh, what a pity it was, Kilmore, he ever went near that fire!"

"Not for the young woman's sake, by all accounts. However, the thing is to get him out of her way, and then I daresay he will forget all about her."

They talked in this fashion a little while longer, and settled the train by which Lady Kilmore and Annette Gower were to start for Eastcliff in the morning. But when during the evening Lady Kilmore mentioned this to Annette, she visibly shrank from the idea of going.

"I will go if you wish, Aunt Jeanie," she said, with downcast eyes, "but—"

"Would you rather not go, Annette?" inquired Lady Kilmore.

"I think Clair perhaps might—" hesitated Annette.

The truth was that Annette had also heard from Mrs. Dighton that Eva Moore and her daughter were at Eastcliff, and knew only too well, as she did so, what had been Clair's attraction to the place. He had gone to see this beautiful girl whom he admired so greatly, and Annette's heart sank within her as she recognized the fact. And she felt, too, that to go to Eastcliff, to run the chance of perhaps seeing Clair with Miss Moore, would be very painful. And perhaps Lady Kilmore guessed something of her thoughts, for after looking a moment at her young niece's downcast face, she said in her kindly way:

"Or will you stay and take care of your uncle, Annette, and Barton can go with me?"

"Just as you like, Aunt Jeanie," answered Annette, but Lady Kilmore saw she did not wish to go to Eastcliff, and therefore arranged to take her maid with her instead.

And the next morning Lady Kilmore started in the first train to join her son, and arrived at Eastcliff about twelve o'clock, and drove direct to the principal hotel in the place. She inquired if Lord Clair were staying there, and was informed that a gentleman who gave the name of Clair was.

"Has he had an accident to his foot?" asked Lady Kilmore.

"Yes, the gentleman has sprained his foot," answered the waiter of whom Lady Kilmore was making these inquiries.

"Then I wish to see him. I am his mother," said Lady Kilmore.

"The gentleman is at present out, madam," replied the waiter; "he drove out, but he said he would return for luncheon. Shall I show you to his apartments?"

Lady Kilmore therefore installed herself in Clair's rooms and waited for his return to lunch. But she waited in vain. The lunch hour came and passed and there was no appearance of him; the afternoon likewise waned, but still Clair came not, and each moment added to his mother's uneasiness. At length, about half-past seven, Clair limped into the room, leaning on a stick, having heard downstairs that a lady was waiting for him, and was at once clasped in his mother's arms.

"My dear Clair, how did this happen?" she asked, anxiously.

"I slipped on the rocks," answered Clair, smiling, "so I thought it best to telegraph to you; but, mother, dear, there was no reason why you should have taken the trouble to come."

"My dear, of course I came, and I shall stay with you until you are well enough to return with me," answered Lady Kilmore, and it must be admitted Clair's face somewhat lengthened when he heard this announcement.

"But it's nothing, mother; there is no occasion for you to stay," he said.

"Dear Clair, I will not leave you. But do not stand; sit down here and tell me all about it."

Clair accordingly sat down and detailed his adventure on the rocks, omitting various details that he thought it unnecessary to mention. Lady Kilmore heard nothing of the white sunshades in the distance that had lured his unwary feet into the pitfall. But she listened in her gentle, sympathizing way, and it was not until after dinner that she ventured to approach the subject nearest to her heart. Clair was then lying on a couch, and his mother sitting on a chair near him, and twice she essayed to mention Miss Moore's name, but her courage failed her. We all know how easy it is to fix beforehand to say unpleasant things, and how painful and disagreeable it is to do it. Lady Kilmore had decided on the very words she intended to use to Clair when she remonstrated with him on the subject of "that girl," but she found that these words did not readily flow from her tongue.

At last, however, with a decided effort she commenced.

"I was talking to Mrs. Dighton yesterday, Clair," she said, "and she told me that her daughter and that other young lady, to whom you were so kind during the fire at Holly Hill, are staying here. Have you seen them?"

"Yes, mother," answered Clair, quietly.

"My dear," rejoined Lady Kilmore, quickly, "I wish to speak to you about this acquaintance. Clair, it is not a wise one. Take your mother's advice, and do not see anything more of this young lady."

"Why, mother?" asked Clair, moving slightly on the couch.

"Dear Clair, the reason is obvious. She is not in your position of life, and any attention you pay her might be misunderstood; it is unkind even to the poor girl."

"You are quite mistaken, mother," answered Clair, raising himself up, while a flush crossed his face; "Miss Moore is a lady in every sense of the word, and not at all a person to misunderstand anyone's attentions."

"Still, dear Clair—"

"I think I am old enough to choose my own friends, you know," interrupted Clair, as his mother paused, and then he smiled and held out his hand. "Don't say anything more about this, please," he added, and then changed the conversation, which Lady Kilmore found it impossible to renew.

She retired to rest, therefore, in great uneasiness of mind, but when she proposed next morning to Clair that they should return the same day to Kilmore he made no objection.

"Very well, just as you like," he answered. "I'm going to make a call this morning, but after that I'll go when you wish."

"Surely, Clair, you are not going to call on—" began Lady Kilmore, in consternation.

Clair made no answer. He limped out of the room, and five minutes later his mother saw him drive away from the hotel door in a cab. She sat still and afraid after he was gone, trying to realize the situation. Clair was no longer a boy to be led, she plainly saw. He had asserted his right to choose his own friends, and had no doubt gone now to bid this young lady good-bye.

"Oh, how mad! how foolish!" murmured Lady Kilmore, speaking her thoughts aloud in their entirety. "And she is probably some adventuress, someone who will try to take advantage of his youth. But his father must speak to him; surely he will have more influence."

In fact, Lady Kilmore spent a very anxious hour before Clair's return. He came back to the hotel looking very bright and happy, and was ready to go home by the train his mother had decided on. His foot was still much swollen, but he made very light of it, and altogether seemed in the humor to take a very cheerful view of everything. Lady Kilmore, on the other hand, felt nervous and depressed. But she did not venture to say anything more to him on the subject of Miss Moore, nor did Clair mention her name; they mutually avoided it, but this fact did not tend to lessen Lady Kilmore's uneasiness.

They reached the Hall in time for dinner, but before that meal Lady Kilmore found an opportunity of speaking to her husband. He listened gravely and then smiled.

"After all," he said, "I don't suppose there is much harm done. Clair, like other young men, I suppose, did not like being lectured; but if he left Eastcliff so readily, it does not look as though he had any very strong attraction there. He talked of going to Scotland the end of this month, and at the Frasers some other pretty girl is almost sure to put this one out of his head."

"I only hope so," answered Lady Kilmore, wistfully. And during dinner, when Lord Kilmore indulged in some mild jocularity on the subject of Clair's sprain, he took it all in very good part.

"Were you assisting some fair damsel over the rocks, Clair," he said, "when you came to grief?"

"No, father, I was alone," he answered, "but I was not looking where I was going."

"A very unwise thing to do in life. 'Look before you leap' are words of wisdom."

Clair laughed good-temperedly. And during the next few days he said nothing about returning to Eastcliff, and

Lady Kilmore began to hope her alarm had been unnecessary. In the meanwhile Clair's sprain was mending, but he was still obliged to lay his foot up, and was thus a good deal thrown with his cousin, Annette Gower; and one day when he was lying on a couch and she was reading at the other end of the room, he noticed how ill, thin and pale she looked.

"Are you not well, Annette?" he asked, kindly, "for you don't look particularly flourishing."

A sudden flush passed over Annette's face.

"Oh, yes, I am very well," she answered. And then to Clair's great astonishment she rose hastily and left the room, and as she did so Clair noticed that her dark eyes had filled with tears.

"Poor little girl, what can be the matter?" he thought; and he was so disturbed at the idea that Annette was ill or unhappy that he spoke to his mother on the subject.

"What is wrong with Annette, mother?" he said. "She seems nervous, and does not look well."

"Yes, she looks ill, Clair; I do not know whether I should tell you, but she got a great shock when she heard of your accident at Eastcliff," answered Lady Kilmore.

"A great shock when she heard of my accident?" repeated Clair, in complete astonishment. "Why, mother, how could that give her a shock?"

"It did, at all events, Clair," said Lady Kilmore, gravely. "I got your telegram, and Annette was in the room, and I foolishly started up and cried, 'Clair has had an accident,' and the next moment Annette grew deadly pale and staggered forward, and would have fallen if I had not caught her in my arms."

A pained and an annoyed expression passed over Clair's face.

"What nonsense, mother," he said; "she is a nervous girl."

"I think she is very fond of you, Clair."

"Yes, of course, as a cousin; as I am of her."

"I do not know," answered Lady Kilmore, so significantly that Clair turned away his head and left the room, leaving Lady Kilmore perplexed whether she had spoken wisely or no.

CHAPTER XII.

JEALOUSY.

In writing to her mother at Kilmore Hall Annie Dighton had not mentioned Lord Clair's visit to them at Eastcliff. She did not do so by the advice of Eva Moore.

"What is the good of telling such a trifle?" Eva had said, carelessly; but after Clair's accident, Lady Kilmore herself mentioned to Mrs. Dighton that her son had sprained his foot on the rocks at Eastcliff.

"I wonder if he saw the girls?" replied Mrs. Dighton. "I told you, did I not, my lady, that our Annie and Miss Moore are there?"

Lady Kilmore gave her no further information, in fact, ignored Mrs. Dighton's remarks, and made that good woman uneasy lest she had taken an unwarrantable liberty. But after Lady Kilmore left the room she at once told her son that the young lord had been at Eastcliff, and Richard Dighton's face darkened at the news.

"What was he doing there, I wonder?" he said.

"I don't think the girls saw him," added Mrs. Dighton.

"I suppose Eva Moore saw him after the fire?" asked Richard.

"Yes, he went to call upon them at Sunny Brow, and walked with them to Holly Hill, and father saw them there. Father thinks a vast of the young lord, Dick."

"Oh, he's well enough. When can we go from here, mother? I'm certain I'd get better far faster at the sea."

Richard Dighton was in truth impatient once more to see Eva Moore, and jealous of Clair, though he told himself it was folly to be so. But he thought the young lord might amuse himself with Eva, and the fact that he had saved her life gave him a claim on her gratitude, though Richard Dighton had in truth a still greater claim.

He was therefore restless to leave the Hall, and his mother also felt she would be more at her ease under her own roof. But the doctor thought Richard still unfit to travel, and advised that no risk should be run.

Things went on thus for a few days after Clair's return

from Eastcliff, and then Clair suddenly announced he was going to run up to town for a few days.

"At this season, Clair?" said his father, looking up from his paper.

"Yes, I want to meet a fellow I was at college with; he's on the point of going out to India, and I want to shake hands with him before he starts; it's Allan Fraser; I think you once saw him in my rooms at Oxford, father?"

"I think I did; I suppose he hasn't time to come down here?"

"No, I'm afraid not; he's awfully busy, but I should like to see the dear old fellow again."

This conversation took place at breakfast the day following that on which Lady Kilmore had told Clair that Annette Gower had nearly fainted when she heard of his accident, and Lady Kilmore moved uneasily when she heard that Clair was about to leave home, and wondered if her words had done anything to hasten his departure.

If so, he gave no hint of this, and parted with Annette in exactly the same cousinly manner with which he always treated her. He went straight up to town, and certainly met his friend there, and wrote to his mother from his hotel, but the day after went down to Eastcliff and was ringing at the door of Sea View House when the clocks were striking five!

He was shown into the drawing-room by Mrs. Appleyard's shiny-faced handmaiden, and found Eva Moore alone there lying on a couch reading, and she rose with a sudden blush to receive him.

"You!" she said, in great surprise, holding out her hand.

"Yes, I told you I would not stay long away," answered Clair, clasping her hand fast in his.

"I am surprised. I thought—"

"What did you think?" asked Clair, with his eyes fixed on her face.

"Oh! nothing," answered Eva. "Annie is out," she added, "but I was lazy."

"Will you be lazy no longer, but go out with me?"

"Shall I? Very well;" and a few minutes later the two were walking together along the yellow sands, and Clair was telling Eva of his love.

"I have been counting the hours until I could see you

again," he said. "Do you know what I came back to say, Eva?"

"How could I know?" she answered coyly.

"I thought you might guess; I came to tell you what I am sure you do know—that I love you very dearly, and ask you to be my wife?"

Eva shook her head.

"You must not ask me that, Lord Clair."

"But why?" said Clair, eagerly.

"For many reasons."

"Tell me one."

"Your father and mother would not like it."

"I love and respect both my father and mother," answered Clair; "but a man has a right to choose his own wife, and I have chosen mine—if I can persuade her to have me."

Eva laughed softly.

"Why talk of it?" she said. "Let things drift on; are you not very happy as you are, Lord Clair?"

"Call me Clair."

"Well, are you not happy, Clair?" and Eva looked at him with her lustrous eyes. "You are too young to marry—too young even to think of it—and are we not dear friends?"

"The dearest friends!" answered Clair, ardently. "But you are so dear to me I cannot bear to think of life without you, or even a day without you, so you see nothing but marriage will satisfy me."

Eva was silent for a moment; then she looked again at his eager, earnest, good-looking face.

"Do your people know that you are here?" she asked.

"No," replied Clair, with an ingenuous blush.

"And they would say to you if they did, 'Why do you run after a girl of whom we know nothing; a girl who may be an adventuress; who does not hold your own position in life?' Is not that true now? Did not your mother say some such words to you when she came here and took you away? That was why I was surprised to see you to-day. I told myself: They will persuade him to drop an acquaintance of which they naturally do not approve."

"Even if they did, Eva, do you think what anyone said could induce me to change to you? You cannot understand what I feel to you if you can think so. If you will give me hope, that is all I ask and care for."

Eva sighed softly.

"You would reproach me perhaps some day if I did."

"No, never, Eva; you hold my future happiness in your hands. Will you throw it away?"

"Let us talk of it some other time. Why don't you ask me all sorts of questions, before you are so rash as to wish to marry me?"

"Because I know what you are without any questions. There is only one I wish to ask, Eva?"

"And what is that?"

"Will you learn to care for me?"

"Have I to learn, Clair?" and Eva smiled.

"Do you mean—am I so happy—"

"Hush, hush, do not go so fast! I mean we are friends, and friends care for each other you know. Let it rest there just now—Ah! here comes Annie just in the nick of time."

"What a pity we are going to meet her," said Clair, as Annie, pretty, blushing and shy, approached them.

Eva said nothing. She met Annie as though she were well pleased to do so, and smilingly looked at Clair.

"Aren't you surprised to see him, Annie?" she said.

"A little," answered Annie, blushing more deeply, as Clair shook hands with her.

"Well, I was a great deal, not a little," continued Eva, still smiling. "And Lord Clair, I suppose you are not going home to-day?" she added.

"Not for many days, I expect," said Clair, "but I did not come from Kilmore, but from town."

"Oh! indeed."

"And I hope I shall be able to stay here for a few days at least," went on Clair.

"And to-day? Where are you going to dine?" asked Eva.

"At the hotel, I suppose," replied Clair.

"Oh! but that will be dull for you all alone. We have dined, but suppose we give him high tea, Annie? It will be fun; will you have high tea with us, Lord Clair?"

"I shall be too delighted."

"Come along, then," said Eva, as though the idea amused her. And all through the evening she was in one of her liveliest moods. And as the hours wore on, the three young people seemed in the highest spirits. But by-and-by when the moon rose, and shed its white beams on the sea and on the shore, Eva went to the window and stood there

for a few moments in silence. And Clair followed her, and
stood by her side in silence also.

"I dare say there are people walking on the sands," suggested Annie.

Still Eva did not speak. Clair was standing very close
to her, she could almost feel his breath on her cheek, and
his near presence stirred a strange emotion in her heart.
She sighed, and Annie Dighton understanding plainly that
she was not wanted, rose and left the room. And as the
door closed behind her Eva looked round, and in doing
so accidentally touched Clair.

"Is Annie gone?" she said, in a low tone.

"Yes," answered Clair, and he bent his head down, bent
it until his cheek rested against Eva's, and again she sighed.

"Why do you sigh?" he whispered.

"Did I sigh?" she said softly.

"Yes—Eva—"

He put his arm round her as he spoke, and for a moment or two Eva did not turn away. She stood there with
her young lover, and did not shrink from his touch. Then
suddenly a memory darted across her mind, and she cried
out impatiently:

"We must not be foolish, Clair; do you hear? we must
not be foolish!"

"Love is not folly," answered Clair passionately; "and
I love you, Eva—Eva, I love you!"

He drew her closer and kissed her, but the next moment
Eva pushed him away.

"We must forget this," she said. "Clair, be wise, go
away from here—and yet—"

"And yet what, Eva?"

"I shall miss you—that is like a woman, isn't it? One
moment I bid you go, and the next I wish you to stay."

"I will stay."

"But trouble may come of it. Mrs. Dighton and her son
are coming in a day or two, and it will come to your father
and mother's ears that you are here."

"I do not care."

"Oh, but you must care; you must care for your own
sake, for mine. No one must know, Clair, what has passed
between us to-day; our only chance of seeing each other,
of being with each other, is that no one knows anything
about it."

"But how can such a thing be, Eva?"

"I live alone; when I go to town you can come and see me, but here you must remember that your father and mother are certain to hear if you are much with me. And if they hear, that will part us. I don't want to part, Clair, though perhaps I should—yes, I know I should."

"I will hear of no parting, Eva, my darling, my darling—"

"No, no, you must not speak so. Let me ring for lights."

"Give me one kiss first, Eva—just one!"

She turned her face to his as he spoke, and for a moment her lips lightly touched his cheek.

"You foolish boy!" she said, half-tenderly, and then drew away from him and did ring for lights, and when Annie Dighton returned she saw there was a strange flush on Eva's cream-like skin, and an unusual light in her dark eyes.

Clair stayed late, and lingered even when he rose to go.

"To-morrow?" he said, as he held Eva's hand, "What time may I call?"

"Lord Clair," she answered gaily, "I have frequently had to remind you, both here and at Sunny Brow, of the existence of a certain Mrs. Grundy."

"Oh! bother Mrs. Grundy," said Clair, half-impatiently.

"But she exists, and we must consider her. Suppose you do not call, but that we meet on the sands at twelve."

"Oh, come earlier than twelve; say eleven."

"Very well, at eleven—and now good-night, Lord Clair."

Then he went, still loth to go, and after he had quitted the house, Annie Dighton said in a half-frightened tone:

"Do you know, Eva, I think it is very strange of Lord Clair coming here again so soon."

"Why do you think it strange?"

"Well, you see—he's not like us."

"Not in our station of life, you mean. That's precisely what I told him."

"I think he must be in love with you; but, of course, nothing could come of it."

"Of course not!" laughed Eva, rather bitterly.

"And I am afraid people will talk."

"Well, perhaps you had better not leave the room any more when he is here, Annie."

"I think I had better not."

They agreed to this, yet nevertheless when they met Clair

by appointment on the sands the next day and Annie remained steadily by Eva's side during the whole time, and
also when he came to call upon them in the evening, Eva
admitted to herself she felt it was a little wearisome. As
for Clair, he could scarcely conceal his impatience in the
bounds of politeness.

In vain he tried to draw Eva apart, there still was the
apparently inevitable Annie! This went on for two days,
and then Eva either took pity on herself or Clair, for one
afternoon she informed Annie that she meant to go out by
herself.

"What! with Lord Clair, Eva? You know he said he
would call at four," answered Annie in a shocked tone.

"Yes, even with Lord Clair," rejoined Eva, with a little
laugh. "Don't look so alarmed, Annie, I am not going
to run away with him."

"Still—"

"My dear, I mean to go, so don't say anything more; I
find that two are company and three are not; and now I
am going to dress for my walk." And with another laugh
Eva turned away.

And when Clair called he found only Eva waiting in the
drawing-room to receive him. Annie Dighton, who felt injured, had retired to her bedroom, and to Clair's intense
satisfaction Eva announced she was not going out to walk
with them.

"Then I shall have you to myself for once," said Clair,
joyously.

Eva laughed, and the two went out together along "the
ribbed sea-sand." Clair was happy and excited, but Eva
was more subdued than usual. It was a somber day for
one thing, the sky clouded and gray-tinted, and the sea
broke on the shore with a melancholy moan.

"It sounds as if it were angry," said Eva.

Clair turned round and looked at her with his bright
smile.

"But you are not angry, are you," he said, "to be alone
with me?"

"No, I am not angry, but somehow I feel rather sad.
Have you ever presentiments of coming evil, Clair?"

"No, I can't say I have."

"I have felt them, and the evil came; I wonder where

they come from? If our good or our bad spirit sends them?"

"And do you think we each have a good and a bad spirit in constant attendance?" laughed Clair.

"I think we are dual creatures at all events; that we have a good and an evil nature within us at constant warfare. One wins one day, and the other the next. This accounts for the contradictions in our actions; for our unstableness of purpose."

"But you are not unstable, Eva?"

"Yes, I am. What says the proverb? 'Unstable as water thou shalt not excel.' That accounts for all my failures and shortcomings."

"I will not listen to such heresy! Let us go and sit on the rocks, Eva, for I have so much to tell you; what I've been thinking of these two days when that tiresome little Miss Dighton would not leave us alone."

In the meanwhile at Sea View House "that tiresome little Miss Dighton" was receiving a great surprise. This was no less than the unexpected arrival of her father and mother, and her brother Richard. The doctor had the night before given Richard leave to travel, and he insisted on at once availing himself of this, and the family party had started in the morning from the Hall.

"We thought we would give you a pleasant surprise, my dear," said Mr. Dighton, while kisses and handshakings were being exchanged. "And where's your friend, Miss Moore? Here's Dick all anxiety." And the farmer laughed heartily.

"Oh!" replied Annie, still smarting from the slight she had received about going out to walk. "Eva's out with Lord Clair."

"Out with Lord Clair, my lass?" repeated Mr. Dighton, in genuine astonishment. "Why, Lord Clair's in London; his lordship told me so himself this morning."

During this conversation Richard Dighton's face grew a dusky red, and his dark brows met in an angry scowl.

"You must be mistaken, father," went on Annie; "the young lord has been here for days now, and we have often seen him."

"But you never wrote to say so, Annie," said Mrs. Dighton reproachfully.

"No, mother, because Eva said I had better not."

"Well, I must say this beats everything!" exclaimed Mr. Dighton. "The young lord here! Why, Annie, who is he running after? Miss Moore I suppose?"

"I suppose so," replied Annie, with a little toss of her pretty head, while with an angry exclamation Richard Dighton turned indignantly away.

"It was cursed impudence of him to come here at all," he muttered, and as he spoke a certain look of anxiety passed over his father's good-natured face.

"Nay, my lad, don't say that," he said; "young folks will be young folks, even if they are lords, and run after a pretty face."

Richard Dighton made no answer; he sullenly strode out of the room, and his mother looked after him uneasily.

"It's a pity you told Dick about the young lord being with Miss Moore, Annie," she said; "he doesn't like it, and I think she ought not to go walking about with the like of him; I always said so."

"But, mother, you mustn't forget she owes her life to him," replied the farmer.

"Our Dick did more and fared worse." said Mrs. Dighton, with some indignation; "and it's a queer business, the old lord telling you, father, that the young lord was in London, and us finding him here. Don't you think it has a queer look?"

"Pretty odd," said Mr. Dighton, with a perplexed look. "But I think, mother, you had better go and look after Dick now."

Mrs. Dighton followed her husband's advice and found her son in a very angry and excited mood up-stairs.

"Don't mind, Dick, about the young lord; it's just all nonsense, I dare say," she began, by way of consolation.

"But I do mind. He had no business to come here running after the girls, and Annie had no business to keep it a secret. It's an insult to us all, and I won't have it!"

He strode angrily to the room window as he spoke, and the first sight that met his eyes was Eva Moore, fair and smiling, and Clair close to her side, approaching the house.

"Curse it! here they are," exclaimed Dick Dighton, and upon this Mrs. Dighton at once hurried to the window also.

"Well, to be sure! It's the young lord, and no mistake. And how he's looking at her, just as if he could eat her, I declare. And she's a smiling and coquetting up in his face! I wouldn't think of her any more, Dick; she's not fit for a decent man's wife if she's ready to carry on like that," said Mrs. Dighton, commenting on the young couple below.

"Don't talk folly," answered Richard, sullenly, with his gloomy eyes also fixed on Clair and Eva. "But I'll bring him to book for all this. Lord or no lord, I'll let him know what I think!"

CHAPTER XIII.

VERY DISAGREEABLE.

In the meanwhile, Eva and Clair, quite unconscious of the storm within, were smilingly approaching Sea View House, and stood talking together in the porch what seemed a very unnecessary time to several eyes that were watching them.

Even the good-natured farmer felt disturbed as he noticed from the dining-room window the lingering hand-clasp and lengthened parting of the young pair.

"This will never do," he muttered to himself, and when at last Eva entered the room and saw Mr. Dighton, the expression of his jovial face was not as its wont.

"Mr. Dighton!" exclaimed Eva, advancing with outstretched hand, "this is quite an unexpected pleasure."

"Well, my dear, how are you?" answered Mr. Dighton. "So the young lord was with you, was he?"

"Yes," said Eva, with a pretty little shrug and a smile; "he's been here a day or two, and he's nothing to do."

"Except to walk about with you, seemingly," said Mr. Dighton; "his father does not know he's here; he told me he was in London."

"So he was a day or so ago, and he's going back directly, I suppose; that is how Lord Kilmore made the mistake," replied Eva calmly. "Nowadays, you know, Mr. Dighton, young men do not write home every day to tell where they are going."

"No, indeed," said Mr. Dighton, shaking his head.

"He's a very pleasant companion," continued Eva,

"Yes, yes, so he is—but still, my dear—"

At this moment the room door opened, and Richard Dighton entered with a frown on his brow.

"Oh! you here too!" said Eva, going toward him with a smile, and holding out her hand. "I hope you are better, Mr. Dighton?"

"It wouldn't matter much to you whether I am or not," answered Dick sullenly, and as he spoke Eva opened her large dark eyes wider, and looked at him in surprise.

"Why do you say that?" she said. "It does matter—it must matter I think, when you were so dreadfully injured in trying to—help me," and Eva gave a little shudder. "I have never had the opportunity of personally thanking you yet," she went on the next moment, "but I do thank you now with all my heart."

"Oh! I did nothing," said Richard, still sullenly; "I failed." And he sneered.

"I thank you all the same, and I have grieved very much to hear of all the pain you have gone through on my account. But I hope the change here will make you quite strong."

"Oh! yes, Dick will soon pick up here," said Mr. Dighton, pleasantly. "Well, young folks, I don't know what kind of housekeepers you are, but I feel uncommonly peckish. But mother has come armed with hams, and eggs and butter, as we thought we would surprise you; so we won't starve, anyhow." And Mr. Dighton laughed his jovial laugh.

"My dear Mr. Dighton," cried Eva, who liked the farmer, "you make me quite hungry by talking of all these lovely country things! But I assure you Annie has not starved me; she is a famous little housekeeper."

"Well then, Annie, see about something to eat," said Mr. Dighton, "and I'll go and look after mother and her good things, for I can tell you we all want something after the journey." And saying this, he left the room, closely followed by Annie, and Richard Dighton and Eva Moore were left alone. Almost from the very first sight of his sister's friend, Richard Dighton had conceived a passionate admiration for her, which had quickly ripened into violent love. It was quite true, and he knew it, that Eva had never given the slightest encouragement to his somewhat awkward advances. But in spite of all the young farmer had cherished the most romantic hopes. He was really in love with Eva, and his desperate attempts to save her during the fire had proved this, and now his heart felt very bitter within him at her seeming forgetfulness of what he had gone through.

He turned away his head as his father and Annie left the room, and then the next moment looked at her, still with anger in his rather deep-sunken eyes.

"So," he said, "you've had the young lord here to amuse yourselves with—or to amuse him."

"Both, Mr. Richard," answered Eva, airily.

"That's well!"

"Yes, Lord Clair has nothing to do here, and we have nothing to do, so it has been a mutual accommodation," said Eva, and she laughed.

Her mirth jarred on Richard's ears, and made him more bitter still.

"Well, I won't let my sister make a fool of herself any longer," he said roughly.

"How has she made a fool of herself?" inquired Eva looking at him.

"I consider any woman makes a fool of herself who allows a man to dangle after her when he means nothing but to spend an idle hour or two."

"But Lord Clair has not dangled after Annie; I was the person he came to see."

"And you say this to me!" exclaimed Richard fiercely; "to me who—"

"Why should I not say it to you, Mr. Dighton?" asked Eva, calmly.

"Because you know—you must know," and the young man's face flushed darkly, and the veins on his forehead swelled, "that I can't bear to hear it; that I can't bear to think of any man making a fool of you; that I shall resent it."

"You have no right to do so, Mr. Dighton."

"Yes, I have; at least you are under my father's roof."

Eva was silent for a moment, then she said quietly:

"I have received great kindness from you all; I am greatly indebted to you—so much indebted I can never repay it—but still, Mr. Richard, this gives you no right to speak of Lord Clair as you are doing."

"I think he has no right to come here; I am sure he has none."

"Why?"

"Because as I said before he only means to amuse himself."

"Well, and if he does, what of that?"

Richard Dighton bit his lips under his dark moustache, and turned his head indignantly away.

"If you look on it in that light—" he said.

"We all seek to amuse ourselves, Mr. Dighton, so why not Lord Clair?"

Richard Dighton said nothing more. He strode hastily out of the room, though only to return to it a few minutes later. Eva Moore possessed to him the old symbol of the moth and the flame. He could not resist the attraction of her near presence, though it only gave him pain.

He sat down therefore to the substantial meal which Mrs. Dighton and Annie presently provided, with a scowling brow and a sullen heart; Eva maddened him; love maddened him. In vain the farmer essayed his most genial jokes. Richard neither ate nor smiled, and Mrs. Dighton's maternal feelings were greatly troubled. She also secretly resented Eva Moore's conduct and blamed her for making her beloved Dick unhappy, though in truth she was not in the least to blame, though her beautiful face might be. At all events this evening meal was not a success, and when as the twilight gathered the house-bell rang, and a few moments later Clair was announced, they all felt—including Eva—that his visit was an ill-timed one.

Nevertheless the farmer rose and welcomed him with the respect due to his landlord's son.

"How are you, my lord?" he said.

"Ah, Mr. Dighton," answered Clair, pleasantly, holding out his hand, "I did not know you were here?"

"Only came this afternoon, and my wife and Dick."

Then Clair looked round, for the room was very dark, and perceived Mrs. Dighton and Richard. He went up to them, but Mrs. Dighton received him stiffly, and Richard more stiffly still. Eva Moore, however, was, or appeared to be, quite at ease.

"We have had a pleasant surprise you see, Lord Clair," she said; "when I came in this afternoon I found in my absence that Annie had got her father and mother and brother all with her again."

"A great pleasure to Miss Dighton, I am sure," answered Clair, pleasantly. "And how are you, Dighton?" he added, turning to Richard. "Nearly well again, I hope?"

"Yes, nearly," answered sullen Dick.

Upon this Clair sat down by Eva Moore on the couch, but Eva did not remain long by his side. She rose, crossed the room, and drew a chair near the farmer's.

"I want you to tell me all about my pets at Holly Hill, Mr. Dighton," she said. "How is Rover, and Dobbin, and Rose, and my little pet pig, and last, but not least, is the puppy old enough that you promised me for me to have him now?"

The farmer laughed aloud.

"My dear, how many questions have you asked me at once?" he said, good temperedly. "The horses are well, and the cow, but I don't know which was the pet pig. And the puppy? He's growing a very handsome fellow, and I daresay you could have him now."

"I tell you why I ask. Now that you and Mrs. Dighton are here, I am no longer needed to chaperon Annie," said Eva, with a little laugh. "So in a day or two I propose to leave your hospitable roof."

"Nay, nay, my dear, don't say that. Annie will feel lost without ye. Stay at least as long as we are here."

Eva gently shook her head.

"You are very good, but I should not have stayed so long only Mrs. Dighton could not be here to look after Annie. I have enjoyed my visit to you very much, Mr. Dighton."

"Not so much as we've enjoyed having ye, I make sure of that," said the hearty farmer. "Come, Miss Moore, promise to stay a bit longer with us."

While this conversation was going on, to which Richard Dighton was eagerly listening, Clair was talking in rather a disjointed fashion to Mrs. Dighton and Annie. But his heart was not in it, and it did not progress very satisfactorily. Then suddenly Eva rose and left the room for a few minutes, and on her return she resumed her seat by the farmer. Altogether, no one seemed enjoying themselves particularly, and, somehow, Clair felt that his presence was not overwelcome to the family group. He therefore, after a short stay, said he must go, and no one pressed him to prolong his visit.

He shook hands with the rest, and then advanced toward Eva, who rose as he approached her.

"I want a word with you for a moment, outside," she said.

"Yes, most certainly," answered Clair, only too well pleased.

She followed him, therefore, to the door of the room, while all the eyes in it followed her, and, without going out into the hall, she put a small note into his hand.

"I want you to study that," she said, smiling. She did not expect her action would have been seen, but as the hall lamp was lit and the room nearly dark, it was; and a fierce pang of rage and jealousy darted through Richard Dighton's heart.

"Thank you, I shall," said Clair, and then they shook hands and parted, and Eva returned to the room and began to talk of something else, as though she had done nothing out of the way. But this was not the opinion of Mrs. Dighton. She cleared her throat, and (for her) began in a somewhat severe tone—

"You seem very friendly with the young lord, Miss Moore."

"I like him," replied Eva carelessly.

"And has he been coming here much?" continued Mrs. Dighton.

"Oh, no; we have seen him outside once or twice. But how stupid we all are! Annie let us sing them a song, and try to enliven them."

She thus changed the conversation, but not the current of Richard Dighton's thoughts. He remained sullen and moody during the rest of the evening, and when the party broke up for the night, he hardly spoke to Eva. In the meanwhile Clair, at his hotel, was studying the little note Eva had put in his hand. It was very brief but significant.

"Dear Clair:

"Don't come here any more just now; that young rustic, Richard Dighton, has been making himself remarkably disagreeable, and for the short time I now mean to stay here, I do not want any quarrels. I will see you once before I go, and will write and tell you where we can meet.

"Yours,

"Eva."

CHAPTER XIV.

AN ANONYMOUS LETTER.

Clair read Eva's brief note many times, and was absolutely reading it again the next morning after breakfast, when a waiter entered the room, and asked him if he would see a gentleman who had called.

"Certainly," answered Clair, and a few moments later Richard Dighton was ushered into the room.

"Ah, Mr. Dighton," said Clair, rising politely, and holding out his hand, but Richard did not take it.

"I have not come on a visit of ceremony, Lord Clair," he said sullenly, with downcast eyes.

"Ah—then may I ask—"

"I have come to ask you not to come hanging about my sister or her friend any more," answered Richard roughly. "You mayn't look on them as ladies, but I mean to see them treated as such."

Clair opened his gray eyes a little wider, and stared at the angry young man opposite to him in complete surprise.

"I utterly fail to understand your meaning," he said.

"It is this," retorted Richard Dighton fiercely, "you've been walking about with Miss Moore and my sister day after day, and going to my father's house in an underhand way, and I won't have it! They are not in your station of life, Lord Clair, and you had better keep to ladies who are."

"You are extremely rude, and are speaking in a manner utterly improper and uncalled for. And you are also much mistaken. I regard Miss Moore in my own station of life —as a lady—or I should not have sought her society."

"That's all very fine! But as long as she is with us—"

"Would you kindly leave the room?" interrupted Clair, coolly. And with a half-muttered curse Richard Dighton did so, leaving Clair feeling greatly annoyed.

Nay, he was more than annoyed—he was angry. That this young Dighton, the son of one of his father's tenants, should presume to speak to him in such a manner absolutely amazed him. Clair, at Kilmore, and indeed through all his young life, had been accustomed to be treated with respect, which his own kindness and sweetness of disposition had certainly merited. He had known Richard Dighton from boyhood, and they had always exchanged pleasant words with each other when they chanced to meet. "And for him suddenly to turn round thus, and absolutely insult me," thought Clair, indignantly.

"I suppose he is jealous about Eva. What impudence of him ever to think of her," went on his reflections. Indeed, this last idea ruffled him still more.

"It is monstrous," decided Clair; "and from Eva's note he has evidently been talking folly to her also. But I am glad I ordered him out of the room, the rude cub."

It took Clair quite an hour to get over the irritation of Richard Dighton's visit. Then he went out and wandered on the sands in the hope of meeting Eva and Annie Dighton. But no; none of the Dighton family were to be seen, and Clair returned to his hotel for lunch in anything but a happy state of mind.

But he found a note lying in his room from Eva, which instantly restored his good temper. It was very brief, but it asked him to meet her that very afternoon, and that was sufficient to bring the sunshine back to Clair's heart.

"Dear Clair:
"For certain reasons I have decided to leave this place to-morrow, so will you meet me this afternoon to say good-bye? Come to the rocks where you had your unfortunate stumble about four o'clock, but please do not stumble again!
"Yours,
"Eva."

Even the news of this note did not displease Clair. Eva was leaving Eastcliff, and Clair was not sorry for this, after his unpleasant interview with Richard in the morning. He felt that he could not go to the Dightons' house now, but he felt that he could go wherever Eva was going, and then he could see her and be with her without "that idiot," as he mentally dubbed Richard Dighton, "talking folly."

So he went with a light heart to the rocks, where he had his mischance, long before the appointed hour, and sat there watching for Eva's slender, graceful figure to appear. And presently he did see her advancing in her white gown along the sands, and he rose and went eagerly forward to meet her.

"You got my note?" said Eva, as she took his hand.

"Yes, I was awfully glad to get it," he answered.

"And yet we are going to part."

"Only to meet again very, very soon though."

"I don't know. Clair," continued Eva, looking at him earnestly, indeed sadly, "I've been thinking over things; I owe much to you, and I don't want to repay it badly."

"How do you mean, Eva?"

"It would be better for you, wiser for you—not to see me again."

"Eva!"

"Listen to me, Clair, and do not be angry. It is not that I should not like to see you again, for indeed I should. But, if you like me in the way you said—"

"I do not like you, Eva, I love you with my whole heart!" answered Clair impetuously. "Do not talk any more thus, please. Not see you again! I do not know what I should feel if for a moment I believed that."

"Still—"

"Eva, you are leaving here to-morrow, you say; now tell me where you are going?"

"That is just what I have been making up my mind not to do; just what I have been telling myself I should not do. You had far better forget me, Lord Clair, far, far better for yourself."

Eva spoke these last words with some emotion, for her lips quivered, and her voice faltered.

"I could not forget you if I would," replied Clair, also agitated. "Eva, why do you torment me thus? You know I love you, yet you are saying things that you must also know give me great pain."

"I do not wish to give you pain—here are the rocks; let us sit down, Clair, and I shall tell you what I think."

They sat down together on a shelving brown rock, near which there was a deep fissure, into which the sea swept and gurgled, raising the brown sea-weed, and passing over the sea flowers. With that changeful mood of hers Eva pointed these out to Clair, talking of the beauty of their coloring, while the young man's heart was hot and restless, thinking of other things.

"You were going to tell me something," he said, at length, almost impatiently.

"Yes, so I was," she answered, looking round. "Clair—if I tell you where I am going—if you come and see me, we must just be friends, you know."

"You mean—"

"Well, to put it in a different way, you—must think of me as a woman older than yourself—"

"I do not believe you are older," quickly interrupted Clair.

"Not in years, perhaps, but in mind, in everything, far, far older! You have had no troubles. I have had heaps —troubles and sorrows, Clair."

"Let me shield you from them all," he answered, ardently, clasping her hand.

"You would if you could, I believe, Clair," answered Eva, softly.

"I will, and I can—give me the right to shield you, Eva, and you shall see."

"And so bring them on yourself, perhaps. Clair, you must not talk thus—you must promise, and then I shall tell you where I mean to go."

"Well, tell me!"

"Well, promise!"

"I promise not to say anything you do not wish to hear for—ever so long."

Eva laughed.

"Ah, Clair, Clair!" she said, shaking her head.

"Do tell me, Eva."

"I know I should not; however, I will. You must know, Clair, since Mr. Richard Dighton came down here he has made himself most remarkably disagreeable. He affects to be angry about you; perhaps he is jealous."

"But you have given him no cause to think—"

"Certainly none," said Eva, decidedly; "but from the time I went to Holly Hill, he, I suppose, admired me a little."

"And you?"

"I certainly did not admire him. I never liked him, yet he took upon himself to lecture me on your visits."

"Impertinent fellow!"

"It was rather cool, I must say. Certainly he tried, I believe, to help me on that dreadful night at Holly Hill.

He was hurt, you know, in trying, so they told me; and this, I suppose, gives him, he thinks, a certain claim. But not to be rude, and he was rude, and so I am glad to go away, and I do not wish Mr. Richard to know where I am going."

"Do not tell him."

"I do not mean to; I mean to go to Brighton for a day or two, and write to Annie from there, and then go to my own house in town. I wish, in fact, to drop Mr. Richard entirely, for I am getting rather frightened of him."

"Frightened?"

"Yes, he looks so savage and sullen there is no saying what he might do, and therefore I mean to keep out of his way."

"He had the impertinence to come to me this morning, and to request me not to go near you and his sister any more."

"Had he really? That's just what I say; he has taken some folly or other about me into his head, which I suppose he will forget if he does not see me, but in the meantime it is very disagreeable. Therefore, when you come to see me, come to Kensington."

"When, Eva?"

"I shall be there in a week. This is the address."

"Then in a week I shall see you?"

"Yes, if you wish to do so, with no Mr. Richard Dighton to watch you and make himself disagreeable. I live alone."

"Alone?"

"Yes, quite alone; does the idea make you afraid, Clair?"

"Why should it?"

"That I have no chaperon; no maiden aunt, no friend to look after me? I am a solitary being, Clair, and if you are wise, you too will leave me alone."

"Then I shall not be wise, Eva."

She sighed softly, and leaned forward and rested her cheek against her hand.

"Things are so strange," she said musingly.

"Why do you say that?"

"I was thinking that when I went to Holly Hill, when I danced that first day with you in the tent, that I little imagined such a short time afterward I should be talking to you and treating you quite like an old friend."

"Then from that day, Eva, do you know what I felt to you?"

She slightly shook her head without looking up.

"I was thinking of you, dreaming of you, that night when I first saw the red light in the sky that warned me of the fire at Holly Hill. So you see from the very first, Eva, what you were to me."

"Was it fate?" she said, now glancing up with rather a sad smile.

"Yes, you are my fate, my beautiful fate," and he put his hand on hers.

"Take care I am not your baneful fate—but no, no, I must not be that, Clair; I will not, I must not injure you."

He answered by some impassioned words; he sat there gazing at her, his young heart all aglow with love. Her vague warnings against herself fell on deaf ears. He could believe nothing ill of her; to him her soul was pictured in her face.

And when she rose to leave him, and held out her hand, he would not let it go. Neither of them suspected that at this moment jealous eyes were watching them, and yet this was so, for with bitter emotions raging in his breast, Richard Dighton had followed Eva at a distance when she went to meet Clair, and at a distance also now saw the two standing handclasped on the rocks.

He could scarcely restrain his rage, crouching down there behind them, hidden by a jutting crag, and yet he did so. The rebuff he had received from Clair in the morning was still rankling in his heart, and he felt that if he made his presence known to Clair now he would only be treated as he had been before. So he watched them, and the jealous anger within him grew and grew as he did so. And to do him justice he really believed that Clair was only amusing himself with Eva Moore. It never entered his imagination that he would marry her if he could.

"He wishes to make a fool of her," he told himself darkly, "but he shall not, if I swing for it."

And had he heard what Eva and Clair were saying of him, he probably would have been more angry still.

"I must go, Clair," said Eva, smiling; "consider if I were to encounter my rustic and most unpleasant swain, Mr. Richard Dighton."

"Oh, confound the fellow!" answered Clair.

"It's best to keep out of his way, I feel sure; he has a sullen, dangerous look in his eyes that I don't quite like."

"He had better not come in my way, I can tell him, or do anything to annoy you."

"He won't annoy us in Kensington; so please leave him alone."

Then, after a few more words, Richard Dighton saw them part, and he remained where he was until they both left the rocks. But an idea had entered his brain there; an idea which he believed would soon end the acquaintance of Lord Clair and Eva. He would write anonymously to the earl, and tell him how his son was conducting himself at East-cliff, and he believed that this would effectually separate them.

In the meanwhile Eva was walking toward Sea View House, and as she did so her expression changed and saddened.

"Poor fellow," she murmured more than once to herself, "poor, poor Clair."

And when she reached Sea View she went straight to her bedroom and locked the door behind her after she got there.

"I should not have told him," she was thinking in self-reproach. "I meant not to tell him, but he looked so dear, so honest, that I could not resist. It's folly, madness—but I am afraid I like him too well."

She sat down and sighed wearily, and it was not until Annie came and rapped at the door to tell her tea was ready that she roused herself. She did this with an effort, and went downstairs, where she found Mrs. Dighton and Richard.

"Well, Miss Moore, so you have been out for a walk, Annie tells me?" said Mrs. Dighton as she entered.

"Yes, a short walk," replied Eva.

"I hope you enjoyed it?" remarked Richard, disagreeably.

"Not particularly," said Eva, and then she began talking of her journey on the following day to Brighton, and Richard sat listening, wondering if Clair would follow her there also, and determining at the same time to do so himself.

And he did not go to bed until he had accomplished his idea of writing to Lord Kilmore. And this letter took him much time and thought to compose. It was written in a vindictive spirit, and he could hardly disguise this in his words. He commenced it again and again, and could not satisfy himself. He wanted to abuse Clair, but his common-sense told him this was unwise. He must write a friendly warning, and not let Lord Kilmore suppose that it was written by an enemy of his son. At last as he could make no better of it, he sent the following lines, going out to post his letter after the rest of the family had all retired for the night:

"My Lord," began Richard, "this is written to warn you that your son, Lord Clair, is here, and paying marked attention to a young lady named Miss Moore, whom it is said he assisted to rescue during a fire. This is written by a friend who feels sure that your lordship would not approve of his conduct, the young lady being in a completely different position of life to himself, and her friends also greatly object to an intimacy from which no good can result.—And I remain, your lordship, your obedient servant,

"A Friend."

Richard having posted his letter felt happier, having no doubt that it would at once cause his parents to look after Lord Clair. Therefore at breakfast the next morning he was not quite so sullen in his manner to Eva as he had been since his arrival at Eastcliff. She was going away, too, and the real love, or rather passion, in his heart made him anxious to remove any bad impression he had made from her mind. And she looked so handsome, too, as she sat opposite to him, that he could scarcely take his eyes from her face. She was going to start in an early train, and Richard asked if he might escort her to the station, to which Eva smilingly assented.

"Annie is going with me, too," she said, "but I am very sorry to go."

She was not really, though. She was half afraid of this young man, and of the jealousy he had so plainly shown of Clair. She knew something of the darker passions of men's hearts and felt it was playing with fire to arouse those of Richard Dighton. She was pleasant and gentle in her manner to him, therefore, but this was all. She had in truth never encouraged his admiration; in fact, despised it. But she did not show this; she simply ignored it.

"And how long will you stay at Brighton?" Richard aske

going to her side, as she stood a few minutes at the window looking out at the sea.

"I am not sure," she answered, turning round.

"If I go there to see you, will you cut me?" went on Richard.

"Certainly not; why should I cut you, Mr. Richard?"

"That's all right then, I will go," said Richard, and Eva decided at this moment, what she had indeed intended before, that her stay at Brighton should be a very brief one, and after she left there that her future residence should be a secret from the Dighton family.

But she gave no hint of this. She thanked Mr. and Mrs. Dighton for their kindness and hospitality very prettily, and the farmer more than once told her that she would be always a welcome guest on their return to Holly Hill. Then the cab came to take her to the station, and Annie and Richard accompanied her there. Eva had asked Clair not to go to see her off, as the Dightons were sure to be with her, and Clair unwillingly had promised not to appear.

And at the very time when the brother and sister were taking leave of her Richard's letter to Lord Kilmore was being opened at the Hall. Breakfast was over and the post bag had just been brought in, and among other letters was one bearing the Eastcliff postmark. Lord Kilmore glanced at it, opened it carelessly, and then read it and frowned as he did so. But he said nothing. His wife and Annette Gower were in the room, but Lady Kilmore noticed that he looked annoyed, and when he rose and gathered his letters together to leave the breakfast-room and go to the library, he beckoned to his wife to follow him.

Lady Kilmore did so, feeling anxious, for her thoughts had at once flown to her son, and there was something in her husband's manner that made her uneasy. When she reached the library she closed the door behind them, and looked at Lord Kilmore.

"Any news, Kilmore?" she said.

"Yes," he answered, gravely; "if the news in this letter be true, it is a great blow to me, Jeanie, for I must cease to believe in Clair."

"In Clair!" repeated the mother, and her face paled.

"Yes; this letter states that he is now at Eastcliff; that he is constantly with that girl, Miss Moore; and yet the last letter I had from him was from his club in town. He must have gone there purposely to deceive us."

"Oh, Kilmore, this cannot be true!"

Lord Kilmore answered by placing the letter in his wife's trembling hand, and when she had read it tears rushed into her eyes.

"Oh! this is terrible," she said. "You must go to him, Kilmore; you must try to save him!"

"I am very much disgusted with him," replied Lord Kilmore; "I did not think our son would have acted a lie."

CHAPTER XV.

A FATHER'S WARNING.

Lady Kilmore caught her husband's hand imploringly, as he uttered these harsh words.

"Oh! don't speak thus, Kilmore," she said, tremulously, "thus of our boy!"

"I have very good reason to be angry with him, Jeanie."

"He has been foolish, but consider how young he is, Kilmore, and this woman may be some artful person—besides this letter may be false."

"It does not seem to be so," said Lord Kilmore, again reading the anonymous letter; "it is probably written by some one who knows us, by name at least, and thought it only kind to let us know about Clair, though," he added after a moment's pause, "I admit I do not like anonymous letters."

"Nor I; if there is anything to tell, why not do it openly?"

"Still there is no doubt that this ought to be inquired into. If Clair has been at Eastcliff—and what motive could the writer have if he has not?—he has intentionally deceived us, and it is my duty to see into this. I will go to-day."

"I will go with you then, Kilmore—but are you well enough to go, dear?"

"I should rather you did not go, Jeanie; I should rather see Clair alone. Besides I wish my visit to be kept as quiet as possible, which could not be if you went also."

After some further anxious conversation Lady Kilmore

agreed to this plan, and Lord Kilmore started for the station in time to catch the mid-day train to Eastcliff, leaving his wife in a most unhappy state of mind. She tried to hide this from Annette Gower, but could not, for she was so restless and disturbed, and unlike herself during the whole day.

"Is there anything the matter, Aunt Jeanie?" at last asked Annette.

Lady Kilmore hesitated for a moment.

"Something has worried me a little," she then said, and Annette immediately began to think, Could it be anything about Clair?

And so the hours passed anxiously for both the aunt and niece, and when Lord Kilmore arrived at Eastcliff his mind was also anything but relieved on the subject of his son.

It chanced that almost the first persons that he saw on the platform as he left the train at the seaside village were Mr. Dighton, of Holly Hill, and Richard. The farmer saw the earl alight, but did not intrude himself until Lord Kilmore's eyes fell upon his substantial and well-known form. Lord Kilmore at once bowed, and then Mr. Dighton approached his landlord.

"Ah, Mr. Dighton," said the earl, "so you are here, are you?"

"Yes, my lord, for a day or two. I brought my wife and Dick down, you see," answered the farmer.

"And how is your son getting on?"

"Oh, very well, my lord. Dick, come along, my lad; here is his lordship and you must thank him for all his kindness to you at the Hall."

Richard Dighton accordingly now approached his father and Lord Kilmore, who asked him kindly after his health.

"And have either of you seen my son here?" he added, inquiringly.

"Yes, my lord," replied Mr. Dighton, with a certain uneasiness of manner which did not escape Lord Kilmore's notice; "the young lord has been here for a day or two, and I saw him the first day we came."

"I saw him yesterday," said Richard Dighton, without looking up.

"Ah!—I'll find him at some hotel, I suppose; perhaps either of you gentlemen would be good enough to direct me to where he is likely to be found, for I have not been to this place for many years, and I hear it is greatly changed."

"That it is, my lord; new-fangled and the like. Lord Clair is staying at the North Star, isn't he, Dick?"

"Yes, father."

"We will walk to the North Star, then," smiled Lord Kilmore; and accordingly the three proceeded together to the new part of the town, where Clair had been staying. And on the way the earl inquired about the repairs at Holly Hill, and alluded to the fire.

"Is the young lady still with you," he asked, "who so nearly lost her life?"

"No, my lord, she left this morning," replied Mr. Dighton; "she's gone to Brighton."

"Ah!—she had a narrow escape. I'm told she is a handsome girl?"

"That she is, and no mistake; and she's a nice one, too, my lord," said the farmer.

"Yes," answered Lord Kilmore, and then he changed the conversation. He did not wish the farmer to suspect his motive for coming to Eastcliff, though Richard Dighton of course knew it well.

The father and son parted with Lord Kilmore after pointing out the North Star, and when the earl arrived there and inquired for Lord Clair he was told that his lordship had left Eastcliff in the mid-day train for town.

"For town?" asked the earl quickly.

"Yes, sir," answered the waiter to whom Lord Kilmore was addressing his inquiries; "his lordship's luggage was directed to his club in town."

There was nothing further therefore to ask. Clair had been at Eastcliff and had left on the same day as this Miss Moore, reflected the earl grimly enough, and Brighton was very accessible to London. Altogether the affair looked very unsatisfactory, and Lord Kilmore ate the dinner he ordered at the hotel with an uneasy heart, and started back for the Hall by the very first train he could catch.

It was late when he arrived there, but he found his wife up, and anxiously awaiting him. And the moment Lady Kilmore looked on her husband's face she saw he did not bring good news.

"Have you seen him?" she asked quickly.

"No, he had left Eastcliff to-day, but he had been there for several days as far as I could gather."

"Oh! Kilmore—and this girl?"

"The girl also left to-day; she went to Brighton, and Clair to town; in fact, Jeanie, I think it very unsatisfactory."

Lady Kilmore clasped her hands, and her lips quivered.

"Oh: if after all our hopes, he wrecks his life!" she murmured, in great distress.

"We must try to prevent him doing so. I shall go up to town to-morrow and see him, and I shall point out to him the extreme folly and imprudence of his conduct. Come, Jeanie, don't cry; I will use all the influence I have to stop this affair going any further."

But Lady Kilmore could find small comfort. She was devoted to Clair; had been from the time when his baby eyes first looked into her face, and to think of this infatuation for an unknown girl was most grievous to her heart. She put no obstacle in the way, therefore, of her husband going up to town on the following day, and entreated him, if possible, to bring Clair back with him. And Lord Kilmore did go. He was in indifferent health, and rarely left the country, but this business about Clair seemed to him to be too urgent to be neglected for a day.

He started therefore on the following morning, and reached London about seven o'clock, and drove at once to the club, of which he also was a member, where he expected to find or at least hear some news of his son. Lord Clair was there, he was told, in the smoking-room, and thither Lord Kilmore proceeded, and seated in a divan chair, smoking and reading the evening papers, he found Clair, who started up in great surprise, and it must be admitted, some consternation, when he saw his father approaching him.

"Why, father, whoever expected to see you!" he exclaimed.

Lord Kilmore gravely shook hands with him, and there was something in his father's manner that made Clair sure that he had come on no ordinary purpose.

"Is there anything the matter?" he asked quickly. "Is my mother—"

"Your mother is well, Clair," answered Lord Kilmore, as Clair for a moment paused. "But I have come up to town on purpose to see you, and you had better go with me to the hotel where I mean to stay."

Clair made no objection to this plan, and together they drove to the hotel, Lord Kilmore's manner still continuing very grave during the drive, and when they found themselves in a private room, Lord Kilmore did not hesitate to announce his purpose to his son.

"I have something very serious to say to you, Clair," he began.

Clair's face slightly flushed, but he looked with his gray eyes steadily in his father's face.

"Yes, father," he answered.

"It is this; you left home to see your friend, young Fraser, before going to India, you told me, yet I find you in reality went down to Eastcliff, and have been there some days. Is this true, Clair?"

"Yes," said Clair, after a moment's hesitation, "I did see Fraser, and then I went to Eastcliff."

"And your motive?"

Again Clair hesitated.

"Your motive," continued Lord Kilmore severely, "was to run after and constantly be with the young woman you rescued during the fire at Holly Hill. Is this right, Clair?"

"I see no harm in it, father."

"No harm! What right have you to trifle with the affections of any young woman to whom you possibly could have no honorable intentions?"

"I certainly did not mean to trifle with Miss Moore's affections," answered Clair, sturdily.

"But you are doing so. What you did for her gives you a certain claim on her regard, and you have no right to take advantage of this, by paying her attentions that can mean nothing. I received a letter, an anonymous letter, informing me that you were constantly with her, and that her friends objected to your being so."

"That is utterly untrue, whoever wrote it. Did you bring the letter, father?"

"Yes," said Lord Kilmore, producing Richard Dighton's letter from his coat-pocket, and handing it to Clair, who grew very red as he looked at its contents.

"I think I know who wrote this," he said, angrily; "it's a piece of monstrous impertinence."

"But it states what is true, I suppose?"

"No it does not, father; Miss Moore had no friend at Eastcliff to object to any attentions of mine. The one person who did I believe wrote this letter, merely for the purpose of making mischief."

"Even if that is so, you see your conduct is exposing this young person, Miss Moore, to injurious remarks."

"That is impossible."

"But it is so; Clair, as a gentleman you have no right to act thus."

Clair began to walk up and down the room impatiently; then he suddenly stopped and stood before his father with a certain nobleness of expression on his good-looking face that the earl did not fail to notice.

"You are mistaken, father," he said bravely. "You are speaking as though I meant to do Miss Moore some injury. But this certainly is not so, for I have asked her to be my wife."

"Asked her to be your wife!" repeated Lord Kilmore aghast. "Are you utterly mad, Clair?"

"I see no madness in what I have done, and, moreover, she refused me."

"Boy," said the earl, in strong indignation, "how dare you trifle thus with the family honor?"

"I do not consider that I have done so."

"Then I tell you that you have! Who is this girl that you have invited to take your mother's place, and what do you know of her? Absolutely nothing!"

Lord Kilmore was a man who prided himself on his philosophic calmness of temper under all the aggravations of life. But this was a little too much for his philosophy. That his son, his heir, should have dared to ask a young woman to marry him, who was, and must be in a perfectly different position to himself, almost took the earl's breath away. He looked at Clair with his eyes full of anger, and not a little contempt. He was thinking he was a fool, and an obstinate fool to boot.

"Do you tell me," he repeated, "that you have absolutely asked this girl to marry you?"

"Yes, father," answered Clair, sturdily.

"Then I tell you," shouted the earl, "that I will not allow it! I'll see this girl, and tell her you won't have a penny during my lifetime if you commit an act of such outrageous folly. Marry a girl whom you met staying with a tenant farmer, indeed! It's preposterous; you must give this up, Clair; I insist on it."

"I told you she refused me, father."

"I don't believe in her refusal; that is probably a clever move to make a soft young fool more in love with her; for you are a fool, Clair, to make such an ass of yourself."

"Really, father, you are using very strong language."

"No language, in my opinion, can be too strong for such folly. That you, my heir, the future head of the house, should for a moment have thought of such a thing is to me inconceivable. Even if you were what is called in love with her you should have some self-control. You owe it to your birth, to your name."

Clair was silent, but the earl perceived no signs of yielding in his face.

"I have some claim upon you, at least," continued Lord Kilmore, "and your mother has some claim. Promise me, Clair, for our sakes to give up this insane idea, to see this young woman no more."

"I cannot do so, father."

"You cannot?" cried the earl, again raising his voice. "You tell me this to my face? You, almost a boy, dare to put your will against your parents, and talk of marrying a girl of whom you know nothing? Who is she? Who are her friends, and where does she come from?"

"I cannot answer such questions; they are an insult to Miss Moore."

"Because you don't know, I suppose," said the earl, with a bitter and derisive laugh. "She's some handsome adventuress, I'll be bound for it. There are scores of such to be met with in the world, and that you'll find out before you're many years older. I should not be surprised if it were a regular scheme to get hold of you. She may have heard from her friend, Miss Dighton, that the young heir of Kilmore was coming of age on such and such a day, and have absolutely gone down to Holly Hill on purpose to try to make a conquest of you. Oh, yes, you may smile and sneer, whichever you like, but I have not the least doubt that this is the truth."

"Well, in justice to Miss Moore, I must tell you that she especially requested me not to pay her any attention; that far from trying to entangle me she threw cold water on all my advances."

"Oh, yes, I dare say, and then little by little relented. Clair, I know the world and such women better than you do, and before I married had my temptations and follies like the rest. But when a young man in your position talks of marrying it is a different affair."

"But, father—"

"My dear boy, do not speak such folly any more. If you want a wife, choose one in your own position of life; one who has no secrets in the past, whom you can take from her father's house. Such marriages only are satisfactory, and it would be a miserable thing for your mother and myself if our only child were to make a fool of himself with an adventuress."

"But Miss Moore is not an adventuress," said Clair, indignantly.

"Whatever she is, she is no match for you. Clair, come home with me. Keep out of this woman's way, and some day you will be thankful that you followed my advice."

Again Clair was silent. He was fond of his father, and he had never seen him angry and what he thought unjust before. Lord Kilmore, in truth, was a kind and affectionate husband and father. But Clair's "folly" had provoked him out of his usual frame of mind, and he was certainly not acting with his usual good sense to speak to Clair as he was doing. Clair perhaps felt naturally indignant to be treated as if he were a boy, though he suppressed his anger out of respect to his father. But he speedily excused himself from remaining any longer at the hotel, as he said he had a dinner engagement he was bound to keep. Thus Lord Kilmore dined alone, and after dinner wrote to his wife, telling her he had seen Clair, but suppressing, out of consideration to her feelings, the painful—to him—nature of the interview.

But the more he thought of Clair's words, the more uneasy he became. That Clair was warmly attached to "this girl," as he mentally designated Eva Moore, he plainly perceived. And he also believed that no young woman in her position of life would really hesitate to marry his son if she could possibly do so. Her refusal of Clair was all nonsense, he told himself, and only showed she was deeply designing. Altogether the whole affair was most vexatious— more than vexatious—and after spending a restless night the earl telegraphed next morning for his son to come to him.

Clair went, but this meeting was equally unsatisfactory as the former one. Nothing that his father could say would induce him to promise that he would give up his acquaintance with Eva Moore.

"I think it is a subject on which no man has a right to dictate to another," he said.

"And you are such a very old man, Clair," replied Lord Kilmore, a little scoffingly.

"I am old enough, at least, to choose my own friends," retorted Clair, and in the end a very serious disagreement arose between the two, and they finally parted on anything but good terms.

"If you have anything to do with this woman you will bitterly repent it," was the earl's parting admonition to his son. But Clair merely bowed, and muttering that he was an obstinate fool, Lord Kilmore turned away, and, as he was feeling anything but well, and saw that his words and advice were quite wasted, he decided to leave town, and went back to Kilmore carrying his ill news with him to the anxious mother.

CHAPTER XVI.

A QUEST.

Eva Moore had scarcely gone from Eastcliff when an overpowering restlessness took possession of Richard Dighton's heart to see her again. A letter to Annie arrived from her two days after she had left, dated from Brighton, and telling Annie vaguely she hoped she would soon see her again. But she gave no especial invitation, and never mentioned the name of Lord Clair. Annie showed this letter to her brother, and he read it eagerly, noting the address, and mentally determining that he would find some excuse to go to Brighton to see her. Eva said nothing in her letter about leaving shortly; in fact, inferred that she meant to make some stay. The Misses Richards from Sunny Brow were coming on a visit to Annie for a few days at Eastcliff, and Richard Dighton took advantage of this, and told his mother that as he "could not bear those two women" he meant to go to Brighton while they were with them.

Mrs. Dighton sighed uneasily at this announcement. She knew quite well why her son wished to go to Brighton, and she was not at all satisfied in her mind about Eva Moore and Lord Clair.

"Don't you think it will seem rude to them for you to go while they are here?" she suggested.

"Don't care whether they think it rude or not," replied Richard.

Again Mrs. Dighton sighed, but she said nothing more. She wished Richard to be happy, but she saw he was not, and she was uneasy. She told her husband that she was afraid Miss Moore was quite unsuited for a farmer's wife, and that she did not believe that she would "settle down with Dick after carrying on with the young lord."

"My dear, in my opinion she won't have Dick," replied the farmer. "But don't cross the lad; let him try his chance if he has a mind to, and if Miss Moore does marry him she's not a girl, or I'm much mistaken, to look at anyone else."

Thus Richard Dighton met with no opposition from his parents regarding his proposed visit to Brighton, and just one week after Eva Moore had gone there, he also proceeded thither, and, having engaged a room for a week at the Grand, went with a fast-beating heart to the address that Eva had given Annie in her letter.

He found the house, which was not a pretentious one, and, having inquired for Miss Moore, was told to his dismay that she had left two days before.

"Left!" repeated Richard. "Why, she only came a week ago."

"Yes, I know, sir," answered the servant who had opened the door; "she took the rooms for a week, but she said she had to go to London quite suddenly, and so she went last Tuesday."

Richard Dighton's heart sank within him as he listened to these words.

To London! And Lord Clair was in London, and these two might meet! Perhaps she had gone there to meet him, thought Richard, with a bitter, jealous pang.

"Did she leave any address?" he asked, harshly.

"Not that I know of, sir, but I'll ask the missus," replied the maid, and presently the landlady appeared, who was red of visage, and apparently of uncertain temper.

"You're asking for Miss Moore, I understand, sir," she

began; "but I know nothing of her, and I don't think she behaved as I expected."

"How was that?" said Richard.

"Well, she came here and took the rooms for only a week certainly, but I understood her that if they suited she meant to stay on. But she just stayed four days exactly, and then packed up and was off. I don't call that exactly good behavior."

"But she would pay for the week, I suppose?" inquired Richard, who was anxious to prolong the conversation in the hope of hearing something more of Eva.

"In course she paid for the week," said the landlady, irately. "She shouldn't have stirred from here unless she had done what's honest. But I consider she was doing the rooms an injury just to stay four days, as if she wasn't comfortable, though that's impossible."

"And she gave you no address where she was going to in London?"

"Not a word. She just said one morning, 'Mrs. Midge, I am going to-day; I've been suddenly called to London,' and off she went before twelve o'clock in the day in a cab, taking her luggage with her; but if she was called suddenly to London it was not by letter, for none came for her when she was here."

"No letter? Did any telegram come, then?"

"Not one, sir; my opinion is she came intending only to stop four days, and I don't call it good behavior."

"Did anyone call to see her?"

"Not a soul crossed the door, sir. If she has any friends," added Mrs. Midge, spitefully, "they weren't particular in their inquiries."

"She has friends," retorted Richard, who did not like the landlady's tone. "My sister and my mother are friends of hers."

"Eh, dearie me, sir," said Mrs. Midge, now dropping a curtsey and changing her manner. "Don't think I'm saying anything against the young lady, for she was always pleasant spoken. But being a widow, with many calls, for them rates and taxes are just enough to break a lone woman's heart, I can't afford to stand empty, and I felt hurt that Miss Moore should go so soon, when I hoped for a month at least."

Richard Dighton put his hand into his pocket and produced half a crown.

"Will you take that?" he said, which offer Mrs. Midge accepted with avidity. "And you are quite sure she left no address lying about her rooms?"

"None that I know of, sir, but come in and look and welcome, and I'll be pleased to show the rooms."

Richard accordingly followed the landlady upstairs, and was ushered by her into the drawing room, the door of which she opened with some pride.

"It's a nice room, sir," she said, looking round her apartment, "and was fresh papered two years ago last October, and I had a new rug and irons at the same time, though, as I was saying, all these things press very hard on me in my present state, and any little help is very acceptable. Yes, sir, that is the desk where I have seen Miss Moore sit a-writing; you can open it, sir, perhaps there may be an address inside, for I have never looked."

Richard Dighton on this permission eagerly opened the little ordinary desk, which stood on a little ordinary table near the window, and inside he found a few scraps of paper which had apparently been used to cover some small parcel. He examined the torn pieces of paper closely, and on one was written the word "Kensington." The rest of the address, if there had been any, was not there. Only this single word, and as he looked at it Richard remembered that Eva Moore had been at the same school at Kensington as his sister Annie. This was then probably part of the wrapper of some old parcel. Still Richard Dighton took it away with him.

"May I keep this?" he said.

"Oh, certainly, sir," replied Mrs. Midge, affably. "And as I was saying, sir, any little help is most acceptable."

Upon this hint Richard produced a second half-crown, and after looking all round the room he took leave of Mrs. Midge, and returned to his hotel in a very desponding frame of mind.

He had gone to Brighton on purpose to see Eva Moore, and he had missed her, but there was a certain obstinacy in his disposition that made him determined to find her, and his jealousy of Clair grew yet stronger as he remembered that Clair might know where she was, though he did not.

He started to his feet, he bit his lips, as this idea stung

his heart. He hated the young lord; hated him for his good looks, for his easy grace of manner, which Richard Dighton knew that he himself did not possess. And he easily persuaded himself that Clair meant to wrong Eva, and that he, with his truer love, had a right to defend her. He finally determined to go to London to try and find her, though he had no chart to help his quest, except the one word "Kensington," and the knowledge that Eva had been a boarder at a school there where his sister Annie had finished her education.

But he would try. So he left Brighton, and went up to town, and took rooms near the street where Annie had been at school. He called upon the lady who kept this establishment, and having announced himself as the brother of her late pupil Miss Dighton, said that his sister was anxious to know where her friend Miss Eva Moore was now living and had asked him to call and inquire.

But the lady shook her head. She had never heard of or seen Miss Moore since she left her roof, and had no information whatever to give. Thus Richard Dighton gained nothing by his visit, and used to wander up and down the streets and squares of South Kensington in the vain hope of meeting or catching a glimpse of Eva Moore.

A fortnight passed thus. The weather was hot and sultry, and Richard Dighton's funds were running low, and he was becoming impatient and irritable, and still he could see or hear nothing of Eva. Then he took to going to different stations and watching the passengers leave the trains, eagerly scanning the different faces as he did so. But all were strangers to him, and disheartened and weary he would turn away. This went on day after day. His people at home were becoming uneasy about him, and still Richard Dighton lingered in town. At last one night, while he was standing idly outside Earl's Court station, looking at the passers-by, at the women with their baskets of half-faded flowers, at the stir and bustle of the street, suddenly a soft laugh fell on his ears which made him start and turn quickly round.

A train had arrived a minute before in the station below, and the passengers were now coming up, and this laugh— low, musical and sweet—proceeded from one of them. Richard Dighton knew that laugh, and in the semi-darkness he eagerly scanned the little crowd passing him on their way from the station, and his eyes quickly fell on Eva Moore and Clair!

He recognized them in a moment. They passed him closely, but never saw him, and just as they went by Richard heard a few words fall from Eva's lips.

"What a boy you are, Clair," she said, looking smilingly up in her companion's face.

Clair! The word echoed through Richard Dighton's heart with a fierce pang of jealousy and rage. What, it had come to this, then, he thought. She called him Clair; she was with him, alone. And as the two, unconscious of his presence, passed on, Richard Dighton followed them, dogging their footsteps at a sufficient distance to prevent them noticing him.

They passed the conservatory a little distance from the station; they went on down the main street for some distance and then turned into a side street, finally stopping before a pretty-looking small house with a balcony and a red-striped awning. Clair rang the bell of the door of this house, which was opened, and the two entered together, and then the door was shut, and Richard Dighton stood outside in a state of mind almost impossible to describe.

He himself could scarcely realize it. Rage, hatred, jealousy, some of the darkest passions of our nature, were all surging together in his soul with overwhelming force. He at once put the worst construction on this intimacy of Clair and Eva. They were living together, he told himself. This scoundrel of a lord had taken advantage of the service he had done Eva to ruin her life. Richard set his teeth hard and clenched his hands, and vowed bitter vengeance as he stood there in the quiet street in the starlight. And presently he heard voices above him—Eva's voice—though he could not hear the words. They were out on the balcony, talking and laughing, little guessing of the dark-faced listener below with black despair on his brow and heart.

It was all over, he felt, at this moment of extreme bitterness. This woman, whose beautiful face had cast a spell over his life, was unworthy of a thought. But none the less did Richard Dighton think of her; none the less did he vow to avenge her wrongs.

It was an insult to them all—to his mother, Annie, and himself. Lord Clair had met Eva Moore when a guest under his father's roof, and this was the respect he had shown to them all!

A snatch of song from above broke in upon his dark reflections. It was Eva singing a pretty verse, and by-and-by she went inside and played the melody of the song, and then came back to the balcony and sang it through. Then Clair clapped his hands in applause and cried "Bravo!" and Eva's soft laugh floated on the night air.

This mirth and seeming light-heartedness maddened Richard Dighton. What! She could laugh and jest, could she, in her dishonor? This woman, who had darkened his life and made it all bitterness to him, felt neither pity nor regret. He had risked his life three times to save hers, and she never gave him a thought. But she shall rue her sin, swore Richard Dighton, and even as the oath lingered on his lips the house door opened, and, to his surprise, Lord Clair came out.

He appeared so suddenly that Richard had not time to make up his mind how to act. And as he hesitated Clair whistled for a hansom, and one came up, and the next moment he was gone. To attempt to follow him was, Richard knew, useless. Should he force his way into the house and upbraid Eva? But that, too, would be useless, Richard thought, darkly. She would probably again disappear if she thought she were watched. He could not take his vengeance so easily if his presence were known. He would watch and wait, and so gloomily he paced up and down the street for hours, until the city clocks chimed midnight; until the first faint tinge of dawn spread on the summer sky. But he saw and heard nothing. The lights had been all put out in the little house with the balcony soon after Clair left, and he did not return.

"But to-morrow," thought Richard Dighton, darkly, "to-morrow I shall know."

CHAPTER XVII.

A PROMISE.

Richard Dighton drank heavily before he finally flung himself down in the early hours of the new day to take a few hours' rest. He drank to drown the gnawing pain in his heart; the intolerable sense of shame and pain by which he was pursued. And he slept a heavy sleep, but awoke in the morning with the pain in his heart still, before he fully realized what caused it.

When he did its full bitterness was not diminished. He recalled Eva as he had seen her first—the graceful, beautiful girl, so unlike all those whom he had ever seen before. He remembered the languid light in her lustrous eyes the evening she came to Holly Hill, and how from that night her image had never been absent from his heart. All this came back to the unhappy young man as he lay there with throbbing brow; all his hopes, his love, and then his angry jealousy at the attentions of the young lord to Eva at the dance in the park, where from the first he had distinguished her above all others.

Then he thought of the fire; how when they had roused him from his sleep, and told him of Eva's danger, he had rushed into the burning house, ready to give his life, if need be, for hers. Three times he had tried to ascend the flaming staircase and fell with it; and then this other man—this lord—and a fierce oath burst from Richard's lips, had come, and with no danger to himself had saved her—for what?

He sprang out of bed, unable any longer to endure his thoughts, and began hastily to dress himself with his trembling hands. He had forgotten to wind up his watch the night before, and did not know the time until he went down to his sitting room, and was amazed when he got there to find it was so late. It was past eleven o'clock, so he hurriedly drank some tea and then went out, going direct to the neighboring street to the one in which was the house where he had seen Eva Moore enter with Clair.

He stood at the corner of this street, out of sight of the windows of the little house with the balcony where he had watched the night before. But this morning he had not

long to wait. Before twelve o'clock he saw a hansom drive
up to Eva's house, and Clair sprang out of it dressed in riverside costume. He entered the house, but three minutes
later Eva, in white, with a large hat trimmed with red pop-
pies, and with a red silk sash round her slender waist, came
out of it, closely followed by Clair, who was carrying some
wraps.

He handed her into the cab, he seated himself by her side,
and then a maid-servant brought a luncheon basket from
the house and placed it beside them.

They were evidently going on a country excursion; probably down the river; and the fiercest passions flamed forth
afresh in Richard Dighton's breast as he realized this fact.

He turned away with unutterable bitterness in his soul as
the cab containing the young pair disappeared from his
sight. He seemed to see them together on the shining
river flowing placidly by its willowy marge; he seemed to
see Eva's face, and to hear her low laugh, as she listened
to her lover's words.

*   *   *   *   *   *   *

But let us for awhile leave the half-distracted man, wild
with jealousy and hate, nursing his dark thoughts and plan-
ning his dark deeds, and follow the two on whose faces was
the sunshine of love.

From the time of Eva's return to town Clair had been a
constant visitor to the little house which she had taken furnished, where she lived alone, excepting the two servants
she had engaged.

Clair asked no questions as to the reason of this retired
and solitary life. She did not wish to be troubled by Mr.
Richard Dighton, she told him, smilingly, and Clair was but
too happy to be allowed to see her; to sit by her side, and to
hope that some day her love would be warm and tender as
his own.

But she would not allow him to talk of this.

"No, no forbidden subjects!" she would cry, gayly, when
Clair was led away by his feelings and began to speak some
impassioned words. "We are friends," she told him; "it
was an agreement when I told you where I was going to
live."

"I never quite promised," answered Clair one day, smiling.

"Oh, that is mean; abominably mean," said Eva, still gayly. "Well, promise now, then."

Clair shook his head.

"I only said I should not say what I thought would worry you, and Eva—does it worry you to hear I care for you so much?"

Many such words as these had passed between them during the time Eva had been in town, and though she affected not to like to listen to Clair's declarations of affection, she in truth found pleasure in them, and was happiest when he was by her side.

And while Richard Dighton, with knitted, gloomy brow, was thinking of her with rage and despair, Eva was smiling brightly on her lover, bent on enjoying the river excursion which they had fixed to take the night before.

It was one of those days, fresh and beautiful, when the first breath of autumn cools the summer heat. They drove to Paddington and went by rail to Henley, and soon found themselves upon the shining water.

Eva was in extraordinary spirits, and insisted on first rowing the boat they had engaged, and they spent two or three hours most enjoyably. Then the luncheon hour came, and they pulled to the shore and landed by the meadows; and here Eva unpacked the basket, spreading out the good things she had brought, and was seemingly in the happiest possible mood.

The excitement and the fresh air had heightened her beauty, and as they sat together beneath some trees, Clair suddenly caught both her hands in his.

"Eva, how long are you going to keep me waiting?" he said, passionately.

"For what are you waiting, Clair?" she answered.

"For you to be my wife; for you to be with me always."

"Clair, this is folly."

"No, it is not. Why should we wait?"

"There are many reasons why, as I have told you before."

"But I do not care for any of the reasons."

"But then I do."

"Oh, Eva, you tantalize me! You allow me to be with you, to love you, and yet you will not go a step further."

"Would you rather never see me, then?"

"How can you ask such a question? How can you say

such words? Not see you! I could not live now if I did
not see you, but I am not made of stone."

"But, Clair, there are many reasons why—we cannot
marry just now, at least. For one thing, your parents would
naturally object, as I am not in your position of life."

"I will take any position of life you like until I give you
mine."

Eva sighed uneasily, and glanced shyly at Clair.

"If I were a good woman," she said, after a little pause,
"I would not listen to you, Clair."

"You overestimate things, dear Eva; there is really no
difference between us except that my father is a peer, and
that is a very small difference indeed."

Again Eva sighed; but she let her hand rest in his, and
looked vaguely at the sparkling river beyond.

"Clair," she said, presently, "do you believe that if we
were very good, very self-denying, that we should be happier?"

"I suppose we ought to be, at least."

"I don't think I could. I am not self-denying; I am selfish. I think of present enjoyment, and not of other people.
I am afraid I am very bad, Clair."

"Your badness is very charming, then."

"You think so because you are young, and I am, I suppose, good-looking. But if you could see into my heart."

"I see into your heart; your character is written on your
sweet face."

"Then I must be very ugly," said Eva, with a little laugh.
"I hope my character is not written on my face; I wish my
face to be a mask to hide my soul."

"Oh, Eva!"

"I want you to understand me—and yet I don't. That is
what is so strange about me. I want to be quite honest,
quite true to you, and yet I have not strength of mind to see
you change. For you would change, Clair, if—"

"If what?" asked Clair, uneasily, for at this moment his
father's warning words recurred to him.

"If you knew what a bad temper I have," said Eva,
quickly, for her sensitive ears had caught the alteration in
his tone. "I am so variable, Clair."

"I am not afraid," answered Clair, in a relieved voice;
"that makes you only more charming, I think—the light
and shade."

"Let us go back to the light, then, and leave the shade. After all, life is so short we should try to enjoy it; to knock some pleasure out of it, for there is plenty of care."

"What cares have you, Eva?"

"Let me see—oh, no, I won't think of them. Let us go on the river again, Clair, and make the most of our holiday."

After this they spent most of the afternoon on the water, and then had tea at the hotel, and lingered there until it began to grow dusk. Then they returned by train to town, and drove from the station to the little house at South Kensington, where Eva had ordered supper to be prepared for them.

And as they traveled together in the gathering dusk, Eva was sweet and gentle, almost tender in her manner, and Clair's heart was full of happiness. He had never felt so sure that she cared for him as during these hours. They sat side by side; they spoke in love's soft whispers, and strange joy filled their souls. Eva seemed to have forgotten her warnings—her gloom. Her dark eyes were fixed on her young lover's face, her hands were clasped in his. There were moments of delicious silence, but they needed no words. The journey seemed far too short; the spell broken only too quickly. They both sighed softly when they reached home. They never saw a dark form crouching near the doorway; never heard the hiss of a suppressed oath as Clair handed Eva from the hansom, and for a moment drew her against his breast.

They went into the house with light hearts, and sat merrily down to the meal which Eva had ordered to be ready for them.

The wretched watcher outside saw the house all alight, and could even hear the murmur of voices and laughter as he pressed against the iron railing in front. Then after an hour or so he heard the piano and a man and woman's voices singing together. It seemed to him as if this song would never end. The blood rushed to his head, the veins in his neck swelled, and such a fierce whirl of passion rent his soul that his senses seemed to reel. The song stopped at last, and he drew a deep breath, moved on a step or two, and then returned to his watch.

In the meanwhile, inside, Eva and Clair were taking leave of each other.

"I suppose I ought to go," said Clair, looking regretfully

at the clock on the mantelpiece, which indicated the fast
passing hours.

"Absolutely nearly eleven!" cried Eva, now also looking
at the clock. "Indeed you ought to go, Clair."

He went up to her and took her hand.

"Have you enjoyed yourself to-day, Eva?" he asked, tenderly.

"Yes, Clair."

"And we must have many other holidays?"

"Yes, Clair."

"What a good little girl you are to-night!"

"Quite a pattern of meekness and sweetness, am I not?"

"Quite a pattern! Well, good-night, then, dear—Eva,
my dear, dear love, give me one kiss?"

She smilingly shook her head.

"Do not impose, sir!" she said.

But Clair caught her in his arms and kissed her fair face,
in spite of Eva's not very strong opposition.

"Good-night, my dearest," he said, "I will see you to-
morrow."

And so he left her, and Eva, after he was gone, stepped
out into the balcony to watch him pass below.

She had scarcely got there, Clair had scarcely advanced a
few steps down the street when a shot was fired, and then
another, in quick succession.

Eva gave a sudden cry of alarm and looked anxiously
over the balcony, and saw to her dismay and terror by the
lamplight in the street below that Clair had stopped, that he
reeled slightly, and then fell forward.

With another cry she sprang back into the room, ran
down the stairs, and, calling to the servants as she passed
the dining room, who were removing the supper, she opened
the front door and hurried into the street, and two moments
later was beside Clair, who was trying to stagger to his feet.

"Clair! What has happened?" she asked, breathlessly.
"Are you hurt?"

"A shot has struck me, I think," he answered, faintly.
"Did you hear it?"

"Yes. Lean on me, Clair, and come back into the house,"
said Eva, putting her arm round him; and as Clair tried to
do this the two servants also came running up.

"He has been hurt; help me to lead him," said Eva; and

as one of the women took Clair's arm to assist him, a slight cry escaped his lips.

"It is broken, I think; do not touch it," half whispered Clair, and he staggered forward towards the house, Eva holding him by the other arm; and when they reached it Eva saw by the hall lamp that her white dress was stained with blood.

"Run for Dr. Sidney," cried Eva, excitedly, to one of the maids. "Tell him to come at once; that a gentleman has been shot."

The maid hurried away to obey her, and with the assistance of the other Eva succeeded in leading Clair into the dining room and placing him on a couch.

"Dear Clair, who has done this? How did it happen?" she asked, tremulously.

But Clair seemed too faint to make any reply, and Eva hastily called for some brandy. He drank a little of this and it revived him, but the blood was streaming fast from his side, and Eva's agitation was excessive. She knew not what to do, as each moment appeared to increase the bleeding, and one arm hung helpless by his side.

"You run for a doctor, too, Cooper," she said to the other maid, and as the woman left the room she was alone with Clair, and kneeling down beside him she clasped both his hands.

"Dear, dear Clair," she murmured.

He looked at her with a tender light in his gray eyes and saw she was trembling.

"Don't be afraid, my dearest," he said, "I shall be all right —and Eva, even if—"

"If what, Clair?" she asked, with a choking sensation in her throat.

He did not speak; he pressed her hand with the one hand he could move, and Eva bent down and kissed his brow, while tears rushed into her eyes.

"Oh, if the doctor would only come," her heart was praying, but the minutes seemed hours to her, and all she could do to help him was to hold the brandy to his lips. But at last she heard someone ascending the door steps, a man's footfall, and a moment or two later Dr. Sidney entered the room.

He was a tall, good-looking, rather elderly man, who lived

in the neighborhood and had attended Eva for some slight
ailment since she had lived in her present house.

"There has been an accident, I hear, Miss Moore," he said
as he went forward.

"Yes," faltered Eva, "this gentleman has been shot just
outside the door."

"Shot?" repeated the doctor, in surprise.

"Yes, I heard the shots; I was standing on the balcony,
and—and—they must have struck—"

The doctor by this time was bending over Clair, and,
asking for scissors, he proceeded to cut up the coat sleeve
upon the injured arm.

"I think perhaps you had better leave us alone, Miss
Moore," he said, and, greatly agitated, Eva left the room
and went up to the drawing room, and stood there trembling violently.

"Can—can he have done this?" she was asking herself,
with a heart full of terror. "Clair, dear Clair, have I brought
this on you?"

She wrung her hands together and walked up and down
the room in extreme agitation.

"No, no, he could not know," she told herself the next
moment; "it must be an accident, and yet—and yet—"

One of the servants came into the room while she was
thus debating some most painful question in her mind, and
she looked hastily up.

"Cooper has brought in another doctor, miss," said the
maid.

"That is right. Have you heard them say anything?"
asked Eva.

"I heard Dr. Sidney say to the other doctor, miss, that
his arm is broken, and that he is badly wounded in the
side—"

"Oh, how dreadful! How dreadful!" interrupted Eva,
clasping her hands.

"It's an awful business, miss, that it is."

Eva made no answer. She began pacing restlessly up
and down the room, holding her hand to her side, where
she was feeling a severe physical pain brought on by agitation. It seemed hours that she walked there; hours of
racking anxiety; but in reality it was not an hour when Dr.
Sidney rapped at the door and came into the room, looking
certainly serious.

"Well, my dear young lady, we have done all we could for him at present," said the doctor in answer to the mute inquiry in Eva's dark eyes. "He is severely, though I trust not fatally, wounded, and the great thing in his present condition is that he should be kept perfectly quiet, and not removed from this house."

"Of course not—of course not," answered Eva, in a trembling voice.

"But he will not consent to this until he has had an interview with you," continued the doctor; "a private interview," he added, with a smile, "and I advise you to grant him this. I understand he is not a stranger to you, but an intimate friend?"

"Yes, I know him well."

"Then will you see him at once? And I propose that a bed be taken down to your dining room, so that there will be no carrying upstairs, and I shall send in a professional nurse to attend him; and between us I hope to pull him through. He is a fine-looking, healthy young man, and that is greatly in his favor. What did you say his name is?"

"Clair," faltered Eva.

"Well, then, I hope Mr. Clair will recover from the effects of the shot of his cowardly assailant, for he has been shot from behind. But will you come to speak to him now?"

Eva followed the doctor downstairs with trembling footsteps, and paused at the dining room door while Dr. Sidney entered the room and spoke in a low tone to the other doctor, who was standing by the couch on which Clair was lying. This other doctor looked round at Eva as Dr. Sidney spoke to him, and then nodded, and a moment later they both advanced to the doorway where Eva stood.

"Will you go in now, Miss Moore?" said Dr. Sidney, in a low tone. "And do not on any account excite him. Comply if you can with any wish of his."

Eva made no answer. She walked forward into the room with her eyes fixed on Clair's white face, while the doctor gently closed the door behind her, and she was thus alone with him.

"Clair," she said, in an agitated voice, and she knelt down by the side of the couch and laid her hand on one of his, "do you feel better now?"

"Yes, dear, I am not so faint," he answered, in a very low, weak voice.

"The doctors say, Clair," went on Eva, "Dr. Sidney says that you must stay here, and of course you must stay."

"I can only do so on one condition, Eva—this is why I asked to see you—if I stay you must promise to be my wife. We must tell these doctors we are engaged to each other—or—"

"Oh, what matter is it what they think?" prayed Eva. "Only get well, dear Clair, and I care for nothing else."

"But I care for something else, my dearest. I care for you far more, and will risk my life certainly sooner than that anyone should be able to speak an untrue word of you."

"Oh, Clair!" and Eva laid her head upon his breast.

"Let me tell the doctors you are my betrothed wife, Eva, or I must go?"

"But they say it will be dangerous, Clair," half whispered Eva, "and Clair, dear, Dr. Sidney called you Mr. Clair—"

"So much the better. Eva, if you care for me ever so little, promise to be my wife. I may die, you know, dear, and if they take me to a hospital my father and mother may hear, and they will take me away from you. Will you let me die without you?"

"No, no!" cried Eva, passionately. "What matter is it what happens to me. Try to get well, dear Clair. I will nurse you and be near you—say what you like."

"You will promise to be my wife, then?" asked Clair, eagerly.

"Yes," answered Eva, in a stifled voice, and again she laid her head on his breast.

"My darling!" said Clair. "Kiss me, Eva. Now I will get well. I feel sure I shall get well!"

She lifted her face and kissed his lips, and she shivered slightly as she did so.

"You have made me so happy, darling," whispered Clair. "Kiss me again, Eva—my own love—my dearest wife."

Again Eva slightly shivered, but she once more pressed her lips to his and then rose from her knees.

"I must go now, Clair, and see about things. I will arrange everything with Dr. Sidney and then come back to you. Try for my sake to get well."

She looked at him with a strange gaze in her shadowy eyes as she spoke—a gaze half of pity, and yet of love.

"It is for his sake," she was telling herself; "if I am doing wrong it is to save his life."

CHAPTER XVIII.

MR. GOWER, Q. C.

Naturally since the time that Lord Kilmore had parted with Clair in anger there had been great anxiety on his account at the Hall. The day following her husband's return Lady Kilmore had written to her son entreating him to return to them, and urging him in the tenderest words to give up an attachment which was causing them all the keenest pain.

"Whatever this young lady may be to you, my dearest Clair," wrote Lady Kilmore, "can she be so much to you as those who have loved you and tended you from childhood? Your dear father is far from well, and this affair has been and is very trying to him. It grieves him also that you, who have always been so good a son, should positively disobey him, and I assure you that your conduct has caused us both great and bitter sorrow."

To this letter Clair wrote an affectionate and respectful answer, but in it he showed no signs of yielding to his parents' wishes.

"There are some subjects, dearest mother, on which a man himself alone can judge. I am very sorry, more than sorry, that I am giving you pain, but I assure you there is no true cause for it. I will not write on this subject any more, and I ask as a great favor that you and my father will also forbear doing so."

"He is bent on making a fool of himself," said Lord Kilmore after he had read this letter. "And he is of age, so what can we do? It's a thousand pities, but I'm afraid there is no help for it."

"He may change; he may get over his infatuation," answered Lady Kilmore, with a sigh.

"No, my dear; the clever woman who has caught him in her mesh will take good care he does not get over his infatuation. She will not often have such a chance, and we may be sure she will not lose it."

"It's terrible to think of it. If I went to him, Kilmore—"

"It would do no good, Jeanie."

Tears rushed into Lady Kilmore's eyes.

"It is hard—hard," she said. "Hard on you, hard on me —and—"

"You are thinking of Annette Gower?" said Lord Kilmore, as his wife paused.

"Yes," she answered, almost in a whisper; "she does not know what we do, but I think she fancies something is wrong—poor girl!"

Annette more than fancied something was wrong with Clair—she felt sure. Her even-tempered aunt was restless and unhappy, and her uncle was gloomy and taciturn. Yet weeks passed on and nothing apparently happened. Clair wrote to his mother, and Lady Kilmore answered his letters, but by her husband's advice she said nothing more about Eva Moore.

"I am convinced it would be useless," said Lord Kilmore. "We have said all we could to him; it is wasting time to say anything more."

"When is Clair coming back, Aunt Jeanie?" one day asked Annette, unable any longer to keep silent on a subject so near her heart.

"I do not know, my dear," answered Lady Kilmore, gravely.

"But—has anything happened to him? Has he quarreled with Lord Kilmore?"

Lady Kilmore hesitated a moment or two, then she said yet more gravely:

"Do you remember that girl whom he saved at the fire at Holly Hill, Annette?"

"Yes," faltered Annette.

"Well, his father is angry with Clair because he has carried on his acquaintance with this young lady; because he refuses to give it up."

Annette's face grew very pale, and then a sudden flush dyed it.

"I knew he admired her very much," she said, as if forcing herself to speak. "Do you mean that—he wished to be engaged to her?"

"The strangest part of the affair is that he told his father that she had absolutely refused him. I cannot credit it, but he told Kilmore this."

"Refused him?" repeated Annette, in absolute astonishment.

"So he told his father."

"Then—then she may be engaged to someone else—she must be!" said Annette, with strong conviction.

Lady Kilmore was silent for a moment or two, then she said, slowly:

"That may be so, Annette; I never thought of this, yet it may absolutely be the case.　I pray and trust it is."

"And where is she now?" asked Annette, eagerly.

"She went to Brighton, so Mr. Dighton told your uncle, and Clair is staying in town, as you know.　When your father comes next week I wonder if he will be able to give us any news of him?"

Annette's father, Mr. Gower, a famous Q. C., spent annually a part of his vacation with his sister, Lady Kilmore, at the Hall.　He was a shrewd, hard-headed, hard-working man, and it had floated through his mind also that his daughter Annette would make a very suitable wife for his nephew, Lord Clair.　Perhaps his sister had unconsciously put this idea into his brain; at all events, it was there, and when he arrived on his usual visit he was not over-pleased to hear that Clair had had a disagreement with his father about some young woman, and was not at the Hall.

"And who is the young woman?" inquired the Q. C. in his sharp tones, with his keen eyes fixed on his sister's disturbed face.

"That we cannot tell, Arthur," answered Lady Kilmore; "she came to this part of the country to stay with a farmer's family, one of our tenants, and Clair met her at the tenants' ball when he came of age; then the same night there was a fire at the farmer's house, and with great bravery and danger to his own life Clair saved this young lady's."

"Most romantic!"

"That is the worst of it.　I fear the very romance of the affair has led poor Clair into all this trouble.　At all events, he followed her to Eastcliff after she left here, and refuses to give up his acquaintance with her.　It has made us both very unhappy."

"I do not suppose he contemplates matrimony?"

"But, Arthur, he declared to his father that she had refused him!"

"Very unlikely that the friend of a farmer's should refuse a young lord.　There is something behind all this, Jeanie. Does Annette know anything of it?"

"Just what we know. She has had no private communication from Clair."

"And where is he? And where is the beloved one?"

"Oh, Arthur, don't jest about it! It is too serious. It has changed Clair entirely; he used to be so good, and never worried us at all; but since he knew this young lady he will not listen to us."

"He is asserting his manhood," answered the Q. C., with his somewhat harsh laugh. "It's always the young cockerels that crow the loudest. But you have not answered my question: Where is he? Where is she?"

"He is in town and she is at Brighton, I believe."

"Most convenient for both! At this season, too. Well, Jeanie, I'll look Clair up when I go back to town, and be able to report on the state of his mind. In the meanwhile I should not worry myself if I were you. Most likely the affair will all end in smoke; and as for her refusing Clair, I simply don't believe it, nor do I believe he ever offered to her."

"But he told his father he did, Arthur."

The famous Q. C. shrugged his shoulders.

"Most likely from some Quixotic notion of defending her reputation he invented that little fable for the benefit of Kilmore. He's at the age of Quixotism, you know, in theory, but you will see."

Lady Kilmore sighed restlessly. Her brother's words gave her little comfort. To her idea it was cruel of Clair to behave as he was doing to this young lady unless he meant to make her his wife, and cruel to them if he did. Mr. Gower spoke as a man of the world; a man who was used to its undercurrents and pitfalls, and who had a professed belief in the selfishness of all the inhabitants of the earth.

"It's instinct," he would say. "We all think of self, and what's best for self, and this feeling guides almost every action of our lives. And it is the same with beast and bird. Does the wild duck stay by the side of his shot mate struggling madly in the water? No, he is away, and his mate dies alone; his self-love is as ours."

"There is love stronger than selfishness, Arthur," Lady Kilmore one day replied. "Mothers have died for their children; lionesses for their cubs."

"I am speaking from a masculine point of view, my dear," answered Mr. Gower, with a laugh.

Nevertheless, though he so persisted in the selfishness of humanity, Mr. Gower was not without some tenderness in his nature. He was really fond of his only daughter, Annette, and sincerely anxious for her welfare. He had earnestly desired that she should marry her cousin Clair for her own sake, and perhaps a little for his own. And he quietly determined, as he listened to his sister's account of Clair's infatuation for Miss Eva Moore, to find out as much as possible about that young lady. He spoke to his daughter also on the subject, and his acute eyes soon perceived that Annette cared for Clair only too well.

"So your cousin has got into trouble about some young woman?" he said.

Annette's dark, piquant little face flushed violently.

"I—believe he admires some one," she answered, hesitatingly.

"Have you seen her? Is she handsome?"

"She is very handsome, and Clair saved her life—I think that is how he came to think of her."

"Precisely, but it's folly. However, I'll see him when I go back to town, and try to laugh such romantic nonsense out of his head."

Annette sighed. She did not believe that her father's words or laughter would have any influence on Clair, but since her aunt had told her that Eva Moore had refused her cousin a sort of saddened hope had sprung up in her breast.

"She must love someone else," she had told herself again and again. No one whose heart had been free would have refused Clair, she firmly believed.

"It must be painful to poor Clair," she thought, "but still—"

She tried to be sorry for her cousin and his supposed disappointment, but she knew she was not honestly so. And she tried, too, not to think of him except as a cousin, but she knew that she failed in this also.

Her own feelings humiliated her, for a woman who loves unsought cannot well be proud of her affection.

And Annette was a sensitive girl, who hid as best she could the emotions of her heart. But unconsciously she betrayed them. Her aunt knew and her father guessed her secret.

"When will he come back, I wonder?" she thought, gazing pensively out of the window of her own room on the park shortly after this conversation about Clair with her father. "He will weary of a vain pursuit, and then—" And again Annette sighed, thinking sadly of the cousin who at this moment was lying grievously ill, with his hand fast clasped in Eva Moore's!

CHAPTER XIX.

A SUDDEN BLOW.

Scarcely had Richard Dighton, in his mad jealousy and rage, fired the two cowardly shots which laid Clair low, than remorse and fear seized upon his trembling soul. He saw Clair fall, and then turned hastily away, dreading, however, to walk too quickly lest he should attract suspicion, and to his consternation a few minutes later, though after he had turned out of the street where Eva lived, he encountered a policeman who stopped him.

"Beg your pardon, sir, but did you hear two shots fired somewhere in this direction?" said the policeman.

"I heard something," answered Richard, with faltering tongue, and as he spoke the policeman observed him with attention.

"I could have sworn there were two shots," he continued. "What street have you come out of, sir?"

Richard named an adjoining street, but not the one where Eva lived, and then walked on, and the policeman looked after him as he did so.

"That fellow looks rather queer," he was thinking, "and not up to much good; I think I'd know him again." And then he also walked on, little dreaming, however, that he had just met the man who had fired the two shots, and under whose ulster at this moment lay concealed the very weapon he had used.

As for Richard Dighton, this encounter made him realize more keenly what he had done. On he fled now with swift steps, glancing backward to see if he were pursued; and a sick, cold feeling crept over him—a feeling partly of remorse, partly of fear.

It came in place of the hot passion which had filled his soul not a quarter of an hour ago. Had he killed the young lord? he asked himself, with pallid lips. He had wounded him, at all events. Suspicion might fall on him, and Richard shuddered as he thought.

He wandered aimlessly along for some time, not knowing where he went. Then the idea struck him to get rid of his revolver, which he only purchased in the morning. He sought a quiet square for this purpose, intending to push it through the iron railings in the center, and leave it there unseen. He stopped, thinking to do this, but a couple approached him as he did so, and Richard walked on. In fact, he found it by no means easy to find a place suitable for its concealment.

At last he did drop it over the railings, and then hurried away. He was bodily weary with his long watch before Eva's house, and he went into the first tavern he came to and drank two glasses of whisky, which seemed to put some life into him. Finally he returned to his lodgings and there drank more whisky and then tumbled into bed.

He slept until the morning, but when he awoke a grim terror seized him. The cold dew broke out on his brow; his heart beat violently. A ghastly vision rose before him— the scaffold, the hangman, and the rope—and with a groan Richard Dighton turned his white face to the wall.

What had he done? He remembered at this moment his father and mother, and the homestead where he had been born. Until Eva Moore had come with her wonderful beauty and changed all his life, Richard had liked and had been proud of the acquaintance of the young lord. Many a day, as boys, they had fished together in the river Ayre, which flowed past the end of the park, and as young men their acquaintance had continued.

"She has done it all, curse her, muttered Richard, darkly, and then he thought what must he do.

He must go away, he decided, and he rose and with shaking hands dressed himself and went down into the sitting room and rang for breakfast, scarcely having courage to open the morning paper, which, as usual, lay on the table awaiting him.

With an effort he did this, but there was no mention of the murder or injury to Lord Clair in its columns. Richard scanned it all through, holding it in his trembling hands, and then gave a kind of gasp of relief. Yet he had seen the young lord fall.

It seemed to him now as though he had been mad. It was a mad action, he told himself. No woman was worth it, and again Richard swore as he uttered Eva's name.

She was not worth it! Yet even as he said this the passion in his heart rekindled. With a groan he flung his head on the table near him, and her beautiful face seemed to take form and coloring before his eyes.

"I'm glad I killed him!" he muttered, savagely, but the next moment the grim vision that he had thought of before he rose struck terror in his heart.

But he could not rest. He felt impelled, as it were, to go to the scene of his last night's crime, and try to learn how it had ended; and he actually did this. He went to the very street where he had watched Eva and Clair start on their riverside excursion, and he had not stood there five minutes when he saw a carriage drive up to the door of Eva's house. And from this carriage a gentleman descended; a tall, grave, good-looking man, unmistakably a doctor. The door was opened quickly, and he disappeared; then another carriage drove up to the door, and from this second carriage another doctor emerged.

Then Richard understood. He had shot Clair, and he had been actually carried into Eva's house, and he was not dead. Richard Dighton realized this fact with various almost overwhelming feelings surging in his heart. The young lord was with her, he might live, and he was safe now from his (Richard's) vengeance.

He turned away from the sight of the house and his spirit was dark within him, and there was despair on his soul. He had sinned, and the bitterness of his sin had fallen on his own head.

He could do nothing more, and with a brow black as night he returned to his rooms, paid what he owed, which almost left him penniless, and then took the train to Eastcliff, where his mother and Annie were still staying at Sea View House.

Mrs. Dighton received him at first with delight, but his gloomy face and manner soon filled her warm maternal heart with great anxiety. It was evident to them all that something had gone very wrong with Richard, and they naturally concluded that his wooing had failed. But Richard made no explanation and never mentioned Eva Moore's name. Once Mrs. Dighton tried to approach the subject, but Richard stopped her so roughly that she never again attempted it.

In the meantime the victim of his ungovernable passion was lying very ill at Eva's house in South Kensington, filling her heart with wearing and constant anxiety. Eva felt that Clair's father and mother should know the condition he was in, but when she said this to Clair he would not hear of it.

"What good would it do, dear?" he asked. "It would only make my mother unhappy to know I was lying here. She would come; they would take me away from you! Eva, if I am going to die, let me die with my hand in yours."

"But you are not going to die, Clair."

"No, I don't think I shall, when I have got so much to live for," answered Clair smilingly and lifting Eva's hand to his lips and kissing it.

Clair, in fact, bore the pain of his wounds with extraordinary sweetness and patience. The doctors and nurses said he was the best patient they had ever attended. He had two nurses, a night nurse and a day nurse, and Eva was also constantly in the room.

They were to be married, it was understood, in the household, as soon as he was able to go through the ceremony. Clair used to talk of his coming marriage to both doctors and nurses, but Eva said nothing on the subject. Still she did not deny it. She had promised Clair, and seemingly she meant to keep her word.

She grew very fond of him during those anxious days. To part with him now she knew would be a great and bitter blow to her heart as well as his. And the idea that she had brought all this suffering upon him was most grievous to her.

"Clair," she said to him one night in the gathering twilight, "who do you really think it was who shot you? Do you suspect anyone?"

"Yes," answered Clair; "I don't want anyone else to know this though, Eva, but I suspect Richard Dighton of Holly Hill."

"Oh. Clair!"

"I told you he was very insulting to me about you at Eastcliff, and that night, just as I left the door here I saw a fellow crouching on the other side of the street whose figure certainly reminded me of Dighton's, then I heard the report and the shots struck me. Yes, Eva, I believe it was Dighton who fired the shots, and his motive was jealousy about you."

"The wretch! Just as if I would ever have looked at him."

"I know you never would, dearest, but that did not prevent him from looking at you, you know. But I mean to leave it to his own conscience; and after all he has drawn us closer, has he not, Eva?"

"Yes," she whispered.

"And after we are married he will come to his senses a bit. Eva, will you send to the club now, dear, to see if there are any letters from my mother?"

Eva did send, and the messenger brought back two letters from Lady Kilmore and a card from Mr. Gower.

The Q. C. had fulfilled his promise and "looked Clair up" on his return to town, and was told that Lord Clair had not been to his club for several days.

"Ah—do you think he is in town?" inquired Mr. Gower.

Yes, they believed his lordship was in town was the reply he received, as some clothes and necessaries had been forwarded to him to an address at South Kensington.

"Ah," said Mr. Gower, but he asked no more questions, and slightly shrugged his shoulders for his own edification as he turned away. Nor did he write to his sister on the subject.

"The young fool will come to his senses by-and-by," he told himself; "at present interference would do no good."

But Clair was not over pleased to receive his uncle's card. He guessed the probable motive of this attention, as the busy barrister had little time to spend on idle ceremonies. He had been sent by his people at home to look after him, and at present Clair did not want to be disturbed by family interference.

"After I am married it will be all right; they will all love Eva. Just now they will only worry us," he thought, and for the same reason when he answered his mother's letters he dated his replies from his club, and made no mention of his severe injuries.

It was his left arm that was broken, so he could use his right hand, yet Lady Kilmore noticed the feebleness of his handwriting, little dreaming however that he was lying as he was; but she was very unhappy about him. There had leaked out in the neighborhood somehow a report that the young lord and his father had had a serious quarrel, and that this quarrel was about a woman.

Lady Kilmore's sensitive ears sometimes caught a curious inflection in the tone in which her friends inquired after Clair. Naturally people were interested in him as the young heir to a large property, and hitherto he had been known to be the pride and darling of his parents. And his continued absence from home, no doubt Lady Kilmore knew, created remark.

And this absence went on week after week and still no startling news reached the Hall from Clair.

Mr. Gower kept his ideas to himself, and Lord Kilmore began to hope that his son's infatuation for Miss Moore had not gone to the extent of marriage.

Altogether it was a most trying and unsatisfactory autumn at Kilmore, and the earl's failing health added to Lady Kilmore's uneasiness.

Clair, in the meanwhile, was slowly recovering from his injuries, and was being nursed and tended upon so well at the little house at South Kensington that he would often whisper to Eva he had never been so happy in his life. But there was a heavy cloud sometimes on Eva's fair brow when she was alone that she was very careful he did not see. And when he talked of their speedy marriage she often suppressed an uneasy sigh.

And things went on thus until the chill October breezes were filling the squares with russet leaves in town, and at Kilmore sighing through the fading brackens and the ferns. It had been a beautiful autumn, but sad hearts and clouded brows had been beneath the stately roof-tree of the Hall.

Then a sudden blow fell there, and the earl one afternoon while sitting in his library alone was stricken with paralysis, and when his wife went to look after him she found him lying insensible on the floor.

The greatest alarm at once prevailed; doctors were telegraphed for, and Annette Gower with trembling lips uttered in her aunt's ears, who was kneeling by her husband, the single word "Clair!"

Then Lady Kilmore turned her agonized gaze from the

changed face of the husband of her youth and looked at Annette.

"Send for him," she said, hoarsely; "telegraph for him to come at once—tell him—" And again she looked at her husband and Annette understood.

So she sent a telegram to Clair, telling him that his father lay stricken nigh unto death, and bidding him come without delay. She sent this telegram to his club, with directions to forward it at once to wherever he might be, and the same day Clair received it, as it was sent on by a special messenger from the club.

By this time Clair had so far recovered that he was able to leave his sick-room, and it chanced that he was seeing Dr. Sidney in Eva's drawing-room when the telegram from Annette was placed in his hand.

He opened it with a slight apology to the doctor, and as he read it an exclamation of horror and alarm broke from his fast whitening lips.

"No ill news, I hope," said the doctor.

"Terrible news!" cried Clair, forgetting everything in his great anxiety; "my father, my dear father, has been struck with paralysis."

For a moment the doctor made no answer; he looked at the agitated young man before him and remembered that at the time of Clair's wound he had suggested to Miss Moore that it would be as well to inform "Mr. Clair's" parents of his injuries, and that she had made no reply and seemed embarrassed, and he had therefore thought it judicious not to say anything more on the subject.

"This is very sad news," he now said after a slight pause; "we must hope it is not a serious attack."

"But I fear it is," continued Clair in a state of painful excitement; "this telegram is from my cousin, and she says I must go home at once—I must go."

"You are not yet fit to travel," said the doctor, gravely.

"But I must; I must go to him," went on Clair in increasing excitement. "I must go to-day—and Eva—"

"Will Miss Moore accompany you?" asked the doctor with pardonable curiosity.

"No," he said, "she will not go—but it was about leaving her I was thinking—leaving her before our marriage."

"May I ask, does your father know of your engagement?" said Dr. Sidney.

10

"He knows I wish to marry her, but—"

"Perhaps he does not entirely approve? In that case any agitation might be very injurious to him, and perhaps he does not even know of your injuries?"

"He does not." And Clair began walking up and down the room hastily in his agitation, and then suddenly stopped. "Excuse me, doctor," he said; "I must see Miss Moore at once; I have arrangements to make—"

"But I am your doctor, and protest against a hasty, and perhaps a long journey. Where is your home?"

But Clair made no answer; he was thinking of his stricken father, and he was thinking also of the reputation of the fair woman he loved. He therefore left the room without any further apology, and hurried to a small morning-room where he had left Eva when the doctor arrived. She was still sitting there as he re-entered it, and she looked up with a smile from her book as he did so; but her face instantly changed when she saw his expression.

"What is the matter, Clair?" she asked, rising hastily. "Has anything happened?"

"Yes, dear Eva," answered Clair, clasping her hand. "I have had a telegram from Annette Gower, and my father is dangerously ill."

"Oh! Clair—"

"And I must go to him; but first, Eva, let us be married; let us be married to-day—in an hour."

Eva's face grew very pale.

"That is impossible, Clair," she said in a low tone.

"Let us try to manage it. I shall be miserable unless we are."

"There is no time," went on Eva, gravely, though with some agitation. "You must go to your father, Clair, and promise me one thing before you go."

"What must I promise, Eva?"

"Promise not to speak of—our engagement at Kilmore? Clair, remember this, if you do we shall never be married."

"Do not speak thus, Eva; we must be married—we shall be married. You know what you promised when I consented to stay here?"

"Yes, I know, and I will keep that promise, but one condition is that at present it must be kept a secret. Therefore, Clair, at the Hall you must not speak of it."

"I should rather tell the truth, and that is why I wish to be married before I go away."

"It cannot be before you go away; but do not be afraid, I will not go back."

"But I do not like to leave you. I am afraid—"

"Of what?" asked Eva, looking at him steadily as Clair paused.

"Of what people might say—"

Eva gave a sort of laugh.

"If you are afraid of what people say you had better not marry me."

"Oh, Eva!"

"I don't want you not to think of me, Clair," said Eva with unconscious tenderness; "I—I want you to love me and to be with me always. Don't let them turn your heart away from me when you go home; only don't talk of it. I wish to be everything to you—but in secret."

"But that could not always be, dearest."

"At present it must be; and, Clair, what will you say about your wounds? How will you explain, and does the doctor think you are fit to go?"

"I left him grumbling about it; but I must go, Eva; I should never forgive myself if I did not see my poor father. Eva," and again he clasped her hand, "you will not deceive me? I shall find you here when I come back?"

"You will find me here, Clair."

He drew her to his breast and kissed her passionately.

"My dearest, my sweetest," he murmured, with his lips on hers; "I ought to go—but it is hard to part—"

"Yes," whispered Eva, fondly.

"But you will write every day? Twice every day?"

"I will write every day."

"And I will not be long away. But give me the keys of my desk now, Eva. I must face the doctor before I go or he'll think I have run away."

Eva handed him the keys, and Clair presently returned to the drawing-room where he had left the doctor in rather a ruffled state of mind; but at the sight of the large fee that Clair placed in his hand, his expression mollified.

"Pardon me for leaving you so abruptly, doctor," said Clair, "but I wished to persuade Miss Moore to marry me to-day, at once, before I leave, but she says there is not time."

The doctor smiled.

"The young lady is right. There is certainly not time to-day, if you persist in going."

"I have no choice; the telegram from my cousin is imperative."

"Have you a long journey before you then?" again inquired the doctor.

"Not very," answered Clair with a certain reserve in his tone which the doctor thought he understood. "My home is in the Midlands."

Dr. Sidney made no further inquiries. He perceived there was something that this young man wished to suppress, and he shrewdly guessed that his rank was higher than he had admitted to him. He was wealthy at all events, for the manner in which he had recompensed his professional services told this, and therefore the doctor confined his remarks to strict injunctions to Clair concerning the care of his health.

Then, after he was gone, Clair began hurriedly to make preparations for his departure. Eva went into his room to assist him, and as she was kneeling down packing something in his portmanteau, Clair saw her eyes suddenly fill with tears.

"Eva, my dearest," he said, laying his hand on her shoulder.

Then she rose, and without speaking a word, fell sobbing into his arms and hid her face on his breast.

"My darling, my dearest, does my leaving grieve you so much?" whispered Clair, tenderly encircling her waist with the one arm he could use.

She did not answer for a few moments, while sobs shook her slender form. But after awhile she looked up in his face with her dark eyes all wet with tears.

"You may believe this, Clair," she said, "that unless I loved you—loved you most dearly—I should not part with you thus."

CHAPTER XX.

ANNETTE'S PRAYER.

Clair felt extremely exhausted long before he reached the railway station nearest Kilmore. The shock of his father's sudden illness, and the emotion and agitation of parting with Eva, all had tended to weary him in his present condition of weakness.

The doctor had given him some restorative to take on the journey, and again and again he applied to this. Still when he arrived at the station he found one of the servants from the Hall waiting on the platform for him, as he had telegraphed to Annette Gower what train he expected to arrive by. It was all he could do to ask after his father.

"His lordship has rallied slightly, my lord," answered the servant, respectfully touching his hat.

Clair breathed a little quivering sigh of relief.

"The carriage is waiting outside the station, my lord," continued the servant, and walking feebly, leaning on a stick, Clair made his way to it.

It seemed strange to him to be among all the familiar surroundings after his varied experiences during the last few weeks. The carriage rolled into the Park and presently stopped at the entrance of the Hall, and the butler, an old family servant, ran down to receive him, and nearly started back when he looked on the changed and pallid face of the young heir.

It was well known in the household, we may be sure, that there had been a disagreement between Lord Clair and the earl, but nothing had been heard of his illness, and therefore the butler's surprise was very great. Clair leaned on his arm as he stepped out of the carriage, and his footsteps faltered even then, and his arm was in a sling.

"I beg your pardon, my lord," inquired the old family servant anxiously, "but have you had an accident?"

"Yes, rather a serious one," answered Clair, "and my father—"

"His lordship is slightly better this evening," said the butler.

But at this moment Annette Gower, who had been standing at the door of the morning-room watching Clair enter, came forward with a pale and quivering face.

"Clair!" she said, breathlessly, "what is this? Are—you ill?"

"I have been, Annette, and the journey has knocked me up a bit. But my father is better?"

"We hope so—yes, we hope so," repeated Annette, still with her eyes fixed on Clair's face. "Come in here, Clair—lean on me—you look quite faint."

"I do feel rather queer," said Clair, sinking down on the chair nearest to him.

Upon this the butler ran for brandy and Annette called for water, and presently Clair revived a little and looked kindly at his cousin.

"Did I give you a fright, my dear?" he said.

"You looked very pale," she answered with quivering lips. "But, Clair, what is the matter with your arm?"

"I'll tell you by-and-by," said Clair, glancing at the servants. "But tell me about my mother, Annette? I fear my father's illness has been a great shock to her."

"A terrible shock, Clair! It was so sudden, though he has not seemed well for some little time."

Clair felt these words were a tacit reproach to him, and Annette grieved the moment after she had spoken them.

"Aunt Jeanie will be so pleased to see you," continued Annette, "but I had better tell her you have been ill before she sees you. How—how did it happen, Clair?"

The servants had by this time discreetly left the room and the cousins were alone.

"It was a very strange thing," said Clair; "but I was shot either by accident or design in the street."

"Shot!" repeated Annette in horror.

"Yes, shot, and I was carried into a house in South Kensington, and have been there ever since until I received your telegram this morning!"

"And you never told us!"

"It would have done no good; only grieved my mother," said Clair.

He had made up his mind on the journey to give this explanation of the change in his appearance, but he had also made up his mind to obey Eva's earnest request and not to mention her name.

But Annette was thinking of her as she gazed with her

dark wistful eyes at Clair. She believed, as we know, that Eva Moore's only motive for refusing Clair—if she had done so, as he had told his father—must be that she was bound to someone else.

Could this other lover have shot Clair in a fit of jealous anger? thought the quick-witted girl. All this passed through her brain in a moment, and the thought was a very painful one. But she said nothing.

She told Clair how his father's illness had occurred, and the doctors they had sent for, and then she suggested that she should go and tell her aunt of his arrival.

She did this, and a few minutes later Lady Kilmore hurried into the room, and after gazing a moment in her son's face clasped him in her arms with a cry of pain.

"Clair! my dearest—dearest boy!"

All his shortcomings were forgotten. He was near her again, her son, her darling; near her after danger and suffering, and she looked into his altered face with unutterable tenderness.

"Why—why did you keep it a secret?" she asked, plaintively. "Why have I not been with you, Clair?"

"Dear mother, you have had enough trouble," answered Clair, carressing her.

"But, dear, it was my place to be with you—with my son —and who did such a dreadful thing, Clair? Who dared injure you?"

"I have no idea, mother; probably some madman. I was shot from the back, but cannot tell you by whom."

Lady Kilmore sighed deeply. She too, as Annette Gower had done, was thinking of Eva Moore; was wondering if evil had come to her son through her influence. But she asked no further questions. She looked again anxiously in his face and saw how worn and weary he seemed, and then at once suggested that after he had taken some refreshment that he should retire for the night.

But Clair could not eat. His forehead was throbbing painfully, and he was glad when at last his head rested on his pillow. But he had a bad night. The excitement and the journey had been too much for him, and he tossed and tossed wakefully with snatches of fevered dreams. And in the morning he was worse. He felt, in fact, incapable of rising, and when his mother saw him she insisted upon him at once seeing the doctor, who had remained overnight at the Hall in attendance on the earl.

The doctor declared him to be very feverish, and ordered him to remain in bed, and during the day Clair did not improve, and Lady Kilmore's anxiety and Annette Gower's increased hourly.

A letter came for him the next morning; a letter from town in a woman's handwriting, and Annette, who had opened the letter-bag, gave it into his mother's hands, and for a moment the two women looked at each other, though neither spoke.

Lady Kilmore carried it to Clair, who received it eagerly, read it, and then placed it beneath his pillow.

But he said nothing, and seemed very ill, and toward nightfall the fever rose higher and he became delirious at intervals.

Annette Gower was in the room, half-hidden by the curtains, when he first began to call for Eva Moore, and addressed her in his wild wanderings in terms of passionate love.

"Eva, my dearest, my dearest, come to me," Annette heard him mutter, and the words cut into the listener's heart as a sword. "No one shall part us—you have promised—Eva, my own, my Eva!"

Then he fancied they were again together by the river, and he rambled on about the shining water, but there was always one refrain:

"Eva!"

Annette sat and heard that name repeated a hundred times, and always in terms of the most tender endearment. She turned faint and cold; she leaned back, and a bitter and terrible idea darted into her heart.

"He had better die," she thought; "I would rather he were dead."

She clasped her hands together and a moan escaped her pale lips. If he lived he would marry this girl; he would bring her here—she would see their daily life—and again Annette moaned.

The thought was terrible to the poor girl, and she rose hastily and left the room, glancing at her unconscious cousin as she passed the bed still babbling fondly of his sweetheart's name!

She went up to her own room, locking herself in, and then flung herself passionately on the floor.

"Oh, God! let him die; he is better dead!" she prayed in her agony, forgetting everything in her cruel grief.

But even as she writhed there, with great darkness on her soul, a violent rapping suddenly came to the room door, and she heard her aunt's voice in evident agitation.

"Annette, come—open the door—Clair is worse!" cried Lady Kilmore.

Then Annette rose, trembling, tottering, and went to the door and unlocked it, and outside stood Lady Kilmore, her face all wet with tears.

"Oh, Annette!" she wept, grasping Annette's cold hand, "Clair does not know me; he is talking in the strangest way —wandering—oh, Annette!"

Lady Kilmore was terribly overcome, and as Annette tried to comfort her, her own heart was stabbing her meanwhile in keen reproach.

"Better dead"—she had said he were better dead, Clair, so young, so beloved, in whom his mother's heart was bound.

The selfishness of her cry—it could scarce be called a prayer—now rose before Annette's mind in all its blackness.

"He will get better, Aunt Jeanie; let us go to him," she said, and together they returned to Clair's sick-room, who was now talking very wildly.

"How dare you look at her?" he was saying, addressing some imaginary being near, "You!"

He spoke the last word as if in great scorn, and as he did so his mother softly took his hand.

"Clair, my darling Clair," she said, tenderly.

But Clair took no heed; he went on speaking loud and menacing words, and it was terrible both to his mother and his cousin to hear him.

And presently Annette crept away and again returned to her own room, and this time knelt down on her knees and prayed earnestly for Clair's life.

"Oh, spare him, Almighty Father, spare him!" she cried, "and forgive me! I have sinned—let him be happy—even with her—only let him live!"

CHAPTER XXI.

ALWAYS JEANIE.

But for some days after this there seemed great doubts whether poor Annette's prayer would be answered, for Clair continued very ill.

The wound in his side broke out afresh, and the greatest uneasiness and anxiety prevailed at the Hall.

As for Annette, she seldom left his side, and many a piteous silent prayer for his recovery was offered there. She was ashamed now, most bitterly ashamed, of her own selfishness, and tried in every way to atone for what she called her wicked thoughts.

However, after days of semi-delirium and great pain and prostration, Clair began to mend. But he was extremely weak and unable almost to lift his hand. And when with a pallid face and faltering lips Annette laid on his bed a packet of letters which had arrived—all in the same hand-writing—day by day since his return to the Hall—Clair was almost incapable of opening them, and certainly of answering them.

They were from Eva Moore, and each succeeding one showed increased anxiety at his unlooked-for silence. At last in one she urged him to tell her the true reason why he had not written.

Clair read letter after letter with great uneasiness, and then looked anxiously at Annette, who was watching his changing face from the other end of the room, as she had left the bedside after placing the letters on it.

"Annette," said Clair at length in his weak voice, "will you do me a favor?"

"Of course, Clair," she answered in a low tone, approaching him as she spoke.

"These letters are from—someone who is surprised at not hearing from me," continued Clair. "Will you telegraph what I dictate, as I am not strong enough to write?"

"Yes, Clair."

"Telegraph to my club then that I have been very ill, and ask them to forward the telegram to the same address to which they sent your telegram to tell me of my father's illness. Say in the telegram I will write the moment I am able."

A choking sensation arose in Annette's throat, but she suppressed all signs of emotion.

"Very well, Clair," she said, "I will get the telegram form and you dictate what I am to write."

She did this, and knew very well as she did so that the message was really intended for Eva Moore, and that Clair intended to keep her address a secret.

But she nerved herself to go through the task her cousin had asked for, and Clair's telegram was sent, and also duly forwarded to the little house in South Kensington, where Eva Moore had during the last few days been enduring a perfect fever of anxiety at not hearing from Clair.

The first day of his absence had seemed very dreary, for we scarcely realize what a gap a beloved presence makes until it is gone. Eva felt restless; she had the rooms rearranged; she put any little thing belonging to Clair carefully away, and she kept wondering if it were possible to receive a letter from him by the last post.

The last post arrived and brought three circulars, two lists of prices of coal, and no letter from Clair.

"In the morning," thought Eva, hopefully, flinging her letters into the wastepaper basket.

But the morning came bringing more circulars, more prices of coal, and some new winter fashions from the shops.

Why will people torment householders as they do? Investments, mine shares, business circulars of every description pour in every day, and no one ever looks at them. They weigh down the postman, they irritate the servants, who have to answer the postmen's knocks, and they worry the mistress, and fill the house, and yet still they come.

The letters we watch for come often slowly enough; the letters we hope for very often never at all, but the letters we don't want arrive in shoals, and the waste of labor and postage stamps is truly deplorable.

Eva Moore, during the next three or four days after Clair's departure, went through various phases of female emotion. She was anxious the first day, and afraid the journey had been too much for him; she was angry the second day and thought he certainly ought to have written; on the third day she began to be exceedingly unhappy.

"They have influenced him against me," she thought. "His dying father may have influenced him, and yet he seemed to care for me so much."

She had no one in whom she could confide her doubts and fears, and this perhaps made them worse to bear. Thus several days went on, Eva writing to Clair each day as she had promised, and then his telegram to the club was forwarded to her, and Eva knew the cause of his silence.

He had been very ill! She stood with clasped hands reading these words, trying to realize what could have happened to him, her heart filled with all sorts of painful apprehensions. Oh! how she longed to go to him; to attend upon him once more. She thought of what Clair had said when he was first wounded, how he had told her that if his parents knew that they would take him away from her; that he might die without his hand in hers.

If he were to die—if she were to lose him now! Eva walked up and down the room in a very agony of grief at the thought.

"Clair, Clair!" she cried, "I love you. Oh! come back to me, my love! I have no right to love you, I know," she added a moment later, "but I do—and you will forgive me, Clair."

Then she sat down to write to him, telling him all her anxiety and unhappiness. She asked him to telegraph when he got this letter, and waited uneasily and impatiently until he could do this. His next telegram, which also came through the club, was more reassuring. He was better, and a day or two later she received a few lines written by his own hand.

Clair, however, recovered slowly, and the earl had rallied and was able to be up days before Clair was well enough to see him. When he was first told that his son was at the Hall, and that he had come there to see him when he heard he was ill, a faint smile passed over Lord Kilmore's pallid features.

"Poor Clair," he said, in his altered voice, which was still very inarticulate.

"He came when he was very ill himself to see you, dearest," said his wife, bending over him and taking his chill hand.

"And that—girl?" asked the earl.

"He has never mentioned her," replied Lady Kilmore.

"I—hope it is ended," faltered Lord Kilmore, and then he sighed.

But it was days after this before Clair was strong enough to walk to his father's room, and when he was the two were both so shocked at the change of each other's appearance that they clasped each other's hands in silence.

"You—have been ill?" at last faltered the earl.

"Yes, some madman, I suppose, shot me in the streets," answered Clair, trying to smile. "I am glad to see you so much better, father."

The earl did not speak; he sighed, thinking he had much to say to his son, and yet feeling incapable of any mental exertion.

The interview, however, made them feel more at ease, and after this Clair went every day to his father's room for a short time. They both continued to improve in health, and all painful subjects were for the time ignored. Lady Kilmore said nothing to her husband of the letters that arrived daily for Clair, feeling that any agitation would be most injurious to him, and Clair was thankful to escape all questions, and it was not until he suggested to his mother that he thought he might now leave his father with safety for a few days that any allusion was made to the past.

"Oh, do not go, Clair," said Lady Kilmore, imploringly. "Your presence here makes your father so happy, has done him so much good."

"I want to go for a few days, mother; only for a few days," urged Clair.

"But, my dear, we cannot tell what may happen in a few days; wait at least for another week before you think of leaving him, and I am sure also that you are not fit to travel."

And Clair did wait another week, but in the meanwhile he wrote to Eva imploring her to marry him during the few days he could arrange to be absent from his father's side.

"His health is most precarious, my dearest," he wrote, "and my mother is miserable at the idea of my being absent from home, and I am miserable at the idea of being away from you. Let us be married then, dearest Eva, and then nothing can part us. I have not mentioned your name here, as I promised not to do so, and it has not been mentioned to me, and if you wish it our marriage can be kept a secret for the present. But do let us be married when I come; let me feel when I return to my father's side that you are indeed my own—my very own."

A great struggle took place in Eva's mind after she read this letter, but it ended in her love for Clair overpowering all other considerations.

"I will run the risk," at last she decided; "I cannot bear to lose him now."

She therefore wrote to him to tell him that when he came to town if he wished it she would marry him if he would faithfully promise that this marriage should be a secret one. This Clair, under the circumstances, was only too happy to do. Indeed, he felt it would be impossible at the present time to do anything that would certainly agitate his father.

They agreed then that their marriage was to take place as soon as Clair was able to arrange to leave Kilmore.

But he found it very difficult to do this. Whenever he approached the subject his mother's face changed and saddened, and she always entreated him to remain. At last he fixed the time, and Lady Kilmore was forced to tell her husband that Clair thought of leaving them for a few days.

"For a few days?" repeated the earl.

"Yes, dearest, he assures me he will return in a few days," answered Lady Kilmore, soothingly. "He has some business to see after."

The earl's face twitched uneasily.

"It is not business," he said.

"But, dearest, we cannot expect that a young man of Clair's age should never leave home. He came to us, you know, poor fellow, when he was very unfit, and he has been very good and kind."

For a few moments Lord Kilmore did not speak, then he said with evident agitation:

"Jeanie, must I speak to him before he goes about—"

"No, dear Kilmore, it would disturb you, and you know the doctors say agitation is so bad for you. He has promised to return in a few days, and I am sure he will not break his word."

"Still if I thought it would do any good—perhaps now my words would have more influence on him?"

"Dearest, it would make you ill, and throw you back,

and it would distress me so if you had any further quarrel with Clair. Let us leave it to God!"

The earl sighed uneasily.

"It is hard to think that those who come after us—" he said falteringly, and then paused.

His wife bent down and kissed his brow, and murmured some endearing words, and for a few moments the earl did not speak. Then he looked up in his wife's face.

"I have always you at least, Jeanie," he said, and they both felt the comfort of these words.

They indeed loved each other with a tender and enduring affection which had known no change all through the long years of their wedded life. And these years had been singularly peaceful and happy ones, and not until the great trouble about Clair had any serious cloud darkened their existence.

But Clair's attachment to Eva Moore had been a great and bitter blow to them both. Lady Kilmore had fondly hoped that her darling son would learn to love her favorite niece, Annette, and the earl naturally had not been without ambition that his heir should marry suitably in life.

He was not exactly an ambitious man; he valued worldly greatness with too true a gauge to be so; but still that Clair should have allowed himself to become entangled— to use Lord Kilmore's ideas on the subject—with a girl whose acquaintance he had picked up while she was the guest of a tenant farmer, irritated him more than he could have believed his equally balanced mind would have permitted.

We are all, as we know, apt to be very calm and philosophic about the troublesome things in life until the troubles absolutely tap at our own door.

Had any fellow nobleman's son wished to marry a girl so much socially beneath him in station as Eva Moore was to Clair, Lord Kilmore would probably have said with a shrug and a smile:

"Ah, well, young fools will be young fools!"

But it was very different when the young fool happened to be his heir. He had fretted and fumed, and worried himself about Clair's "infatuation," until he had absolutely made himself ill. And now, broken down in health as he was, he was miserable about it still.

But he took his wife's advice. Clair went to bid his

father good-bye before he left the Hall, it must be admitted with a sinking heart. He was afraid he might be urged to give up Eva in terms that to him would be intensely painful:

"For your dying father's sake!"

Clair feared to hear these words, but he did not hear them. Lord Kilmore merely said:

"Your mother tells me you are going to leave us for a few days, Clair?"

"Yes, father," answered Clair with a flush which the earl noted.

"Let it be only for a few days then, my boy," continued Lord Kilmore, "for my health, as you know, is precarious, and if anything were to happen I should not like your mother to be alone."

These words affected Clair; he put his hand into his father's; he looked on the earl's altered face with his honest eyes.

"It shall only be for a few days, father," he said, "but I hope when I come back to find you much stronger."

"We must hope so," answered the earl, with a somewhat sad smile.

And so they parted, and Clair went away on an errand, which, had he known it, would have broken his father's heart!

CHAPTER XXII.

IN A FEW DAYS.

She was watching for him—Eva—watching for her lover, in the gathering twilight of the same day, with a flush on her fair cheeks and a glad light in her dark eyes.

He had telegraphed that he was on his way, that he would be with her early in the evening, and now she was impatiently awaiting his arrival.

She was dressed in white—Clair loved white—with a flower at her breast and in her hair, and she was excited, and full of fitful joy.

"How long he is," she thought as hansom after hansom passed her door. They were beginning to light the street lamps before one stopped. With a fast beating heart Eva saw Clair spring out, and the next moment ran into the hall to meet him with outstretched hands.

"Clair!" she said in a glad voice.

He did not speak; he drew her into the little dining-room and closed the door, and then caught her passionately in his arms.

"My darling, my darling!" he murmured with his lips on hers.

Then for a few moments there was silence between them—the silence of a great content—and Eva was the first to break the charm.

"And are you quite better, Clair?" she said, drawing back and looking at him. "What a terrible fright you gave me when you did not write!"

"I am nearly well; I was off my head, you know, darling, for days. And so Eva was uneasy?"

He tenderly stroked her cheek as he spoke; he kissed her dark eyes, but with a smile Eva drew away from him.

"Come, I must see after your creature comforts," she said. "You must be both hungry and thirsty."

"I have been hungry and thirsty to see you," answered Clair, ardently. "Oh! how long the time has seemed, Eva."

"And your poor father?"

"He is better; I left him better."

"Then your mind will be more at ease. Come, Clair, dinner will be ready in five minutes, and then you must tell me all your news."

They dined together, and after the servant left the room Eva proposed to go upstairs to the drawing-room, which was softly lighted when they entered it.

"Then everything is settled, Eva, for to-morrow?" asked Clair eagerly as the door closed after them.

"Yes, everything," she answered, "except you must see the clergyman to-night if—"

"If what, Eva?"

"If, Clair," and she put her arm through his and looked up in his face, "if you have no fears, no doubts. Do you love me really well enough to—what shall I call it—run certain risks?"

"Eva, I never can understand you when you talk like that."

"Well, there are always risks you know about unequal

11

marriages, and ours is an unequal one. And Clair, before I marry you, you must sign a paper—a paper in which you bind yourself to keep our marriage a secret."

"For a time?"

"For as long as I wish it to be so. Clair, you must promise this."

"But, Eva, to keep it a secret for any length of time would be unjust to you, unjust to—"

"Clair," said Eva, pulling her arm from his and standing before him, "I want you to understand this: I am marrying you, not because you are Lord Clair; not for anything but for yourself. If I did not love you—well, too much—no, don't be foolish, Clair, for these are very serious words, but if I had not loved you as I do, if I had not felt I should me miserable without you, I would not marry you."

"Not even for my sake?" he asked, taking one of her hands and kissing it.

"Oh! you would be far better without me, my dear, let there be no mistake about that. No, I am not marrying you for your sake, but for my own. I am marrying you because I am a selfish woman, and like you too well to lose you, and could not bear anyone else to have you! There, that is high-minded love for you, isn't it? Not self-sacrificing love, but love for all that—yes, Clair, love!"

"Then I am content," he answered, and again he clasped her to his breast.

"But you must promise to keep the secret?"

"Yes, dearest, anything you like; and now about the parson?"

"Well, Clair, the parson as you call him is, I assure you, a very charming man. He called upon me two days ago, and I hinted to him then that probably I should soon require his services, and I told him a gentleman would most likely call on him this evening, and he said he would be at home after eight."

"Then I had better go now," said Clair, looking at his watch, "it is half-past eight o'clock."

"Wait until you have signed the paper, sir!" cried Eva, half in jest, half in earnest. "Here it is," she continued, taking out a note sheet, on which something was written, from a drawer in her writing-table. "Now, Clair, shall I read it to you?"

"And so you wouldn't trust my word?" said Clair, half reproachfully.

"Oh, yes I would, but there is something more business-like in pen and ink. This is it," she continued, reading from the paper:

"I, Clair, faithfully promise and vow to keep my marriage with Eva Moore a secret until she gives me permission to announce it."

"You see it's nothing very serious nor solemn, and you have just to put your name here, Clair, and it will be all right."

"Very well," answered Clair with a little laugh.

It seemed more like a jest to him than anything else; and when Eva handed him a pen he signed the paper and gave it back to her.

"Well, is that right?" he asked smiling. "Does that satisfy you?"

"Clair," said Eva, reading the signature. "Yes, that is right, and now I shall lock it away."

"And I shall go and arrange with the clergyman. What time shall we be married, Eva?"

"As early as possible, so that no one may see us. Shall we say ten?"

"Just as you like; and now tell me the parson's name and address!"

"He lives close here, in this street, and his name is Onslow. He lives at number eighteen."

"Then I shall go; I won't be long. Good-bye for the present, dear."

"But be sure, Clair, you make Mr. Onslow understand that this is a secret marriage, and you must bind him by his honor as a gentleman to keep it a secret. You can tell him—"

"Any more orders?" laughed Clair, going to the door of the room, and then he smiled, nodded, and went away, and Eva Moore was alone.

The expression of her face changed in a moment after he was gone, and she sank down on a low seat by the fire.

"Is it fate?" she murmured in a low tone; "but no one will ever know—no one must ever know—and I could not, no I could not part with him now!"

In the meanwhile Clair was ringing at Mr. Onslow's door,

who was the vicar of the parish where Eva lived. Even in London, to a certain extent, we get to know something of our neighbors' appearance and take a slight interest in their affairs.

Eva Moore was so handsome it was almost impossible for anyone who had seen her once to forget her face, and Dr. Sidney had talked to his friend, the vicar, of the beautiful young woman who was engaged to a young fellow called Clair, who had been carried wounded into her house, and had had a very narrow escape of his life.

The vicar had become interested in his fair parishioner, and he had called upon her, and alluded to the report of the injuries that her betrothed, Mr. Clair, had received, and Eva had smilingly hinted, as she had told Clair, that their marriage was likely to take place soon.

Thus when Clair inquired if Mr. Onslow were at home, and was told that he was, the servant having asked his name, he replied simply "Clair" and the servant naturally announced him as "Mr. Clair," when he opened the library door, where the vicar was sitting reading.

The vicar, a fine, benevolent-looking man of some fifty years, rose smilingly to receive his visitor, whose errand he guessed, and held out his hand.

"Mr. Clair," he repeated, "the gentleman to whom I believe my parishioner, Miss Moore, is engaged?"

"Yes," answered Clair with his ready, pleasant smile, "and I have come to ask you to marry us to-morrow, Mr. Onslow."

"To-morrow?" repeated the vicar in some surprise.

"Yes; my father is ill," said Clair, "and I am uncertain about my time, as I can only leave him for a few days, and I am most anxious to be married at once."

Mr. Onslow looked thoughtfully on the young man's ingenuous face as Clair spoke, with his benign gray eyes.

"And there is another thing," continued Clair, with some slight embarrassment, "for family reasons, Mr. Onslow, both Miss Moore and myself wish for the present our marriage to be kept a secret."

"A secret?" said the vicar, slowly, still looking at Clair.

"Yes; my father is very ill, and—"

"I presume then he does not approve of your marriage?"

Clair hesitated a moment.

"To tell the truth he does not," he then said. "He is prejudiced—"

The vicar looked grave.

"It is a stupid prejudice," continued Clair, quickly; "a mere class prejudice, because Miss Moore does not belong to his order—"

"Order?"

"Yes, I wish to tell you, Mr. Onslow, I have been called Mr. Clair here, I believe, but my father is the Earl of Kilmore, and as his son I bear the title of Lord Clair, and of course I must be married in my proper name."

"Then you are Lord Kilmore's eldest son, his heir!"

"Yes, I am his only son."

"And you wish to marry against his will? Lord Clair, permit me to say so, but this is a very serious matter."

"I think every man has a right to choose his own wife, Mr. Onslow. My father has no real reason to object to my marrying Miss Moore, and as I am of age he has no authority to prevent it."

"No certainly not, and Miss Moore is no doubt a very charming young lady; but still as you are your father's heir his wishes ought to carry weight, and a secret and hurried marriage is very often an unwise one."

"Mine, at all events, must be secret and hurried," answered Clair with some anger in his tone, "but if you do not wish to perform the ceremony, Mr. Onslow—"

Mr. Onslow smiled.

"You are jumping at conclusions," he said; "I only thought it my duty to point out that in a family of your rank marriage is a very serious affair, and involves serious consequences; but of course if you are determined—"

"I am determined; nothing shall prevent my marrying Miss Moore!"

"Then I shall say no more. And you wish this marriage to be kept a secret?"

"For the present—yes. I trust to your honor as a gentleman, Mr. Onslow, not to mention it."

"I see; have no fear, Lord Clair, your secret is safe with me until the proper time comes to reveal it. And now as that is settled, let us go into details."

After this they arranged all about the ceremony for the next day. His curate, on whom he could perfectly depend, would give the bride away and act as the witness, the vicar said; and Clair returned to Eva with a light heart to tell her everything was settled.

He found her looking pale and uneasy, and she put her hand in his with a restless sigh.

"What is the matter, darling?" he asked tenderly.

"I don't know. I feel half afraid," answered Eva, "now when it is so near."

"You are not afraid I'll turn out badly?" smiled Clair.

"No, no, I've no fear of you, Clair; none, none!" cried Eva with sudden emotion. "It is not that," and she rose and began walking slowly up and down the room. "If things don't turn out well it won't be your fault, I know that. But it is too late to talk thus," she added, and she once more went up to him and put her hand in his. "Clair, for good or evil—even if you knew it would be for evil— do you wish me to be your wife?"

"For good or evil, even if I knew it would be for evil," repeated Clair, "I wish you, and no other, to be my wife."

*   *   *   *   *   *

They were married the next day, and by Eva's wish went for three days to a quiet, old-fashioned, half-town, half-village by the sea.

"Let us go somewhere we have never been before," she said; "somewhere where no one has ever seen us before;" and Clair did not in the least care where he went so long as he was with her.

So the young pair wandered together among the bays and coves and watched the waves breaking on the crisp sea-sand. Everything in these days had a charm for both— the crimson sea-sand, the hardy flowers raising their modest heads among the rough herbage on the banks, the boat of a solitary fisherman, the wild bird on the wing. They watched these, and then looked in each other's face and smiled.

"If we could only be here months instead of days," said Clair one evening wistfully, as they gazed at the shadows gathering over the desolate sea. The purple light had died out in the west: the night was drawing near, a chill wind swept over the dark restless waters creeping almost to their feet, and Eva shivered and pressed nearer to Clair as he spoke.

"They have been happy days, Clair," she said in a low tone.

"It is so hard to have to leave you so soon."

"We have one more day at least—one whole long day."

"Yes—Eva, I want to ask you something—if a chance should arise, a favorable chance of telling my father and mother that we are really married, you will grant me leave to do so, will you not?"

But Eva drew back in sudden alarm at the very suggestion.

"Clair," she said sharply, "did you not promise me that you would not do this?   Did you not sign the paper binding yourself not to do so?"

"Yes, but Eva—"

"Clair, there must be no doubt about this, no uncertainty. Our marriage must be a secret one.   I would not have married you unless you had promised that it should be."

"But I cannot understand—"

"Perhaps not, but there it is.   You married me on these conditions, and I beg you will not even speak of breaking them."

Clair said nothing more; the moaning sea went on with its restless tossings, the wind grew more chill, and a strange feeling of doubt suddenly crept into the young man's heart.

"It is turning cold," he said in an altered voice; "we had better go in."

Eva put her arm through his and they walked together in silence to their hotel, and when they got there she rang for lights, and began talking to Clair in her usual manner. But there was a cloud upon his brow still which did not pass away as quickly as she expected.

"You look quite cross," she said, going up to him presently and putting her hand caressingly on his shoulder.

He could not resist the sweet face so near to his; he bent down and kissed her, but still there was an uneasy feeling in his heart.

"I have no secrets from her," he was thinking, "none, and yet she must be keeping something back from me."

But the next day Eva managed to charm away Clair's brief doubts.   It was the last day of their "honeymoon," she called it, and her spirits, always changeable, were very bright and gay.   It was a boisterous, almost stormy day, and the rough waters of the German Ocean were tumbling and tossing in wild confusion, and Eva clapped her hands in glee as she watched their rough play.

The wind blew back her bright hair and brought the color of a wild rose to her smooth cheeks.

"She was fair, exceeding fair," and so thought her lover —her husband of three days!   They stood hand-in-hand on the brown rocks, and Eva sung little snatches of song to the music of the waves.

"It is the end of our holiday," she said gaily, "so we must enjoy it. Sing with me, Clair."

And the two sang by the sea, in their youth and in their love: sang of hope and joy, yet the dark shadows were gathering round them, though the encircling clouds seemed far away.

CHAPTER XXIII.

AN AWKWARD MEETING.

Clair returned to Kilmore the next day, after accompanying Eva to town, and then proceeded direct home. He found his father improved in health, and his mother was delighted with the change in his own appearance.

"Why, Clair, you look quite brown!" she exclaimed, after she had kissed him, looking in his face; "as if you had been by the sea?"

Clair blushed a little and laughed.

"I feel much better," he said; "I hope soon to be quite well."

And he looked happier too, his mother also noticed, though he was somewhat restless and excited.

"And Annette?" he asked, looking round as though he missed his cousin; "where is she after all her kindness?"

"Annette does not look very well; her father wishes her to go home to him for a time, but I shall miss her dreadfully if she does," answered Lady Kilmore.

"We shall all miss her," said Clair, heartily; and as Annette entered the room at this moment Clair went up to her and shook her hand warmly.

"You have just come in time to hear us all singing your

praises, Annette," he said, smiling, and Annette's small, pretty dark face flushed deeply as he spoke.

"I am glad to see you look so much better," she said.

"Thanks, very much; yes, I am better; the little change has done me good."

Annette suppressed a sigh; and she, too, observed during the evening that Clair was very restless. His quiet home seemed in truth very dull to him after the excitement and happiness of the last few days. He was always thinking of Eva, picturing to himself what she would be doing at that moment; in fact his thoughts never left her.

He went the next morning to the bridge across the Ayre, where he used to meet her in the days of their early acquaintance, and stood looking down into the water thinking that she was now his wife. And as he leaned over the parapet there he suddenly remembered with an uneasy pang her extreme anxiety that their marriage should be kept secret.

"I can't make it out," thought Clair; "my darling loves me, I am sure, and we would be so much happier if we were together here and everything were known. Of course, just now, on account of my father, it is best kept quiet, as any excitement might do him harm; but it must be known some day—"

Clair's reflections were interrupted by hearing steps on the bridge behind him, and turning round he saw the ruddy face of Mr. Dighton, the farmer at Holly Hill, and by his side his son Richard.

Richard Dighton started violently as Clair turned quickly round and he recognized him, and a sickly pallor at once spread over his face. But the elder Dighton received the young lord with many expressions of sincere and cordial satisfaction.

"Why, my lord," he said, pulling off his low-crowned hat, "I'm truly pleased to see you out again, and looking so well. We heard your lordship had a bad accident."

"Scarcely an accident, Mr. Dighton," answered Clair, fixing his eyes steadily on Richard Dighton's changing face. "Some madman, or worse, shot me intentionally in the streets."

"Shot ye in the streets!" repeated Mr. Dighton, in extreme astonishment.

"Yes," continued Clair, still looking at Richard Dighton, "and I mean to put the affair into the hands of the police and have the fellow punished, for I have a good notion who it was."

Clair said this purposely to see the effect of his words on young Dighton, and they were very marked. Richard turned almost green, and his knees shook under him.

"The scoundrel! he deserves hanging, nothing short," exclaimed the genial farmer. "Shot your lordship! I never heard tell of such a thing!"

"Yet it is a fact," answered Clair. "And how are you getting on, Mr. Dighton, and how is Mrs. Dighton, and your daughter?"

"Both nicely, thank your lordship; our Annie's in a bad way though because she's heard naught of her friend Miss Moore for a long time, who your lordship may remember? You haven't come across her in any of your travels, have you?"

It was now Clair's turn to change color, and a dusky red stole over his skin.

"No," he said, with slight hesitation.

He hated to be forced to tell this lie, believing that the sullen-faced young man opposite to him knew it to be one, but then what could he say?

And Richard Dighton heard him deny any knowledge of Eva Moore's movements with a sudden surging rush of passion to his heart and brain. What, when he knew— when he knew! The young man could scarcely contain himself, as his father went on in utter ignorance of the truth.

"Why it's a queer thing altogether of the girl to do, isn't it, my lord, and she and Annie such friends too; and when she well nigh lost her life here, but for your lordship; but after she left us at Eastcliff she has just written once to Annie, and Annie's letters to her have been returned through the Dead Letter Office."

"It is very strange," said Clair, and nothing more; and the farmer, who was a shrewd man, saw by his manner that the conversation about Eva Moore was not acceptable to the young lord, and so changed it to the ever convenient weather.

As for Richard Dighton, he spoke no word, nor did Clair take the slightest notice of him in speech. Richard stood biting his under lip, his passion nearly getting the mastership of his feelings of fear and shame for what he had done.

It crossed Clair's mind to call him back and tax him with his dastardly crime after the farmer and he had walked on, but consideration for Eva held him back. Therefore, the father and son disappeared, and Clair stood still, feeling not unnaturally very wroth.

That such a fellow should have dared to look at Eva, and dared to try to murder him, was monstrous, Clair thought, frowning, and striking with his stick at some lichen on the parapet of the bridge to relieve his feeling. But on the other hand, if he accused him it would bring endless troubles: troubles to the kindly farmer and his family, to Eva, to himself. Still for one man to shoot at the other, and cause him great suffering out of an insane jealousy about a woman who had never looked at him, was sufficiently irritating to the man who had been shot.

Clair, in fact, scarcely knew what to do, but finally turned back, left the bridge, and strolled through the Park, and on the terrace—being wheeled by a footman in a Bath chair —he encountered his father, who smiled as his tall, good-looking son approached him.

"Well, Clair, have you been for a walk?" said Lord Kilmore.

"Yes, just to the bridge," answered Clair, laying his hand on the back of his father's chair.

It struck him, seeing the earl thus in the full daylight, how ill and feeble he looked, and Lord Kilmore glancing up saw his son's eyes fixed with genuine concern and anxiety on his face.

"You can leave us for a little while, James," said the earl, addressing the footman, "Lord Clair will call you when I require you."

So the servant went away, and the father and son were alone. The earl's chair was drawn up on part of the terrace which commanded an extensive and lovely woodland view of the wide-spreading Park and lands around. It was a bright day, more like October than November, into which month the year had now advanced, and as the earl's eyes wandered over the familiar scenes he sighed, thinking perhaps that ere another year was on the wane that he no longer would be there to watch its fall.

"The Park looks very well this morning, father," said Clair, thinking to cheer him.

"Yes," answered the earl, slowly, "and this will all soon be yours, Clair."

"Please do not talk thus, father."

"My boy, I know it will be so. I have had my warning, and time has been given me to make ready for the change; and, Clair, you also should prepare for it, as a large property like this brings many responsibilities."

"You have borne them most generously and nobly, father, and I pray and trust you may yet bear them for many years."

"I believe you do, Clair," said the earl, and his eyes softened. "From your childhood you never were self-seeking; it is your very nature that—makes me afraid."

Clair was silent. He cast down his eyes, and his heart began to beat more quickly.

"The very generosity of your nature," continued the earl, "its truthfulness, lays you open to deception, and it is this I fear. A young man, rich, good-looking, and holding your present and future position, is sure to be assailed by many temptations, by many wiles—for your mother's sake, Clair, will you resist them?"

"My dear father—" began Clair.

"I know what you will say," interrupted the earl waving his hand; "that a man has a right to manage his own private affairs. That I do not dispute. But he has a right to manage his affairs only with due regard to the dignity of his position, and of his family. Clair, you know to what I allude, and I pray that my words now at least may have some weight with you."

"Your words always have weight with me, father," answered Clair in a low tone.

Again the earl slightly waved his thin hands.

"On that assurance I shall rest content, Clair," he said; "I shall trust to your honor. And now will you call James?"

Twice Clair opened his lips to speak; twice to say, "Father, I have deceived you," and then his promise to Eva, the state of his father's health, rose before his mind, and he stayed his tongue. He waved to the footman to approach them; he walked quietly by his father's side with his hand still on the chair until his mother came out to join them, and smiled softly when she saw her boy beside his father.

"How pleasant the air is," she said. "Why, Kilmore, you

have quite a color," she added, looking in her husband's face. "After all, I like the late autumn; there is a peculiar charm in a day like this."

"Autumnal beauty and autumnal decay," smiled the earl.

"I see no signs of decay," answered Lady Kilmore, also smiling, and putting her hand through Clair's arm; "only a change. I like to see the mist lying on the lowlands as it is doing over there, and the dew on the cobwebs in the grass. When I was a child I used to make lovely little fairy tales about the spangled cobwebs!"

"What a poetical little mother I have," said Clair, smiling, too, and pressing her arm closer to his.

But though he jested, his heart was ill at ease. He felt he was deceiving his father, and this thought was very grievous to him.

CHAPTER XXIV.

FLIGHT.

Almost at the very time when Clair was walking with his father and mother in the park, Eva was going through what to her were some of the most terrible moments of her life.

She had gone out early to make a purchase; a purchase of a new gown, a gift from Clair. She had spent some time in choosing this, and was leaving the shop in Regent Street where she had bought it, when suddenly she encountered face to face a tall, spare man, dressed as a clergyman, with a dark, rather harsh, countenance, whose eyes had no sooner rested on her than he started slightly and stopped.

"Eva!" he said.

Until he addressed her she had not noticed him. She indeed scarcely ever looked up in the streets when she was alone, conscious, perhaps, that her appearance attracted too much attention if she did so.

But as this man's voice fell on her ears she raised her eyes hastily, and in a moment—almost as though a lightning flash had struck her—she staggered and grew deadly pale.

"You!" she exclaimed, with horror in her voice and eyes.

"My appearance seems to startle you," said the man, with a shade of bitterness, a shade of scorn, in his tone; "but why should it? You knew I was alive?"

"Yes, I knew you were alive," answered Eva, trying to recover herself; "but I did not expect to see you."

"No, probably not; but I rather hoped to see you. I have been to your banker's and ascertained you are living in town."

"It is nothing to you where I live; our lines are parted forever," making a great effort to steady her trembling voice.

"I don't know about that, Eva," answered the man, calmly enough. "I have been round the world since I have seen you, and have had time to consider the whole situation. We both acted foolishly, I believe; I the most so in allowing you to go away."

"Foolishly or not, it is done," said Eva, with quivering lips, "and never can be undone."

"You think so? Well, I don't. I believe now that I have not done my duty in the matter; that it was not right to allow a young girl like you to go alone into the world. Where are you living? And what are you doing?"

"You have no right to ask such questions."

"Yes, I have a right, and you know this very well."

"You gave up your right. You gave me my freedom, and you cannot take it again."

"I think that you will find that I can. You are looking very well. Suppose we take a hansom and drive together to your temporary home; that will be better than arguing such questions as these in the public streets?"

These words seemed to excite Eva almost beyond control.

"No, I will not!" she said, passionately. "You agreed to leave me alone always, not to meddle with me if I left you alone, and I have done so. I live on my own means. I live—with friends, and I am nothing to you, nor you to me."

"Such ties as ours unfortunately cannot be so easily shaken off, Eva, and, as I have told you, I have come to the conclusion that it is my duty to see after you. I ask you again, where are you living?"

Eva hesitated. The man looked greatly in earnest, and it flashed through her mind that the best way to escape from him was to give him a wrong address.

"I am living at present," she said, slowly, after a moment's consideration, "at No. 10 Wyndam Place, Bayswater Square, but I do not wish to see you there."

The man quietly drew out a note-book and wrote down the address.

"I shall call and see you, Eva," he said, after he had done this. "When shall I do so?"

"What good will it do—your coming?" answered Eva, with a ring of defiance in her tone.

"We will see. Are you going home now?"

"No, I am not."

"Well, I shall call to-morrow afternoon at three o'clock, and I shall expect to see you then."

Eva made no answer.

"Will you see me?" persisted the man.

"Yes," said Eva, sullenly, with her eyes cast down; and suddenly she raised them and looked straight into his face. "I warn you again," she continued, "that any meeting between us can do no good, and may do harm; it is utterly useless."

He smiled coldly and bitterly.

"You were always self-willed," he said, "and I gave way to your will once, but this time I shall not do so. I shall see you to-morrow, then?"

"Very well," she answered, trying to speak indifferently. "And now I want a cab. Will you call one?"

The man at once beckoned for a cab and handed Eva in, who gave an address to a shop in Oxford Street, and was driven there in a state of such terrible, almost overpowering, emotion, that it seemed to her as though her mind would give way beneath the strain.

"This is too much—too much!" she murmured with her white, writhing lips. "Now—Oh, Clair! Oh, Clair!"

Then she leaned back in the cab and covered her face with her trembling hands.

"It is hideous!" she cried, half aloud, the next moment, passionately. "I shall die—if Clair ever knows I shall die that day!"

Presently the cab stopped. She had reached the shop she had named, but for a moment she did not dismount. She sat still, trying to think what she must do; trying to recall her thoughts from the terrible position in which she found herself.

"I must escape," she whispered to herself, her breath coming fast and quick, and her bosom heaving. "I will change my cab here, and yet again, and then—go home—but not to stay. I must leave London to-night—must telegraph to Clair—to—to my Clair!" and she wrung her hands as if in absolute misery.

But with a great effort she succeeded in partly composing herself. She changed her cab, and went along the crowded streets with a white, quivering face and staring eyes. In all these streets there was not a more tortured heart than hers!

The meeting she had just passed through had filled her whole being with horror and dismay.

"I have been living in a dream," she told herself, shudderingly, "and now I am awake—awake to what?"

At last she told one of her drivers to take her to the little house in South Kensington, and she entered it almost with a groan. Her maid looked in her face as she crossed the threshold and asked anxiously if she were ill.

"I feel ill," answered the unhappy woman, faintly, for all her strength seemed suddenly to have left her, and she tottered as she walked. She went into the dining room first, and the maid brought her some wine, and after resting a little she dragged her failing feet upstairs, and having reached her own room she locked herself in, and sat down by the bed with a moan.

She was trying to think—to think where she must go, and how to tell Clair—to explain her sudden departure.

"I must go abroad," she told herself; "but what will he think? Or shall I go to some quiet out-of-the-way place—some village? But people talk in villages."

Then she thought of the old-world town by the sea where they had spent their brief days of happiness.

"It would not seem so strange to Clair to go there," she reflected; "I can tell him I want change; that I went to see again the place where we were so happy. Oh, I was mad to be so happy! But I love him so—my Clair, my Clair—I cannot part from you!"

At last she decided she would telegraph to Clair, and then start at once for Westwold, where she had sung by the sea with Clair. She felt a feverish impatience to be gone; she told her servants she was going to join Mr. Clair, who was not very well, and that the news had agitated her.

Then she hurried through her preparations for leaving town, and left South Kensington early in the afternoon, traveling direct to the sea coast. She breathed more freely when she heard again the sough of the waves breaking on the shore. It was almost dark when she reached the quiet spot which she had chosen; dark, and she was alone, but she was away at least from London, and hope rose in her heart that for a time at least here she would be safe.

She arrived at the quaint, old-fashioned inn where she had spent her short honeymoon, and it naturally created some astonishment at first that she was not accompanied by her young husband.

But Eva explained he would join her in a few days, but at present was with his own people, as his father was ill. This satisfied the old-fashioned landlady, and whatever satisfied the landlady satisfied the landlord.

But everything painfully reminded Eva of Clair. She occupied the same rooms they had shared. There was the couch his head had rested on, the well-thumbed book his hand had touched. And it was so dreary—so dreary to be alone! She sat by the cheerful fire and listened to the moaning of the wind and the sea, and her heart was very sad.

"We can't help things," she was thinking; "we drift on and on. I remember telling Clair so—I did not mean to marry him—I could not help loving him. And how will it end? But he must never know; whatever happens he must never know!"

Altogether it was a dismal evening, and Eva could not sleep when she went to bed for the restless thoughts which pursued her. Something whispered in her ear that she had done wrong, but she tried to still that voice. Fate had been too strong for her, she self-argued, but she knew in her inmost heart she had not struggled to resist fate.

"Was I to have no happiness all my life?" she asked herself. "That was too hard. I risked it—have been happy—happy with Clair, and I shall be happy with him still if only he never knows the hateful truth."

The morning broke cold and gray over the stormy sea, and the dawn found Eva still wakeful. Some fitful sleep, fevered, dream-haunted, she had gained in the dark hours, but the light brought back all her troubles in stern reality.

And she must act—she must face them, she determined;

and scarcely was the bountiful breakfast removed downstairs when she sat down and wrote to her bankers. And in this letter she informed them that probably some inquiries regarding her whereabouts might, during the course of the next few days, be made at the bank by a person whom she did not wish to know her present or future address; and she requested them to answer no such inquiries, as this person had no right to make them, and they were only made for the purpose of annoying her. She directed and sealed this letter, addressing it to one of the heads of the firm with whom she had a slight business personal acquaintance, and then she went out into the rain and wind-swept streets of the little town.

A quaint, old-fashioned spot. The red-tiled roofs, green with the moss of distant years; the irregular streets; the walks crumbled and eaten by the fierce breath of storms that blow inland from the sea. The place lies, as it were, amid the great mass of rolling waters which sweep round the little promontory on which it stands, and had swept over in days of old some of the low-lying portions of the land.

There are legends of a submerged church and a churchyard over which the waves now roll. But the stout headland on which Westwold stands yet rears its lofty crest, and the winter tempests pass over it, and the summer sunshine finds the old houses standing still.

But Eva could scarcely keep her feet on this bleak November morning as she made her way to the postoffice with her letter to the banker in her hand. But she was determined to post it herself without delay; and at length she reached the little shop through which the loves, sorrows, hopes and fears of the dwellers in Westwold sometimes passed.

The postoffice was old world, like the rest of the place. An old woman peered over the counter with horn spectacles mounted on a very inquiring-looking nose, and sold the stamps Eva asked for. Pounds of ancient-looking tallow candles hung suspended from the rafters above, intermingled with sides of bacon and hams, while cheeses and lard were displayed on the counter for sale.

Everything was primitive, and reeked, as it were, with the odor of the sea. And the primitive failing of curiosity was not absent in the place.

The old postoffice woman remembered the face of the pretty bride, and speculated mentally as she looked at her why she had returned to Westwold so soon. She looked curiously, too, at Eva's letter when she stamped it. It was nothing to her, but it interested her as a daughter of Eve. Then Eva made some inquiries as to the time the first post came in, and having done this, and dropped her letter in the box, she started once more through the wind and rain.

A letter had arrived for her in her absence; a letter from Clair; and with eager, trembling hands Eva tore open the envelope and read the tender lines it contained.

"My dearest love," Clair wrote, "I have just received your telegram to tell me you are starting to-day back to Westwold, and this news has filled me with some anxiety. Why have you made this hasty move, my dear one? Surely at this season the North Sea coast must be very bleak for you, and your comfortable little house in town far pleasanter. You telegraph, also, you are not feeling very well, and I need not tell you how the thought of this distresses me. I would start to-day to join you, my Eva, but it seems almost impossible at this moment for me to leave here. My father was out in the grounds this morning in a bath chair, and on his return to the house did not seem so well. Every little thing seems to upset him, and he spoke to me very despondingly this morning about the state of his own health. I most earnestly hope he is mistaken, but you can understand how anxious all this keeps my mother and myself. And now the idea of you being ill and my not being with you makes me quite miserable. Write at once when you receive this and tell me really why you have left town, Eva. Is anything worrying you, dearest? Tell me everything, and if you want anything, and believe me, my darling wife, to remain always

"Your affectionate and loving husband,
"Clair."

Eva kissed the concluding words, and her eyes grew dim with tears.

"Poor fellow," she murmured; "dear, dear Clair."

Then she sat down and wrote to him, and explained that she had felt weak and languid, and had suddenly taken a fancy once more to go to Westwold, "where we were so happy, dearest Clair. But come to me when you can," she added; "and till you come I shall spend the time thinking of you, and walking about the coast where I wandered with you."

Tender words—almost as warm and loving as his own, and the heart that dictated them was loving, too. Eva kissed the letter she had got from him, and kissed the words she sent.

"Tell him I love him," she whispered to the written lines. "If I have done wrong it was for love."

And this thought seemed to console her. Her step was lighter when she again faced the wind-swept streets.

"We love each other," she whispered to her heart, and pressed her hand against her breast where she had placed Clair's letter. This great love between them seemed now to blot out all the rest.

"He would forgive me, I think," she thought, softly, and when she slipped her letter in the letter-box she sighed softly, too.

Meanwhile the old woman in the postoffice, when she heard the letter fall, peered over the box and saw the pretty bride again. She liked to look at the letters left in her charge, though this was against the rules; but she had a sort of tacit agreement with the postman who came for them that she might have a peep before he carried them away.

For this privilege she paid in kind, presenting the postman occasionally with snuff, and on very cold mornings with a glass of rum.

"She seems to send a vast of letters," she thought, inquisitively, as Eva turned away, and she determined the morning was cold enough to give the postman a glass of rum when he called, and later on she carried out this intention.

But Eva went back to the inn without ever remembering the postoffice woman; and as the day did not improve she remained indoors during the rest of it, trying to while away the time as best she could.

But she could settle to nothing, and when three o'clock came she kept excitedly thinking of the forced appointment from which she had fled, and wondering what the man would do when he found she had played him false.

What really happened was this: Exactly at three o'clock the tall, clerical-looking person whom she had met in Re-

gent street arrived at and rang the door-bell of the house in
Wyndam Place which she had given as her address. The
door was opened by a neat maid-servant, and the clergyman
outside inquired for Eva in the following words:

"Is Mrs.—" and then he checked himself, and a dusky
color rose to his dark-complexioned face. "Is Miss Moore
at home?" he added a moment later.

"Miss Moore?" repeated the maid-servant.

"Yes; Miss Eva Moore?" said the inquirer.

"No, sir; we have no Miss Moore staying here," answered
the maid.

"No Miss Moore?. Are you sure?" asked the man,
sharply, and the dusky flush on his face faded as he spoke.

"Not staying here. I am quite sure there is no lady of
that name; among the visitors, though, I cannot say."

"Can I see the lady of the house? What is her name?"

"Her name is Miss Sprigge."

"Ask Miss Sprigge to see me, then. Take in my card
to her," said the man, producing a card-case from his pocket
and drawing out a card on which was inscribed:

REV. GEORGE TEMPLE,

HARLAXTON VICARAGE,

DORSET.

The maid took the card, and as she did so Mr. Temple
continued his inquiries.

"Is this a private house?" he asked.

"In a way, sir; mistress takes in ladies and gentlemen to
board. Very select," added the maid, anxious to keep up
the character of the establishment.

"All right. Give her my card, and I will wait until you
come back."

The maid gave an uneasy glance at the umbrella stand,
and then another at Mr. Temple, for she had heard of im-
postors assuming even a clerical garb. But there was nothing in the hard, cold, severe face before her that gave her
the idea of deception of any kind. She therefore hesitated
no longer, but left the umbrellas to their fate, and retired to
a back parlor to seek her mistress.

Miss Sprigge, a thin, spare, middle-aged woman, was engaged over her accounts; dotting down one item after the

other; trying the hard task of making both ends meet with
an uncertain income and a weary heart!

A heavy task life had been to this poor lady; heavy and
sad to bear.   In one of the upper rooms of the house there
was an inmate who did not pay; an inmate who made her pay
and spent her small earnings with a somewhat lavish hand.
This was her father, a fraudulent bankrupt, who, after breaking his wife's heart and ruining his family, still lived at ease.
He was not seen at the "select table" downstairs; he laughed
at the old maids, or old cats, as he called them, who gave
his daughter, and, through her, himself, bread.

He was a graceless ne'er-do-well.   Yet Miss Sprigge bore
it, and when her friends remonstrated with her on her patience, she only answered very gently, with her sad eyes
cast down:

"He is my father," and seemed to consider that this rela-
tionship gave him a claim to the protection and care which
should have come from him.

She looked up from her accounts as the maid entered the
room carrying Mr. Temple's card in her hand.

"There's a gentleman, a clergyman, miss, wants to see
you," said the maid, handing her the card.   "He's been inquiring for a Miss Moore, but I told him we had no lady
of that name here."

"Miss Moore?   No," said Miss Sprigge, rising and reading the name and address on the card as she did so.   "The
Rev. George Temple, Harlaxton Vicarage.   What sort of
gentleman does he seem, Jane?"

"He looks quite the gentleman, miss."

Upon this Miss Sprigge proceeded to the dingy mirror
over the mantelpiece, and looked somewhat disconsolately
at her livid face and shabby gown.

"I'm not very tidy," she said, for in many middle-aged
female hearts the very name of a clergyman brings a tender
and expectant flutter.   "But I'll see him.   Ask him to walk
in, Jane."

Accordingly the Rev. George Temple was ushered into
Miss Sprigge's back parlor, who made her best bow as he
entered.

"I called to see a lady—Miss Eva Moore—who gave me
her address at your house," said Mr. Temple, also bowing.

"Miss Moore?   We have no Miss Moore at present, Mr.

Temple, but the lady may be coming," replied Miss Sprigge, hoping for a new boarder.

"True."

"Or she may be coming as a guest to one of my ladies to-night to dinner," continued Miss Sprigge; "I have notice for three extras; Miss Moore may be one of them."

Mr. Temple stood silent, knitting his dark brows.

"She has played me false," he was thinking; "but I will trace her through the banker. I have her safe."

<hr>

CHAPTER XXV.

AT MISS SPRIGGE'S.

In the meanwhile Miss Sprigge was gazing with timid admiration at Mr. Temple's gloomy face, whose cold gray eyes were cast down.

"He looks sad," she was thinking in her gentle way. "I fear he has some secret grief."

"I am sorry to have troubled you," presently said Mr. Temple, looking up.

"Oh, no trouble at all, Mr. Temple; quite the contrary; and I'm sure if you think that the lady you are inquiring after—Miss Moore—is at all likely to be a visitor to any of my ladies this evening, I shall be proud if you will be a guest at my table on the occasion. I have a very pleasant and select circle, and of course a clergyman is always welcome."

Mr. Temple bowed gravely.

"It is a very remote chance, I fear," he said, "that Miss Moore should be present as a guest this evening, as she distinctly told me she was living here at present."

"Perhaps—excuse me suggesting it—but perhaps you have mistaken the date that the lady said she might be living here," said Miss Sprigge, a little eagerly. "Mistakes about dates are easily made, and she might have said she would be living here at a later date."

"True."

"In that case she may be coming here this evening as a

guest, and with a view also of seeing if the society and establishment would be likely to suit her. It is a chance, at all events, and in that case perhaps you will honor my table, Mr. Temple?"

Again Mr. Temple bowed.

"You are very good," he said.

He was considering if it were a chance. Eva might have had some motive for naming this especial house, and in that case someone who knew her might be living here. He knew very few—almost no one—in town, but he was nevertheless determined to trace Eva.

"Well," he said, after a few moments of hesitation, "if you are so kind as to allow me to take the chance, I shall gladly be your guest this evening."

Miss Sprigge's faded skin colored softly.

"I shall be most pleased, most proud to see you," she said. "I have a great respect and honor for the church. In other days—before my poor father was unfortunate—I used to take a great interest in the parish in which we resided. Now, of course—"

And she sighed.

"You have too much to see after, I presume?"

"Yes, Mr. Temple, I have; an establishment like this requires a great deal of looking after—constant superintendence, in fact. Of course, in other days—"

And again she sighed.

That sigh was given to a hazy vision which at this moment passed before her of the one romance of those "other days."

She saw herself again a young girl, with a consumptive-looking curate by her side, going to early services, decorating fonts, embroidering slippers.

It was a common story; the curate was lying in his grave, the young girl was a middle-aged woman toiling for her daily bread, and the daily bread of the worthless father beneath her roof. But it was a romance still! It perhaps made those faded eyes look sweet and gentle even amid the carking care which harassed her present life.

She had loved and been beloved, and the fragrance of the past lingered, as the scent clings to the dead rose.

The remembrance of the curate also made everyone in the garb of a clergyman a person of interest to Miss Sprigge. She felt pleased that Mr. Temple was to be her guest, and when he had taken his leave after promising to return to dinner at half-past seven o'clock, she made haste to add some little delicacies to her table which she did not as a rule indulge in. She put on her bonnet and went out to purchase fruit and flowers, and before the dinner hour came she arrayed herself in her best silk gown. Mr. Temple, however, did not arrive until after the dinner-bell rang, and Miss Sprigge's boarders had mostly taken their places at the table. These boarders consisted of a very varied collection of human beings, being principally composed of spinsters and bachelors. There were, however, a sprinkling of widows, and one widower, a navy man, tall, white-haired and mild, but also sly of visage. He was said to be very well off, and in consequence received a great deal of attention from the ladies of Miss Sprigge's establishment. But Mr. Waldron was proof against the wiles of maids and widows alike. He was affable to them all, but he entrenched himself by his general affability. One widow lady, large, fair and handsome, once believed, it was said, that he was about to succumb to her attractions. But no; Mr. Waldron suddenly was called away to attend the bedside of a sick friend, and remained away so long that the widow gave him up. Then he reappeared, smiling and wary as usual, and he had remained with Miss Sprigge for several years, and still showed no signs of changing his condition.

The appearance of Mr. Temple in his black coat, tall and gentlemanly-looking, as he was ushered down the side of the long table by one of the waiters to the seat by the side of Miss Sprigge, created quite a little sensation. Everyone in the house nearly knew each other by sight, and a clergyman was an unusual visitor. They as a rule mostly marry, and not a single married couple lived at Miss Sprigge's.

Miss Sprigge herself rose, smiling and blushing, to receive her visitor, and the boarders looked up from their soup with interest. They concluded Mr. Temple was a new boarder, and was about to become one of themselves. They also noticed the unusual flutter in Miss Sprigge's manner and her eager wish to pay Mr. Temple every attention.

Presently Miss Sprigge addressed him with some timidity.

"Is there anyone at the table," she said, "that reminds you of the lady you were inquiring for this afternoon?"

Already Mr. Temple's dark, stern, gray eyes had traversed twice up and down the long table before Miss Sprigge made this inquiry, and now before answering her he looked again. But among the many women present there was none like the fair one for whom he sought. There was not much beauty, if the truth be told, to be seen at Miss Sprigge's. There was one fine-looking girl with bright, fair hair and a piquant face, but as a rule a general air of middle-agedness prevailed.

"No," answered Mr. Temple, and again his eyes fell; "there is no one like her here." No one with the charm, the lustrous eyes, the supple, graceful form of Eva Moore. She was a woman with a personality of a distinct type; a woman who could not be overlooked; and Mr. Temple felt this as he glanced at the faces round Miss Sprigge's table.

Presently Miss Sprigge introduced him to the lady seated next him, who proved to be a pleasant, agreeable, middle-aged woman named Miss Onslow.

"My brother is a clergyman also," smiled Miss Onslow.

"Indeed?" replied Mr. Temple. "May I ask if he holds a town or a country living?"

"He is vicar of a parish in South Kensington," said Miss Onslow; "St. John's, and I think he has some very nice people among his parishioners."

"He is fortunate, then."

"Yes. He was telling me of quite a romantic marriage he had at his church lately—a young nobleman and such a lovely girl. But he did not tell me the young gentleman's name; in fact, he was bound to secrecy not to do so."

"An unequal marriage, then, I presume?"

"Yes, I suppose so; but by my brother's account the bride was handsome enough to turn any man's head."

Mr. Temple sighed restlessly.

"Beauty is sometimes a curse," he said.

"But a very pleasing curse to a woman, after all," smiled Miss Onslow, who had been, and still was, good-looking. "Fancy how delightful to look charming on every occasion without any trouble."

"But it has brought much evil in ancient and modern times alike."

"That is true. Well, we must hope this lovely bride won't bring any evil to her young husband. My brother, who is a bachelor, indeed quite fell in love with her, and she had such a romantic name, too—Eva."

"Eva?" repeated Mr. Temple, quickly, and his dark skin slightly paled.

"Yes; my brother would not tell me her other name; that was part of his secret; but her Christian name was Eva."

"This grows interesting; a secret marriage, a romantic name."

"Isn't it? Well, we shall know the secret some day, I suppose; probably when the young man comes into his inheritance."

"Yes, probably. Eva," Mr. Temple again repeated; "it is a name I once knew well."

Upon this Miss Onslow began to talk of women's names, and so the conversation drifted on until the dinner was over, and some of the boarders went to the drawing room and some to their own rooms. Mr. Temple went to the drawing room, where part of the ladies got up a card table, which, however, he declined to join. He talked to Miss Sprigge a little, and to Miss Onslow. These two suited his grave nature better than the laughing widows and the wary men. Neither of them affected anything, and took sober, sensible views of life, and before he left Miss Sprigge pressed him to come again.

"You are very good," he replied.

"And my brother, I am sure, will be very pleased to make your acquaintance," said Miss Onslow. "Let me see—the Rev. George Temple, Harlaxton Vicarage, Dorset, isn't it? May I ask where you are staying?"

"I am staying at the Grosvenor Hotel for the present," said Mr. Temple, drawing out his card-case and presenting a card to Miss Onslow. "I shall be very pleased to know your brother."

Then they shook hands and he went away, and Miss Onslow and Miss Sprigge said a few words about him after he was gone.

"He is a very quiet, gentlemanly man," remarked Miss Onslow. "How was it you got to know him, Miss Sprigge?"

"He came to inquire after a young lady who had given her address as staying here," replied Miss Sprigge; "a Miss Eva Moore."

"Miss Eva Moore," said Miss Onslow, with interest; "he seemed very much struck with the name of Eva—and this young lady is not here, and yet gave her address as being here? It is quite a little romance. I wonder if she has been playing him false?"

She spoke these words lightly, but they were a realization of the old adage that "Many a true word is spoken in jest."

CHAPTER XXVI.

THE BANKER.

"She has played me false," also thought Mr. Temple, as he walked along the street after leaving Miss Sprigge's house. "Whatever she was she used to be truthful, but yesterday she evidently purposely deceived me. She must have some reason."

He thought of what that reason could be, and his brow darkened.

"She is too handsome; I should not have left her alone, and yet I cannot believe she would degrade herself by any folly," he reflected. "She is too proud—too cold."

But she did not wish to see him again; she had told him so; and this was now very evident.

"She prefers a careless life of freedom, I suppose; but I committed a grave error when I gave way to her folly. I should have borne with her—conquered her—but this shall come."

"This shall come," he repeated, and he looked up to the dark sky as he spoke, and his face was very resolute and grave.

It was very resolute also the next morning when he went to the bank where he knew Eva had an account. He asked one of the clerks quietly at first if he could obtain Miss Eva Moore's address there.

The clerk replied he did not know.

"Can I see one of the heads of the firm?" then inquired Mr. Temple, presenting his card.

The clerk said he would ask, and retired into an inner room, but returned in a few minutes.

"Mr. James Ford," he said, "the junior partner, son of Mr. John Ford, senior partner, will see you, sir, if you will walk this way."

Then Mr. Temple followed the clerk through various passages, and finally came to a green baize door, at which he rapped.

"Come in," said a voice from within, and the clerk thereupon pushed open the swing door and held it back for Mr. Temple to enter the room.

He did so, and found himself in a luxuriously furnished apartment in a business way. But everything was of the very best, and seated in a divan chair, with the morning papers in his hands, was a tall, handsome, dignified-looking man, who rose and bowed as Mr. Temple entered.

"Mr. Temple, I presume?" said the banker, fixing a pair of keen hazel eyes on the clergyman's face.

"Yes," replied Mr. Temple, "and you are—"

"I am Mr. James Ford. May I ask what I can do for you?"

"I have called to make some inquiries regarding the address of a lady who banks with your firm—Miss Eva Moore. Can you furnish me with it?"

A smile flitted over Mr. Ford's good-looking face. He had received Eva's letter, for he was the partner in the bank with whom she was personally acquainted, and to whom she had written from Westwold, and he had therefore been prepared for some such inquiry, and he was, moreover, a man of the world, and a great admirer of beauty.

"This is rather a strange request," he said, "and one I do not feel myself justified in complying with."

Mr. Temple's dark face flushed.

"I cannot look on my request in that light," he said; "I know the lady and I wish to see her, and if you will be good enough to let me know where she is I shall feel greatly obliged."

"But suppose the lady does not wish to see you?" smiled Mr. Ford.

"I cannot suppose so, and you can have no reason for thinking so, Mr. Ford," replied Mr. Temple, with some anger in his tone.

"I may have some reason," said the banker, quietly raising a paper-cutter which was lying on a table near his chair.

"Then do you mean she has instructed you not to tell me where she is?" asked Mr. Temple, in increasing anger.

"If she had done so I should feel bound not to tell you;

if the lady had wished you to know where she is she would
have informed you herself."

"You are playing with me, Mr. Ford," said Mr. Temple,
"and I did not come here to be played with. I have a right
to know where Miss Eva Moore is."

"No man has a right to know where a lady is who does
not wish to see him," replied Mr. Ford, slightly waving the
paper-cutter.

The blood rushed hotly into Mr. Temple's dark face as he
listened to these words, and he looked at the handsome
man before him with a sudden suspicion in his heart.

"Do you know this young lady personally?" he asked.

"That is also a question," answered the banker, "which I
consider you have no right to ask.

"I have a right!" cried Mr. Temple, in quick anger. "A
right I can enforce—this lady is my wife!"

Mr. Ford opened his hazel eyes a little wider, but expressed no astonishment at this announcement.

"Even if this were so," he said calmly, "I should certainly
not give you the information you ask for. It is evident this
lady wishes to withhold it, and in that case no gentleman
would act contrary to her wish."

Mr. Temple fixed his cold, stern, gray eyes on the banker's face with an expression which was not very pleasant
to behold.

"You will make me suspect you have some motive for
all this secrecy, Mr. Ford," he said.

"How so?"

"I have told you what this lady is to me—"

"Yes, you have said your wife."

"I can prove she is my wife."

"Yet you speak of her as Miss Eva Moore?"

"That is the name she bears at present; the name she
adopted when—"

"I presume she parted with you? Pardon me, Mr. Temple, but I can give you no information as to her place of
residence, and do not mean to do so. I wish you good-
morning."

After this there was nothing left for Mr. Temple to do but
to bow haughtily and go away, and Mr. James Ford smiled
softly to himself as the swing door closed after his visitor.

"So," thought the banker, "the fair Eva has a past, then?
A peculiar past, apparently—a parson." And he once more

looked at Mr. Temple's card. "Harlaxton Vicarage; he does not look a humbug, but she evidently wants nothing to do with him, and I am glad she has such good taste. As for being his wife, I suppose that's all moonshine—but I'll write and let her know what he said."

And he carried out this intention without delay. He admired Miss Eva Moore excessively, as indeed he admired all pretty women, and moreover she had over twenty-five thousand pounds lodged in the bank.

This money had been left her by her uncle, Mr. Moore, an Indian merchant, who had resided in Calcutta, and with whom, in her childhood and early girlhood, she had lived. This much Mr. Ford knew of Miss Eva Moore, and he had on two occasions seen her. He was a married man, but this did not prevent him from being very desirous to see her again, and he considered that now he might have an opportunity of doing so. He therefore penned the following lines, and addressed them to Miss Eva Moore at Westwold:

"Dear Miss Moore:—I received your letter, and a gentleman, whose card I enclose, called here a short while ago and was most anxious to obtain your address. This, of course, I refused to give him. He was exceedingly persistent and stated he had a right to the information he required—a legal right. I need not tell you that I obeyed your wishes to the letter, and Mr. Temple left without hearing a word about you from me. And I write now to tell you that if I can be of any use or service to you in suppressing this very inquisitive person, you have only to give me your commands. It seems that he called here a short time ago, and inquired if you were in town, and one of the clerks said yes; but luckily this clerk did not know your address in South Kensington.

"If you will write personally to me now on any business matter I think it will be safer, and I shall have the greatest pleasure in assisting you in any way in my power.

"And with kind regards,
"I remain yours very sincerely,
"James Ford."

When this letter reached Eva at Westwold it threw her into the greatest state of excitement and anger.

"What!" she cried, passionately. "He is going to hunt

me down, is he?　But he shall not.　I hate him—I hate him
—I wish he was dead!"

She caught up the card as she spoke on which was engraved Mr. Temple's name, and which had fallen from Mr.
Ford's letter, and thrust it into the fire, watching the flames
scorch and destroy it with dilated eyes.

"I was mad—mad," she muttered, "a mad child, and
the curse has fallen on my womanhood, when I might be
so happy.　Oh, Clair, my Clair!" and she burst into a sudden and passionate fit of tears, rocking herself to and fro in
her bitter distress.

"I must leave England," she murmured, between her
sobs; "Clair will think it strange, but I am safer away—and
this banker will help me.　I must write to him.　Oh, how
well I wrote."

She dried her eyes; she tried to comfort herself, and
then sat down to reply to Mr. Ford's letter:

"Dear Mr. Ford," she wrote, "I thank you very much indeed for your kind letter, and for treating the person who
called to inquire for my address as you did.　I earnestly entreat you never to let him know it.　He has no right—no
legal right to do so, and the greatest annoyance and pain
would come to me if it were possible for him to see me
again.　I will trust you implicitly, and no one need know
my address but you, and I feel sure you will not tell it to
anyone.　I am thinking of going abroad, but I shall of
course let you know before I do so.　In the meantime I
shall remain at this quiet place, as I am afraid to return to
town, so great is my horror of the person who called on you.

"Once more thanking you for your great kindness,
"I remain, with kind regards,
"Sincerely yours,
"Eva Moore."

She felt a little happier after she had posted this letter,
but still she was very restless.　She had nothing to do, and
did not know how to pass the time, and then she was so
utterly lonely.　Outside the sea was moaning—a great waste
of gray-green, restless water—and the melancholy sound
did not tend to make her more cheerful.

She kept walking up and down her little room trying to

think of and solve the problems of life—wondering if the tangled skeins would ever become straight.

"Is anyone happy—really happy?" she asked herself. "They say there's a skeleton in every house. Mine is a grim enough one, at all events. That woman I met yesterday whose husband was drowned didn't look quite miserable as she stood watching the sea. She said he was safe with God —this is what they call faith, I suppose. But I have none; I cannot understand it. I think we can't help ourselves any more than the leaves driven before the storm. We must do things; they are fated. Or why did I ever meet my Clair? I have had many lovers, but I cared for none of them until I saw him. I could not help caring for him. I tried not. I never sought him, but I just went drifting on— and now—and now life is utterly desolate without him."

Up and down the room she went, still thinking of Clair. What was he doing? Was he thinking of her? A soft blush stole to her cheeks.

"Yes, he is thinking of me," she whispered; "Clair, my own, my darling, can you feel me near you? Clair—" She stretched out her arms, her bosom heaved, she closed her eyes, and a sensation she had never felt before passed thrilling through her frame.

"Clair!" she cried again, in a sort of rapture.

Far away at Kilmore at that moment Clair was indeed thinking of her with intense and passionate love. All day he had been wearying for her presence; all day picturing her fair and lovely, as she was to him. And now, as he leaned by the window of his room, looking out on the misty park, it seemed to him he heard her whisper, "Clair."

He slightly started. Was he dreaming? No, not dreaming, yet, though the room was empty save himself, he did not feel alone.

"Eva!" he said aloud, but there was no answer. Only the sough of the wind through the trees; only some raindrops pattering on the panes.

But Clair felt strangely disturbed. Was she calling him? he asked himself. Was she in trouble or pain, and had her spirit come nestling near him for help?

He began walking restlessly up and down the room. It seemed intolerable to him that he could not go to her. His wife, his love! He must see her again, he told himself. He could not wait.

13

He kept moving about the room, full of impatience, trying to think what reason he could give for leaving Kilmore. And while he was doing this a rap came to the door, and his mother's gentle face appeared.

"Your father has been asking for you, Clair," she said. "Will you go and read to him a little while?"

"Yes. But, mother, there is something I want to say to you. I want to leave Kilmore for a few days. I must go," he answered, and there was impatience in his tone.

. His mother looked at him in pained surprise.

"Your father is very ill, Clair."

"He is no worse," said Clair, still impatiently; "and I cannot stay always here; I have other—"

"Your duty here may not last long, Clair," answered Lady Kilmore, reproachfully, as Clair paused, and her words touched his heart.

"Don't say that, and don't be vexed with me, mother, but —something has made me very anxious."

"You will make your father unhappy if you go. Should he not be your first consideration?"

"Of course I think of him—but—"

Lady Kilmore said no more. Again she raised her eyes reproachfully to her son's face, and then turned and left the room, leaving Clair unhappy enough, but still determined to see Eva. She was his wife—she had the first claim upon him; a claim greater than father or mother, and somehow he felt she was longing to see him as much as he was longing to see her.

Presently, however, he went to his father's room, and found the earl irritable and restless. It was one of his bad days, and he was impatient under his sufferings. Clair tried to read to him, but Lord Kilmore interrupted him with something between a groan and a sigh.

"I can't listen to-day, Clair," he said, and when Clair spoke some commiserating words he scarcely answered.

Clair left the room when his mother entered it, and went to seek his cousin Annette. He had made up his mind to ask her to break to his mother that he was about to leave Kilmore for a few days without seeing her again.

He found Annette sitting by the library fire—a pensive figure, with an open book lying on her knee. But she was not reading. She was thinking of her cousin Clair, and a flush came to her small face when she heard him enter the room.

"Annette, I have been seeking for you," began Clair; "I want you to be a dear little thing, and do something for me?"

"And what is it, Clair?" smiled Annette, with a soft look in her dark eyes.

"I must go away to-day for a few days; I can't help myself," went on Clair, hurriedly, "and when I said something about it to my mother she made no end of objections. But I must go, so I mean to catch the first train up to town, and I want you to tell mother after I am gone that I was obliged to go, and that I did not wish to disturb her or my father about it any more. I shall only be away a few days, and if you will do this for me, Annette, it will save a lot of trouble."

Annette's face flushed and then paled as she listened to this request.

"But, Clair—" she said, and then paused with parted lips.

"It is absolutely necessary that I should go," continued Clair; "some one—some business—requires my presence, and I do not wish to worry my mother."

"I fear it will worry her," said Annette in a low tone.

"I am very sorry, but I cannot help it."

"And if your father is worse?"

"Oh, Annette, don't worry me, too! If I could help it I would not go, but I can't—I am very anxious—in fact I must go."

Annette did not speak for a moment or two, and then she said, slowly and painfully:

"If you will tell me what to say I will tell Aunt Jeanie."

"Just say that I asked you to tell her that I was obliged to go, and that I will be back at latest in a day or two."

"And—if they require you here?"

"Just telegraph to the club. A telegram will find me there. Thank you, Annette. And now good-by, dear, for I mean to be off to the station in half an hour."

He shook hands with her, and noticed that her little fingers were very cold and trembled in his own. But his heart was too full of the idea of soon again seeing Eva for nything about Annette to make more than a momentary impression on his mind.

He hurried from the room, and in less than half an hour

he was on his road to the station, and was in town before nightfall. He did not write nor telegraph to Eva.

"There is no need," he thought, fondly; and after a restless night he went the next morning, by the very first train he could catch, to the little old-world fishing town by the North Sea where he had spent the happiest days of his young life.

Shall we follow his eager footsteps along the storm-swept, irregular streets? It was blowing a hurricane when he reached Westwold, and the sea was breaking with a sullen roar along the coast.

But Clair neither heeded the rain nor the wind. On he went, with bright eyes and a beating heart. His bride, his darling, was waiting for him, and the world seemed full of hope and joy.

They remembered him again when he arrived at the old-fashioned inn. The young husband, they said, had come back, and the primitive landlady received him with smiles.

"Your lady is well and nicely, sir," she said. "She has your old rooms."

Clair needed no second bidding. He ran bounding upstairs, he reached the sitting room door, rapped and then opened it, and the next moment Eva was in his arms.

"Clair, my Clair!" she cried.

She had been singing softly to herself as he went in. The storm outside excited her, and there was a flush on her lovely face, and she wore a loose white gown. A beautiful woman, and most beautiful in the eyes of the young man who clasped her so passionately to his breast.

"And you never told me," she murmured, raising her head after a few moments of silent joy; "never said you meant to come."

He pressed his lips to hers before he answered her.

"I did not mean to come," he said; "but Eva—I thought I heard you call for me."

She looked up with startled eyes into his face.

"When, Clair?" she asked, quickly.

"Yesterday afternoon. I could have sworn I heard you, darling."

"Oh, Clair, I did! I did call!" she cried. "I cried to you to come; I felt somehow that my spirit had gone to yours— but now—I am half afraid. Can such things be?"

"I seemed to hear you, Eva."

"I—I wanted you so much; I was so lonely, Clair—and you came. Clair, promise me one thing?"

"What is it, darling?"

"That if ever you are away again—if ever we are parted—no matter by what—that you will come if you hear me call?"

"Yes, I promise," and again he kissed her.

"Remember, it is a promise—a solemn promise," she continued, looking at him with her lustrous eyes. "Our souls must be very near akin, Clair—very near."

"I always felt it was so."

"And nothing can part us. Say nothing shall part us."

"Nothing—I swear it."

"Then I shall be happy again. I will be happy, Clair—I have been unhappy, but now I shall throw it all to the winds. And you have come to stay?"

"Yes, for a few days, at least."

"They shall be golden days! Oh, Clair, I am so glad—so glad to be with you once more!"

CHAPTER XXVII.

GOLDEN DAYS.

They were golden days that the young pair spent together by the wintry sea. Days when love made the sunshine, and filled for them the whole world with warmth and joy. Eva half forgot the grim shadow that stalked behind her path. She would not think of it; she was with Clair, he loved her, and she was happy, and she tried to forget all else.

But sometimes in the cold dawn—that hour of memories —she would awake with a start, and shudder when she thought. "It might be so brief, so brief, all this joy," said a chill whisper in her ear. But no, she would not listen. "Life, too, was brief," she answered, defiantly; "let us be happy while we may."

And so they were happy, the young husband and the young wife. The fisher-folk used to look after them with a kindly smile on their bronzed faces. But the old ones sometimes shook their heads.

"It would not last," they were thinking. To them had come the time of change and sorrow, of separation and pain. And so it would come to these two—the earthy heritage which none escape. But not now; not when the bloom of youth was on the bride's fair cheeks, and on the bridegroom's the flush and glory of his young manhood. To all outward seeming for them the evil days were far away. They were rich, also, for they gave with lavish hands, and many blessings followed their footsteps.

"Some folks have everything, seemingly," one day said a bleared-eyed old woman, as they passed her cottage door.

"Ay, till their time for sorrow comes," answered her gossip, who was bent, aged, and decrepit. "I mind the time when I and my Jim were jest as fond as they are, and for thirty years now the salt sea has rolled over him."

"I wonder why troubles and sorrows are made in the world?" Eva was saying at the same moment to Clair, for they had seen the two old crones cowering over the poor fire as they passed the cottage.

"That's a question which no man could answer, Eva," said Clair, smiling.

"But still wouldn't it have been better, now, if we just had brief, happy lives; all sunshine instead of worries, and bothers, and troubles, like those two old women? Wouldn't they have been far better dead long ago, instead of living with aches and pains all over them?"

"They mayn't think so, dearie; and, besides, there's another life to live for, you know, Eva."

"Oh, I don't believe it," she answered, shaking her head. "We know nothing about it, at any rate. Don't look shocked, Clair, you know I was what is called badly brought up, and I've made, I'm afraid, an apt pupil."

"Don't talk such nonsense, Eva."

"It's not nonsense, Clair, but a sad fact. My mother died when I was born, and my father, who was an Indian officer, died of sunstroke when I was about three, I believe, and then an old heathen of an uncle took me to live with him at Calcutta. He lived for one thing—money—he worshipped it, and he had no other creeds nor beliefs. He said it bought everything in this world and that there was no other. There was a nice rearing for me!"

"My dear," answered Clair, almost gravely, and he took

her hand, "another rearing will, I trust, come to you some day."

"Do you mean love? That has come to me; that has made me think sometimes—of other things—but it's best not to think, Clair."

"Not sweet thoughts, Eva?"

"Yes, sweet ones, but not serious ones."

Clair did not speak. He looked at her fondly, and thought, perhaps, as the fisher-people did, that her time for serious thoughts had not come. Himself in the heyday of youth, life naturally wore its brightest aspect for him, but still underlying this Clair often remembered his mother's words, his mother's prayers. From his earliest childhood, almost babyhood, he had lisped his simple petitions at her knee. She had taught him to believe and trust in God, and Lady Kilmore's own pure and noble life had unconsciously influenced him through the follies and temptations of his young manhood.

He did not care, therefore, to hear from Eva's lips expressions of doubt or unbelief. But he said nothing. "She does not mean it," he thought. "Some day my mother will talk to her, and all these wayward fancies will pass away."

"You look quite grave," Eva said, smilingly raising her dark eyes to his face.

He pressed her arm, which was through his, closer to his side before he answered.

"What is the matter?" asked Eva.

"I was thinking—do you know, Eva, I've been here four days; four such happy days, and I've heard nothing from home. I told Annette Gower to telegraph to the club how my father was, but—" and here Clair stopped and suddenly bit his lips.

"What a fool I've been!" he cried the next moment. "I declare, I believe I quite forgot to give the club people my address here. I was thinking so much of seeing you, Eva, everything else went out of my head, and I never remembered until this moment they haven't got it."

"I daresay it will be all right," answered Eva, calmly.

"Still I should have remembered, for my father wasn't at his best when I came away, and my mother is always very anxious about him. Eva, I must run up to town to-day, dear, and see if any telegrams have arrived."

"Don't you think if you wrote to the club it would do?"

"I don't know. I think I would rather go, for, you see, writing would lose a day. I'll be back all right this evening."

"Still—"

"Little woman, you must not stop me," said Clair, fondly. "You alone are to blame for my doing such a stupid thing; I could think of nothing but Eva."

"Foolish Clair!"

And talking thus—in love's sweet, tender words—they returned together to the hotel, and Clair shortly afterwards started for town. Eva walked with him to the station, and watched the train that bore him away until it disappeared. Then she went back to the hotel and sat still thinking of him until the early winter afternoon began to darken in. And somehow—she could scarcely tell why—a great sadness came over her heart, in place of the excitement and joy of the last few days.

In the meantime Clair had reached town, and, having driven direct to his club, after he got there inquired at once if any letters or telegrams awaited him. He was told two telegrams did, and his heart began to beat a little faster when he heard this. They were given to him, and he tore one open. It was from his cousin, Annette Gower, and was dated the day after he left Kilmore. It was as follows:

"Return at once. Your father was attacked by another fit last night, and is lying dangerously ill.
"Annette Gower."

Clair grew pale as he read these brief words, and his hands trembled violently as he opened the second telegram. It was briefer still:

"Your father is dead."

Dead! Clair could not realize it; could scarcely believe it. Yet there the fatal words lay written before him on the thin pink paper, signed also by his cousin's name. It was a terrible shock; and he had been so happy, so careless, he thought, with a bitter pang, while his poor father's last moments were ebbing away. He looked at the date of this also; it was two days ago; his father had been dead two

days, and he had not known. What must they think of him
at home—his mother, Annette—not to have been with them
in their great sorrow?

A kind of groan escaped Clair's lips, and he covered his
face with his hand, and just then a man he knew who had
been watching him open his telegrams went up to him.

"Sorry to hear of your father's death," he said.

Clair did not speak for a moment; then he said slowly:

"I did not know; I have had a great shock."

"Yes; sad thing, isn't it? But Kilmore looked very ill
when I saw him last; I suppose you will be going down
directly?"

"Yes, of course," answered Clair, huskily. "Yes, I will
go at once," he repeated, and then he turned away, and
with a sort of strange, new, benumbed feeling at his heart,
he lifted up a railway guide and began looking for the
earliest train that would carry him to Kilmore.

He had to wait nearly two hours. But he telegraphed at
once to his mother and to Eva. To his mother he sent
this message:

"Just received the sad news of our great loss. Will be
with you to-night."

In his telegram to Eva he told her that his father had
died, and that the news of his death had been a great shock
to him, and that he was starting for Kilmore.

He also wrote a few lines to her, telling her of the sudden
blow he had received. Even to write to her required a
great effort. He thought as he did so of the quarrel with
his father for her sake; and that for her sake, also, he had deceived him. Their last conversation on the subject rose
vividly to his mind, and there was great self-reproach in
his heart.

"I should not have left him," he thought, and he remembered his mother's sad warning that his duty to his father
might not be for long. This had been only too true, and
now Clair blamed himself in vain.

At last the time came for him to start for Kilmore, and
the journey was a long and inexpressibly dreary one. He
telegraphed on the road for a carriage to be waiting for
him at the station nearest to his home, and he reached this
station on a dark and blusterous night. A carriage was

outside, and the station-master took off his hat to the new peer.

But Clair pulled his hat over his brow, and walked on without a word. He could not speak of it, he felt, and he did not until he reached the Hall. There the butler, Gregson, was waiting at the entrance to receive him.

"How is my mother?" asked Clair, hastily.

"I am very sorry to say my lady is very ill, my lord," answered the butler. "My lord's sudden death was a great shock to her, and she is very prostrate."

"Where is my cousin, Miss Gower?" next inquired Clair, who was much agitated.

"I had orders to inform Miss Gower when your lordship arrived. She is with my lady."

"Tell her at once; I will wait for her here," said Clair, going into the breakfast-room. But many minutes elapsed —endless minutes, they seemed—before Clair heard Annette's footsteps, and when she did enter the room her face was very grave and reproachful.

"Annette!" cried Clair, going up to her with outstretched hand, "this is very terrible!"

But Annette did not take his hand; she raised her dark eyes and looked in his face, and Clair understood how much she blamed him.

"I only got your telegrams to-day," he said, hastily. "I have been out of town."

"And why were they not forwarded?" asked Annette. "The anxiety you have caused her has nearly killed Aunt Jeanie."

"I'm so dreadfully sorry—I—forgot to leave my address at the club, and when I remembered this, I came up to town and got your telegrams. It has been a terrible shock to me. I never thought of such a thing for a moment, or, of course, I should not have gone away."

"It has been terrible for Aunt Jeanie; she thought something must have happened to you also, and she has been nearly out of her mind. You left me a bitter task, Clair, when I had to tell her you had gone against her wish; gone without bidding her good-bye."

"I was forced to go—I could not foresee—"

"Your father took the fit the same night, and he never rallied; it has been most dreadful."

"I had better see my mother now," said Clair, in great distress.

"You cannot see her," answered Annette, and she burst into tears. "She—she thinks the news that you had left Kilmore as you did killed your father—she—"

"Good heavens! How can you say such a thing?"

"It is true," sobbed Annette; "she told him, and he got greatly excited, and then the fit seized him, and—he never spoke again."

Clair groaned aloud; he was terribly upset, but Annette said no word to comfort him.

"At all events I had better see her," he said at length.

"She does not wish it, Clair; it would only make her worse; she could not bear it."

Clair did not speak; that his mother, his fond, devoted mother, had turned against him, cut him to the quick, and after a moment or two of silence he left the room and went to his own, which he found ready prepared for him.

It was all very terrible—his dead father and his broken-hearted mother, both beneath the roof, and he could do nothing. His own conscience, too, reproached him, and Annette's words had stabbed his heart. Had he really killed his father? Had he, for the sake of his own selfish happiness, for the love he bore Eva, brought death and sorrow to those to whom he owed his birth? Clair asked himself these questions, and a chill presentiment stole over his soul.

"We were too happy," he thought, still thinking of Eva; and so in this sad and gloomy fashion ended the golden days that Eva had promised him.

CHAPTER XXVIII.

HIS NEW NAME.

The next morning his new responsibilities were forced upon him; his new name. He had spent a miserable, restless night, and when he went down to breakfast he had to take it alone. But it was scarcely over when the butler informed him that Mr. Jepson, the late lord's land agent, wished to see him.

"You can show him in," replied Clair, though in his heart he shrank from this interview.

A few moments later Mr. Jepson entered. He bowed respectfully, but not sympathetically, and Clair felt that his manner, also, was changed. The respect was due to the man on whom his future income depended; the sympathy was lacking to the son, who had neglected his father in his fatal illness.

"We meet on a sad occasion, my lord," he said.

"Terrible, and so utterly unexpected," replied Clair.

"Lord Kilmore's health had been long failing."

"Yes, but I never dreamt, never thought of this sudden end."

Mr. Jepson did not speak; he knew that the young lord had offended and grieved his father by his infatuation for some girl, and that he was supposed to have left Kilmore on some fool's errand just before the late earl's fatal seizure, and that he had let days elapse after his father's death before he had returned to the side of his bereaved mother. But it was no business of his, Mr. Jepson told himself; his business was with the estates, not the family differences; and besides, the young lord was master now, and his—Mr. Jepson's—own bread and butter was to be considered.

"I am glad you have returned, my lord," he said, after a few moments' painful silence. "Of course there are many sad details to be considered, and I could not venture to act on my own responsibility, and her ladyship has been too ill to speak of such things. We have therefore waited for your lordship's orders regarding the funeral; but I ought perhaps to tell you that the tenants wish to express their deep regret and respect for his late lordship by attending it."

"Of course," answered Clair, deeply moved, and turning away his head to hide his emotion; "let everything be done, Mr. Jepson, to show the greatest honor to—my dear father."

Clair's voice broke and trembled as he uttered the last few words, and the man of business began to think that the young lord had some feeling after all.

"Young men will be young men," he thought. He said, "Then am I to conclude, my lord, that you wish everything done suitably to the late earl's rank—that expense has not to be considered?"

"Certainly not; arrange everything, Mr. Jepson—and when—"

"We thought the day after to-morrow, my lord; any further delay would not be advisable."

Again Clair turned away his head, and his lips quivered. He rose quickly from his chair and went to the window, and Mr. Jepson was just considering whether he should withdraw, when Clair turned hastily round.

"Where is he, Mr. Jepson?" he said, with a ring of intense pain in his voice. "I have not seen him—I—wish to see him now."

"His lordship is reposing in his own bedroom, my lord," replied Mr. Jepson, not unmoved. "It was her ladyship's orders that it should be so; her ladyship, I am told, scarcely leaves the room, and carries the key; but of course if your lordship wishes, I can no doubt procure it."

"I do wish it; I wish to look once more on my father's face."

"I will see about the key then," replied Mr. Jepson, and he accordingly left the room, and after some delay returned.

"Will you come with me now, my lord?" he said, and so Clair followed him to the familiar room, where he had last seen his father, and where the earl now lay in his unbroken slumber.

The light was dim, and for a moment or two Clair could scarcely see the still, waxen face that rested on the satin pillows. When he did, his own eyes were soon blinded by his tears. The earl's hands were crossed meekly on his breast; his expression was calm and peaceful; the silent dignity of death hovered round his placid brow.

"Father, dear father," half-whispered Clair, and he bent down and kissed the cold hands. Mr. Jepson was also much affected, for over twenty years he had faithfully served the dead man lying before him, and such old ties are not broken without infinite pain. But he had at least nothing to reproach himself with. But Clair's heart on the contrary was smiting him with cruel pangs. He was remembering all his father's love and kindness; the boyish days when there had been no quarrel between them. Until Eva Moore's fair face had crossed his path Clair had ever been guided by his father's wishes; and the earl had been alike just and generous to his son.

"And I deceived him," thought Clair, remorsefully; "would that I had told him the truth—but I had promised Eva."

"Perhaps you would rather be alone, my lord," presently said Mr. Jepson, considerately, glancing at the young man's agitated face.

"Yes, thank you," answered Clair, without looking up, and Mr. Jepson accordingly quietly withdrew. Then, after he had gone, Clair sank down on his knees by the side of his father's prostrate form.

"Oh! father, forgive me!" he cried out aloud in bitter grief. "Father, if you can hear and see me you will know why I acted as I did; I meant no wrong—none, father—God is my judge."

At this moment the dressing-room door adjoining the room where the earl lay was noiselessly opened, and a white-faced, hollow-eyed woman appeared, but Clair never raised his head. It was his mother, and as Clair, without knowledge of her presence, continued to entreat his dead father's forgiveness, Lady Kilmore advanced slowly into the room.

"Clair," she said, and at the sound of her voice Clair started to his feet.

"Mother!" he cried, and he went forward and clasped her hand, and then fell on his knees before her.

"Oh! you forgive me, too, mother!" he prayed, looking up at her altered face; " I did not mean to grieve you—mother; say you will forgive me now."

She opened her quivering lips to speak, but no words came forth, and then she bent down and kissed her son.

"Mother, my dear mother!" said Clair, rising and clasping her in his arms, and Lady Kilmore's head fell on his breast.

"Help me to bear it," she murmured. "Clair, Clair, it has broken my heart!"

"I know, it is terrible; let me try to comfort you, mother."

"Let us look at him," whispered Lady Kilmore; and so the two went hand-in-hand and stood by the side of their dead, gazing at the placid features.

"He looks happy," murmured Lady Kilmore. "Oh, Clair, I wish I lay still beside him."

"No, no, you must live for my sake," answered Clair; and with many tender words he presently led her away, and Lady Kilmore did not feel so utterly crushed and desolate when her hand lay in her son's.

But her husband's loss had been a terrible blow to her.

Their married life had been a singularly happy one, and Lord Kilmore's sad and sudden death had, as she told Clair, broken her heart.

"I have lost all interest in everything," she said a few days later, gazing with her dry, tearless eyes out on the park; "and yet the world goes on the same."

Just the same, though it seems all dead to us! In the first blank hours of loss and grief we think only of the new-made grave. Lady Kilmore felt this when they bore away from her the husband of her youth, the love of her life. These were, indeed, terrible moments; terrible to the bereaved woman, terrible to Clair.

Everything was conducted in the most stately fashion, and a long line of mourners followed the earl to his grave. Amongst these Clair—the present earl—stood foremost. He was naturally forced into this position, and had to receive the friends and neighbors of his dead father. Upstairs Lady Kilmore lay white and speechless, the muffled sounds from below mercifully shut out from her strained ears by the loving hand of Annette Gower. She never left her aunt, and showed the most tender affection and consideration for her in her bitter sorrow.

Among the tenants who received invitations to the earl's funeral were the two Dightons at Holly Hill. Lord Kilmore's death, we may be sure, had been much talked of at the various homesteads, and the young heir's absence from his father's death-bed had also been freely commented on. Richard Dighton heard all this conversation with a gloomy brow and an angry heart. He knew, he thought, at whose side the young lord lingered; for whose sake he had left his father. But he never spoke of these things. He hated Clair, but he also feared him, and when they had accidentally met on the bridge over the Ayre after Clair's return home, and old Dighton had been inquiring after his injuries, there had been a look in Clair's eyes, when he told the farmer that some coward had shot him in the street, that struck absolute terror into Richard's soul.

And now he was the earl—their landlord—thought Richard bitterly, and she—where was she? Richard, as we know, had put the very worst construction on what he had seen of the intimacy between Clair and Eva. He never dreamed that he would marry her, or think of marrying her. He had disgraced and would probably abandon some day the girl he had met while staying under their roof. Often Richard Dighton had reflected darkly, but by his own mad act his lips were stayed.

He did not dare to tell what he knew, and still less now. He scowled when his father said that they had better both follow their late landlord to the grave, and discussed the mounts for the occasion. Richard Dighton felt he could not go and see the young lord raised so far above him. And, though he did not know it, his parents guessed something of his feelings to the new earl.

"I'm sure," said Mrs. Dighton, in matrimonial confidence to her husband, "I wish it may be all right between Eva Moore and the young lord. You mind how from the first he ran after her; and what with him saving her at the fire, and then following her to Eastcliff, and then her disappearing like, I wish it may be all right."

"Well, we've naught to do with it, my dear," replied the farmer, putting on his nightcap; "he's our landlord now, and least said is easiest mended."

"Our Dick's never been the same lad since she was here," said kindly Mrs. Dighton with a sigh. "I'm sure I wish she had never come."

"Perhaps he'll marry her."

"The young lord!" answered Mrs. Dighton in great disdain; "not he. She was good enough to make a fool of, but not a wife. He'll marry some grand lady, and some day Eva will find herself left out in the cold—she'd better have married Dick."

"It's no good talking of it."

"I know that, father; but I would like to know what's become of the poor motherless girl, though I never quite took to her like the rest of you did."

Mr. Dighton moved uneasily. He, too, would have liked to have known what had become of the pretty girl who had always been a great favorite of his, and he also had his suspicions that Eva's disappearance was somehow connected with Lord Clair. But, on the other hand, the term of his lease was running low, and moreover, he was meditating asking a renewal of it at a reduced rental.

"We can make no better of it," he said, and then presently composed himself to sleep, with the fullest intention of attending his late landlord's funeral on the following day.

And all the country-folk gathered up to do the same. Mr.

Jepson had arranged that the mounted tenantry had to follow the carriages in the procession, and that they were to assemble at the Hall by two o'clock. It was a great gathering. Lord Kilmore had been a quiet man, and had led a very retired life, but he had been a good landlord, and personally popular among his people, and they all wished to pay him this last respect.

But Richard Dighton would not go. He affected to be ill, and his father therefore set out without him. The farmers were received by Mr. Jepson, and a cold collation was spread out in the large dining-room for their refreshment, as many of them came long distances. This was partaken of with much solemnity, while in another room the personal friends and neighbors of the late lord also were entertained.

At last, however, the long procession moved away, Clair following in the carriage next the hearse as chief mourner, accompanied by his uncle, Mr. Gower, who had come down from town for the ceremony. The shrewd barrister also felt much interest in his nephew, and as they drove together to the church where the family vault of the Kilmores was situated, Mr. Gower was wondering what use the young earl was likely to make of his new wealth and position.

"It will greatly depend on his marriage," thought the Q. C.; "I hope he has not got into any trouble about that girl they talked of."

Clair, or Kilmore, as we must now call him, was very grave and silent. He had not yet recovered from the shock of his father's death, and his new responsibilities were by no means to his liking. He had heard from Eva that morning, and she—knowing that Lord Kilmore was dead—had again entreated him to be sure to keep their own marriage a secret."

"Do not breathe such a thing, my dearest," she had written. "I do not want to be my lady, or to be known as such, and I would rather, far rather, that you had been born in a very different rank. But we cannot help these things; only I do not wish to share your honors—only to have your love. Mind, all your love, Clair, for I shall be content with nothing else."

Clair had kissed these lines, and yet they disturbed him. But for the present he also thought it would be better for their marriage to be kept a secret.

14

"It would add to my mother's trouble just now," he told himself, "but of course later on it must be known."

Thus, when his uncle was mentally speculating on his future, Clair, also, was thinking of it, and of the fair young wife whose fate was bound up in his. He thought of her even when they entered the church and the solemn words of the burial service fell on his ears; when he stood by the grave and laid the wreath his mother had entrusted to him on his father's bier. She was, in truth, ever present in his mind, and as the dead man had truly loved his mother, so his son now truly and faithfully loved the woman he had chosen.

At last it was all over. The funeral guests after leaving the church returned to their homes, and talked of the young earl as they went.

"He's a nice-looking fellow," said one.

"He seemed really cut up about his father's death," remarked another.

"He's come into a fine fortune, I suppose?" speculated a third.

These and other comments were exchanged, as is ever so when one man comes into another's possessions. The old lord was dead, but the Earl of Kilmore still lived, and the interest naturally followed the title.

But while his neighbors and tenants were talking of him, the new earl returned to the Hall, and at once went to seek his mother. He found Lady Kilmore utterly prostrated with grief, and her expression as she looked at her son as he bent over her, cut him to the heart.

It might be fancy, but he thought there was reproach still in her sunken eyes. "Why did you do this?" they seemed to say. "Clair, you killed him, and have broken your mother's heart."

CHAPTER XXIX.

THE BANKER'S VISIT.

During the sad days at Kilmore that followed the late earl's funeral, at Westwold Eva had a visitor that much surprised her. This was no other than Mr. James Ford, the banker, who had greatly admired Eva's beautiful face when he had seen her, and was also interested in her on account of her fortune. He wanted to know, too, something more of the mysterious visitor at the bank, Mr. Temple, and taking advantage of a business transaction regarding the investment of some of her money, he went down to Westwold, and having arrived at the old-fashioned hotel where she was staying, he inquired for Miss Eva Moore.

At the hotel, during the first days after their marriage, the young couple had passed, to avoid any remark, as Mr. and Mrs. Clair. But Eva had given directions that if any letters arrived addressed to Miss Eva Moore, that they were to be delivered to her, as this was her maiden name. She had done this, meaning to keep her marriage to Clair a secret from the banker, and indeed from everyone connected with her. When, therefore, Mr. Ford inquired for Miss Eva Moore, the dingy-looking waiter replied there was no lady of that name staying at the house.

Mr. Ford looked and felt greatly surprised. He had written to Eva here, and she had answered his letter, and told him she would let him know of any change of address.

"Are you sure?" he said to the waiter.

But before the man could answer, the landlady, who had been listening behind her bar to the question by the stranger (the bar being close to the entrance of the hotel), put her head through the little open glass window, which she could raise and close at will.

"Ye'll be meaning the young married lady," she said, "Mrs. Clair?"

The banker stared, but merely prudently said:

"I inquired for Miss Eva Moore."

"Yes, sir, she was Miss Eva Moore, and sometimes letters

come for her by that name still; but she's wed now; she's Mrs. Clair."

"Mrs. Clair?" repeated Mr. Ford, in great surprise.

"Yes, sir, she and her husband are staying here, but he's away just now, he's gone to his father's burial."

Mr. Ford listened to all this in extreme astonishment. Then, after thinking a moment or two, he drew out his card and handed it to the waiter.

"Ask the lady if she will see me," he said.

"Yes, John, ask the lady," directed the landlady, "and give her the gentleman's card."

John accordingly disappeared for the purpose, and the landlady made a few affable remarks on the weather to Mr. Ford. Then John returned.

"The lady will be glad to see you, sir," he said, addressing Mr. Ford; "if you'll be pleased to follow me."

This Mr. Ford accordingly did, and the landlady looked after the tall, handsome banker with mild curiosity.

"He'll be one of her relations come to look after her," she was reflecting; "I always thought those two had run away."

In the meantime Mr. Ford was following the waiter up the broad, old-fashioned, irregular staircase, and at the first landing the waiter stopped, and rapped at a sitting-room door.

"Come in," cried Eva's clear, sweet voice.

The waiter accordingly opened the door, and Mr. Ford entered the room, and Eva rose to receive him with a blush and a smile.

"This is quite a surprise," she said, pleasantly.

"Yes, I thought I should surprise you," answered Mr. Ford, smiling also and holding her hand, and thinking how lovely she was; "but the truth is I thought I should like to see you personally about that investment I wrote to you of, and so I ran down. What a charming view you have here: a magnificent sea view."

"Yes, I am very fond of the sea."

"You have plenty of it here at all events," smiled Mr. Ford. Then he looked again at Eva; he was wondering if what he had heard downstairs was true; wondering if Eva was really Mrs. Clair.

"I have just heard some news about you," he said,

"News!" And Eva's face suddenly paled. "Not about the man who went to the bank?"

"No, but they told me downstairs that you are married, that you are Mrs. Clair."

Eva's cream-like complexion grew scarlet.

"You must not believe everything you hear, Mr. Ford," she faltered.

"That is true; then must I not believe this?"

Eva tried to prevaricate.

"If you speak to anyone they say absurd things," she said, with downcast eyes.

"That is true also—well, all I can say is that if it were true Mr. Clair should be the happiest man on earth."

Eva tried to laugh; she turned away her head from the bold, handsome hazel eyes fixed on her face, and she began to speak of the money Mr. Ford affected to have come about.

"And you think it would be a good thing?" she said.

"Yes," answered Mr. Ford. He was a man of the world, and he quite understood he was to ask no more questions about "Mr. Clair," and he understood also that Miss Eva Moore was apparently a young lady who not only had a "past," but a present affair, and he smiled.

He sat down beside her and talked to her, but he said nothing more either of Mr. Temple or Mr. Clair. He thought her beautiful, and he wished to let her know that he thought this, but he made Eva only feel nervous and uncomfortable. She was afraid not to be civil to him, as he had so much in his power, and yet there was something in his manner she did not like.

It was the afternoon, and presently she asked him if he would have some tea. He accepted this offer, and talked well and agreeably, but still Eva did not like it; she wished him to go away, but Mr. Ford seemed to have no idea of going. After it grew dusk, however, he rose with a smile.

"I must go and speak to the landlady," he said, "and see if she can give me some dinner and put me up. It is too cold a night to travel," and he gave a little shrug.

Eva felt exceedingly disconcerted, but what could she say? Mr. Ford, however, was perfectly at ease.

"As we are neighbors for the present in this out of the world spot, may I come in and have a little chat with you

after I have dined?" he asked, leaning both his hands on
the back of the chair from which he had just risen.

Eva visibly hesitated.

"I am afraid that will be late," she said.

"Oh, no, and I shall stay a very short time; good-bye
for the present then," and he bowed and went away, leaving
Eva in a very unhappy frame of mind.

What should she do? she asked herself. Take this man
into her confidence so far as regarded Clair? But the
danger of this, she knew, would be very great. On the
other hand, if Mr. Ford made any inquiries down-stairs
about herself and Clair, what would he think? At last
she determined to risk his bad opinion rather than run
any chance of her marriage becoming known. And as she
sat meditating the difficult question, Mr. Ford was actually
making the inquiries she dreaded. He did this in his easy
and self-assured way while he was arranging with the landlady to remain all night at the hotel.

Having ordered his dinner, he said, as if casually:

"It must be very dull for your visitor upstairs when Mr.
Clair is away, I should think?"

Upon this the landlady at once told him everything he
wanted to hear. How devoted the young couple were to
each other; how they went about on the shore hand in
hand like two children; how he was a handsome young
man, and she a beautiful young creature.

"I think she has a face just like a flower, sir," added the
landlady, who had sentimental tendencies, and the banker
also agreed in this tribute to Eva's loveliness.

And during his lonely dinner which followed he sat revolving in his own mind the strange story he had just heard.
If Miss Eva Moore were actually married to this Mr. Clair,
then she was evidently keeping her marriage a secret, and
she must have some motive for this secrecy.

"And the parson?" reflected Mr. Ford. "Could there
be any truth in Mr. Temple's story that this pretty woman
was his wife? In that case she had probably run away with
Mr. Clair, and was hiding from the husband who was
naturally looking after his wealthy wife."

"So wags the world," thought the banker with a somewhat grim smile.

His own life was by no means a clean record. He had
also married a wife in the days of his youth, and had wearied

of her, or rather had never cared for her except as a stepping stone to help on his own fortunes. He was a rich man now, and he could afford to spend as much money as he cared to do on his own pleasures, and he did not take his poor wife much into account. She was older than he was, she was plain, and Mr. James Ford's conscience was of a very elastic description.

And Eva's beauty, the confidence she had placed in him, and these two men—Mr. Temple and Mr. Clair—excited some very peculiar feelings, partly of curiosity, in Mr. Ford's heart.

"I wonder if she would like a third lover?" he thought, and again he smiled. Then he rose from the table—still smiling—and went and looked at his own handsome visage in the faded green-tinted mirror over the mantelpiece.

A fine-looking man this, stalwart and keen-eyed, and he might perhaps be forgiven the complacency with which he evidently regarded his own features.

"I think I could cut out the parson at all events," he reflected, and then he gave a little shrug of his broad shoulders. He did not believe much in women, except in their beauty, and beauty had to him an overpowering attraction.

"I must find out all about it," he decided, "but not to-night; it never does to be in a hurry when there is anything to unravel."

And then after another glance at himself in the mirror he quitted the room where he had dined, and went to the one occupied by Eva, and rapped softly at the door.

With a sinking heart Eva said "Come in," and the banker entered, well pleased.

They say that admiration is dear to every woman's soul, but there are times when it is certainly very embarrassing. Eva knew she was a pretty woman, and she knew that Mr. James Ford admired her, but she certainly wished at this moment that he did not. She was afraid; afraid of the bold, smiling hazel eyes fixed on her face, and of a certain gleam in their expression which was not over-respectful.

"What must he naturally think of me?" she thought with a little inward shudder. And she thought, too, of Clair; of Clair whom she loved, and for whose sake she had run a great risk, and who might not care to hear of Mr. Ford's visit.

"Will you forgive me for intruding on you again?" he said.

"I dare say you find this place very dull," answered Eva.

"On the contrary, I am charmed with it, and your landlady gave me an excellent dinner."

Eva smiled.

"Which is one item to produce content," she said.

"It is, doubtless, but I am not a man devoted to the pleasures of the table. There are other things in life to my mind so far beyond mere eating that I never think of it unless food is before me."

"And then I suppose you do?" laughed Eva.

"In moderate fashion only," answered Mr. Ford; "and to-night I did not think of it at all."

"No? How was that?"

"I was thinking—that I hoped to see you again."

Eva blushed, and slightly frowned.

"Forgive me; I am too bold," a moment later said Mr. Ford, and then he changed the conversation, and being a clever and agreeable man, when in about half an hour he rose to take his leave, he had made rather a favorable impression on Eva.

And the next morning he returned to town, but before he did so he again paid Eva a short visit. He spoke first of business, and then mentioned Mr. Temple's name.

"If the clergyman—Mr. Temple—again calls at the bank, I presume you still wish your address to be kept a secret from him?" he said.

"Certainly," answered Eva, and a scarlet flush mounted to her very brows; "he has nothing to do with me; he has no right to ask after me, and I never wish to hear of or see him again."

Mr. Ford shook hands with her.

"He shall not hear of you through me," he said; "good-bye, you can quite trust me."

CHAPTER XXX.

THE PORTRAIT.

When Eva wrote to Clair, or rather Kilmore, though he would always be Clair to her, she told him of the banker's visit.

"He came to see me about investing some money of mine," she wrote. "You know my uncle left me money in India, and there is loss in the exchange," etc., and so on, and Kilmore kissed the paper on which these words were written, not knowing of the secret anxiety in which they were penned.

Eva, indeed, ever since his father's death, had realized more than ever the dangers of her position. Now, as Earl of Kilmore, she knew Clair's actions would be noticed, and her own connection with him more likely to be discovered. She had hidden herself away, but for how long, she asked herself with a restless heart, as she paced her room after the banker had left her, and she felt now that she was committed in his eyes.

"I wish I had been differently brought up," she thought with clasped hands; "brought up to be a good woman—fit for Clair's wife. Ah, I am beginning to think there is something in what we hear in church; something in trying to do right, even when we want to do wrong. I loved Clair, but I should not have married him—my dear, dear Clair."

In the meanwhile that grim Nemesis which so often dogs the footsteps of our wrong-doings was stealing nearer and nearer on her path. Miss Onslow had told her brother that she had met a clergyman named Temple at Miss Sprigge's, and that he had gone there to inquire after a young lady called Miss Eva Moore.

"Miss Eva Moore!" repeated Mr. Onslow, in a tone of great interest, which instantly struck his sister.

"Yes, do you know her?" asked Miss Onslow.

The vicar was silent; he had seen the death of the Earl of Kilmore in the papers, and he naturally at once remembered the secret marriage of his heir.

"It will be acknowledged now, I suppose," he thought, but he of course still felt bound by his promise not to mention the affair. But he naturally felt curious about the clergyman who had inquired after Miss Eva Moore, and wondered if she were the same person who now rightfully was the Countess of Kilmore.

"He is a tall, dark, rather severe-looking man," explained Miss Onslow, "and he is staying at the Grosvenor; I said perhaps you would call upon him."

"Well, perhaps," smiled the kindly vicar, and so the conversation ended; but a day or two later Miss Onslow and her brother at a picture gallery in New Bond Street actually encountered Mr. Temple.

Miss Onslow recognized him at once and bowed, and Mr. Temple raised his hat. Then Miss Onslow stopped and introduced her brother.

"This is my brother, Mr. Temple," she said, "of whom I spoke to you at Miss Sprigge's; the vicar of St. John's, South Kensington."

The two men bowed, raised their hats, and looked at each other steadily. At the same moment both their minds were going back over twenty years.

"Not Temple, of Trinity?" cried Mr. Onslow, extending his hand. "Yes, surely it is!"

"Yes, I am George Temple," answered Mr. Temple; "and you are Alfred Onslow; I remember you perfectly."

They had been at college together, and on fairly friendly terms while there. And now they again shook hands; they talked of their old days, their old comrades. It was a pleasant meeting; pleasant to the genial vicar of St. John's and even to the more reserved George Temple."

"And are you married?" presently asked Mr. Onslow, smiling.

"Yes," replied Mr. Temple, but his tone was so grave, so cold, that the vicar of St. John's asked no further questions on the subject.

It ended by Mr. Temple going to dine with the vicar at his bachelor establishment at South Kensington, and after dinner when the two men were alone, Miss Onslow having also dined with them, Mr. Temple grew a little more communicative regarding his past life.

He had been three years absent from his vicarage in Dorset, he told Mr. Onslow, having established a curate there before he left England, and during these three years he had been a great traveler.

"And Mrs. Temple?" the vicar ventured to say.

A dusky red rose to the harsh, dark countenance before him.

"My wife and I quarreled," he answered, after a moment's pause; "I married a child—a foolish, lovely child—unknown to her only surviving relation, who then lived in India. She was totally unsuited to me—wayward, spoilt—perhaps I was harsh, but our married life was one perpetual scene of disagreement and recrimination. At last she proposed, nay, entreated me to allow her to return to her uncle in India, who did not know of our marriage, as Eva was afraid if he did that he would not leave her a fortune, as I was a poor man, and Mr. Moore hated poor men. I foolishly consented to her wish; Eva started for India, and I went to Africa, and before we parted we agreed to separate for good. I was away three years—in various lands—and during these years I had time to reflect. I came to the conclusion that I had done wrong; that I had no right to leave my young wife alone in the world; and I heard also on my return to England that her uncle in India was dead; that he had actually been dead three years, and that thus Eva must have been alone during my absence."

"What was her name?" asked Mr. Onslow, who had listened to the story with deep interest.

"Eva Moore," answered Mr. Temple; "her uncle was Mr. Moore, of Calcutta, a merchant there, and a wealthy man, and I conclude that Eva must have inherited his fortune, or a portion of it."

"And have you seen her since your return to England?" asked Mr. Onslow quickly.

"Yes, I met her by chance in the street; I knew she was in town, for I heard this at the bank where she used to have an account, before and after her marriage to me. She resumed her maiden name when we separated, as her uncle in India did not know of our marriage for the reason I mentioned to you. I inquired for her, therefore, as Miss Eva Moore, and was told she was, the clerk believed, in town, but he did not know her address. But soon after this I met her."

"Yes?"

"I knew her instantly, for she is little changed; I told

her that I had repented of our separation; that it was not
right, and that she must return to me. She refused to do
so; refused to tell me where she lived, but finally, on my
persisting, gave me an address—a false address, as I afterward found—at Miss Sprigge's, in Wnydam Place, where
I met your sister, and I have never seen her since."

"Then she means to elude you?"

"I am determined to find her, and to insist on her living
with me again. She is my wife. I have right on my side,
and I am determined to enforce my rights."

Mr. Onslow was silent for a few moments; then he said
slowly, almost painfully:

"What is she like?"

"You mean in appearance?"

Mr. Onslow nodded.

"She is tall and slender—a beautiful young woman with
regular features, a white, cream-like skin, and large dark
eyes and dark hair. She is little changed from her young
girlhood; handsomer, I think—too handsome to be alone
and without a protector in the world."

Something between a groan and a sigh escaped Mr. Onslow's kindly lips. The description of the Eva Moore he had
married to the young lord in secret was too accurate to be
mistaken. She had been married first then to this man—
George Temple—he was her legal husband, and what should
he, Mr. Onslow, do?"

"And you have heard nothing more?" he said, presently.

"Not yet, but I am determined, as I told you, to do so.
I went to the bank again where her money is placed, and
saw one of the partners of the firm, a Mr. James Ford, and
this man evidently knows where she is, though he affected
not to do so. He, in fact, must know, as she must receive
her money through the bank, but he declined to give me
the information I asked for; but I believe I can compel him
to do so. I am taking legal advice on the point, and I think
there is no doubt I can force him to speak."

Mr. Onslow rose from the table and began walking slowly up and down the room. He was a good man, God-fear-
ing and just in all things, and the position in which he
found himself suddenly placed was a most trying one. He
was a High Churchman, also, and believed in marriage as a
sacred institution, not to be broken by the will of man.
And this lovely young woman had, he feared, committed

bigamy when she married Lord Clair. It was an ugly word; ugly in its consequences against the law, and in the eyes of this Churchman a heavy sin.

"And you were actually married to her?" he said, after taking a few turns across the room in silence.

"Most certainly I was," answered Mr. Temple. "I was married to her at one of the city churches here in London, and I can show you the register. When I met her first she was a school-girl; her uncle had sent her over to England to finish her education. Then she went to board with a lady, and during this time we were married. It was a private marriage on account of her uncle, but the lady with whom she lived knew of it."

"And this lady?"

"Is unfortunately now dead. I went to her house immediately on my return to England, but she died some time ago, and I could hear nothing of her but the bare fact of her death. No, it is through the banker that I must trace Eva, and I mean to do so."

"It is a strange story."

"You mean about our separation? Yes, I blame myself now. I should never have permitted such a thing, but she was strangely self-willed and was always regretting the luxuries she had been accustomed to in India. She had been badly brought up, I fancy, as her mother had died during her infancy, and her father also I believe. But to me now my duty is plain; she must return to her husband, and the law can force her to do this—but I have wearied you with this long story?"

"No, you have not," answered Mr. Onslow, and again he sighed.

He saw indeed at this moment again before him the young couple in their beauty, their happiness and their love, that so short a time ago he had wedded before the altar of God. He remembered the look of devotion in the young lord's eyes, and the soft blushes and sweet smiles on the bride's fair face. Then he looked at Mr. Temple, at the harsh, dark, stern countenance of the man advanced into middle age. And this was her husband; he would take her from her young lover; he would turn her life into misery and woe.

"But it is a sin," the next moment reflected the Churchman; "a deadly sin. She must have deceived Lord Clair, and led him into sin also—a painful duty, I fear, lies before me."

Nevertheless he said nothing to Mr. Temple of his almost certain conviction. He must be sure, quite sure, before he took any steps in the matter. He asked the name of the clergyman who had married them in the city church, and found he was an acquaintance of his own.

"We had better look him up and see the register," he suggested.

Mr. Temple was quite ready to agree to this, and before they parted he had made an arrangement to meet on the following day, and go together to the city church.

"I will know her signature," thought Mr. Onslow. "You have strangely interested me," he said; "have you a portrait of your wife?"

Again that dusky blush crossed the dark face opposite to him.

"Yes," answered Mr. Temple, after a moment's hesitation. "It may seem folly to you that the portrait of the woman I could not live with, that I continually quarreled with, yet accompanied me in all my wanderings. I have it at my hotel now, and if you like I will show it to you; you may by chance have seen her?"

"It may have been so; yes, I should like to see it."

After this they settled that Mr. Onslow should call the next morning at Mr. Temple's hotel for the purpose of seeing the portrait, and that they should afterward proceed to the city church at which Mr. Temple asserted he was married to Eva Moore. Then Mr. Temple went away, leaving the vicar of St. John's strangely disturbed.

But if this were so, if this unhappy young woman had deliberately led the man into sin, what could he as a priest, a servant of God, do? he asked himself. There was but one answer—his duty—and this duty was most grievous to his kindly heart.

He said nothing to his sister of the communication he had received. He placed her in a cab and bade her good-night, and Miss Onslow could not help wondering why this visit of Mr. Temple's had brought such a sudden cloud on her brother's brow. Then Mr. Onslow returned home, and spent the rest of the evening in solitary and very painful reflections. But he was up betimes in the morning and at the appointed hour arrived at the Grosvenor Hotel and inquired for the Rev. George Temple.

He was within, and a few minutes later the two met, and shook hands almost in silence. Indeed, Mr. Onslow affected no particular pleasure at the meeting, and Mr. Temple wondered somewhat at the gravity of his manner. Before him on the table where he had been writing as Mr. Onslow entered the room was an old travel-stained leather desk. This, after a few words of rather strained conversation, Mr. Temple unlocked and took out from it a worn and discolored envelope. This also he opened, and then Mr. Onslow perceived it contained a photograph, worn and discolored too, which, after glancing at Mr. Temple handed toward him.

"This is my wife," he said in a rather husky voice.

Mr. Onslow took the photograph almost nervously and fixed his eyes on the lovely face it portrayed. A girl's face, almost a child's, on the threshold of her womanhood. But there was no mistaking the fair lineaments; the broad, low, white brow, the straight nose, the dark marked eyebrows, and the large lustrous eyes. There could be no other face like it, thought the vicar of St. John's, with an uneasy pang darting through his heart. Yes, this was the fair woman he had wedded to the young lord; this was the Eva Moore and no other, who, if George Temple's story were true, had married when she knew her other husband was still alive!

"But she may not know," the next moment thought the kind vicar; "she may have believed him to be dead, and in that case the sin does not lie at her door."

"She is handsome," said Mr. Temple, gravely, holding out his hand to receive back the portrait; "you will smile I suppose at such an exhibition of human weakness as that I should have carried this about with me so long? But it was so, and perhaps looking at it in my loneliness first changed my feelings toward her, and led me to believe that it was an actual sin to live any longer apart from my wife."

"It was a dangerous experiment to leave so beautiful a woman," answered Mr. Onslow.

"Not as regards her falling into any folly; she is too cold, too proud for that. But what I feel now is that not only her temporal but her spiritual welfare should be my care. Her ideas on religion were most vague, if she had any at all, and the uncle with whom she was brought up was an atheist."

"It is a terrible state of things; without an Anchor, and a Guide, God knows to what we may not drift," said Mr. Onslow, solemnly.

"That is so; we are ever surrounded, I believe, by those, who for their own dark purposes, would tempt us to evil, and is there one of us can say we will not fall?"

"Not one; without Help no man nor woman is safe."

They talked a little longer in this strain. George Temple's ideas, the kindly vicar of St. John's perceived, were narrow and somewhat warped. Women he considered decidedly inferior to men; inferior mentally and physically, and he believed and argued that they should take no place in the world but in their husband's households. They were to be guided and protected, and their place in his eyes was literally to "love, honor, and obey." He forgot or ignored the eminent women of science, literature, and art. He was essentially of the old-fashioned school, and had been reared in a Scottish manse, and some of the rigidity of the early home clung to him still. His mother, whose Bible and cookery book had formed her library and her literature, was still to him a pattern among women. He was completely behind his time, and with a certain obtuseness of nature failed to see this.

The vicar of St. John's, on the other hand, accustomed to the life of great cities, to the society of polished and intellectual men and women, could scarcely forbear a smile at his crude and narrow thoughts. No wonder a young Anglo-Indian girl, fresh from the easy school where she had been brought up, had revolted and rebelled against such a hard taskmaster, thought Mr. Onslow. The astonishing thing was how she had ever married him, but this presently Mr. Temple partly explained.

"I used to do a great deal of hard work among the very poor in the East End in those days," he said, "and Eva was very generous and charitable with her money, and sometimes went with me to the houses of the destitute. And I suppose," he added, with a suppressed sigh, "she endowed me with qualities which I did not possess. At all events, from the very first our marriage was an unhappy one, and yet—" And again he sighed.

Mr. Onslow in his large and generous sympathy understood. And yet this harsh-mannered man, with his narrow, tyrannical views, had loved the beautiful girl his treatment had repelled. He had not understood the warm, impetuous nature that sought homage and not rule. It had been one of those fatal mistakes when, without any consideration of character, men and women rush into indissoluble bonds.

Then after a while, and after, Mr. Onslow remarked, Mr. Temple had again carefully locked away the portrait, the two started for the city church where Mr. Temple asserted this unhappy marriage had taken place. Mr. Onslow personally knew the incumbent of this church, and no difficulties were placed in their way regarding the examination of the register. Mr. Onslow had looked over his own book of registration of marriages in the morning before he started on this expedition, and carefully noted the signature of Eva Moore. He now saw it again; the same handwriting, though unformed, but still the same. There was no doubt now. With a heavy heart Mr. Onslow turned away. He, however, still preserved his reticence on the subject to Mr. Temple. He must think before he acted, he decided, and he parted with his brother clergyman without coming to any decision.

But during the night that followed he did. His duty—to this man a most painful duty—plainly pointed one way. The young lord who had unconsciously wedded the wife of another man, must be informed of this grievous fact, and Mr. Onslow determined himself to be the bearer of the evil tidings.

In the announcement of the death and funeral of the Earl of Kilmore in the newspapers, Lord Clair, his eldest and only son, had been mentioned as being present. The funeral had taken place from Kilmore Hall, and therefore Mr. Onslow concluded that in all probability the young earl would still be there. At all events he would go there, as he would be almost sure to learn something of the present Lord Kilmore's movements.

And he did go. He waited another day—he wished to be quite certain that he was doing right in his own mind—and then he started. He arrived at the station nearest Kilmore in the afternoon, and having engaged a cab, drove through the country lanes, where the mist hung on the leafless hedgerows and lay like a white cloud above the river bed. It was a gloomy day, and the good man's heart was also full of gloom.　He was going to the house of sorrow, from which the old master had been but lately borne away, and he was carrying with him the news of fresh sorrow—of sorrow most bitter, most tragic in its pain.　Once his heart almost failed him.

"I cannot do it," he told himself; but after a struggle with his conscience he went on.

"My sin would be great if I kept this back," he decided. "God give me strength to do what I know is right."

CHAPTER XXXI.

MORE BITTER THAN DEATH.

At length Mr. Onslow reached the hall, and having arrived at the entrance presented his card, and inquired if he could see Lord Kilmore.

The footman replied that he believed that his lordship was within, but that he would ask, and accordingly disappeared with the card, but returned in a few minutes.

"His lordship will be happy to receive Mr. Onslow," was the message he brought, and in anything but a happy frame of mind the vicar followed the footman to the library.

The new Lord Kilmore rose to receive the clergyman as he entered the room.　The moment he had glanced at the card he remembered Mr. Onslow's name.　He had married him to Eva, and with a certain amount of anxiety in his manner he now went forward to meet the vicar.

"Mr. Onslow?" he said, holding out his hand.

Mr. Onslow took it, but there was something in the expression of his face that still further alarmed Kilmore.

"You have lost your father since we met?" began Mr. Onslow with faltering tongue.

"Yes, it has been a great blow to us all; a terrible blow, especially, to my poor mother."

"Yes, indeed.　I grieve, Lord Kilmore," and here the vicar's voice again faltered, "to come to a house of mourning as the bearer of ill news."

"Of ill news?" repeated the young earl quickly, and his face paled.　"Not about—"

"Lord Kilmore, I married you, as you remember, a short time ago; you requested me to keep your marriage a secret, and this, of course, I have done."

"Yes, my poor father objected to the marriage, and he was so ill at the time, I feared to worry him in any way. But now this cause of secrecy is gone, and I am only waiting for a little time to elapse after my father's death to announce it."

"I expected some such course from you, I hoped for it, but now it only makes my task more bitter."

"What do you mean? I do not understand."

"A painful duty has fallen upon me; so painful I can scarcely speak the words. Lord Kilmore, it has come to my knowledge, and I am not speaking without full knowledge, that the lady you married in my church that day was already the wife of another man."

"It is a lie! What folly!" cried Kilmore, starting to his feet in overpowering excitement. "Forgive me, Mr. Onslow, but you are speaking under some unaccountable delusion."

"Would that I were; would that the pain I am giving you had no real cause! But I fear I cannot be mistaken; that there is no doubt."

"I do not and will never believe it! What ground, what possible ground, have you for such an absurd assertion?"

"The lady you married was Miss Eva Moore, was she not, and she was the niece and heiress of a certain merchant in Calcutta, named Moore also?"

"I married Miss Eva Moore, certainly," answered Kilmore, with some haughtiness; "but I never heard of her being an heiress. You are mistaking one person for the other, Mr. Onslow."

"I fear, unfortunately, I am not. By one of those strange chances of life, if we can call them such, I met two days ago a man I had not seen nor heard of for over twenty years. He was an old college acquaintance of mine and his name is George Temple; the Rev. George Temple. He dined with me, and after dinner he told me something of his life."

"But what has all this to do with—my wife?" interrupted Kilmore, impatiently.

"If you will listen to my story you will see it has, unhappily, Lord Kilmore."

"I will believe nothing against her, listen to nothing against her," said Kilmore, loyally.

"God forbid that I should speak against her, for I trust and hope that the sin she has committed was done unwittingly. But some four or five years ago, when she was but a child, she married this George Temple, and the man is living now."

"But what proof have you of such a thing?" asked Kilmore, in great agitation, for Mr. Onslow's manner was very earnest.

"I will tell you; George Temple dined with me, and told me a strange story; he had married, he said, I think it was some four or five years ago, while a curate in London, a young girl, an Anglo-Indian, who had been sent to England to finish her education. It was a secret marriage;" Kilmore visibly winced as he listened to these words; "a secret on account of the young lady's uncle, who was a rich merchant in Calcutta, and who would not have approved of his niece marrying a poor curate. The young lady's name was Eva Moore."

"There may be many Eva Moores in the world."

"True; but the name struck me and startled me; and then Mr. Temple went on with his tale. His marriage proved a particularly unhappy one; they were unsuited to each other in every way, and finally, when Mr. Temple was appointed to Harlaxton, in Dorset, his young wife positively refused to accompany him there. She insisted, in fact, on returning to India, and several violent quarrels took place between them. At last they mutually agreed to separate for good; she going back to her uncle in India, bearing her maiden name, and he going out to Africa for an indefinite period, after appointing a curate to take charge of his vicarage. He was abroad three years, and during this time his ideas changed regarding his wife. He blamed himself for leaving her, and he determined to claim her once more. He came back to England, and heard through the bank where his wife had kept an account in her maiden days, and in her maiden name, that Miss Eva Moore was in town."

"What was the bank?" asked Kilmore, breathlessly, and his face flushed, and then grew pale.

"Ford & Ford, Lombard street."

"Ford!" echoed Kilmore, aghast, for he had received Eva's letter telling him of the banker's visit.

"Yes, Ford & Ford; but to go on with my story, one day unexpectedly, quite recently, Mr. Temple met his young

wife in the streets; he told her he wished her to return to
him, which she refused, and he asked her for her present
address.   After some hesitation she gave him one; gave him
a false address, to a lady's boarding house where my sister
lives, and through her I again met George Temple.   Lord
Kilmore, I regret deeply to grieve you, but I have a duty
to fulfill I cannot shirk from; I asked him to describe this
young wife, and his description corresponded only too ac-
curately with the beautiful young lady whom I fear you had
the misfortune to marry."

"I cannot believe it, and yet—" faltered Kilmore, his face
blanching, and his mind going back to Eva's earnest and
constant desire for secrecy; to the banker's visit—Mr. Ford's
visit—and a hundred little things which had often puzzled
him.   He remembered at this moment her warnings; her
unwillingness at first to marry him; her telling him that she
had been badly brought up—brought up in India—and a
sort of groan broke from his quivering lips.

"I would not have come on such an errand as I came
to-day, without a sure conviction," continued Mr. Onslow,
who was greatly moved by the young lord's deep and
unmistakable agitation.   "But I asked Mr. Temple to let
me see the portrait of his wife—I saw it—and I grieve to
say there is no mistake.   It was the face, and there are few
such, of Miss Eva Moore, to whom you were married so
brief a time since."

Again a groan burst from Kilmore's lips, and he covered
his face with his hand.

"I saw, also, the register of her first marriage, and it is
written in the same hand-writing as her second—"

"You saw this!"

"Unhappily, yes; then I felt bound to act as I have done;
to come to you and tell you the truth."

"And," asked Kilmore, in a broken tone, "does this man
know—know where she is?"

"No, he does not; he saw one of the heads of this banking
firm, Mr. James Ford;" Kilmore started; "after his wife had
given him the false address, and the banker, he supposes
under her orders, refused positively to give him her present
address, though he was convinced that he knew it.   And I
also gave no hint to him of the dreadful certainty that had
crept over my mind.   I determined to see you first; it is, of
course, for you to act."

"For me to act!" cried Kilmore, passionately, beginning to pace the room in violent agitation. "Do you know what this is to me, Mr. Onslow, if it be true? More bitter than death! God is my witness, I would rather be lying by my poor father than have lived to listen to such a tale."

"It is, indeed, a terrible blow."

"No one knows what it is!" continued Kilmore, with intense emotion; "I—I loved her too well—for her sake, my mother thinks, I broke my father's heart; for her sake—but why speak of it?" and he abruptly broke off, and for some minutes continued his restless pacings in silence, with bent head and knitted brows, and Mr. Onslow also forbore to speak, feeling that no word of his could at this bitter moment give any consolation to the unhappy young man.

Up and down the room Kilmore strode; up and down. He was trying to think; trying to realize the position in which he found himself, and then he stopped suddenly before Mr. Onslow.

"Until her own lips," he said, with a certain sternness and hardness of manner new to him, "have confirmed this shameful story, I will never believe it. You must go with me and face her; not come and blacken her character to me behind her back."

"I am quite ready to face her," answered Mr. Onslow with some dignity, raising his head; "I only came here from a strong sense of duty, and no one would rejoice more than myself if this unfortunate young lady can clear herself from this dreadful charge. But I have no hope of this; my one hope is that she acted unknowingly; that she believed her first husband to be dead when she married you."

"But even that—" began Kilmore, and then once more he paused. "I will believe nothing," he added, "neither judge nor condemn her except from her own words, and I will see her at once. I will go to town by the next train, and will you accompany me, Mr. Onslow?"

"Most certainly, Lord Kilmore."

"We cannot see her to-night, there is no late train to Westwold, where she is staying. But the first train to-morrow we can go down by. There is a train passes the station nearest here at six; we can travel by that; in the meanwhile you will require some refreshment—the butler will see to it; you must excuse me."

Mr. Onslow bowed gravely and Kilmore was just hastily

leaving the room, when he turned round and once more faced the vicar.

"Until we know, let this painful subject be spoken of no more," he said, and again the vicar bowed silently, and Kilmore then quitted the library, going direct to his own bedroom, and when he got there he flung himself into a chair in a perfect paroxysm of wretchedness.

If this were true! The thought seemed to shatter at one blow all his future life; to darken every hope of his young manhood. Kilmore loved the woman that he secretly and fondly called his wife with an extraordinary depth of passion and love. It had blinded him to everything but her. Now, sitting alone in his misery, he recalled certain scenes and words; he remembered Eva's restlessness the night before their marriage; how she had asked him if he were not afraid to run certain risks; if he were willing to marry her for good or evil; and he remembered, too, in the very first days of their married life how, when he had asked her if a chance should arise to tell his father and mother of their marriage, that she had become almost angry; that she had reminded him of his promise, and that a strange doubt at this moment had crept into his own mind.

"She kissed and smiled it away," thought Kilmore, bitterly. What could she not kiss and smile away? But if she had good cause for all this secrecy? If she were the wife of another man! Kilmore started to his feet; the thought stung him like a scorpion. His Eva—his beautiful one; the bride he had longed to bring to his stately home in the pride and fondness of his heart. He had thought of her fair and gracious—the young countess who would grace the position he had given her, and become a loving daughter to his mother; a comfort to her after her great and bitter loss.

"And now?" Kilmore groaned aloud as the haunting words rose ever before him—if this were true! It meant shame, disgrace, and then Kilmore started; it meant crime. If Eva had married him knowing her first husband to be alive, she had put herself in the power of the law. She might be tried, imprisoned—he knew not what. The thought was maddening, and a half-suppressed cry broke from his pallid and quivering lips.

Then he remembered his mother; he must think of her. Lady Kilmore had never recovered her husband's death, and had never left her own rooms since he had been carried away from them. She used to sit in a listless attitude by the windows for hours, gazing out vaguely on the park. In vain Annette Gower and her son had tried to rouse her. It was very pitiful, the unbroken mourning that her manner and face betrayed. She spoke very little of her loss; she was gentle always, but Annette knew, and Kilmore knew, that her interest in life was gone. It lay buried with the lover of her youth, the husband of her happy and maturer years. And it was to this broken-spirited woman that Kilmore was now forced to go, to say, "Mother, I am about to leave you," and thus, perhaps, add a fresh pang to her sorrowful heart.

He roused himself to do this; he went to her rooms and asked to see her, and Lady Kilmore, who was sitting by the windows as usual, looked round with a faint shadow of a smile on her pallid features as her son approached her.

"I find I am forced to start for town, mother, this afternoon, and have come to say good-bye," he began in that forced, unnatural way in which we speak when we are trying to hide inward emotion, and something in his tone struck his mother, for she raised her languid eyes and looked up in his face.

"This afternoon? That is sudden, Clair," she said.

She still always called him Clair—the name of his happy boyhood and youth—and had not yet been able to bring her lips to call him Kilmore—the familiar Kilmore!

"Yes, it is sudden, but I cannot help it; I must be in town to-night; a gentleman has come for me," answered her son, with downcast eyes.

Lady Kilmore made no further remonstrance; she sighed merely, and then turned her gaze once more on the misty park. Beyond the leafless trees a gray spire rose—the church of Kilmore—and in this church, within the family vault, the last lord slept, and her widowed heart seemed nearer to him when she could watch the spire.

"I am very sorry to leave you, mother."

Again that wintry smile passed over her pale lips.

"It is no matter, Clair," she said, gently.

"Good-bye, then," and he stooped down and kissed her cheek; kissed it, and could not suppress the bitter sigh that seemed to rend his heart in twain.

That sigh was echoed. He had not seen his cousin, Annette Gower, who was sitting in the shadow, so overpowering had been the emotion with which he had entered his mother's room. But Annette had seen him and heard his words, and now as she looked in his face she saw there the shadow of some great and terrible pain.

"Good-bye, Annette," he said, and would have shaken her hand, but she rose and followed him from the room.

"What is the matter? Has something happened?" she asked, when they were outside the door; but Kilmore made no answer.

"Do tell me," urged Annette; "I am sure something is wrong with you."

"I cannot tell you," said Kilmore, hoarsely, "look after my mother;" and he turned away, with the black cloud upon his brow.

CHAPTER XXXII.

"BETWEEN MY LOVE AND ME."

Not one word was spoken on the dreary journey to town between Kilmore and Mr. Onslow of the absorbing thought of both their hearts. Few words, indeed, of any kind were exchanged; Kilmore sitting gloomily with his traveling cap pulled over his brow, and not making any pretense to exchange common courtesies with the good man who from a sense of duty had stabbed him so cruelly. And Mr. Onslow respected this silent suffering, and forbore to speak when he knew his words would be of no avail. The wound was too fresh, too bitter for consolation, and Mr. Onslow understood this, and did not attempt to offer any.

They parted for the night when they arrived in town, but before they did so Kilmore said with gloomy significance:

"You will not fail me to-morrow; you will go with me by the first train to Westwold?"

"I will not fail you," answered Mr. Onslow, and held out his kindly hand, but Kilmore did not take it. In a few brief, abrupt words he named the time and the station where they were to meet, and having settled this he drove to his club, to spend long, restless hours of misery and suspense which seemed literally to have no end.

At length the morning, the gray, cold winter dawn, broke

over the great city, and found Kilmore sleepless, wretched. One by one when he awoke from his broken slumbers a grim array of condemning thoughts and facts had risen up before him, and he found it difficult, mentally, to repeat the words to which, in spite of all, he had tried to pin his faith.

"Unless she tells me so with her own lips I will not believe it," he had said more than once to Mr. Onslow, and a hundred times to himself.

"But if she were to swear falsely," something now seemed to whisper in his ears. He put the thought aside, he would not listen, but it was still there. It haunted him and filled his soul with inexpressible humiliation and pain. Then before it was quite light he arose, for to think was too terrible, and began hastily to dress, and afterwards paced backwards and forwards in his room, until he could possibly make his appearance downstairs.

Long before the proper time he was at the station, impatiently awaiting the arrival of Mr. Onslow; again and again looking at his watch, and at the station clock, and counting the minutes as they slowly passed on in their appointed course.

When it wanted only ten minutes to the time that the train started, he could scarcely control himself—then seven minutes was all the grace left, and Kilmore determined to enter the train alone, and wait no longer for Mr. Onslow. But just when he had come to this determination his eyes fell on the somewhat stately form of the vicar, and he hurried forward to meet him.

"I thought you were never coming," he said, in so impatient a tone that Mr. Onslow raised his eyes to his face in grave surprise, and at the same moment drew out his watch.

But that glance at the young man's haggard countenance swept away any feeling of anger from the vicar's heart at his curt mode of address. He saw that Kilmore had gone through almost more than he could bear; that the mental strain had nearly been too great for his endurance.

Mr. Onslow therefore replied gently and quietly, and soon the two were seated in a railway carriage affecting to read the morning papers. But the vicar noticed how the hand trembled with which Kilmore held his, and that he was actually holding it to screen his twitching face.

It was not a long journey, and before mid-day the train had reached the little town by the sea where Eva and Clair had lived their brief hours of joy. He remembered at this moment of almost intolerable suspense their first going there; the warm clasp of her little hand. But with a mental and bodily shake, as it were, he roused himself. He hailed a porter, told him to call a cab, and was in it before Mr. Onslow could realize that they had arrived at Westwold.

"Come, make haste," said Kilmore to his companion, and a few minutes later they were driving hastily through the irregular streets on their way to the hotel where Eva was staying.

It was a fine winter's day, cold and fresh, and the sun was shining and the sea a steely-blue. But neither Kilmore nor the vicar glanced at sky or wave. Kilmore's heart was too full of overpowering emotion to notice anything around him, and the vicar's feelings of pity, sympathy and anxiety were too strong to allow him also to notice his outward surroundings.

On they went, up and down the steep streets, and then the cab suddenly stopped. They had arrived at the old-fashioned hotel that Kilmore knew so well, and everything grew dazed before his eyes. He flung a sovereign to the driver, who thought he was mad, and began fumbling in his pocket for change. But Kilmore sprang past him, and, followed by Mr. Onslow, entered the hotel, and was at once recognized by the landlady, who was sitting, as usual, behind her glass window at the bar.

"Oh! Mr. Clair! good morning, sir," she said, pleasantly; "you'll find your good lady all right. She's in the sitting-room, sir."

Kilmore made no answer; he ran up the broad, old-fashioned stairs, he reached the sitting-room; he opened the door, and as he did so Eva, who was sitting reading in an easy chair by the fire, looked hastily up, and then sprang to her feet.

"Clair! Clair! my own dear Clair!" she cried, and then ran forward and clasped him in her arms. "How happy I am to see you, how glad," she murmured, with her face upon his breast. She never saw in her excitement and joy that someone had followed him; never saw the black-coated man standing on the threshold; saw nothing but her love!

She was dressed in a white serge, trimmed with otter; her

bare arms gleamed through the long loose sleeves bound with the dark fur. Her shining, auburn hair fell all loose around her. She was beautiful in her joyous abandonment, in her eager, welcoming love; and the vicar's heart, as he looked at her, smote him with a remorseful pang.

"Have I come to end all this?" he thought, and he would have turned away, but as he did so Kilmore looked round.

"Speak to her," he said hoarsely, addressing Mr. Onslow; "ask her to say it is a lie—all false!"

As he spoke Eva raised her head and saw Mr. Onslow, and her expression changed.

"What is this?" she asked, and her white arms fell from Kilmore's neck.

"Eva," continued Kilmore, his voice broken and trembling with excitement, "you know who this is—the clergyman who married us?"

"Yes," came slowly from Eva's lips, and her large, dark eyes were fixed uneasily on Mr. Onslow's face.

"Tell him now, then," went on Kilmore in increasing excitement, "that the story he came to me yesterday with is totally untrue. He said that he had discovered that you —you were the wife of another man."

"What!" And Eva staggered back and grew ghastly white as she uttered this single word.

"It is an error, of course; say it is an error!" cried Kilmore entreatingly, and he grasped her hand. "He has mistaken you for someone else."

"What has he got to say?" said Eva, forcing herself to speak with her pallid lips.

"This," said Mr. Onslow, now advancing into the room, "and I deeply grieve to be forced to speak such words; but it came to my knowledge by a strange chance that you were married some four or five years ago, to a man with whom I was at college—"

"What man?" asked Eva, still in that forced, unnatural voice.

"George Temple, the Rev. George Temple," answered Mr. Onslow.

"How do you know this?" said Eva, with sudden passion, "and what have you to do with it if you did! I deny it; I know of no such person; and what right have you to try to come and make mischief between my Clair and me?"

"God knows I did so most unwillingly, but my sacred calling left me no choice."

Eva gave a scornful laugh; her eyes were blazing now, and she stood defiant like a hunted creature at bay.

"Your sacred calling!" she repeated bitterly. "Does that mean a mischief maker, a meddler?"

"No," answered Mr. Onslow with dignity; "it means that having taken certain vows in the service of the Most High, I am bound humbly to do what my duty points out to me. I met this George Temple, and he told me his story; told me of his young wife, whose maiden name was Eva Moore, and how he had parted with her. The name struck me; I asked to see his wife's portrait, and I saw yours."

"Do you believe this, Clair?" said Eva, now turning round and looking at the man who loved her, and who had been an agonized listener to these words.

"Only from your own lips; I will believe nothing unless you tell me," answered Kilmore.

"You hear; he does not believe you; now go away," said Eva, again looking at Mr. Onslow, and pointing to the door.

"Are you willing to meet this George Temple, then?" asked Mr. Onslow, gravely. "To stand face to face with him; to deny you are his wife in his own presence!"

Eva visibly cowered.

"Send him away, Clair," she said, "will you send him away?"

"But Eva—oh! Eva speak the truth! Is that man anything to you? Is this story a lie or not?" cried Kilmore, passionately.

"I have told you," answered Eva, with her eyes cast down.

"Then why not face him?" went on Kilmore, still more excitedly. "You must face him, Eva; my wife shall have no such slur on her name as this. If this Mr. Temple is nothing to you, then let Mr. Onslow send for him here, and I shall force him to speak the truth."

Eva did not speak; she looked from one man to the other; her bosom was heaving, and there was a desperate gleam in her dark eyes.

"Mr. Onslow, telegraph for this friend of yours," continued Kilmore; "I am determined that this story shall be cleared up."

"I will do so," answered Mr. Onslow; "this is the best course, Lord Kilmore."

"No!" cried Eva, suddenly raising her arm commandingly, as she listened to these words. "No, you shall not send for him, and face him I will not! You want to hear the truth, Clair," she went on with thrilling passion, "the truth of a child tricked into a marriage—then you shall. I was married to this man when I was too young to know what marriage was; I was married to this George Temple before I was sixteen, and it has been the curse and misery of my life!"

Kilmore staggered back as he heard these words, and a cry escaped his whitening lips.

"You never should have known," continued Eva; "I meant you never to know," and she caught his arm, but he pushed her aside. "But for this meddler we might have been happy still! You shrink back, Clair—that is hard, hard, when for your sake I have risked so much."

"Why did you do it?" gasped Kilmore, hoarsely. "Why did you bring this shame to me?"

"Why! Because in my folly, my love, I told myself this man was dead to me, and he is dead, for I shall never see him more. We had been parted for years; we agreed to separate forever, and not—not till I was married to you did I actually know that he still lived."

"I thank God for this," said Mr. Onslow, solemnly; "then unknowingly you committed this sin?"

"I neither knew whether he lived or was dead; to me he was dead, and, Clair—you turn away your head—but do you not remember, I warned you? Did I not ask you if you loved me well enough to run all risks? Did I not tell you you were better without me? You know I did, and you know your answer."

"But not this," said Kilmore, hoarsely; "had I known—"

"You would not have married me?" asked Eva, bitterly. "Well, then, you are free again; I have cost you nothing."

Kilmore sank down on a couch near with a moan, and covered his face with his hands.

"You see what you have done," cried Eva, pointing to him, and looking at Mr. Onslow. "In your self-righteousness you have come between my love and me; you have broken our hearts."

"I grieve—" began Mr. Onslow.

"What good will your hypocritical grieving do?" interrupted Eva, passionately. "But go, now; you have done your worst; leave us to our misery." And once more Eva pointed to the door.

Mr. Onslow hesitated. But there was something so tragic in this beautiful woman's attitude and expression; something so full of grief and scorn, that he felt he could no longer dispute her will. He bowed, therefore, and withdrew, and Eva and Kilmore were alone.

She turned as the door closed behind the vicar, and made a step nearer to the couch where Kilmore sat with his bowed head.

"Clair," she said in thrilling accent; but Kilmore never raised his head.

"Clair," she repeated, but he made no answer.

Then she went up to him; she knelt down before him; she laid her head against his knee.

"Will you forgive me?" she said, looking up pleadingly in his covered and averted face. "Forgive me for my love's sake—I loved you so well, Clair?"

Then he did look at her.

"Is it love," he said, hoarsely, "to blight a man's life; to bring disgrace and shame to his name?"

"I have brought none to you, only to myself," answered Eva. "You are not married to me; as this wretch, George Temple, is living, the ceremony which passed between us is null and void; it binds you to nothing; when you are tired of me you can send me away."

"How can you speak thus; how dare you speak thus!" cried Kilmore, in sudden passion and anger, and he sprang to his feet, and pushed her clinging hands away. "You, the woman I loved and honored; the woman for whose sake they say I shortened my father's life! Yet you speak like a wanton; as if what you have done was but some passing caprice!"

"It was no caprice," answered Eva; "I loved you and still love you, and what you know now need not change our love. I am willing for the sake of that love to sacrifice what is called my good name, and I am not afraid of the parson's hard words. And you will lose nothing; a man, as you know well, loses nothing in this just world, by such a connection as ours in future must be. It all falls on the woman's head, whether the woman, as in our case, is the chief sinner or no. Your friends will receive you—your cousin will smile on you—"

"Will you be silent!" cried Kilmore, sternly; "this is no time for gibes or folly. Do you know what you have done? You have committed bigamy; you are liable to be arrested—to be punished by the law."

Eva, who had still been kneeling where he had left her, now rose and drew herself up to her full height.

"That is enough," she said; "if I am arrested, I can bear it better than your words. But do not be afraid; I won't be arrested, nor will the name and home of which you are so proud be dragged into the dust or the law courts by me! I will bear my own burdens, and leave you to your honors!" And without another word she swept out of the room with her head thrown proudly back.

"Eva!" cried Kilmore, as the door closed behind her. But there was no answer; Eva was gone.

CHAPTER XXXIII.

"GOOD-BYE, CLAIR."

He did not attempt to follow her; he felt he must have time to think; to let the terrible shock of the knowledge of her unworthiness calm down in his mind before he could take any action in the matter. His brain was a sort of chaos, and whirling through it one painful and humiliating thought after the other passed with cruel rapidity. He felt almost as if he could not breathe—suffocated with the overwhelming nature of his discovery.

He went to the window and threw it open, and the cold wintry air blew in on his heated brow. It was a sort of relief; it suggested that outside his mind might be clearer, and acting on this idea he seized his hat, and a few minutes later found himself facing the keen north-east wind on the shore, with the sea thundering and tossing the blue, white-crested waves lying before him.

He went on and on, and as he did so a sort of change came over his heart. His first anger, passion and shame cooled down. He remembered Eva's plea, "for my love's sake I did it." He remembered that love—the love that he had just rejected—with its moments of untold, infinite happiness and joy. Between these two lay that mysterious tie —call it what you will—which binds one soul to the other in strange affinity.

Then he thought of her youth; not sixteen when this hateful hidden chain had been bound! A feeling of compassion came over him, and it seemed to put self aside, and made him think only how he could best protect her. Would this man be divorced, and then he could again marry her? But it was this unhappy marriage of hers to him that stood in the way. This Temple might sue her for bigamy, and a man who had already acted as he had done was not likely to be self-sacrificing now.

And presently, too, Kilmore thought of his mother, the widowed woman with her heart lying in her husband's grave. All this he knew would inflict fresh pangs on her bruised soul. And his dead father's words also seemed to rise before him when he bade him remember the honor of his name, on which honor Kilmore felt had now fallen so dark a blot.

But something must be done. He could not leave the woman who had lain on his bosom to face her terrible position alone. This man—her husband—and Kilmore's lips quivered, might trace her—might insist on her return to him. He was a poor clergyman, Mr. Onslow had said, and Eva had a fortune, and for the very sake of that fortune he might try to force her to go back to him.

But perhaps his silence might be bought. This thought brought some little consolation to Kilmore, and he determined to see Mr. Onslow and try what could be arranged.

This idea having struck him, he turned to retrace his steps, and then for the first time noticed where he was. In the agitation and confusion of his mind he had walked on miles and miles ahead, and neither felt the fatigue nor remarked the distance. Now he remembered he must have been some time absent from the hotel, and glancing at his watch saw it was approaching three o'clock.

"I may have frightened her—my poor, poor Eva," he thought with returning tenderness. He sighed; it could never be the same, but still—

At this moment, however, he saw Mr. Onslow approaching him, and he therefore hurried his steps to join him. The vicar looked grave, but spoke very kindly.

16

"I have been looking for you everywhere, Lord Kilmore," he said. "I am sure you must be quite exhausted; you have had no refreshment of any kind since the early morning."

"I forgot all about it," answered Kilmore, with a half smile, and to tell the truth I had no breakfast either—but I have been so frightfully upset by all this."

"That is indeed only natural."

"But the thing now is what is best to be done; I mean for her," continued Kilmore, nervously. "She cannot, I am certain she will not wish to return to this man."

"He probably would not wish it when he knows the circumstances; he seemed to me to be an austere man, and to take very hard and rigid views."

"He does not know where she is?"

"No, he does not."

"And, Mr. Onslow—forgive me saying this—but may I ask you, may I beg of you not to tell him?"

"I promise not to do so, Lord Kilmore; I have thought this over; it may not be quite right, but still I cannot add further to this poor lady's troubles. But the thing is, he may trace her, and in that case—"

"Well, what?" asked Kilmore, quickly.

"He is just the man, I fear, who might prosecute her for bigamy; he gave me to understand that it was his hardness of character that had so totally alienated the affections of his young wife."

"He might be bought," said Kilmore, with a frown, for he could not bear to hear Eva called this other man's wife.

Mr. Onslow shook his head.

"I would give any sum, whatever he chooses to ask, to save her from further annoyance," went on Kilmore. "It's terrible enough as it is; we must try to make it no worse."

"And—yourself, Lord Kilmore?" said Mr. Onslow with hesitation.

Again Kilmore frowned; he thought the vicar had no right to ask such a question.

"I shall return to my mother, to Kilmore," he answered, after a moment's hesitation; "and she—Eva, I think for the present had better go abroad—but, of course, she must decide for herself."

"Yes," said the vicar, slowly; he was wondering if he had done much good; if he had not better have left this tangled web alone. But he said nothing further. He spoke of the sea coast, and of the submerged churches over which it was said the sea had swept. He was a man of cultivated and refined tastes, and under ordinary circumstances Kilmore would have felt pleasure in listening to his conversation. As it was, he contrived to answer him, and so the time passed on until they again reached the old-fashioned inn at Westwold. When they appeared at the entrance, however, the landlady behind the bar received them with the greatest surprise.

"Why, Mr. Clair!" she cried with uplifted hands; "whoever expected to see you again to-day? Didn't you meet your good lady at the station, where she went to join you to catch the two o'clock train?"

"What?" said Kilmore, in a startled tone, and he grew very pale.

"She ordered a cab and went, so I suppose she has missed you, or you have missed her?" went on the voluble landlady. "What a pity!"

"Did she take any luggage?" asked Kilmore in a faltering voice.

"Only a hand-bag. She said she was only going for a day, but she paid for her rooms and everything, which I am sure she had no need to do, and her going away, too, for such a short time."

Kilmore did not speak; he looked at Mr. Onslow, and the vicar also was silent. But just at this instant a young railway porter entered the inn, and went up to the landlady at the bar.

"Have you a Mr. Clair staying here, missus?" he asked.

"That's Mr. Clair," answered the landlady, pointing to Kilmore.

"Then I've a letter for you, sir," said the porter, producing a letter from his corduroy jacket. "A lady left it for you who went by the two o'clock train up to London; I would have brought it before, but I haven't been able to get away from the station until now."

Kilmore put out a trembling hand and took the letter.

"Then she is gone?" asked Mr. Onslow of the porter.

"Yes, sir; I put her into a first-class carriage myself," he replied.

"And the next train to town?" said Kilmore, with a sort of gasp.

"Not till five o'clock, sir," answered the porter; "we've very few trains on this line, especially in the winter time."

Kilmore asked no more questions; he turned and went slowly up-stairs with a sort of faintness creeping over him, leaving Mr. Onslow to reward the porter, who had been already handsomely remunerated by Eva for his services.

When Kilmore reached the sitting-room he tore open the letter with his trembling fingers, and read with a fast-beating, troubled heart, the following words:

"Good-bye, Clair. I am going to leave you as I said I would, for I am not a woman to listen twice to such words as I have heard to-day. I will trouble you no more, and forgive me what I have cost you for the sake of the love I bore you. For it was love, Clair, and it is love, for such love does not pass away. I shall never see you again until my spirit calls you to come, and then if it does, you will know I am in some desperate need.

"Your

"Eva."

In these brief words she bade him farewell, and Kilmore's first feeling as he read them was an overpowering feeling of disappointment. She could have taken no better way to keep her power over him than to leave him thus after his first harsh words. He had but one consolation, that she loved him still. "For it was love, Clair, and it is love, for such love does not pass away." He read and re-read these words; he pressed his lips to them; they were a sort of balm to his heart.

But he must find her. He must protect her at least from this man and find her some safe refuge. And the first thing to do now was to return to town. She might have gone back to her own house in South Kensington. At all events he might hear of her there. Thus thought Kilmore with a hot and restless heart. But his reflections were shortly interrupted. A rap came to the room door and Mr. Onslow entered.

"Pardon me for intruding on you," he said in his courteous fashion, "but I have taken the liberty of ordering some lunch or dinner sent up to you, for I am sure you greatly need it."

"I am not hungry," answered Kilmore. "I—I have heard from her, Mr. Onslow."

"So I concluded."

"And in this letter she bids me good-bye; she gives no address."

"Then you think she means—"

"To leave me? Yes."

"She is acting rightly, Lord Kilmore."

"But I cannot leave her unless I know she is safe from this man; unless I am sure of it."

"He does not know where she is, and now we do not; he may never find her."

"He will try through the banker."

"Who probably will be instructed to keep the secret. When do you propose to return to town, Lord Kilmore?"

"By the next train; the porter said it starts at five o'clock, did he not?"

"Yes. Then we will travel back together, by your permission. Ah, here comes the lunch, and do let me persuade you to break your fast."

<hr>

CHAPTER XXXIV.

A DANGEROUS CONFIDANT.

The same day, late in the afternoon, the banker, Mr. James Ford, was sitting alone in his handsomely furnished private room over the bank, thinking of Miss Eva Moore.

"I can't get the little witch out of my head," he was reflecting complacently. "What is it, I wonder, about her that charms me so? She is wonderfully handsome, certainly; but she is something more than that, she is bewitching—yes, that is the word."

The thought pleased him; he smiled, and leaned back in his divan chair, picturing to himself Eva's beautiful face. Then the mystery about her kept puzzling his brain.

"She's a naughty little girl, I'm afraid," he thought, still smiling. "I wonder what that parson fellow really is to her! Ah, well, such pretty women are sure of many lovers; it is their birthright."

At this moment someone rapped at the room door, and when Mr. Ford called out, "Come in," a young man entered, bearing a small, tightly folded, three-cornered note.

"A lady has brought this, sir," he said, "and asked me to give it to you at once; she is outside in a cab waiting for an answer."

Mr. Ford turned the gas a little higher and put his glasses on his shapely nose; then he opened the note, and his face slightly flushed with pleasure as he read the contents.

"Dear Mr. Ford: Can I see you and alone? I am in great trouble, and perhaps you will help me.
"Yours sincerely,
"Eva Moore."

"Is the lady outside, did you say?" he asked, after he had finished reading these brief words.

"Yes, sir; she's waiting outside in a cab," replied the young man.

Mr. Ford looked round for his hat; it crossed his mind at this moment to go down to the cab himself to escort Miss Eva Moore to his room, but on second consideration more prudent thoughts prevailed.

"Tell the lady," he said, "with my compliments, that I shall be pleased to see her; that I am disengaged."

The clerk bowed and withdrew, and Mr. Ford stirred the fire into a more cheerful blaze and glanced at himself in the mirror over the mantelpiece; pushing his thick brown hair, tinged slightly here and there with gray, into a more becoming wave over his handsome forehead. Then he pulled down the blinds, and stood waiting to receive his visitor.

A few minutes elapsed and the clerk once more opened the room door.

"The lady, sir," he said, and Eva Moore, thickly veiled, entered as he spoke, and as she did so Mr. Ford advanced with outstretched hand.

"Ah, how are you?" he said pleasantly, but not familiarly, as he was conscious the clerk was within earshot, and of course knew he was a married man. "I am charmed to see you," he added in a lower tone, as the door closed behind the clerk; "but I am sorry to hear of trouble. You must let me help you, and you know I shall only be too happy to do so."

"Thank you," said Eva, in a low tone also, and she sat wearily down on the chair nearest her, and put her hand up to her hat, and unfastened the thick black gauze veil that she wore, and as it fell on her knee Mr. Ford saw her face was very pale.

"How tired you look!" he exclaimed quickly. "You must have some wine before you talk, and tell me what is the matter."

Eva did not refuse this offer; she felt, indeed, physically and mentally exhausted with what she had gone through, and so almost in silence she drank the sparkling draught that Mr. Ford speedily presented to her.

"I shall feel better in a moment or two," she said. "I have come to ask you to help me, Mr. Ford."

"And I promise to do whatever I possibly can," he answered.

Eva sighed; sat still a moment or two, and then rose restlessly from her chair.

"You must think me a very strange person?" she said.

"I think you are a very charming person," Mr. Ford replied with a smile.

"You will not think so when you have heard what I have come to tell. Mr. Ford, you remember when my uncle died, more than three years ago?"

"I perfectly remember the time, and the transfer of your fortune from Calcutta to this bank."

"But you did not know—no one knew but the lady with whom I lived—that I was then a married woman."

"A married woman!" said Mr. Ford in surprise. "Why, at that time you were a mere school-girl."

"Yes," answered Eva, bitterly; "a school-girl who had been tricked into a marriage, for I can call it by no other name, by a man almost old enough to be my father. It was so, Mr. Ford, and the terrible consequences of this act of folly have now fallen on my head."

"You did not marry the clergyman who came here—Mr. Temple?"

"Unhappily, I did; I was at a day school when I first made his acquaintance, and he knew Mrs. Bouchier, the lady my uncle had sent me to when I came to England. My uncle knew this lady, had known her in India, and he thought I was quite safe under her charge. To make a long story short, Mr. Temple used to meet me going to and from school, and gradually he obtained a sort of influence over me. I believed him to be a good man for one thing; he went about among the very poor, and I knew nothing of the world. At last he asked me to be his wife, and I, in my childish ignorance, accepted, with some vague longings, too, that I had after better things, for my poor uncle believed in nothing beyond this world, and had brought me up also to believe in nothing. But his ideas never, even in those days, quite satisfied my mind. And I thought, as I told you, that Mr. Temple was good; that he might teach me to be good, and so I married him. Then I found out what I had really done, I had married a narrow-minded, tyrannical man, who wanted to rule me in everything: who had no sympathy nor forbearance for my childishness, my waywardness. I, a spoilt Anglo-Indian girl, accustomed to flattery and admiration, got nothing but sternness and hardness. We quarreled from the first; I was miserable from the first, and about eighteen months after our marriage he was appointed to a country vicarage. I positively refused to go with him there, and we had a bitter quarrel, which ended in my writing to my uncle to recall me to India. I ought to tell you my uncle never knew of my marriage; we dare not tell him because he intended me to marry well in a worldly sense, and not a poor clergyman. Mr. Temple quite agreed to the prudence of this course, and had no wish for me to run the risk of losing my uncle's money by acknowledging my marriage with him. Thus I was only known as Eva Moore, and as Eva Moore I returned to India after Mr. Temple and I had agreed to part forever."

"He agreed to this?" inquired Mr. Ford.

"He distinctly agreed to it; I think he had got to dislike me by this time almost as much as I disliked him, and was glad to be rid of me. Thus, when my uncle wrote for me to return to India, we parted for good. I went to India, and he in a fit of disgust, either at me or the world in general, started for Africa. This is more than three years ago, and I never heard of him or from him during this time. He might have been dead for anything I knew; I hoped he was dead—would that he had been!"

Eva clasped her hands together as she said this, and her

pale face flushed, and Mr. Ford bent forward with a commiserating expression.

"But, unfortunately, he is not?" he said.

"Unfortunately, he is not. But to go on with my story. When I reached Calcutta I found my poor uncle had died of fever the day before I arrived there. But he had, as you know, provided for me, and I returned to England with independent means, but bound by this hidden chain, which I did not, in fact, know really existed or not. By this time my friend, Mrs. Bouchier, was also dead, and I knew none, and had never known any of Mr. Temple's friends or acquaintances except her. I made no inquiries; I wished to make none, and I hoped never to hear of him, or see him again. He was dead to me, I told myself, if he were not dead in reality, and I tried to forget that he ever existed."

"It is a great pity that he ever did," remarked Mr. Ford, dryly.

"I went to board at a ladies' school in South Kensington; I thought it would not be so dull as being alone, and that I would find friends and companions among the girls. I did find one, a simple-hearted, pretty girl, the daughter of a farmer, who had been sent up to London to finish her education—but I weary you."

"No, you delight me."

"The reason that I name this girl, Annie Dighton, is, that indirectly through her all this terrible trouble has come upon me. We corresponded after she left school, and I went abroad, and led a sort of wandering life; but still I always wrote to Annie Dighton. Finally, being in their neighborhood, I proposed to pay them a short visit, and I meant to invite Annie back to stay with |me. They lived at a place called Holly Hill, and I found a comfortable English farm-house—for these Dightons are well off—and a kind homely family to welcome me, and I enjoyed the first few days I was there. Mr. Dighton was a tenant farmer, and his landlord was the Earl of Kilmore."

Mr. Ford nodded.

"Yes, I know," he said; "he died lately."

Eva sighed. "He died lately," she repeated, "but when I was at Holly Hill he was not dead. His son, Lord Clair, came of age then, and a banquet and dance was given in the Park on the occasion to the tenants. I went with the Dightons, and thus I met Lord Clair."

"Ah!" exclaimed Mr. Ford with strong interest; at that moment he remembered Mr. Clair at Westwold.

"I met him and danced with him," continued Eva, and a sort of pathos crept into her voice as she spoke; "and that night he saved my life. A fire broke out at Holly Hill, and the part of the house I was sleeping in was cut off from the rest by a burning staircase. Young Dighton tried to save me, and the staircase fell in with him as he was endeavoring to ascend it. There was no ladder long enough to reach the window—I had given myself up for lost when Lord Clair arrived. He managed to fling a rope up to me, and he crept up by this, and then lowered me from the window. In fact, he saved my life at the risk of his own, and this naturally made me regard him with interest."

"I understand," said Mr. Ford; "this is Mr. Clair?"

"Yes," answered Eva, and a flush stole to her face; "we met again and again after this. I—I did not wish to go on with our acquaintance after I left Holly Hill, but—Lord Clair wished it, and it is hard to refuse the request of one who has saved your life. I saw him at the seaside first, and then in town. He—he asked me to marry him, but at first I refused—"

"To marry him! You surely did not?" interrupted Mr. Ford.

"I was led into it; he was shot one night in the street on leaving my house at South Kensington, and he was brought in. He was dangerously wounded, but for my sake, for he is ever generous," and her voice faltered, "he would not remain, though the doctor said it would be a great risk to remove him, unless I promised to be his wife. At last I did promise—I—I cared for him very truly, Mr. Ford —I tried to forget the past. I did forget it, I think. At all events we were married, secretly married, for his father was dying, and naturally objected to such a marriage for his son."

"But, my dear girl, do you know what this is?" cried Mr. Ford, starting to his feet.

"I know now; this is why I have come to you; I am going to disappear, but I could not do so without money, without letting you know where I am, and so I am going to trust to your honor, Mr. Ford."

The banker's good-looking face slightly fell; this confidence was not quite so flattering to his vanity as he had hoped.

"But does Lord Clair, or rather now the Earl of Kilmore, know of this former—marriage?" he asked.

"I will tell you; after our marriage, which took place at South Kensington, Clair and I went to Westwold; then he returned home to his father, and I went back to South Kensington. And one day—Mr. Ford, I can scarcely speak the words—I met George Temple! I met him in the street; met the man I had hoped was dead, that I never thought to have seen again! He told me he had changed his mind about our separation; that I must return to him—I, Clair's wife! It was too horrible; it nearly drove me mad, but I deceived him. I gave him a false address and then left town. I went back, as you know, to Westwold, and wrote to you from there to ask you to tell no one my address."

"I remember," said Mr. Ford.

"He—Temple," continued Eva, with rising agitation and excitement, "went to the house, the address of which I had given him—the false address, and found I was not there, and then he went to you. You refused to tell him where I was, even when he said he had a legal claim to know."

"I did not believe him."

"You know now. Mr. Ford, it would kill me to see this man again, nor do I now wish to see Lord Clair—"

"Lord Kilmore."

"I think of him always by the old name; but my story is not yet told. I gave Mr. Temple a false address, as I told you; an address to a boarding-house kept by a lady that I had heard of. He went there, and met there the sister of the clergyman who married me to Lord Clair! It seems as if my sin were fated to find me out, for George Temple and Mr. Onslow, the clergyman, had been at college together in their youth, and they renewed their acquaintance, and Temple told Mr. Onslow his story; how he had married a young girl named Eva Moore, and that he had parted with her. Mr. Onslow naturally remembered marrying an Eva Moore to Lord Clair, and he asked Temple if he had a photograph of his wife. He had kept one, why or wherefore I cannot tell; it was mine, and then Mr. Onslow knew; knew I had deceived Clair, and he went to him, and told him the whole story."

"Very officious, in my opinion."

"He said he did it from a sense of duty, but as I told him, his sense of duty has broken two hearts! They came to me at Westwold—Mr. Onslow and Clair—Clair would not believe Mr. Onslow's tale until he heard it from my own lips. I tried to deny it—I will keep nothing back—until they said they would bring me face to face with George Temple. Then I confessed the truth; Clair knows now; he upbraided me, and when he was out I left the place, leaving a few lines to bid him farewell. I do not wish to see him again, and I wish to hide myself away from everyone, and so I came to you to ask you to help me."

"I need not say I will do everything in my power. This Temple, this parson, has, however, an awkward claim against you."

"I know," said Eva, "they told me plainly this morning he could have me arrested for bigamy if he knew of my marriage with Lord Clair."

"Then he does not know?"

"Not yet at least; so far to him Mr. Onslow has kept the secret."

"We must hope he will continue to keep it, but even if this is so, if he could find you this Temple would probably try to force you to return to him."

"That I never shall!" cried Eva, passionately. "I would die before I did so; I should kill myself!"

"My dear girl, do not talk in such a dreadful manner. Let us consider what it will be best to do; you wish, I understand, to hide yourself away from both these men?"

"Yes, I do; Clair reproached me; he shall not reproach me twice."

"Well, I shall not reproach you," said Mr. Ford, smiling; "it seems to me you have been more sinned against than sinning. And this Lord Clair, or Kilmore—what is he like?"

Eva's lips quivered.

"Do not ask me," she said; "he is all that is generous and noble. Yes, it was cruel, wicked of me, to deceive him. I see it all now, and must bear the punishment."

"He will probably soon get over it," answered Mr. Ford, calmly; "he is very young, and love or passion at his age is not generally deep-seated. He is, in fact, not married to you, and if you really mean to keep out of his way he will probably soon marry."

Eva did not speak, but these words seemed to strike a fresh blow into her heart. And Mr. Ford, noticing the expression of her face, rose and began slowly walking up and down the room.

"Of course," he continued, "we must come to a direct understanding if I act in this matter. Lord Kilmore has no right to interfere with you, but the other man undoubtedly has. But are you quite sure—you wish to give up Lord Kilmore?"

"I am quite sure," answered Eva.

In that case I advise you to change your name for the present, and we must find some quiet home for you."

"I wish to go abroad; I thought of Switzerland."

"My dear girl, you cannot go to Switzerland in mid-winter, and besides, you cannot go alone."

"I should not be afraid if I were out of England."

"You are much safer in England; safest in London. I have been thinking of someone whom I think you could live with—for the present. A lady who lives in a small house in the North-West. She is—a distant connection of mine, and I feel sure if I were to recommend you she would receive you."

"But you must tell her nothing of who I am; nothing of my story?"

"Do not be afraid," and again Mr. Ford smiled. "You see this is a somewhat awkward affair to be mixed up in, and both for your sake and my own I shall certainly be silent. This Temple will probably return here to make inquiries about you, and if he absolutely proved himself to be your husband, which I now know he is, he might make himself disagreeable regarding your money. He has no right, I believe, to interfere with it; it was lodged here in your maiden name, and your checks have always been signed by that name. But still he might make himself disagreeable, and I must positively affect not to believe what I know now to be a fact. Therefore I wish you for the present to be somewhere where I could see you if necessary, until things settle down a bit—and this lady's house that I mentioned, I think, would be convenient."

"Well, if you think she would take me, and that I should be safe, I do not care where it is."

"I am almost sure she would take you; she lives in one

of the new houses up Hampstead way. It is quiet there—out of the way, in fact—and the air is good.”

“How shall I arrange it then?”

“Let me see; you had best not go near your house in South Kensington nor to an hotel to-night, as there are sure to be inquiries made.”

“The house in South Kensington is shut up.”

“Well, you have a cab here, have you not? Go down to that now—I shall see you down—and direct the driver to stop at the end of the street. I will join you there in five minutes, as I have some orders to give here before I leave the bank. Then we can drive together to the lady’s and I will see her first and arrange with her. And on the way,” he added, smilingly, “we can fix on a new and suitable name for you.”

“Very well,” said Eva, and she rose. She was frightened, but what could she do? She was forced to make a confidant of Mr. Ford, for she had no one else to whom she could turn, and she could not live without the money that was lodged in the bank.

So she did as he directed her. He escorted her down to the cab, and then she waited for him to join her at the spot he named. He did not keep her long, and she speedily found herself driving through the lighted streets with Mr. Ford by her side.

“And what is the pretty new name to be?” he asked presently.

“I don’t know; something commonplace will be best,” answered Eva.

“But nothing commonplace will suit you.”

“Oh, that is no matter,” said Eva wearily. An intense dreariness had indeed come over her heart; in her first excitement and indignation against Kilmore she had said she would leave him, would hide herself away from him, and she had done so; but a reaction had now set in. She was thinking of him as she sat there by Mr. Ford, thinking of him with wistful regret, while Mr. Ford was flattering himself he was making himself highly agreeable to her.

It was a long drive; presently they left the streets, and drove through quiet roadways and up steep hills.

“I almost forgot to tell you,” said Mr. Ford, “that the lady I am now taking you to is called Madame de Cimbri.”

“Is she French, then?” asked Eva,

Mr. Ford almost imperceptibly shrugged his shoulders.

"Her husband was, I believe," he answered. "No, the lady herself is English. But about your name? I must introduce you, you know."

"Scott is a common name; will that do?" answered Eva.

"Excellently well; Mrs. Scott, then—Eva Scott—keep the Eva, as you are accustomed to it. Ah, here we are; this is the garden gate of madame's house."

He called to the driver of the cab to stop, and then got out and rang the bell of a door in a high wall.

"If you will wait for me in the cab," he said, "I will go in and speak to madame first," and as he spoke he got out of the cab, and presently the door was opened, and he was admitted.

He was quite a quarter of an hour in returning, but at last he did so, and handed Eva out of the cab.

"Madame Cimbri will receive you as a boarder," he said; "but remember, be careful, Mrs. Scott."

CHAPTER XXXV.

MADAME.

Mr. Ford led Eva up a long garden in front of the house, and as he did so she saw the hall door was open and the hall lighted within. She saw also that a tall, handsome woman was waiting in the hall, and peering out with a curious, excited expression into the darkness.

"That is Madame de Cimbri," whispered Mr. Ford.

By this time they had almost reached the house door, and madame made a step forward to receive them.

"This is my young friend, Mrs. Scott, madame," said Mr. Ford, pleasantly; "and, as I have been telling her, I am sure you will be pleased to have her as an inmate of your house for a short while."

Madame bowed on being thus addressed, and continued to look curiously at Eva, who, however, was too thickly veiled for her really to see her face.

"I hope it will not inconvenience you to receive me?" said Eva. "Of course we must arrange terms."

"Oh, that will be all right," answered madame, but not in the soft, sweet tones of Eva. "You have come a journey, Mr. Ford tells me," she continued, "and I suppose are tired, so you had better go up to your room at once, and then we can have some dinner; but you mustn't expect much on so short a notice."

"Oh, anything will do," smiled Eva; "if I could have some tea I should like that best."

"Well, to tell you the truth, high tea would suit me better than dinner; but here's Mr. Ford to be considered, and he, like all men, is fond of a good dinner," and madame laughed and showed her large, strong, white teeth.

"Come, madame, don't take my character away in that fashion," said the good-looking banker. "See after Mrs. Scott, and I will take my chance."

"Where is your luggage?" now inquired madame, looking at Eva, who blushed beneath her veil.

"I have none," she answered; "only this little hand-bag, but I shall order what I shall require to-morrow."

"Mrs. Scott has had a misfortune, she has lost her luggage in the train," said Mr. Ford, but madame did not look at all satisfied with this explanation.

"That's a queer business," she remarked. "Well, come along up-stairs. I dare say I can lend you what you want."

She led the way up a circular-lighted staircase, and as she did so Eva noticed that the house was handsomely but showily furnished. The mistress was also dressed handsomely and showily. She was a tall woman with a large bust and a fine figure; her features were regular and her hair and complexion dark. Altogether she was a handsome woman, about forty, with bold, flashing eyes, but Eva saw in a moment she was not a lady. Something indescribable told this; her attitude, the tone of her voice, the construction of her sentences.

"This is the room," she said, looking round the bedroom into which she led Eva with evident pride. It was showy like the rest, and exactly in the same style.

"Now, what do you want?" she continued. "I've plenty of tea-gowns and that sort of thing if you want a change."

"Thank you, but the gown I have on will do very well," replied Eva; "and I brought what I shall require for the night, and to-morrow I can buy what I want."

"Oh! very well, just as you like, of course; you'll want a good wash after your journey, I suppose?"

"I should like to bathe my face," said Eva, unfastening her veil, and when madame's eyes fell on her lovely features she looked anything but pleased.

"Oh! you're quite young, are you?" she said.

"I am not very old," answered Eva, smiling. Then she went to the mirror and unfastened her long auburn hair, which fell below her waist, and madame looked at it more disapprovingly still.

"Have you known Mr. Ford long?" she asked.

"Yes," answered Eva; "he manages my money."

"He told me he was your guardian. Well, as soon as you are ready, ring the bell—it is there—and the servant will come up and show you the way to the dining-room, where you will get something to eat and drink. I have a nice drawing-room, too, but you have taken me in such a hurry it is not lit."

"I am sure everything is very nice."

"Oh! it all cost a mint of money, I can tell you! I got the best of everything; it's the cheapest in the end, and the carpets you see are all Brussels, and the stairs and drawing-room pile. But I'll show you when you come down." And she nodded and went away.

Eva felt relieved after she had gone. There was no doubt she was handsome, but it was a beauty that did not please Eva. She looked so strong, so coarse, and there was something in the expression of her dark eyes that told of violent feelings of either love or hate.

"I wonder who she is," thought Eva; and then with a sigh she remembered her own dubious and uncertain position. "I can't choose," she reflected, bitterly, "my life is as I have made it."

Then presently she bathed her face, and refastened her hair, and rang the bell for the servant, as madame had directed her. A smart, dressy little waiting-maid soon appeared, and informed Eva that "high tea was ready;" and Eva accordingly followed her down-stairs, and was ushered into a room where a table was spread with many good things.

Madame was standing by Mr. Ford on the rug before the fire, and she turned round as Eva entered in the dark serge dress she had traveled from Westwold in.

17

"Oh! here you are," she said. "Where will you sit, and what will you have to drink? Have some champagne, and these are cutlets, and we have stewed oysters, and a fowl, as you see."

Mr. Ford advanced to the table and placed a chair for Eva.

"Sit here by the fire, Mrs. Scott," he said; "I fear you are very tired."

"I am tired," answered Eva.

But in spite of her being tired, Madame de Cimbri saw that her unexpected guest was a young and beautiful woman, and that the banker's eyes rested more than once on her fair face. Eva, however, was very quiet and subdued, and asked leave to retire very early in the evening.

"I will try and see you to-morrow," said Mr. Ford, rising and taking her hand, "I may have some news."

"Thank you; you are very kind," answered Eva, and then she said good-night and went away, and after she was gone madame turned to Mr. Ford.

"Who do you say she is, James, and where is her husband?"

"She is a young woman who has a large fortune," answered Mr. Ford, "and has had the misfortune to marry badly. As I told you, she wants to live here on the quiet for a bit, and I don't think she will be much trouble to you."

"But I don't think I shall like it. Do you think her pretty?"

"She is fairly good-looking, I think," answered Mr. Ford, with affected carelessness.

"But I can't understand you bringing her here?"

"To tell the truth, I did not know where else to take her; she wants to keep out of the way of this husband of hers, and she has such a large sum of money in the bank I cannot very well afford to lose sight of her."

"Oh, it's business then?"

"Purely business."

"I wonder, in that case, you did not take her to the lady in Eccleston Square."

"The lady in Eccleston Square, as you call her," replied Mr. Ford, a little grimly, "would not have done at all. If I had taken her to my house people would have known she was there. Here no one need know, and as I told you, she wishes to be very quiet."

"She has rather good hair."

"Has she? I did not notice it;" and then he changed the conversation, and after awhile went away.

And the next morning, as he sat as usual in his private room at the bank, a card was brought up to him, at which he looked with interest.

"Show the gentleman up," he said to the young man who had brought in the card, and a few moments later Lord Kilmore was ushered in.

Mr. Ford rose and bowed, and Kilmore also bowed, and began the conversation in an agitated voice.

"I have taken the liberty of calling on you, Mr. Ford," he said, "for the purpose of making some inquiries about—a lady."

Again Mr. Ford bowed. He was thinking what a good-looking young fellow this was, and also casting over in his mind what it would be wisest for him to say.

"You know, I believe, Miss Eva Moore?" went on Kilmore.

"Yes, I know Miss Moore slightly; she is one of the depositors in the bank."

"So I have understood. Mr. Ford, you will pardon me asking you, I hope, but do you know her present address?"

Mr. Ford hesitated.

"I have been to her house in South Kensington, which I find is shut up," continued Kilmore; "and I am most anxious to know of her welfare, and her present address."

"I can assure you of her welfare, then," answered Mr. Ford, smiling. "I saw the young lady yesterday; she came here on a matter of business. But as to her address, I am very sorry to be compelled to refuse your request, as I was especially asked not to give it to Lord Kilmore."

"Asked not to give it to me?" repeated Kilmore, blankly.

"Yes; the young lady seemed to expect some such inquiry would be made, and she asked me to decline to answer it."

"But that—might be regarding someone else?" hesitated Kilmore.

Again Mr. Ford smiled; he had decided how to act and felt himself the master of the situation.

"I will repeat Miss Moore's words," he replied, "as nearly as I can remember them. She said, 'If Lord Kilmore calls and inquires where I am, tell him I requested you not to tell him; that I do not wish to see him again.' "

"She said that?"

"She certainly said that; she also requested me not to give it to another gentleman—a clergyman."

Kilmore grew pale and bit his lips.

"And you will not?" he said.

"Certainly I will not; you may judge by your own case that I mean to respect the young lady's wishes."

"And is—she well, is she safe?"

"She seemed quite well, though somewhat agitated, and she gave me to understand she had gone through some trying interview or other."

"And—will you see her again?"

"I presume I shall see her occasionally on business."

"Will you tell her then—that—that if at any time she changes her resolution, if she will see me, I will go to her at once. I wish most earnestly to see her—perhaps you would convey a letter to her?"

"Most certainly, if you wish it."

"I shall esteem it the greatest favor; I shall not know how to express my gratitude if you will."

"It is a very trifling service, and I am only sorry to be compelled as a gentleman to refuse to give you her address. I may tell you, however, she is going immediately abroad."

"Well, I will write; I wish I could see her before she goes—if I enclose the letter to you—"

"She will receive it, and I will convey her answer back to you."

"I thank you more than I can express; and Mr. Ford, there is a strong reason—a far stronger reason than in my case, that if this clergyman should come here to ask after her that he should not know where she is. He might bring her immense trouble and pain, and I ask, I implore you, to keep her secret from him."

Mr. Ford slightly waved his hand.

"Lord Kilmore, if I have proved trustworthy in your case I am not likely to betray her confidence to the parson. To tell the truth, I do not at all approve of the reverend gentleman, and will have the greatest pleasure in snubbing him."

"Thank you very much; then I will enclose my letter to

Miss Eva Moore to you, and you will let me have her answer?"

"I shall have great pleasure in doing so. Must you go? Good-morning, then, Lord Kilmore, I am pleased to have met you."

"And I trust our acquaintance will continue," said Kilmore, frankly, holding out his hand. "I shall always feel myself indebted to you." And then he turned and went away, and once more the banker smiled as the door closed behind him.

"Upon my word, the young lady has good taste," he was thinking: "that's a fine looking young fellow, and a nice fellow seemingly too. But I pretty cleverly countermined him—everything is fair in love and war."

CHAPTER XXXVI.

THE UNANSWERED LETTER.

The same day a letter was brought to Mr. Ford from Kilmore. It contained one addressed to Miss Eva Moore, which was sealed, and also a few courteous lines to the banker himself.

Mr. Ford read his own letter, and then the address of the one intended for Eva, and after he had done so he calmly locked Eva's letter away. He had no intention of delivering it, but he did not read it. Nor shall we. Are there not words that two only should hear, and thoughts too sacred for the common ken? Kilmore had written in the fullness of his heart; written to the woman he loved, and it was like a cry from his soul. He entreated her to see him again, "if it were only to say farewell." He thanked her with passionate tenderness for writing in the letter she had left for him at Westwold, that "her love would not change." "Nor will mine, Eva," he told her, "and do not wait until you are in some 'desperate need' to call me back." It was a letter in truth which might have changed their whole lives, a letter to his love, though she might be an erring one, but it was fated not to reach her hands.

The banker locked it securely away, and then sat down to think. Afterward, he went out and purchased two stall tickets for a successful play, and sent them out to Hampstead by an especial messenger to Madame de Cimbri. "They are for you and Mrs. Scott," he wrote, "for this evening, and I will send a brougham to Norham Villa in time to take you both to the theater. I will try to join you there," he added, "but I can't promise, as I may have a home engagement."

Madame de Cimbri was delighted to receive the tickets. She ran with them in her hand and Mr. Ford's open letter, which was a guarded one, to the dining-room where Eva was sitting.

"Isn't this jolly!" she cried; "Mr. Ford has sent us tickets for the Adelphi to-night, and he's going to send a brougham to take us to the theater. I am so glad!"

Eva, who was sitting by the fire, feeling ill and languid, looked up without interest.

"I cannot go," she said.

"Not go! And when he's going to send a brougham and everything, and if he can get there he's certain to treat us to a good supper after the play. Oh, you must go."

Eva shook her head. "I don't feel very well," she answered; "and I would rather not go."

"Oh, very well, please yourself, of course; but I never refuse a good offer, and as Mr. Ford's messenger is waiting for an answer, I'll write a line to tell him you are not feeling well enough to go, but I will be there."

"Thank you, very much," said Eva, and once more her head fell languidly, and she gazed with listless eyes into the fire.

She was feeling ill, body and mind alike. The blow had fallen so suddenly at the end, and Clair had treated her so cruelly she thought, cruelly at least for Clair! She forgot what a frightful shock it had given him; that he had believed in her and loved her so well.

"Yet I told him I was not a good woman," thought poor Eva mournfully, and then a little shiver ran through her frame. She had taken a chill, probably from sleeping in one of madame's smart, though unaired beds. And then her mental condition naturally affected her health.

"I would be better dead," she thought; "what is the good of my life parted from Clair, and living in constant dread of that wretch finding me out? And I don't like this woman's face; I can't bear, at least, to stay here."

In the meantime Madame de Cimbri had written her note to Mr. Ford accepting his invitation to the theater, and dispatched it with his messenger, who conveyed it straight to the bank.

It was exactly what he expected, and what he had planned to obtain. He knew madame adored theaters; that they gave her unending delight, and that she would be most unlikely to refuse stalls for the Adelphi. And he knew, also, that Eva would be most unlikely to go. He wished to see Eva alone, and had not the slightest intention of joining madame at the play. He was thinking of a younger and fairer woman when he made these arrangements; and about nine o'clock, to Eva's great surprise, he arrived at Norham Villa, and was announced while she was lying on a couch in the dining-room there.

She rose, and a flush came to her lovely face which Mr. Ford noticed admiringly and mistook its cause. She was dressed in a pretty white tea gown which madame had purchased for her in the morning. Madame liked buying things, and Eva had felt too weary and disheartened to go out, and had therefore commissioned madame to buy her some necessaries.

"Mr. Ford!" she exclaimed.

"Yes," he answered, advancing smilingly and holding out his hand, which Eva took.

"I thought you were at the theater?" she said.

"I never had the slightest idea of going," he replied, still holding her hand. "I wanted madame out of the way, and I knew she could not resist theater tickets."

"Have—you heard anything?" asked Eva in alarm.

"Not directly; but I have been making certain inquiries, and therefore I wished to see you alone to tell you the result."

"Yes."

"My dear girl, now I don't wish to alarm you, but I wish to warn you, and entreat you not to be rash. The inquiries which I have made through a legal friend were regarding the punishment of bigamy."

Eva started, and her lips quivered.

"Don't look so frightened; you are quite safe here, but

you must be prudent. I can understand that madame is not attractive to you."

Eva did not speak.

"She is not what you have been accustomed to; she is not a lady, in fact, but she is useful. She is not troubled with over-fine scruples of any kind, and as long as she is paid for her services she knows how to hold her tongue. Do you understand? She is a convenient person for you to be with under your present circumstances, and I advise you just now at least to remain here."

Eva sighed restlessly.

"I should rather go abroad," she said.

"It would be much less safe; while you are here, on the spot, as it were, I can see you, and can give you timely warning if anything like an arrest is attempted. You must not play with fire, you know, my dear girl! You have, I am sorry to say, placed yourself within the power of the law by that foolish marriage with Lord Kilmore, and the consequences might be very serious."

"What could they do?" asked Eva.

"My legal friend assured me that the punishment for bigamy is sometimes very severe. The law is 'not more than seven years' or less than three years' penal servitude.'"

"Penal servitude!"

"Yes; or not more than two years' imprisonment, with or without hard labor."

"It is impossible!" cried Eva, starting to her feet.

"I am sorry to say it is so; and the unfortunate part of it is that you contracted this second marriage with this young lord so short a period after your first marriage. Had seven years elapsed without your hearing of Mr. Temple it would have considerably mitigated the offense."

Eva clasped her hands with a despairing gesture.

"I must have been mad," she said; "I knew nothing of this; I knew it was not right, but—"

"You allowed the young gentleman to overpersuade you."

"I was thrown with him; he saved my life— I'd better have died!"

"Nonsense, nonsense, my dear young lady! You are far too pretty a woman to talk of dying. You must live and be bright and happy, and this ugly sword that is hanging over your head must be warded off. You know you can completely depend on me."

"You are very good."

"I don't set up to be very good," answered the banker, smiling; "but when I like a person, when I admire a woman, I will do anything for her. Don't make a confidant of madame, however; she is a useful person to a certain extent, but you must draw a line. I told her this much, that you were a young lady with a good fortune, and that you had had the misfortune to marry badly, and wished to keep out of the way of your husband, and live on the quiet for a bit. Here you can; but even here I wouldn't walk too much about the streets. You are too handsome in fact—but it's a charming fault."

Eva made no answer; she was not thinking of Mr. Ford and his compliments, but of her own miserable position.

"And Clair—Lord Kilmore?" she said presently, raising her lustrous eyes. "Have you heard anything of him?"

"Not one word," answered Mr. Ford.

"I thought perhaps he might go to you—to inquire," continued Eva. "He knew that I know you, and that my money is in your bank, and I told him of your visit to Westwold."

"Did you? But you do not wish to have any further communication with him now?"

"No, no; what good would it do? Besides, I said I would not; I wrote to him I would trouble him no more."

"It is the wisest, indeed your only course; besides, if this affair of the bigamous marriage with him leaked out he might be dragged into it."

"How? He did not know."

"That would be very difficult to prove. No, my dear girl, you must not attempt to renew your unfortunate acquaintance with Lord Kilmore."

"Unfortunate, indeed!" said Eva with a restless sigh.

"You must try to forget it."

"That I never can—but it's no matter."

"And there is another thing I wish to arrange with you; I may wish to see you; it may be necessary that I should see you without the knowledge of madame sometimes. She goes a great deal to the theater in the evenings and I can see you when she is away, but it would be better she did not know that I did. For instance, this evening do not tell her I have been here."

"But Mr. Ford—"

"It would be wiser, I assure you; she is rather an odd person, and has a jealous disposition, and might not like to think I saw you in her absence."

"But the servants— Mr. Ford, I really cannot do this."

"My dear girl," and Mr. Ford shrugged his shoulders, "such servants as madame's are not difficult to silence. I can arrange all that; and I've no doubt," and he gave a low laugh, "that madame has visitors of which I do not hear."

"I do not know; I know nothing of such things."

"No? And yet—" Mr. Ford paused after he had said these three words, and Eva felt an indescribable feeling of annoyance and anger. She knew he meant more than he had expressed, and was slightly amused perhaps.

But with easy tact the next moment he changed the conversation. He was a well-read man, and had traveled a great deal, and could make himself exceedingly agreeable when he pleased. It pleased him to do so now; to try to make Eva forget for a time at least the absorbing troubles of her life.

He stayed about an hour, and then left her, but before he did so he again cautioned her about Madame de Cimbri.

"Promise not to tell I've been here," he said; "we need not tell madame everything."

"But if she asks me?"

"Most unlikely; and now, my dear girl, good-night."

Then he shook hands with her and went away, and Eva heard a whispered conversation in the hall before the house door closed behind him. He left her still more miserable than she had been before. A vague hope had lingered in her breast that Clair would go to Mr. Ford; that through him he might have traced her, that he might have come to her. But he had not even tried it seemed! And then Mr. Ford had terrified her about the legal penalties she had incurred. Penal servitude! The very words were enough to strike terror into her soul, and if Mr. Ford had meant to frighten her, he certainly had most successfully done so.

She went up-stairs before Madame de Cimbri returned, but not to sleep. She heard her arrive, and she heard her also laughing and talking with her maid. Then followed a restless night, haunted by terrible dreams. She felt so ill and feverish in the morning that she did not go down-stairs, and presently, after breakfast, madame came up to see after her.

"What a pity you did not go last night to the Adelphi," she said. "I did enjoy myself, while you were staying moping at home."

"I was not well enough to go," answered Eva, wearily.

"You do look awfully bad this morning, anyhow. Well, Mr. Ford didn't cast up. I suppose he couldn't get away from his old woman." And Madame de Cimbri laughed.

"His old woman?" repeated Eva.

"Yes, his wife; you knew he was married, didn't you?"

"Yes, I think I've heard so; I'd forgotten," answered Eva, indifferently.

"Oh! he's married sure enough, though he's never to be seen with her. He married a rich old woman for her money, and he knows how to spend it; but he's rich and can afford to be generous."

Eva made no reply, and presently to her great relief madame went away. There was something about this woman inexpressibly antipathetic to Eva. Her coarse beauty, her coarse mind revolted her. So she spent the morning in her own room miserably enough, repining at her fate.

"But for my childish folly," she was thinking, "I should now have been Clair's happy wife—my own Clair—whom I love, and who loves me so well. If my mother had lived she would have taken care of me, and everything might have been different. As it was, I was thrown on the world without a guide, and shipwrecked my happiness. I thought I should defy fate when I married Clair, but fate was too strong for me, and this is the end."

In this unhappy frame of mind she spent hour after hour, and while she was thinking of her lost lover with inexpressible tenderness and regret, he was receiving a blow—seemingly from her—which cut him to the heart.

As early in the morning as he thought it possible to call on a stranger, Kilmore proceeded to Ford's Bank and asked to see Mr. James Ford. He sent up his card and was speedily ushered into the banker's presence.

"Ah, Lord Kilmore," said Mr. Ford, rising and extending his well-shaped hand in welcome; "I am pleased to see you; I hoped you would call."

"I must apologize for coming so early—but I felt anxious."

"Precisely; about the fate of your letter, you mean, to Miss Eva Moore?"

"Yes," answered Kilmore in an agitated voice.

"Well, I am afraid my news will not be very welcome; I saw the young lady last night, and I carried your letter with me when I went to see her."

"And—"

"Well, at first she did not wish to open it, but asked me to carry it back to you."

"Unopened!" exclaimed Kilmore, and his face blanched strangely.

"Finally she did open it; she read it before me, and sent a verbal answer by me. 'Tell him,' she said, 'that it is no use; I cannot see him, and he must not write.'"

"Was that all?" asked Kilmore, with quivering lips.

"There were a few more words to that effect, but that was the gist of them. It was useless and only painful to renew a—broken tie. That was what she wished me to convey to you—and Lord Kilmore, you will pardon me when I remind you in all confidence of the peculiar position of the young lady."

"You mean—"

"I mean her unfortunate and early marriage, of which, on account of business matters, she was obliged to make me cognizant. One day a gentleman called here at the bank and asked to see one of the partners. My father rarely comes to town and I saw him. He was a clergyman, and said he had come to make certain inquires about the whereabouts of Miss Eva Moore, whom he understood had money deposited in the bank. But before he called I had had a note from Miss Eva Moore, with whom I had a slight personal acquaintance, warning me that inquiries might be made about her, but requesting me to give no information on the subject whatever, and especially not to give her address. I received this letter from Westwold."

"From Westwold!" echoed Kilmore, with visible agitation.

"Yes, from Westwold," repeated Mr. Ford, in a somewhat marked manner. "Well, this gentleman, this clergyman, got rather bellicose when I declined to give the information he asked for; he said he had a legal right to know, and finally that she was his wife. This, to tell the truth, I did not believe, and I firmly refused to give Miss Moore's address. I wrote to her to tell her of my clerical visitor, and she replied that he had no legal right to her address, or anything else concerning her. But in a subsequent interview she admitted that she had married this man at a very early age, and that they had been parted for three or four years. But, of course, the marriage tie remains, and under these circumstances—"

Kilmore had listened to this long explanation in extreme agitation. That Mr. Ford should know all this was bitter enough, but that Eva should have planned, deliberately planned, to deceive him was more bitter still. He remembered at this moment Mr. Ford's visit to Westwold; remembered that he must, in all probability, have heard of himself there as Eva's husband, and he understood Mr. Ford's allusion to "a broken tie" only too well.

"Then," he said, with faltering lips, "I am to understand that—Miss Moore does not wish any further communication with me?"

"That is what she commissioned me to express. And she is equally anxious to see and hear nothing further of this husband of hers. I shall certainly refuse to give him any information if he comes here, but at the same time I fear there may be some trouble about it. You see his claim is certainly a legal one, and he could no doubt compel her to return to him."

"She will never return to him," said Kilmore, excitedly.

"Not willingly, I am sure; but the safest plan for her is to keep out of his way and out of his ken, and to do this she must keep out of England at present. Thus you see her decision is wise, Lord Kilmore, regarding yourself."

Kilmore bowed haughtily and bit his lips. His heart was full of inexpressible bitterness and pain, and after a few more words he took leave of the banker, who smiled softly to himself after he was gone.

"I think I have ended that," he thought, and he prided himself on his cleverness in having done so.

But there was no smile on Kilmore's lips as he passed out of the bank and went into the crowded streets. His heart was out of tune with the whole world. Nothing is so terrible as to lose faith in one we love, and yet go on loving still. This was Kilmore's state, and with a gloomy brow and oppressed with miserable thoughts he left town the same day.

"What is the good of staying?" he told himself. "She won't see me, she won't write to me, and yet she could confide in this man."

He traveled down to Kilmore by the first train he could catch, and arrived there during the afternoon. He was not expected, and he walked from the station and soon found himself on his own land; on the broad acres that had descended to him, and which had been inherited by his father with such pleasure and pride.

But Kilmore felt neither pleasure nor pride as he looked on the wide grass lands, on the wooded park, on the gurgling Ayre. A woman's love had spoilt everything for him, and gloomy and dissatisfied he strode on, and in one of the walks in the park he suddenly encountered his cousin, Annette Gower.

The girl started violently when she saw him, and her face flushed crimson and then grew pale, and Kilmore could not help noticing her agitation.

"You did not expect to see me?" he said, as he shook hands with her.

"No," faltered Annette.

"How is my mother?" then asked Kilmore.

"She—is the same, I think," answered Annette, but still in a very agitated voice.

"Where were you going? Will you turn with me?" said Kilmore. He, too, was disturbed by this meeting, and remembered his last parting with his cousin when he had gone on his dreary errand to learn the bitter truth at West-wold. It had been as he had told Mr. Onslow, "more bitter than death," and now he was returning after drinking this cup of gall.

So the cousins, each with their own sad secrets hidden in their hearts, turned and walked on together through the darkening park. Annette asked no questions, and Kilmore made no explanation. She saw by his gloomy brow, by his brief answers and general bearing, that he had returned no happier a man than when he left.

"Something terrible has happened to him," thought the girl, as she glanced at his clouded face, and with a troubled heart she, too, returned to the Hall.

CHAPTER XXXVII.

A PAIR OF GLOVES.

Two days later, in the evening, Mr. Ford once more arrived at Norham Villa. Madame de Cimbri had evidently no idea he had been there on the night that she had gone to the theatre, and welcomed him with effusion.

"Well, what a stranger you have been!" she cried, as she entered the showy drawing-room about half-past nine o'clock. "I was beginning to think Mrs. Scott here must have frightened you away."

And she laughed and showed her white teeth.

"You must have known that was impossible," answered Mr. Ford, advancing to where Eva sat, and holding out his hand.

"And you didn't cast up at the theatre that night also," continued Madame de Cimbri. "Well, you know when 'the cat's away the mice will play,' and I picked up a friend."

Mr. Ford looked annoyed, and madame mistaking the expression of his face, added hastily:

"Oh! it was only young Ludlow; he's very harmless."

"Perfectly," said Mr. Ford, sarcastically.

"And what will you take?" went on madame. "You want something after all that long drive."

"Let me see," answered Mr. Ford, as though considering the matter. "Have you any of that sparkling burgundy still?"

"That you sent me? Oh, yes; I only keep that for high days and holidays. I'll go and get you a bottle."

"Thanks," said Mr. Ford, and as madame hurried out of the room to get the wine he quietly put a piece of folded paper in Eva's hand after she was gone.

"Read that in your own room presently," he said; "and we must see how we can arrange it."

Eva took the paper with a sinking heart. She waited until madame returned with the burgundy and then left the room, and went to her own, and there read the note Mr. Ford had given her.

"I wish to see you alone and talk to you," he had written.

"The parson has been to the bank and made himself remarkably disagreeable. I wish to tell you what he said and how I answered him; and so we must try to arrange to meet alone. You must help me.

"F."

These words naturally threw Eva into a state of agitation, and it was some time before she could sufficiently compose herself to return to the drawing-room. When she did, Mr. Ford was sipping his burgundy, and madame was standing smiling beside him.

"Now, Mrs. Scott, isn't he good?" she said. "He has brought us more theatre tickets, and you must go this time."

Eva shook her head.

"Now don't you think it would do her good?" she continued, addressing the banker. "She's got a cold, but I always say it does no good to coddle a cold."

"I am very sorry you have a cold," said Mr. Ford, looking at Eva. "Well, suppose we fix another day for you to go to the theatre with madame. These tickets are for tomorrow."

"And waste the tickets, James! I call that a sin," exclaimed madame. "You've paid for them, so what's the good of throwing the money away! If Mrs. Scott's not well enough to go, I am, and perhaps you can go, too?"

"No, I am going to a dinner party to-morrow," answered the banker, "and I cannot get out of it."

"What a bother! Well, never mind, I'll go, and I dare say I'll get someone to call the carriage for me if you treat me to one, or get me a cab."

"Perhaps the accommodating Mr. Ludlow," smiled the banker. "Yes, I shall be most happy to treat you to a carriage, as you call it. What time shall I order the brougham to be here for you?"

"Oh! I like to be there early. I don't like to miss the first piece; so order it in time for that, and thank you very much."

"Then that is arranged," said Mr. Ford, quietly, "and it shall be there for you when the play is over;" and as he said this he gave one glance with his bright hazel eyes at Eva.

She understood its meaning; he had arranged to get madame out of the way, and he meant to come to Norham

Villa in her absence, and tell her what "the parson," as he called him, had said.

This is exactly what he intended, and exactly what he did. The brougham arrived for madame at the appointed time, and scarcely an hour after she was gone a ring came to the house door bell at Norham Villa, and a few minutes later Mr. Ford was announced.

He advanced into the drawing-room where Eva was sitting, smiling and holding out his well-shaped hand.

"I have come very early," he said, "in the hope of having a long and very charming evening with you."

Eva rose pale and agitated to receive him.

"You have come to tell me—" she said nervously.

"About the parson—forgive me—about the Rev. George Temple, of Harlaxton Vicarage, Dorset. Yes, my dear girl, I have come to tell you about that learned gentleman, and I must say I cordially enter into your feelings regarding him, for a more disagreeable, self-righteous person I never encountered."

"And—what did he say?"

"What did he not say, you mean?" answered Mr. Ford with a low laugh. "He began by demanding to know your place of residence; by declaring he had a legal right to know—the old story in fact—and I replied by intimating pretty strongly that I did not believe what he was saying, though at the same time I knew it was perfectly true. Then my gentleman got in a rage; he threatened me with law proceedings, and I assured him that he had no ground to go on. He said I was holding his wife's money which he was entitled to share—this is the gist of his anxiety to trace you I verily believe—away from him, and that I must know and tell him where you were to be found. I smiled, and said I was absolutely ignorant where you were to be found, as you were traveling from place to place on the continent; but that you had been to Hamburg, Frankfort, Cologne— in fact a dozen places. He said I must send you money. I said no, I gave her letters of credit before she started, and that I had no idea where you were at the present time. 'I will trace her,' he said fiercely, 'if she is above ground!'"

Eva slightly shuddered.

"Don't look so frightened, my dear girl, for I've led him a pretty dance. He asked where I had last heard from you, and I said Cologne, and he was going to start the same

18

night for that evil-smelling town. So you will see you are quite safe. He will go hunting all over for you, while you are living quietly here, and he will never think of your being here."

Eva did not speak for a moment, and then she gave a restless sigh.

"It's a dreadful life to lead," she said, "a hunted life!"

"It doesn't matter being hunted if you are not caught," answered Mr. Ford, smiling; "and caught you shall not be."

"And—" asked Eva, hesitating and looking down; "has—anyone else been to you to make inquiries?"

"You mean Lord Kilmore?" said Mr. Ford, quietly. "No; I have seen or heard nothing of him."

Again a restless sigh was suppressed on Eva's lips, which Mr. Ford heard, but did not appear to notice.

"So," he said, "now that the Rev. George is disposed of on his foreign quest, there is no need for you to keep so closely immured here. Would you like to go and spend a few days anywhere—say at Brighton?"

"But are you sure he is gone?"

"I am sure he meant to go; but I can find out if he is gone. I will set one of those useful private inquiry people on his track, and we will thus always know where he is."

"I am very grateful to you."

"I told you I would do anything I could for you, and I will. And the only return I ask is—well, that you will give me a little friendship and trust."

"I have already trusted you," said Eva with a wintry smile.

"You will neither repent nor regret your trust some day, I hope. Eva—may I call you Eva?—do you know that you inspire me with a strange interest?"

"I suppose my extraordinary story—"

"No, it is neither your extraordinary story nor, permit me to say, your extraordinary personal attractions, which has raised this interest in my heart. It is something beyond —I can scarcely express it—a charm, a witchery, which is all your own."

"Please do not talk thus, Mr. Ford. I do not care to listen to compliments."

"I rarely pay them; certainly would not pay them to you. No, my words are sincere, and I earnestly wish you to believe that they are so."

"I am sure you mean kindly, but—"

"I mean, and will act kindly, if you only trust me. But about this cold of yours, do you really think a little change would do you good?"

"I will see how I am in a few days—and wait till I hear that—this man has really left England, and then I do think a little change would do me good."

"I shall see about the reverend gentleman's doings at once, then. And now let us talk of something else; we still have time for a charming chat," and he glanced at his watch, "before madame's return."

It is certainly true that when we are unhappy we are very bad company for ourselves. Eva felt annoyed that for the next hour Mr. Ford sat on talking pleasantly, and yet his conversation took her mind away to a great extent from her own troubles.

He was a keen, observing man of the world, and believed very little in the higher aspirations of either men or women. His own moral code was of the most elastic description, and always suited his own convenience. Yet you could not tell this by his words.

He took very good care not to talk to Eva as he would have done to Madame de Cimbri. He drew a line between these two women, though he had no honor for either.

"Here is a lovely woman," he was thinking as he sat by Eva, "who is fretting now for the loss of her young lover, but another lover will soon console her."

But Eva could not tell his thoughts, could not judge him by them. This human tongue of ours is a strange gift, wrapping our inner selves sometimes as in a garment. Here was a man playing his part with ease and discretion, and his listener did not look beyond. It never occurred to her that he might be deceiving her. She regarded him as a middle-aged man who probably said pretty things to every pretty woman he came near.

She had no idea of the feelings with which he regarded her; feelings which were growing day by day.

Again he looked at his watch and then unwillingly rose.

"How tiresome," he said; "absolutely madame will be on her way home now, and I seem only to have been here a few minutes; time flies in your company."

"Time does not fly for me now," answered Eva.

"It may some day; keep up your heart, and now good-bye, but I shall see you soon again,"

After this he went away, and Eva sat still thinking over what he had said. If Temple had really gone abroad in search of her, for a time at least she was safe.

"And why need I stay here?" thought Eva, and then she rose and began walking restlessly to and fro. She was thinking of Kilmore, thinking how strange it was that he had not gone to Mr. Ford to make inquiries about her.

"And yet he cannot forget me," she murmured half aloud. "He cannot forget our love; he may hate me, but he cannot forget."

She was still thinking of him when she heard a carriage stop before the door, and the house bell ring. Then she heard madame's voice, and a few moments later madame herself made her appearance.

"Oh, you are still sitting up, Mrs. Scott?" she said as she entered the room in her elaborately embroidered cloak. "Well, you missed a treat, but I've come home so thirsty. The theatre was very hot, and I think I will have a brandy and soda; I expect there is some brandy here."

She went up as she said this to a little inlaid cabinet which stood at one side of the room, and just as she was bending down to open the doors she gave an exclamation.

"Why! here are a pair of Mr. Ford's gloves, I declare," she said; "however did they come here?"

Eva did not speak.

"I could almost swear these gloves were not here," continued madame, "when I went out," and she lifted up the gloves, which were lying on the cabinet, as she spoke. "He's not been here, has he?" she added, looking sharply round.

"Yes, he has been here," said Eva, coldly.

"Here! when I was out! Here when he said he was going to a dinner party!" exclaimed Madame de Cimbri with sudden suspicion in her tone and manner, and her face grew very pale. "I tell you what, Mrs. Scott, I think this looks very queer; if I thought—"

"Mr. Ford came to bring me some news about my affairs," answered Eva yet more coldly, and madame paused, almost panting with anger, and her dark eyes all aflame with rage.

"Oh! that is all very fine! Affairs indeed! What sort of affairs, I wonder? If I thought I was got out of the way so that you might receive him alone, I'd turn you out of my house this very night!"

"You need not be so insulting, Madame de Cimbri."

"Insulting indeed! And who are you, I should like to know, that he brought here without a single word? A runaway wife he called you? But I won't have it! If James Ford is anything to you, I'm not going to be made a cat's-paw of; I'm not indeed!"

She had worked herself up into a terrible rage by this time, and advanced towards Eva almost as if she were going to attack her personally.

"Mr. Ford is nothing to me," said Eva, drawing herself up to her fullest height, "and I do not understand your insinuations. But I shall no longer remain in your house. I will leave to-morrow!"

And with these words she quitted the room, leaving the angry woman to console herself with several brandies and sodas before she retired for the night.

CHAPTER XXXVIII.

JEALOUSY.

Madame de Cimbri had, however, repented by the morning of her sudden fit of jealousy and anger. It did not, in fact, suit her to quarrel with Mr. Ford, and she was afraid that he might resent her treatment of Eva. She thought of making an apology, therefore, when Eva came downstairs; but Eva did not give her an opportunity of doing this.

She dressed herself early and went out to post a few lines which she had written to Mr. Ford. They were as follows:

"Dear Mr. Ford: Something has arisen which would make it very unpleasant for me to remain a day longer at Norham Villa. Will you, therefore, kindly send me a telegram to assure me that it is safe for me to go to Brighton? You know what I mean; that it is an absolute certainty that G. T. has left England.

"Impatiently awaiting your reply,

"I remain sincerely yours,

"Eva Moore."

Eva concluded that Mr. Ford would receive this note by the two o'clock delivery, and that she would have an immediate answer. And by half-past two a telegram arrived for her and was brought up by the maid.

"Madame sends her compliments, please, Mrs. Scott," said the maid, "and would you come down and have some luncheon?"

"No, thank you," answered Eva, "and then she proceeded hastily to open her telegram. It only contained a few words:

"Do nothing until I see you.

"Ford."

This brief message was naturally very unsatisfactory to Eva. But she was not kept long in suspense. Before three o'clock she heard a cab stop at the outer gate of Norham Villa, and going to the window she perceived the tall and stately figure of Mr. Ford walking up the garden walk. Then followed a long silence, broken, however, presently by a woman's hysterical sobs. A scene was evidently going on downstairs, and Eva heard loud and angry voices. Then came another silence, and in a little while a rap at Eva's bedroom door.

"Come in," she said, and the door opened and Madame de Cimbri entered, with a tear-stained face and a general appearance of unmistakable agitation.

"Mr. Ford is downstairs," she began in a broken voice. "It seems you have written to him to tell him you are going away—" And here a sob choked her utterance.

"I wish to leave," said Eva coldly.

"And he has sent me up," then came another sob, "to say—I am sorry—if I said anything rude—last night. I was put out; I—I did not know why he had come—he says it was about your husband—but—but I am sorry."

Here she burst into a fit of passionate sobbing. She was evidently violently and truly affected, and her distress almost made Eva feel sorry for her.

"It is no matter," she said.

"And," sobbed out madame, "he wishes to see you—he sent me up to ask you to go down—he doesn't wish you to leave here."

"I will go down and speak to him," answered Eva, and

accordingly she went downstairs and found Mr. Ford standing looking out of the dining-room window. He turned round as she entered the room, and there was a frown still on his brow.

"I am very sorry about all this folly," he said, advancing with outstretched hand. "That idiot of a woman has made a nice fool of herself, it seems."

"It is disagreeable for me to be here any longer," answered Eva, "therefore I wrote to ask you if it were safe for me to go."

"My dear girl, I am sorry to say that fellow Temple is still in town," answered Mr. Ford, again taking Eva's hand. "But you shall not stay here to be insulted; only we must be very careful."

"And he is still in town?" said Eva, growing a little paler.

"So the private inquiry man told me this morning. Therefore, you see it would never do for you to run any risks. For anything we know, Temple himself may be employing some of these people to trace you out."

"But I cannot stay here."

"Can you not stay for a day or two? Madame has apologized to you for her folly, has she not?"

"She said she was sorry."

"Well, look over it, then; she is jealous of every woman younger and better looking than herself, naturally."

"She need not be jealous of me."

Mr. Ford gave a peculiar smile.

"We need not discuss it," he said. "But my advice is until we absolutely know this man is out of the country it will be wisest for you to remain here."

"I am very unwilling to do so."

"Surely not on account of madame? What earthly matter is it what a woman like that says?"

And Mr. Ford shrugged his broad shoulders.

"Still in her house—"

"My dear girl, do not distress yourself on that point. Come, let us settle it; remain here a few days, just until we know Temple is gone, and then I will take a house for you, wherever you like."

There was a listener to these last words that neither Eva nor the banker suspected. Madame de Cimbri had stolen downstairs determined to try to hear something of the interview between Eva and Mr. Ford, and when she heard him say that he would take a house for Eva wherever she liked, her very heart seemed to stand still.

She clenched her hands; a dangerous light flashed in her eyes, and she looked at this moment a woman capable of anything.

"I will tell madame to be perfectly polite to you," continued Mr. Ford, madame still listening the while; "and she dare not disobey me. If she is not everything you wish, just let me know."

"Well, for a few days, then," said Eva, unwillingly.

"Then that is settled; I cannot tell you how annoyed I am that you should have had any trouble at all, for you know there is nothing I wish so much as to see you happy —but then a jealous woman—"

And Mr. Ford laughed.

The jealous woman outside heard these words, and heard also the contemptuous laugh which accompanied them.

Then she stole away, and upstairs gave way to a terrible paroxysm of rage and passionate despair. She flung herself on her knees by the bed; she swore she would have her revenge.

"If I swing for it!" she said, clenching her white teeth.

"He dare to speak of me thus!" she went on; "but he'll rue the day; yes, he'll rue the day!"

Then she got up and tried to compose herself, and with her trembling hands smoothed her ruffled hair.

"I've a part to play," she thought vindictively, "and I'll play it."

But she was not a good actress. When she went down stairs again, and Mr. Ford glanced at her white, set face, its expression half-frightened him. She tried to smile, but it was a smile which distorted her features.

"Mrs. Scott has promised to stay on a few days longer, madame," he said, addressing her in a friendly tone; "so I hope you'll take no more foolish fads into your head."

"I'll try not to be—a jealous woman," answered madame in a would-be playful tone, but with rage in her eyes, and the banker felt absolutely uneasy.

"Was it safe to leave Eva here?" he was thinking; "leave her with this passionate, half-frenzied woman?"

He looked at madame again, and again that hideous smile distorted her full lips. She was so pale, too, and her

large dark eyes were gleaming with the passionate anger
of her soul. Altogether, he felt exceedingly uncomfortable, and after considering in silence for a few moments
what it would be best to do, he determined not to quit
Norham Villa while madame continued in her present state
of excitement.

"As I am here," he said presently, affecting a jocularity
he was far from feeling, "suppose we make a day of it?
I'll telegraph for a brougham and take you two ladies for
a drive, and then we can have a good dinner, and go
afterwards to one of the theatres."

"Quite a charming arrangement!" cried madame with
a ring of rage and satire in her tone.

"Then I'll write my telegram," continued Mr. Ford, "and
madame, you can send one of your maids with it to the
telegraph office. In the meantime I think I'll have a smoke
in the garden. Don't forget to order a good dinner,
madame!"

He spoke the last sentence as he was leaving the room,
and in the hall he lighted a cigar and walked contemplatively up and down the gravel garden walk in front of
Norham Villa. He was getting very tired of Madame de
Cimbri. He was a man who detested scenes, and she had
made a most unpleasant one to-day, and altogether Mr.
Ford's reflections were by no means in her favor.

"What a fury she looked, too," he thought, "when she
was raging and crying. I hate crying women; it spoils
their eyes and makes their noses red, and they gain nothing
by it from me."

In the meantime Eva and madame had been left in the
dining-room together, and just as Eva was quitting the
room to go to her own, madame spoke to her, and Eva
was struck with the alteration in her voice.

"I suppose you will go on this drive?" she said.

"I think not," answered Eva, quietly.

"Oh! you had better go," continued madame, but Eva left
the room without saying anything further, and as she disappeared the same evil smile stole over madame's lips.

About three-quarters of an hour elapsed, and Mr. Ford
had time to smoke several cigars, and then the brougham
he had telegraphed for arrived. He went into the house
when it came, and called upstairs to know if Eva and
madame were ready; Eva came out of her own room when

she heard his voice, and went half-way down the staircase to speak to him.

"I think you must excuse me, Mr. Ford." she said, addressing him.

"No, indeed, I won't," he answered, and he came half way up the stairs to meet her. "I want you particularly to go," he added in a lower tone; "and am going entirely on your account."

"Well, if you really wish it?" hesitated Eva.

"I do, indeed," said Mr. Ford earnestly, and Eva, after thinking a moment, said she would go.

She went back into her own room to put on a hat and a thick veil, and when she went downstairs she found madame in the dining-room with Mr. Ford.

"My drive seems most unpopular," said Mr. Ford, addressing her with a smile; "here is madame now says she does not wish to go."

"I have something to do," answered madame, "and I can't manage it. I suppose you won't be very long away?"

"No, it gets so soon dark," said Mr. Ford. "We can go just a little way on the heath; I haven't been there since I was a boy, and it will give me quite a juvenile sensation. That is, of course, if you don't object, Mrs. Scott?"

"It is quite the same to me where we go; but you had better go, too, madame," said Eva.

"No, thank you," replied madame, in sullen tone, "I've business I must see after."

"Come along then, Mrs. Scott," said Mr. Ford, "and I'll keep the brougham for us to go to the theatre in after dinner, madame. Good-bye for the present, then;" and he nodded to her, and then led Eva down the gravel walk to the carriage waiting outside.

He handed her in, and then gave a little sigh of relief.

"Thank goodness," he said, "that woman did not come with us! What a fury she looked in. I was really half afraid of her."

"She did look very angry."

"I see it won't do for you to stay on here any longer. Do you know why I proposed this drive, and going to the theatre, and all that? Simply because I was afraid to leave you alone with her until her tantrums had quieted down a bit."

"It is very disagreeable for me to be here."

"Would you like to go to Brighton?"

"Yes, if you think it would be safe."

"I'll see that private inquiry man again to-morrow, and if Temple is gone it will be all right. At all events he will always let me know what Temple is doing, and Brighton is handy to town, and you'll be out of the way there of this stupid, jealous woman."

While Mr. Ford was talking thus to Eva, Madame de Cimbri had gone to her own room and called for her maid to come to her.

"Shut the door," she said as the smart little maid entered, "though there's no one in the house to hear us but cook, and I suppose she knows. But I want you to tell me something—to speak the truth, and I'll pay you handsomely for it—was Mr. Ford here the first time I went alone to the theatre since Mrs. Scott came?"

The maid hesitated, and cast down her eyes.

"I know he was the second time I went," continued madame, vindictively. "I found out that for myself, and I suppose he bribed you to hold your tongue about the first time? Now, whatever he gave you, I'll give you double to tell me the truth."

"Well, then, he just was," said the maid. "I said it was a shame to cook, and you going away quite innocent like, and then him coming after the other lady. But he called us up into the hall before he went and gave us a pound each to say nothing about it. And because I thought it might make mischief, we didn't."

"Oh! I daresay!" said madame, bitterly, and she drew out her purse. "There's my bribe for the truth," and she put four pounds into the girl's hand. "Give two of them to the cook, and tell her to have dinner ready at six, as we are going to the theatre afterwards. And now I am going out."

And she did go out, but she had returned before Mr. Ford and Eva did. She received them quietly, but Mr. Ford noticed that she still had the same expression of strong, though suppressed, anger on her striking features. But she said very little, and moved restlessly about as though unable for a moment to be still.

"Do I look any younger?" said Mr. Ford, trying to make the best of things. "The air on the heath carried me back to the days of paste-eggs, brambles and all sorts of juvenile things! Oh! those were jolly times!"

"You are looking back a long way," said madame, with a bitter ring in her voice.

"Alas! so I am! To the days of innocence, madame!"

"I never could believe you innocent," retorted madame.

Mr. Ford shrugged his broad shoulders.

"We live and learn," said he. "But here comes Jeanette to announce dinner. I hope you have given us a good one, madame: one of the privileges of middle-age, you know, to which you so unfeelingly allude!"

And he laughed and offered his arm to Eva to escort her into the dining room as he spoke.

Madame made no reply to this; she seated herself at the head of the table and helped the soup, and Jeanette, the waiting-maid, poured out the sherry. Then presently Mr. Ford turned to Eva.

"What wine will you take?" he said. "Champagne or sparkling burgundy?"

"Thanks," answered Eva, "I would rather have some lemon and soda water, which I usually take."

"I thought you would have that, as you always take it," said madame, "so I got the lemons squeezed for you, and sugar in all ready. Open a bottle of soda water, Jeanette, and hand me that jug off the sideboard."

"It was very kind of you," replied Eva, as Jeanette handed madame the glass jug she indicated.

"I will pour out the lemon juice for you," said madame, raising the jug in her hand and pouring some of the contents into Eva's glass.

As she said this, something in her voice attracted Mr. Ford's attention. Then he saw that she was deadly pale, and that her hand shook violently as she raised the jug. He kept his eyes fixed upon her, and the expression of her face became so terrible at this moment that a sudden suspicion darted into his heart as she greedily and eagerly watched the maid pour the soda water into the glass where she had placed the lemon juice.

Eva put out her hand to raise the glass to her lips, but the same moment Mr. Ford sprang up from his chair.

"No!" he said, putting his hand over the glass, "you must not drink this!"

"What do you mean?" asked madame, who was ghastly pale.

"I don't like such mixtures," answered Mr. Ford, who

was now also much excited. "You made it, and you must drink some of it yourself before I allow Eva to touch it!"

"Eva! How dare you call her Eva before me!" almost screamed Madame de Cimbri, starting to her feet. "What do you think I've done with it?"

"Well, drink it yourself, then; I insist upon you drinking it," said Mr. Ford, suddenly recovering his ordinary coolness of manner, and carrying Eva's glass containing the lemon juice and soda water to where madame was standing. "A little lemon juice will do you no harm, and if there is nothing else in it you need not be afraid!"

He held the glass towards her, and madame stood glaring at him with her flashing eyes. Then suddenly she struck it out of his hand, and the glass fell broken in a dozen pieces on the floor, and its contents were spilt on the carpet.

"I thought so," said Mr. Ford, scornfully. "So it was poisoned! Eva, this is no place for you."

Eva had risen to her feet during the scene and stood pale and trembling, while in language that cannot be repeated here madame began to pour forth the vilest imprecations.

"Leave the room; leave her to me," continued Mr. Ford, addressing Eva, and get ready at once to leave this house. Do not be afraid; I brought you here and I will take you safely away. How soon can you be ready?"

"In a few minutes," answered Eva in a frightened voice.

"That is right; I will come for you. And now, madame, answer to me for what you have done!"

Eva ran out of the room, followed by Jeanette, as he spoke, and the two who were left stood facing each other, and there was rage and hate on the woman's part, and defiance on the man's.

CHAPTER XXXIX.

A DIAMOND RING.

About a quarter of an hour elapsed, and Eva stood trembling the while upstairs, and then Mr. Ford, accompanied by Jeanette, rapped at her door.

"Are you ready?" he asked, when Eva opened it. "I

luckily kept the brougham, and Jeanette will help you to pack your things and carry them downstairs. Jeanette, go in and help Mrs. Scott and I will wait outside."

The little maid then entered and she was also trembling.

"Oh! Mrs. Scott, I'm sure I've got such a fright!" she said.

"We had better not talk of it," answered Eva. "Will you help me with these straps?"

Her luggage was soon ready, and then Mr. Ford offered her his arm and led her downstairs.

"Do not be afraid," he said in a low tone, for he felt Eva's hand shaking on his arm. "I have locked her safely in there, and he pointed to the dining-room; "and I have the key in my pocket, and will only give it to the servants as we are leaving."

As they passed the dining-room door they heard loud and passionate sobs from within.

"Fool!" said Mr. Ford, contemptuously. But his face was very pale, and he was agitated in spite of his efforts to seem calm.

Then he gave some directions to the servants, for the cook had now also appeared on the scene, and assisted in carrying Eva's luggage to the brougham waiting outside the outer gate.

But it was all over in a few minutes, and the outer gate of Norham Villa closed behind Eva forever.

"Thank Heaven that you are safe!" exclaimed Mr. Ford with some emotion, as the brougham started, and he seated himself by Eva's side. "I should never have taken you there."

"Was it poison?" asked Eva in a low voice.

"She is a madwoman," answered Mr. Ford briefly. "But do not let us talk or think of her. The first thing to be considered is where you must go to-night; it is too late to think of Brighton."

"I can go to an hotel."

"It is that man Temple I am thinking of. But still we must risk it. Where would you like best to go?"

Finally they went to a well-known West End hotel, and there Mr. Ford engaged a private sitting-room and bed-room for "Mrs. Scott." He also ordered dinner and insisted on Eva taking some.

"You looked fagged to death," he said, "and I must see after you."

Soon after dinner, however, he left her, promising to send her news the first thing in the morning if he had learnt anything regarding Mr. Temple.

Eva spent a restless night; how could it well be otherwise? But before breakfast next morning she received a telegram from Mr. Ford. It was very brief, but to the point.

"Good news. T. started last night on his foreign tour, followed by the man I told you of. Will be with you about twelve o'clock.

"Ford."

Eva breathed a sigh of relief as she read these words, and she also thought gratefully that but for Mr. Ford, George Temple would ere now probably have discovered her, and forced his hateful presence on her against her will. And this feeling made her receive Mr. Ford more kindly than usual when he arrived.

"I thank you very much," she said, holding out her hand as he entered the room. "So he is gone?"

And once more she gave a relieved sigh.

"Yes, he is gone," answered Mr. Ford, smiling, "and my private inquiry man started in the same boat with him, and will let me know his movements from time to time. I had a note from the inquiry man last night, but it was too late to send it on to you, so I telegraphed this morning."

"I am very grateful to you," said Eva, and her lips trembled as she spoke.

Mr. Ford bent down and kissed her hand.

"I am but too happy to have been able to serve you," he said. "And now you can have a little breathing time, for we shall always know where Temple is, and can trim our sails accordingly. You wish to go to Brighton first, you said?"

"Yes; I think the sea air will do me good, for I do not feel very strong."

"No wonder, after what you have gone through. And now shall I go down to Brighton and take a furnished house for you, which will spare you trouble, or would you rather take one yourself?"

"Oh! I can't give you any more trouble, Mr. Ford. I think I will go down to-day and look out for a house. I can go to an hotel first."

Mr. Ford looked at her contemplatively and smilingly. "What a pity you are so handsome," he said. "Wherever you go people will remark on you."

Eva smiled also.

"I hope not," she said; "and Mr. Ford—I think I had better keep the name of Mrs. Scott now?"

"And make all the men envy the unseen Mr. Scott, eh? Yes, I think you are right. Mrs. Scott is a good traveling name, and not likely to be remarked on. Well, I hope Mrs. Scott will sometimes welcome me to her house at Brighton."

"Oh, yes."

"Thanks, very much. Then shall I go with you to Brighton to-day to help you in your search for a house?"

"It is very good of you, but I think I can manage quite well. You see, I am accustomed to go about by myself."

They settled after this that Eva was to go alone to Brighton, but she promised to telegraph to Mr. Ford should she require any assistance or help.

"And I will keep you constantly informed as to Temple's movements," said Mr. Ford. "What a blessing it would be if he should betake himself off to Africa again, but I fear it is unlikely, for he seemed to me a very determined man."

Eva thought of these words many times on her journey to Brighton. "A very determined man," and he was her husband! They made her select the quietest and most out-of-the-way furnished house she could find; they made her shrink as much as possible from public notice, and walk out as thickly veiled as she could be. The lady of whom she engaged the house left two servants in it, and these Eva kept on. She called herself Mrs. Scott and said her husband was abroad, and as she paid a quarter's rent in advance, and gave her banker as her reference, she was regarded as a very desirable tenant.

Thus she found herself once more in a settled home, but the loneliness of her life was very great. She knew no one, and went nowhere, and her one visitor was Mr. Ford, who somehow took good care to remind her that at least she was in a better position than undergoing punishment for bigamy!

He used to go down to Brighton on Saturday evenings very often, and stay over the Sundays at an hotel, and spent many hours at Eva's house when he did so. And gradually Eva got to dislike these visits more and more. There was something in his manner which so constantly reminded her of her obligations to him, and that her liberty was actually in his power. Only through him could she hear of George Temple's continued absence from England; only through him keep her residence a secret. She depended on him, as it were, and Mr. Ford occasionally made her feel this.

One evening they had almost a quarrel about a valuable diamond ring which Mr. Ford had brought from town, and which he begged Eva to accept.

He had often noticed she always wore a wedding ring with a diamond keeper, and he had often wondered also if this wedding ring had been placed on her slender finger by Lord Kilmore, or by her first husband, George Temple.

Yet somehow he had never asked her this question. Indeed, he was conscious that Eva treated him with a species of reserve which he regarded as supremely ridiculous in her position, but which nevertheless he was unable quite to break through.

But in the chill days of the New Year—for time was creeping, if slowly, still surely on—he arrived one Saturday evening at Eva's house, armed with so beautiful a diamond ring that he felt inwardly convinced the woman did not live who would absolutely refuse it. Eva did not expect him, and she was lying on a couch by the fire, dressed in a white woolen tea-gown trimmed with otter, when he was announced. The room was softly lit, and as she rose to receive him, Mr. Ford thought he had never seen her look more lovely.

"I have come to wish you a happy New Year," he said, as he shook hands with her.

Eva slightly shook her head.

"Oh! yes, you must have a happy one," he continued, in answer to this mute gesture; "and I have brought something for this fair hand."

He raised her left hand as he spoke, the hand on which her Clair had placed the wedding ring, and which had never left it night nor day.

"I wish it were in my power—you know that, I am sure —to place a ring like this on your hand," and he touched the wedding-ring. "But you know it is not. I wrecked

19

my life to a certain extent in my young days, as you have done, by making a loveless marriage. But it is in my power to offer you a slight token of my—deep regard— and I hope you will accept this ring?"

But Eva drew back; the glittering gaud was valueless in her eyes.

"No, Mr. Ford, I cannot take it," she said.

"Surely as a New Year's gift? Nay, you won't be so cruel as to refuse what I took so much care and pleasure in selecting?"

"You are very good, and it is very beautiful," answered Eva with embarrassment; "but I never take gifts."

"Never?" smiled the banker, with a marked emphasis on the word.

"No, never now," said Eva, and a flush stole over her cream-like skin.

"But—do not be angry—is not this very foolish?"

"I have no need, no use for jewels."

"Yet you wear two rings?"

Eva did not speak.

"Make an exception in my case," pleaded Mr. Ford. "Come, I have some claims, have I not, on your friendship?"

"I am greatly indebted to you; but please do not ask me to accept anything, for really I cannot."

"But why?"

"You—you know the painful circumstances of my life—"

"Yes; but these circumstances have thrown us into an intimacy, a friendship which certainly entitles me to give you a New Year's gift. Do not be so coy, my dear girl, it is very foolish."

"It may be so, but you will pardon me when I repeat I cannot accept it."

"Oh, very well; just as you like. I'll put my ring back into my pocket, then, and I won't tell you my news from abroad."

He suited his action to his word. He put the ring back into its case and then into his coat pocket, and he rose as though about to go. He felt, indeed, exceedingly annoyed, and began to wonder if this woman meant to be persistently cold to him.

"What is your news?" asked Eva.

"Oh, yes; you want to make use of me, yet you won't accept a small courtesy from my hands," replied the banker with a little shrug.

"It is not that; it is from a feeling of—"

"Of what, Eva?"

"Oh! don't you understand, Mr. Ford, that I am not like other women," replied Eva in agitation. "A sword is always hanging over my head, and I cannot tell when it may fall."

"I have done my best to avert such a catastrophe, have I not?"

"Yes, indeed, you have, and I am grateful, most grateful, but—"

"Well, for the present I will be content with that, but not always, Eva," and again he sat down by her side. "I am not made of stone, you know, and some day you must not be so cruel to me as you are now."

CHAPTER XL.

BABBLING WORDS.

Far away at Kilmore Hall the chill New Year was passing under circumstances of depression, and there were sad hearts under that stately roof.

To Lady Kilmore this time naturally recalled more vividly her great and bitter loss. Last year her husband was with her, and her son, in the flush of his young manhood, made the sunshine of their home.

Now her husband had passed away from her, and there was a constant cloud on the young lord's brow. From the first after his return Lady Kilmore had noticed this, yet she said nothing, even to Annette Gower, of her son's gloomy face, and Annette Gower also did not speak of her cousin's evident depression.

Both these women, however, knew, or at least guessed, by whom it was caused. The beautiful girl who had crossed Kilmore's path so strangely had by some stroke of fate been separated from him, for no daily letter now came for him in the same handwriting as they did during the time of his illness, when Annette had carried them to his sick-bed with a sinking heart.

This unfortunate affair was ended, both his mother and cousin secretly decided, but how it had ended they could not tell. Kilmore remained at home, but was restless and unsettled. At last his mother, remembering the fond love and confidence that had formerly existed between them, did venture to approach the subject of her son's unhappiness.

He was sitting by her one evening in the gloaming, silent and absorbed as usual, when Lady Kilmore suddenly put her thin white hand on his.

"Clair," she said in her gentle voice, for she still found her strength unequal to call him by his father's name, "will you tell your mother something, my dear?"

He moved uneasily on being thus addressed, but a moment later said:

"What do you wish to know, mother?"

"I wish to know why you seem so depressed, Clair? You are not like yourself—and—ever since you came home after the last time you were away, you seem to have no pleasure in your life. What has happened to you, my dear; surely you can trust your mother?"

He turned away his head, and Lady Kilmore felt his hand tremble beneath hers.

"Is there anything I can do?" continued Lady Kilmore. "I will do anything to try to make you happy, Clair."

"There is nothing you can do, mother," answered Kilmore in a low, agitated tone.

"But, my dear, it is so painful to me to see you as you are."

"Mother," began Kilmore, and he rose as he spoke and leaned against the mantel-piece so that his face was hidden from her; "a great blow has come to me—a great grief. But it does no good to speak of it—nothing can do any good; and—I must bear it as I can."

He said no more at the time, and left the room, but during the evening, when they were once more alone, he went up to his mother and kissed her brow.

"Forgive me," he said, "if I was abrupt to you this afternoon, but don't speak of what we spoke of any more. I can't bear it, mother, and it does no good."

So after this Kilmore was asked no questions. He lived a very quiet life, refusing to go into society; but he rode out a good deal, and by Lady Kilmore's wish Annette Gower sometimes accompanied him.

One day they met Mr. Dighton, the farmer, and Richard Dighton, and Annette, timidly glancing at her cousin's face, saw a dark red flush mount to his very brow.

The farmer took off his broad-brimmed hat to the young couple, and evidently expected that his landlord would stop and speak to him.

But Lord Kilmore merely touched his hat and rode on.

"What a sullen looking young man that young Dighton is," said Annette, more for something to say than anything else.

"He is a sullen brute," answered Kilmore, and then he rode on in silence, and Annette guessed the subject of his thoughts.

It was a fine winter afternoon, and the red berries in the hedgerows, the bare branches of the trees, and the brown of the furrows were all lit up by the setting sun, shining above a great bank of clouds behind which it was about to dip. But Kilmore looked neither on sky nor field. At that moment before him rose the beautiful face of the woman he had so passionately loved, and his inner sense seemed to see her as he had seen her in these very lanes. And that she—she who had seemed so fond—should have left the letter unanswered in which Kilmore had poured forth the very inmost emotions of his heart! He could not understand it, yet it must be true, when she knew that a word from her would recall him to her side.

He never for a moment suspected that the banker, Mr. Ford, had deceived him. Like all very young men he regarded a middle-aged man as old, and Eva had said Mr. Ford was married, and therefore it never entered Kilmore's mind to suspect him of treachery or deceit. Yet though she had left him, she had written in those last treasured lines of hers that she would not change.

Even yet Kilmore clung to this hope. Clung to it though he knew if they met again only trouble could come; trouble, sorrow and remorse—and yet, and yet—

He roused himself from his reverie with a restless sigh, and looked at his cousin, who was riding by his side with her head drooped slightly forward, as if she also were indulging in some painful reflections.

"It's a fine evening," said Kilmore, with another sigh.

"Yes," answered Annette without lifting her head.

"How do you think my mother is, Annette?" then said Kilmore. "Do you think she is any brighter?"

"I think she is a little," replied Annette, raising her head, "ever since your return."

"And I—" began Kilmore with a sudden pang of remorse. He was thinking, "I have never tried to comfort her; I have been absorbed in my wretchedness, and forgot that I must have been adding to hers."

But he did not say all this to Annette Gower. He said very little, indeed, during the rest of their ride, but when they reached the Hall he went straight to his mother's room as he used to do in the happy days of old.

"Mother, will you give me some tea," he said, and a little flush rose to Lady Kilmore's delicate features, and a sweet maternal light of love stole to her sunken eyes as she heard his simple words.

"Yes, my dear," she answered, and she rang the bell, and when Annette went into the room after changing her habit, she found the mother and son seated by a little table, and Lady Kilmore was pouring out tea for her boy.

It was the first time she had done so since her husband had left her, and Annette noticed that Kilmore was trying to exert himself to lead his mother to think of other things than her absorbing grief.

He presently took up the daily papers and began to read to her, and Lady Kilmore listened and gave some opinion on passing topics. Altogether this evening was more like the old times, and after dinner Kilmore sat with his mother and cousin instead of retiring to the smoking-room in gloomy solitude, which it had been his habit to do since his great trouble.

But when he did leave them he opened the window and looked out on the dark wintry night, and an intense yearning came over his soul to look once more on Eva's face.

"Only once, Eva!" he said, half aloud, holding out his arms into the chill air; "but once, my love—but once!"

And Eva, to whom he thus passionately appealed, at the same moment also felt an almost uncontrollable longing steal over her again to see her lover.

She began walking restlessly up and down the room; she, too, held out her white arms, and in imagination once more saw Clair kneeling at her feet.

"I will write to him," at last she determined, and she did

sit down and write to him, calling him once more to her side.

"I am so lonely, so miserable, Clair," she wrote; "the whole world is desolate to me—"

Thus far she had written, and then a stinging memory smote her heart. She remembered Clair's words of scorn when he asked her in their last interview if she knew what she had done? She had brought disgrace and shame to him, he had said, and Eva's face flushed as she recalled his words.

"No!" she cried, starting to her feet and tearing up the words she had just penned. "I cannot! I cannot! He has never sought me, and how can I call him back after what he said and what I wrote? I said I would trouble him no more unless I was in some desperate need. Perhaps that need will come," she added with gloomy pathos; "and then I will see Clair before I die!"

* * * * * * * *

The upshot of Kilmore's eager desire to look once more on Eva's face was a brief visit to town on the following day, for the purpose of trying again to see Mr. Ford, and endeavoring to learn if she had made any inquiries about himself, or expressed any wish to see him.

The banker received the young lord in the most urbane manner.

"Ah, Lord Kilmore," he said, rising to receive him, after Kilmore had previously sent up his card. "We are having chilly weather, but seasonable, eh?"

"Yes, indeed," answered Kilmore, and then he paused, embarrassed how to ask the questions he had expressly come to put.

"Have you been long in town?" inquired Mr. Ford, politely.

"No, I only came up this morning. The truth is, Mr. Ford, I came up to see you to ask if you have any news to tell me of Miss Eva Moore?"

The banker put up his well-shaped hands with a little gesture.

"You have come to the worst person in the world then to make inquiries about Miss Moore. She left England immediately after you were here last, intending to travel from place to place, and I have not heard a word from her since. She must, however, have visited Homburg, Cologne, Antwerp, Havre, in fact no end of places. I know this, of course, from her cashing the letters of credit I gave her on the bank."

"And where was she last?" asked Kilmore eagerly.

"At Paris," answered Mr. Ford readily, "but that was at Christmas time, and she probably will not be there now, as when she left England she did not mean to make a long stay anywhere."

"And you can give me no more definite information than this?"

"Indeed I cannot; and I feel hardly justified in telling you as much as I have done. Miss Moore's instructions were positive you know; no one had to know her address."

"And do you know anything of—" and Kilmore paused and hesitated.

"Do you mean Mr. Temple, her husband? No, I know nothing of him, Lord Kilmore."

And this was all the information Kilmore got from the banker—simply nothing. Only the galling fact repeated that she did not wish him to know her address; that she evidently did not care to see him again.

He went back, therefore, to Kilmore in worse spirits than when he had started. But to do him justice he tried to hide this from the fond eyes awaiting him there. He was kind and considerate to his mother, and he asked Annette to sing to him during the evening, but though he applauded it he did not really listen to her song.

Everything, in fact, seemed weary and dreary to him. A shadow had fallen athwart his life, and its gloom clouded his whole existence.

And about a week after his return to Kilmore an incident happened which also greatly disturbed him.

One frosty afternoon he and his cousin Annette were riding on one of the roadways near the Hall, when Annette's horse suddenly slipped and fell, and Annette was thrown violently over the horse's head on the hard and flint-like road.

In a moment Kilmore had dismounted and lifted his cousin in his arms. But Annette, who had fallen on her forehead and injured her face, was unconscious from the shock. Kilmore was naturally greatly alarmed. He sent the groom to the Hall at once for assistance, and he unfastened Annette's collar, and unloosened her habit to give her more air.

As he was unbuttoning the habit at her throat his hand became entangled in a ribbon which she wore round it. He pulled the ribbon aside, and in doing so a locket which was attached to it was exposed to his view. It was a large locket, and Kilmore raised it so that it might not press on Annette's throat. It had a gold back and a glass in front, and as Kilmore held it for a moment in his hand he saw it contained his own portrait.

His face flushed, and an uneasy sensation as of pain shot through his heart. He was fond of Annette, regarding her as the only sister he had ever known.

She had lived so much at the Hall that she had always seemed to him to be one of the family. But as he held the locket in his hand another idea not unnaturally passed through his mind.

Could Annette care for him more than he had cared for her? In his absorbing love for Eva he had never remembered that this poor girl had been thrown constantly with him; that she had nursed him in his illness, and that his mother had said she was greatly upset when she heard of his accident on the rocks at Eastcliff. All these thoughts, one after the other, rushed through Kilmore's brain whilst he knelt on the roadway holding his cousin's head on his arm.

Annette was a pretty girl, though no beauty. She had small, piquant features, and fine, dark intelligent eyes, and Kilmore felt half guilty as he looked on her face, thinking that unconsciously he might have given her much pain.

"Poor little girl!" he thought.

He was very sorry if it were so; he was not vain, and his very fondness for Annette made him grieve to think that she liked him too well. He felt embarrassed also to know what to do with the locket.

Annette would not like him to know, he was sure, that she wore his portrait hidden on her breast. He therefore gently replaced it in her habit, and bent anxiously over her, for she was still apparently unconscious.

"Annette!" he said; "Annette!" and the second time he spoke her name she seemed to hear his voice through her dulled senses. She sighed, and then seemed to try to raise her hand to her forehead, which was bruised and injured.

"Does your head ache, dear?" said Kilmore, taking her hand in his.

She opened her eyes as he asked this question, and when she saw him bending over her a faint flush rose to her face.

"Yes," she answered faintly.

"You've had a bad fall, but you'll soon be all right, dear," said Kilmore kindly. "Poor Rose has cut her knees too," he added, looking at the horse Annette had been riding, and which the groom had pulled up before he had ridden to the Hall for assistance. "But never mind, Annette, it will be all right when you get home again, and I told Jones to send a carriage at once."

Annette did not speak; she closed her eyes again, and lay still with her head on her cousin's arm.

Poor Annette! She knew Kilmore did not love her; knew that he loved, or had loved, another woman, and yet to be near him thus awoke a strange half-painful joy in her heart. He kept her hand in his, and with a half-caressing touch pushed her dark hair from her injured brow. Perhaps the sorrow in his own heart made him feel more tender to her, for his gray eyes were fixed on her pale face with a new softness in their expression, as though a different feeling toward her were stirring in his heart.

But presently the sound of wheels made him look round, and to his great relief he saw one of the Hall carriages approaching them; and bending anxiously from the window, to his extreme astonishment, he perceived his widowed mother.

It was the first time Lady Kilmore had crossed the threshold since her husband's death, but on hearing that an accident had happened to Annette Gower, to the great surprise of all around her she at once said she would go in the carriage that Kilmore had sent for. And when she stepped out of it in her deep widow's weeds and hurriedly approached her son and niece, Kilmore held out his hand to her.

"Don't be alarmed, mother," he said, "Annette's had rather a bad fall; but she'll be all right again presently—and thank you for coming."

"Annette, my dear Annette," said Lady Kilmore, who was trembling in every limb, kneeling down on the roadway and taking Annette's hand in hers. "How is this? How did it happen?"

Annette opened her eyes again on being thus addressed, and a faint smile flickered over her lips.

"Aunt Jeanie!" she half-whispered.

"The truth is, mother, it is far too slippery for riding, and I warned Annette; but she was an obstinate little girl, and so has got a tumble," said Kilmore, trying to speak lightly, but in reality feeling an odd sensation of emotion at the sight of his widowed mother kneeling on the roadway with Annette's hand clasped fast in hers.

"Are you in pain, my darling?" asked Lady Kilmore, bending more closely over Annette.

"My head aches very badly," she answered.

One of Lady Kilmore's women had accompanied her, and had brought brandy and sal-volatile, and Lady Kilmore now wetted Annette's lips and bathed her injured brow with water, and then Kilmore proposed to carry her to the carriage.

"She's a light little thing; I can easily lift her," he said, and as he spoke he raised her in his arms and carried her almost as he would have done a child.

"Lean your head on my shoulder, dear," he said; but a moan of pain broke from Annette's lips with the movement, even though he held her so gently.

Kilmore turned round and whispered a few words in his mother's ear.

"Send for a doctor at once, mother;" and when he glanced again at Annette he saw she had fainted.

She had in fact received a great shock and both Lady Kilmore and Kilmore were very uneasy about her. She was a delicate little girl, and though she had broken no bones, the injury to her forehead was very severe. Her accident, however, roused Lady Kilmore from her deep grief more than Kilmore believed it was possible that anything could have done. Lady Kilmore had always been very fond of Annette, and had planned and hoped from her earliest girlhood that she would one day become her daughter in reality as well as in affection.

Now she took her place by Annette's bedside, and nursed her with untiring love. But two days after the accident fever set in, and at nights Annette became delirious, and Lady Kilmore sat and listened to her rambling words with a sinking heart.

One night she grew very much excited, and began talking

of her cousin; calling him by his old name, "Clair," in tones of the tenderest affection. Lady Kilmore sent the nurse away on some excuse, and then went to the smoking-room, where she knew her son was sitting, who rose hastily as she entered.

"Annette is not worse surely, mother?" he asked anxiously.

"She is very ill, and she is calling for you, Clair," answered his mother. "Come with me, perhaps it will soothe her to see you."

So Kilmore went with his mother to Annette's bedside, but the poor fevered girl did not know him, but kept babbling on with her tender, foolish words.

"He does not love me," she repeated mournfully. "I love him, but he must never know—must never know! Poor Clair! His heart is broken!—like mine!"

Kilmore listened to these words and then turned away his head.

"Mother, I should not be here," he said, and then left the room, and as he passed into the corridor outside his eyes were dim with unshed tears.

CHAPTER XLI.

UNMASKED.

Annette was ill for many days after this, but Lady Kilmore did not again ask her son to go to her bedside. This experiment she saw had only given him fresh pain. Nor did she make any objections, when Annette had been declared out of all danger, to the proposal that Kilmore made that for a while he should go abroad.

"I want a change, mother," he said one day abruptly; "do you think you can spare me?"

Before Lady Kilmore answered she looked anxiously in her son's face, and what she read there determined her reply.

"I think you do want a change, my dear," she said. "Yes, I can spare you, now that dear Annette is going on so well."

"Then that is settled," answered Kilmore with a faint smile, and on the following day he left the Hall, and on the succeeding day England. He went to seek Eva; to try to look once more on the face of the woman he loved.

And from city to city the young lord wandered in constant hope. Sometimes he fancied he caught a glimpse of a form like hers; sometimes a face, but it all ended in disappointment. The woman he was searching for was living her quiet life at home, so Kilmore, with his aching, dissatisfied heart, looked for her abroad in vain.

In the meantime Mr. Ford had somehow learned with undisguised pleasure that Lord Kilmore had quitted England. His plans to part him from Eva had run very smoothly hitherto, and the only obstacle now in his path seemed Eva's persistent coldness to himself. The two men who were seeking her—Kilmore and George Temple, her husband—were both away, and did not know each other by sight even if they should chance to meet.

Therefore Mr. Ford felt his path clear, and he knew that Eva was in his power, and he was not a man to hesitate to abuse her enforced trust.

So the early spring months passed away, and March, stormy and fitful, dawned, and still Eva lived in the retired house that she had chosen, and still Mr. Ford went there, and in half-veiled language tried to make Eva understand that he loved her.

He never alluded to Madame de Cimbri now, nor Norham Villa, after the strange scene which had terminated Eva's residence there; and Eva also never spoke of it. It was in truth a most unpleasant subject to him, for Mr. Ford loved ease and hated worry, and sometimes told himself that Eva was not worth all the trouble he had taken about her.

But in spite of this a strong feeling toward her had taken possession of the man's heart. At first he had begun the pursuit almost in jest. The girl was handsome, and Mr. Ford was accustomed to easy conquests. He was good-looking and rich, and lavish in his gifts and pleasant words, and many women wanted no more. He thought Eva was like the rest, and perhaps had cause not to think very highly of her. But he completely mistook her character. Her very faults were purer than his easy virtues.

At last one day he flung off the mask, and stood before

her as he really was. It was a mild spring night, and the air was blowing fresh and balmy from the sea. It was Sunday, and they could hear the church bells ringing for evening service as they were together in Eva's little drawing-room, the banker leaning against the mantel-piece looking down admiringly at the fair woman, in her white dress, who was sitting on a couch near him, and who was beginning to find his fixed gaze and the long silence very oppressive.

"The church bells sound very pretty at a distance," said Eva at length, not knowing very well what to say.

"Yes," answered Mr. Ford absently.

Then a moment later he quickly raised his head and changed his position.

"Eva," he said abruptly, "how long is this to go on?"

"What do you mean?" asked Eva in some surprise.

"Do you think I am made of stone?" asked Mr. Ford with some genuine passion in his voice. "Do you think I can come here time after time and see you—the woman I love—you must listen! You know it is so, and I can bear it no longer!"

"I am very sorry to hear you speak thus, Mr. Ford," said Eva coldly, rising from her seat.

"You know very well I love you," went on Mr. Ford, approaching her and endeavoring to take her hand. "You must know it! From the time I saw you down at Westwold I have thought of no one else. Give me something in return, Eva—a little love—for all I have given to you?"

"Mr. Ford, this is ungenerous!"

"To love you? Why is it ungenerous? I have done all I could for you; I have sheltered you from the terrible consequences of that foolish act of yours; I have been your best friend, and now you call me ungenerous because I tell you the true feelings of my heart."

"You have been very kind to me, but to speak thus is useless—and is painful to us both."

"You mean you do not love me—yet?"

"I mean I can never love you, Mr. Ford," said Eva firmly. "To speak of such a thing is an insult to me—to me who—"

"Who what?"

"Who am bound by a tie which may be illegal, but which is binding, and always will be binding to every feeling of my heart! My marriage to Lord Clair was perhaps a sin, but it is not less a marriage in my sight!"

"Lord Clair—Lord Kilmore rather—does not appear to find it binding at all events," sneered Mr. Ford.

Eva's head fell, and a half-sigh escaped her lips.

"I heard somehow, I am sure I do not know who told me," continued the banker, "that the young lord is abroad, and going to be married soon—to his cousin, I believe."

"To his cousin?" echoed Eva with a blanched face and a sinking heart.

"So I was told. Is there a Miss Gower related to him?"

"Yes," faltered Eva.

"That's the girl then; she lives with his mother, I believe; and he is wise, Eva. His marriage with you was, as you well know, bigamous, and the sooner he forgets all about it the better for you and him."

Eva made no reply; she sat down with a sort of moan and covered her face with her hand.

"Come, my dear girl," went on Mr. Ford, crossing the room and laying his hand on her shoulder, though Eva shrank back from his touch, "do not be foolish. The little episode of Lord Kilmore is done and gone, and it rests with me how the more serious affair of the parson will end. If you are wise—"

"Don't, don't!" cried Eva, springing to her feet and raising her face with shining indignant eyes. "Mr. Ford, whatever happens I can be nothing to you! I am not fallen so low—"

"Indeed, young lady!"

"You know what I mean. Lord Clair may forget; I cannot."

"Then you actually still retain some sort of feeling for this young lordling who has treated you so shabbily!"

"And how did I treat him?" retorted Eva passionately. "He—who trusted me? If he has forsaken me I deserved it; I was unworthy of his love."

"Really!" and Mr. Ford shrugged his broad shoulders.

"I think you do not understand," continued Eva with a sort of dignity; "but do not let us speak of it. Let this conversation be forgotten."

"I cannot forget it," replied Mr. Ford impatiently. "You make a convenience of me, that is the truth, and I am about tired of it."

"All I ask is for you to leave me alone."

"No, you ask me to keep my eye on Temple's movements; you ask me, in fact, to do everything for you, and when I presume to remind you that I am mortal, that I have a heart to be trifled with, you turn upon me and tell me I have not to talk to you of love."

"I cannot listen to such folly."

"Eva, it is not folly! I repeat I love you—"

"Oh! hush, hush, Mr. Ford," said Eva, putting out her hand deprecatingly; "surely at your age—"

"I am not old," interrupted the banker angrily.

"Too old, at least, to insult a defenseless woman; but I ask you to leave me. Will you go, Mr. Ford?"

Something very like an oath escaped Mr. Ford's lips, but he looked round for his hat, and then stood for a moment scowling at Eva.

"Very well, Mrs. Temple," he said bitterly, "I will go;" and with these words he turned and left the room, and Eva was alone.

With a moan she sank down on the couch after he had left her, and rocked herself to and fro in utter misery.

"Could it be true?" she was asking herself; true that Clair had forgotten her so soon? She remembered all about Annette Gower at this moment; the dark-eyed girl who had sat and watched them when they had first danced together in the Park. "He has never sought me," Eva moaned; "all these long months I have been alone—and now, and now—;" and once more she moaned and wrung her hands in her great and bitter pain.

For a knowledge had come to her—a knowledge terrible, and yet until this moment half-sweet—that a child was to be born to her, Clair's child; and somehow she hoped the little baby hands would draw them closer.

"He will forgive me when he knows," how often she had whispered to herself in the still nights, how often told herself in the dreary days.

This tender tie would break down the barriers between them; he would forget his wrongs, and she her pride. A little child—Clair's child—and he would love it for her sake.

But if these fond and foolish dreams must end? Eva felt the world was then ended for her, and that she must lay herself down and die. But it might not be true? The hateful man who had just gone had a motive, a vile motive, it seemed, to part her utterly from Clair.

"Fancy speaking such words to me!" muttered Eva half-aloud, raising her bent head with an indignant gesture; "to me, who love my Clair—my young, my handsome Clair!"

Then she began walking wearily up and down the room, trying to make up her mind. What should she do? She had a claim upon Clair now, she told herself; a strong, natural claim, and should she stand calmly by and allow another to take her place? Annette Gower could be nothing really to his heart, she felt almost sure. He had loved her, and love does not pass away like the dew on the grass. He must remember her, even if he had been persuaded to ask Annette Gower to be his wife. Over and over again she told herself this, and at last she made up her mind to write.

She almost forgot in her excitement the suspended sword that hung over her head. Only to see Clair again was all she thought of; only to whisper on his breast the secret that now bound their lives.

Mr. Ford had said he was abroad, and she knew not where to address her letter; but if she sent it to Kilmore Hall it was almost sure to be forwarded, she reflected. At all events she would risk it, and at last, with trembling hands, she sat down to write to Kilmore—to call him once more to her side.

"Clair, dear Clair!" she wrote with shaking fingers, "a hundred times I have thought of writing to you, but until now I have not found courage. Now I must, for some one repeated to me to-day a report that you are about to marry your cousin, Miss Gower. Oh! Clair, you must not do this! Our marriage might be illegal, but it was binding at least to my heart and yours, and if I live there will be a new tie ere long between us. Come to me when you get this! Oh! come quickly, Clair, for I am weary with waiting, and I want your tenderness and care to support me now. I have been here all the winter—for many months— and am living in great seclusion, and now I shall count the days until I hope to see you—for you will come, Clair! Oh! yes I know you will, and you must forgive your own
"Eva."

She wrote this letter and then went out and posted it

20

with her own hands. She passed the open door of a church as she went back, and something prompted her to go in and kneel down in a pew near the door, and cover her face with her hands as the clergyman read the prayers.

"If my mother had only lived," she was thinking; "if I had known a mother's love—"

And then a sudden flush rose to her face, and her dark eyes filled with tears. She seemed to foresee in the dim distance the love that she had missed.

CHAPTER XLII.

MR. FORD'S REVENGE.

Mr. Ford was a vain man; vain of his good looks, and of his many conquests, and Eva had wounded him on his tenderest point. She had called him old, reproached him for talking of love at his age, and Mr. Ford left her house more angry than he had ever been before in all his life.

He was pale with rage as he walked back to his hotel, paid his bill, and started in the first train to return to town.

"She shall pay for this," he muttered more than once hoarsely beneath his heavy brown mustache, as he sat gloomily in the train. All his thoughts lately, in business and out, had been given to Eva, and she had rebuffed him, scorned him, and a feeling like hatred toward her was now swelling in his heart.

"She shall not have her young lord back again at least," he reflected savagely; "if I'm not good enough for her I'll teach her a lesson she's not likely to forget."

And in this angry mood he returned to his home; returned to the spacious, handsome town residence where he dwelt with his wife, the unloved wife whom he had married in his early days for wealth.

He opened the door of his house with his latch-key, and crossed the hall without meeting anyone. It was Sunday night, and most of the servants were out, and he was not expected. He had gone down to Brighton full of excitement and love, and he had come back savagely disappointed, and ready for any evil thing; as he turned the handle of the dining-room door and was about to enter the room, this was the sight that met his angry gaze:

On an easy chair by the fire a stout, dark, heavily-built middle-aged woman lay back asleep. Her head was lying back, her lips were apart, and her unlovely features fully displayed. This was his wife! The handsome banker stood and looked at her, and scowled as he did so. A vision of the woman he had left—the woman who had scorned him—rose in his mind at this moment, and added not a little to his disgust. He stood mentally contemplating the two, and his heart was full of bitterness and rage, and he inwardly cursed the poor woman he was about to disturb from her placid slumbers.

His heavy step as he walked into the room awoke her, and she started to her feet.

"Why, James!" she said in an astonished tone as she rubbed her eyes, "I thought you were at Brighton?"

"So I was," he answered, roughly enough, "but I've come back, you see."

"Yes, so I see," said Mrs. Ford; she was unused to him speaking to her in such a tone, for to do him justice as a rule he was civil to her. But to-night he wanted a scape-goat for his wrath, and so he vented his ill-humor on his wife!

"It's a nice house to come back to, I must say," he went on. "You asleep, and the whole house dull and stupid as ditch-water!"

"I didn't expect you; you generally stay over the Sundays when you go down to Brighton; so I suppose you find it attractive," retorted Mrs. Ford.

"And what if I do?" he thundered; "more attractive than I find home, at any rate;" and with these words he turned and left the room, leaving his wife justly indignant.

He went up to his own bed-room, feeling half ashamed of his outburst, but unable still to control himself. All the time he was thinking of Eva, of Eva who had called him old; who had told him that she still loved Lord Kilmore, and on whom he had wasted so much time and thought!

The man felt half-mad with himself, mad at his own folly, and yet the folly was too strong for him.

But he had a purpose before him. In the dressing-room

of his bed-room stood a large strong escritoire, where many valuable deeds and papers were stored. He now went up to this, opened it, and drew out a sealed letter. It was addressed to Miss Eva Moore, and was the very letter that Kilmore had entrusted to his charge, and which he had told the young lord that Eva had declined to answer. As we know, he had never delivered it, and had locked it away unopened. Now he broke the seal, and read the impassioned words of another man to the woman he loved!

He grew a little pale as he did so, and his hands trembled. In this letter—intended but for Eva's eyes—Kilmore had poured out all the deepest and strongest feelings of his heart. No one could have written it who did not love deeply; no one could have received it unmoved. Again Mr. Ford read it, and the evil look grew darker on his face.

*   *   *   *   *   *   *   *

Eva slept better that night than she had done for weeks; she slept and dreamed of Clair, and of the early days of their young love. Once more she fancied she was standing on the bridge over the river Ayre, and Clair was leaning on the stone parapet by her side. He was looking in her face, and there was no reproach in his gray eyes.

It all seemed so plain to her; she heard the gurgle of the water below, and saw the sunshine falling on the green fields that stretched up to the homestead on Holly Hill. She awoke with a smile. This dream seemed a good omen to her; seemed to bring Clair closer to her heart.

"He will come," she told herself hopefully as the dawn crept to her window-panes; "he will take me away somewhere out of England, and I will be with him whatever happens—be with him till I die."

This thought buoyed her up all day; she scarcely thought of Mr. Ford, or his folly, as she called it, of the night before. She kept reckoning how long it would take for Kilmore to receive her letter and come to her It would reach Kilmore Hall to-day, and would probably be forwarded abroad at once to meet him wherever he might be.

He might get it the day after to-morrow, or the day after that. Then he would likely telegraph and come home to her. But to-morrow came and the day after, and there was no foreign telegram or letter for Eva.

It was five days after she had sent her letter to Kilmore

that the anxiously watched for post did bring her something; brought her a letter which she eagerly tore open, and read fond, loving, passionate words, written in the handwriting she knew so well! But Kilmore had evidently not received her letter when he wrote his, for in it he entreated her to see him again; to pardon him for his brief anger and hard words:

"Only see me again, my one, my only love," Eva read with a beating heart, "and surely we can arrange something—surely something can be done! But see me; Eva, my beloved, this estrangement is breaking my heart."

These tender and impassioned words, and many more such, were signed by Kilmore, and as Eva again and again read them, as she pressed them to her lips, laid them against her cheek, as if they were some living thing, she suddenly perceived that in the envelope which had contained them there was another note-sheet. This she too opened and hurriedly read, and as she did so the bloom faded from her face, and a cry escaped her fast whitening lips.

This letter was written apparently by a doctor from Kilmore's sick-bed:

"Dear Madam—I am requested by Lord Kilmore to forward the enclosed letter to you, and to inform you of the unfortunate accident which has occurred to his lordship on the hunting-field. He was thrown from his horse yesterday, and unhappily his arm was broken; but I trust with rest and care no serious consequences will ensue. He is laid up here, as this is the nearest house to the spot where the accident happened, and he is most anxious to see you. He does not wish his mother, the widowed Lady Kilmore, to be informed of the occurrence, from motives which he tells me you will understand. But he asks me to entreat you to come to him at once. And for his health's sake may I urge this, as his mind ought to be kept perfectly quiet, and he is restless and anxious about you. Could you come to-morrow when you receive this? If you start from King's Cross terminus by the 4 express north, and leave the train at Peterborough, a carriage will be waiting for you at the station, as this house is somewhat cross country, and about two miles from Peterborough. Kindly telegraph if you will come, and thus relieve Lord Kilmore's anxiety.

"And I remain, madam,

"Yours faithfully,

"F. L. Page, M. D.

"Address:

"Dr. Page,

"Hurstwood House,

"Nr. Peterborough."

Eva never hesitated after she had read these words. She ran upstairs to her bed-room and hastily wrote a telegram to Dr. Page to tell him she would start by the train he mentioned, and then hurried out to dispatch it. Then having sent her telegram away she returned to her house and began at once to make preparations for her departure. She paid her servants, and left them money to live on during her absence, but she did not give them her address, as she did not wish anyone to know where she was going.

"One of my relations has had an accident," she told them. "I will write when I get to my destination, and I am going to town at once."

She happened not to have very much money in her possession at the time, as she had intended to ask Mr. Ford to cash a check for her the last time she had seen him, but the unpleasant scene which had occurred had put this out of her mind, and she had not cared to write to him since. But she had enough for her immediate necessities; enough to pay her way to Peterborough, and to leave something behind.

"And what matter is it?" she told herself; "Clair will give me what I want until we go away, and then I can write to the bank."

Her heart felt lighter than it had done for months when she started on her journey to town. Her Clair's tender words were lying on her breast; the thought of his unchanged love filled her with happiness and hope. What matter was anything else? She was going to him, going to look again upon his face, to clasp his hand in hers, and the weariness of the past months seemed suddenly to be turned to joy.

She reached London safely, and drove at once to King's Cross. Here she had some tea, and rested quietly in a lady's waiting room until it was time for her to start on her journey. She wore a thick gauze veil, but she did not need this, as she was alone in the carriage in which she traveled.

Every moment was bringing her nearer to him, she kept thinking, and she pictured to herself how he would look. Not as ill as when he lay wounded in South Kensington she prayed. All that time came back to her, when he had wrung her promise to marry him from her half unwilling lips; when she had been by his bedside; and she was going to it now.

On sped the train, but not fast enough for her. At last, as the dusk was beginning to spread its gray shadows over the landscape, they steamed into the station at Peterborough, and Eva alighted, and as she was running forward to see that her luggage was removed from the van, a tall man with blue spectacles and a heavy dark mustache and whiskers lightly touched her arm.

"Are you the lady for Hurstwood House?" he asked. "I am Dr. Page."

"Yes," answered Eva, who was trembling with excitement. "How is Lord Kilmore?"

"Very anxious to see you," replied Dr. Page. "What luggage have you, and I will get a porter to see after it; I have a carriage waiting outside the station?"

Upon this Eva described her belongings, and the porter soon found them.

"If you will come with me I will take you to the carriage," said Dr. Page, "unless you will take some refreshment first."

"Oh, no," answered Eva; and a few moments later she found herself in a carriage alone, as Dr. Page preferred to ride outside.

There were two horses in the carriage, and they started off at a fairly quick pace. But if Hurstwood House were only two miles from Peterborough they took a surprising time to traverse them. It was, in fact, almost quite dark before the carriage stopped before a gray, square, somewhat gloomy-looking house. Then Dr. Page dismounted and opened the carriage door and handed Eva out.

"Here we are," he said; "wait one moment until I open the door with my latch-key."

He did this, and Eva followed him up a short flight of stone steps to the front door of the house.

There was no light in the hall, although it was very dark, but Dr. Page put out his hand and took Eva's.

"This way," he said, "the servants have forgotten to light the lamp; but if you will come upstairs you will find a light and a fire there."

"Where is Lord Kilmore?" asked Eva in an agitated voice, as she began to ascend the staircase, guided by Dr. Page.

"Upstairs; I will take you to him presently, but come in here first, until I settle with the driver."

As he spoke he opened a sitting-room door on the first landing of the staircase and motioned Eva to enter. She did this, and found a large room with a good fire burning in the grate, but no other light.

"Just remain here a moment or two, and then I will return," said Dr. Page. "I will not be long."

Then he left her, and Eva looked nervously round. But she was under the same roof with Clair; in a few moments she would be with him, she whispered to her sinking heart. The few moments passed—a few more—and then she fancied she heard Dr. Page's returning footsteps. She was standing in front of the fire when the handle of the door turned softly, and an instant later she saw a man standing on the threshold.

It was not Dr. Page! The heavy dark mustache and whiskers were not there; the blue spectacles were gone. This man's face was clean-shaven and harsh; he was dressed as a clergyman.

In an instant, by the flickering firelight, Eva's wide-open, horror-stricken eyes took in these details. It was George Temple, her husband, and she knew, as she looked on his face, that she had been betrayed.

"Eva," he said, now speaking in his ordinary voice, and advancing into the room, "I see you recognize me."

She made no answer: her tongue seemed frozen in her mouth, her lips moved, but no sound came forth.

"All your artifices have been in vain," continued Mr. Temple; "the very man you trusted has betrayed your confidence, and at last you are where you always should have been, under your husband's roof."

As he spoke he drew nearer to her and moved his hand as if to lay it on her shoulder, but with a shudder Eva shrank back.

"Do not touch me!" she said hoarsely.

"You came to this house expecting to find your lover, I am well aware," went on Temple bitterly; "instead of which you have been brought here to return to your duty, and if you do this in a proper spirit I am willing to look over, if not to forget the past. I know your whole history, Eva; the shameful and bigamous marriage you contracted with Lord Kilmore; how you induced the banker—Ford—to deceive me and send me abroad to seek you, while you were in hiding at home. All this is known to me; but because to a certain extent I blame myself for having originally left you, left you before you were old enough to steer your course amid the temptations of the world, I am, as I said before, willing to take you back once more as my wife."

"Never!" said Eva in a low, emphatic voice.

"You have no choice," answered Temple calmly. "You have been brought here, and you shall be kept here, and you shall not be permitted to hold communication with anyone except I permit it. You are my wife, and though I could have you severely punished for your bigamous marriage, and Lord Kilmore also, I will not do this if you conduct yourself properly now that you return to me."

"George Temple," said Eva, looking at him steadily with her white and quivering face, "I have not returned to you, and I shall never return to you! I have been lured here by a shameful trick, but it shall avail you nothing! Do your worst; have me arrested for bigamy; but the vilest prison I could be placed in would not be so vile to me as willingly to touch your hand!"

"These heroics are all very fine, but do you know I could have you sent to penal servitude?"

"Send me; only never let me see your face."

"And what about Lord Kilmore?"

"You can't touch him; he married me believing me to be an unmarried girl. I deceived him—more my shame—but I will go into court and swear this, so you are powerless to injure him!"

"You defy me, then; here in this lonely house, miles and miles away from any other habitation?"

"I defy you, so God help me!"

"You appeal to God, whose laws you have broken."

"I have sinned and I have suffered. I married Lord Clair for the love I bore him, and I will be faithful to him now and always. I would rather be in prison with his memory than in a palace with you! Let me go—I will not stay under your roof!"

"You will, and shall," answered Temple with some passion, for he was stung by her taunts. "Here you are, and here you shall remain, and perhaps when next I see you, you may be more amenable to reason."

As he said these words he turned and left the room, and Eva sprang to the door to follow him, but he hastily closed it, and as she seized the handle to turn it she heard him lock the door outside.

CHAPTER XLIII.

THE HIDDEN KNIFE.

As the key turned in the lock, a chill pang of almost absolute despair darted through Eva's heart. She was a prisoner then: she had been trapped, and this was Mr. Ford's revenge. The whole situation flashed through her quick and vivid mind at once. She realized that the letter lying on her breast—Clair's letter—must have been one entrusted to Mr. Ford to deliver, and that he had suppressed it.

But one consolation remained to her—Clair still loved her. His long silence was now accounted for; his tender, impassioned words remained unanswered. What must he have thought? Eva repeated to herself. Their separation had been part of Mr. Ford's scheme, who, for his own vile motive, had not hesitated to break two hearts.

Eva stood by the locked door and thought all this; stood with her hand pressed on her breast, over the spot where Clair's letter lay hid. And now? Would he get her letter, go to her house in Brighton, and find her gone? She had left no address with the servants; the address to Hurstwood House was probably a fictitious one; part of Mr. Ford's scheme, and Dr. Page had no doubt been personated by George Temple.

"And I never suspected it—never dreamed it," moaned Eva; "I scarcely looked at him, and Clair's letter was the lure. I knew he must have written it; no one else could write it, and only in one way could it have fallen into their hands."

After a while she went back to the fire, for she was shivering as if with cold, and leaned on the mantel-piece, trying to think what she could do. Was there any chance of escape? She went to the window, and as she did so the memory of the fire at Holly Hill flashed through her brain, when Clair had lowered her from the window, and so saved her life.

Was there any chance of this now? She tried the window; she undid the clasp. It was nailed down. That precaution had been taken, and so this faint hope was gone. She returned again to the door and examined it; the bolt inside had been removed, the recent marks of a forcible removal were quite plain. She was locked in, but she could keep no one out, and Eva shuddered, and a deadly fear crept through her heart as she made the discovery.

"But I can kill myself," she said with set teeth, and a strange light gleaming in her eyes. "I shall die true to Clair."

Suddenly the thought then crossed her brain that there must be someone in the house beside George Temple. Some woman! If so, could she bribe her by a great sum to take one line, one word to Clair? This idea renewed some hope in her heart.

It gave her courage when about half an hour after she again heard someone outside the door. It opened, and George Temple appeared, followed by an elderly woman bearing a tray. He pointed to the woman to place the tray on the table, and light two candles that stood there.

"I don't mean to starve you, Eva," he said gravely, "though I fear you will find everything rather rough in this out-of-the-way spot. What will you take with your supper? Wine or brandy—I have both?"

In a moment it struck Eva that anything drinkable might be drugged, and she shook her head.

"I only drink water," she said.

"I should advise something stronger than water after your long journey and the excitement of once more finding yourself in your husband's company," answered George Temple still gravely; and then he looked at her fixedly as the woman kept laying the table for supper.

"You don't look as well as when I saw you last," he said slowly. "Have you been ill?"

"No," answered Eva, and a tinge of color passed over her pale face.

"Why don't you sit down?" continued Temple, still with his eyes fixed on her. "Here, sit in this chair," and he handed one to her as he spoke.

But Eva remained standing.

"Is the carriage gone that you brought me here in?" she said.

"Certainly it is gone," answered Temple harshly. "Eva, put all such folly out of your head as that you are going to leave here or me. I have brought you here, and here I mean you to remain. This is your husband's house, and I have taken it for a time; so you had better forget as quickly as possible all about your past life, and begin your new one with me."

"You know that is impossible," replied Eva, raising her dark eyes to his.

"On the contrary, I know it is possible; if I am willing to overlook the past you ought only to be too thankful for my leniency. You cannot deny you are my wife."

"I do not regard myself as such."

"You know you are, so there is an end of it. You will never again see Lord Kilmore, who shall be informed that you have returned to me, so I advise you to make the best of me."

Eva did not speak; she stood there facing this stern, harsh man who had made her young girlhood miserable, and his words that Lord Kilmore should be informed that she had returned to him struck like a knife into her heart. This was part of Mr. Ford's revenge then, she was thinking; he had betrayed her to Temple; recalled him to England; given him Clair's letter that he had suppressed; and now he was about to inform Clair that she had returned to her husband! But if Clair received her letter would he, could he believe this?

"Of what are you thinking?" asked Temple, with his hard, gray eyes fixed on her face.

"Did Mr. Ford give you my address at Brighton?" she asked.

"Certainly he did. Eva, I will make no subterfuges with you or act deceitfully, as you did to me. I am merely claiming my rights, and I was merely claiming my rights when you agreed to meet me that day in the street and then hid yourself away. The man you confided in, the banker, Mr. Ford, purposely deceived me, and led me to believe you were abroad. I went abroad to seek you, and last week I received a telegram from him recalling me to England. I returned. I went to the bank and saw Mr. Ford. He told me that by your request he had deceived me; that you were living at Brighton, and that last year you had formed a bigamous marriage with Lord Kilmore, who, however, was so indignant when he heard of your previous marriage to me that he had at once left you. He also told me that Lord Kilmore had brought a letter for you to him, after your separation, which he had not delivered, as he thought it better that all communication between you and Lord Kilmore should cease. He said you had wished this, and that he still had the letter, but that lately something had led him to believe that you intended renewing your acquaintance with this young lord, and that he had then thought it his duty to send for me."

"His duty!" repeated Eva with curling lip.

"I am merely repeating what he said, and not going into his motive at all. He told me you had confessed the truth about your former marriage to me, but that you had stated to him that you wished to keep your residence a secret alike from me and Lord Kilmore. He said he had weakly agreed to this, as you were afraid that I might prosecute you for bigamy; but that now, when you evidently had some idea of again seeing Lord Kilmore, he had sent for me as your lawful husband, and told me the truth."

"The liar—the miserable liar!" cried Eva in indignant passion. "So this was the garbled tale he told you was it? This! Would you like to hear the truth? It is true, then, that I was forced to go to this man when Lord Kilmore was informed by a friend of yours, Mr. Onslow, that I had already been married to you. Mr. Onslow married me to Lord Kilmore, who was then Lord Clair. This was before

I knew you were alive, before I met you that day, when I never thought to see you more! I believed myself free; you had left me, gone to Africa, and I had not heard of you for years. How could I tell you were living?"

"You made no inquiries?"

"I did not; I wished to believe you dead—to me you were dead—but I know I had no right to marry Lord Clair. But I did marry him, and after our marriage, through Mr. Onslow, he found out I had deceived him. He was very angry—justly angry—and he reproached me, so I left him. I went to Mr. Ford and told him the truth; I was obliged to go, because he held all my money, and I could not live without it, and unless I had told him not to tell where I was, either you or Lord Clair could easily, through him, have learned my address. I did not then wish again to see Lord Clair."

"And you have never seen him since you separated, nor heard from him?"

"I have not until to-day; until you enclosed the letter which that base man must have kept for months! And what do you think was his motive? His vile motive! He has deceived you and Lord Clair alike, and his motive was that on last Sunday evening he made a base proposal of love to me, and because I rejected him with contempt and dislike, his revenge has been that he has sent for you."

"Very possibly; but does not the conduct of this very man, Eva, prove to you how impossible it is for a young and pretty woman to live in the world without the protection of a husband? Mr. Ford may be a scoundrel—I have no doubt he is—but what naturally could he think of you, even judging you by your own confession to his ears?"

"I do not defend myself, but he took a very base advantage of my fault—"

"Your crime," interrupted Mr. Temple.

"My crime, then; call it as you will. He frightened me; he told me I might be sent to penal servitude—"

"So you can."

"I have told you to do your worst. Let me go from here to-night and I will wait to be arrested at the house in Brighton of which you now know the address."

"I do not mean to let you go from here, so such a proposition is useless. I repeat you are my wife, and as such I have a right to compel you to remain under my roof."

"You have no right to detain me against my will."

"You will find I have; but do not let us argue the subject further. Come and have some supper."

"How can you ask me to eat?" cried Eva, passionately.

"Because we must all eat if we go on living."

"I do not wish to live if I am to be a prisoner here!"

"Do not be childish;" and as he spoke he went to the table which the old woman had spread.

There was a cold fowl and some ham, and bread and other necessaries, and Mr. Temple began deliberately carving the fowl.

"Come to the table," he said a moment later, looking around at Eva.

She did not speak for a moment; her lips were parched with thirst, and she felt weak and faint.

"Can I have some tea?" she said at length.

"Yes, certainly," answered Mr. Temple, and he went to the door and outside rang a loud hand-bell.

"The woman downstairs is stone deaf," he said, "but she will surely hear that."

As he was ringing the bell with his back toward her, Eva suddenly crossed the room and went up to the table, and in an instant, before he could turn his head, she had snatched up a knife that was lying near a plate, and had hidden it in the pocket of her dress. She was so quick that Mr. Temple never suspected her action.

He looked around, saw her standing by the table, and then went on ringing the bell.

Presently the old woman came upstairs, and he shouted an order for some tea in her ear. Then he went back to the table and pressed Eva to eat something; but she could not.

"I am so thirsty," she said.

"The tea will be here directly, and then you must try," he answered.

When the tea came, Eva drank some eagerly; it relieved her a little, and then she tried to eat something.

"Your bedroom is ready for you, upstairs," said Mr. Temple, "and as you look exceedingly tired, I advise you to go to bed early."

Eva indeed felt that it would be almost impossible for her to sit up any longer. She was quite worn out with the excitement she had gone through. She therefore expressed her willingness to go to her bedroom, and Mr. Temple lit a candle to show her the way.

"Walk before me," he said, "and I will light you up."

So Eva went up another flight of steps, and came to a fairly well furnished bedroom, where there was a fire burning, and Mr. Temple indicated to her that this was to be her room.

He went into it with her, and looked around as he did so.

"I hope there is everything you want?" he said.

The luggage that she had brought with her was standing in it, but the straps of her two trunks were not unfastened.

"Shall I unfasten the straps for you?" he asked when he observed this.

"No, thank you," answered Eva.

"Then I will say good night to you. Good night, and I hope you will sleep well."

"Good night," said Eva, and then Mr. Temple nodded and left the room, carefully locking the door outside behind him.

The moment he was gone, Eva did as she had done in the room below. She went to the door and examined it. The inside bolt had been recently removed here also, and this room had evidently, too, been prepared for her reception.

There are moments in our lives when no words can describe the despair which overwhelms our souls.

One of these dark moods now swept over Eva. In this lonely house, at the mercy of this hard, harsh man, what was she to expect? She moaned aloud, but the next moment grasped the handle of the knife she had hidden in her dress.

"I can die," she murmured to herself. She sat there and tried to think what such a death would be. A sharp pang; then she would faint, would bleed to death, and it would be all over. And Clair would never know!

She flung herself on her knees and prayed.

"I am a sinner!" she cried; "but Thou who died for sinners do not leave me now! Protect me; have mercy on me, and show me some way of escape which now I cannot see!"

Long she knelt there, and some strength came back to her as she did so. She rose from her knees and dragged the table which stood in the center of the room and placed it against the door. Then she put two chairs also against it, and on these she placed her two trunks. No one could now open the door without overturning these, and having done this, she made up her mind to lie down and rest.

She did not undress; she left the candles burning, and she put the table knife beneath her pillow.

And thus, with Clair's letter on her breast, she fell asleep; fell into a deep, dreamless sleep from which she only awoke when the pale spring dawn of another day was spreading over the world.

<hr>

CHAPTER XLIV.

A GREAT SHOCK.

The letter which Eva had written to Kilmore after her interview with Mr. Ford—the letter in which she recalled him to her side, and told him that if she lived there would ere long be a new tie between them, was duly delivered at Kilmore Hall.

It was then forwarded by Lady Kilmore to her son at Vienna, at which city he was then sojourning, not without more than one restless sigh and uneasy glance at the superscription.

But it never crossed Lady Kilmore's mind one moment to suppress it. She had hoped, she had prayed that the unhappy entanglement, as she always mentally thought of it, between her son and the girl whom she deemed so unsuitable for his position, was ended. That it had cost Kilmore bitter pain she knew, and still she had trusted time would heal the wound. If this letter were from Eva, as she feared, it might renew a dangerous intimacy. But still it was Kilmore's letter, and he had a right to receive it, and he did.

He received it with absolute and unbounded joy. In a moment all life seemed to change to him. His darling was longing to see him again; he was to go back to her. Whatever happened, he would look once more on her dear face.

Half an hour after he had read Eva's letter he started on his journey to England; started full of hope, and with a heart brimful of tender emotions. He would take her away, he told himself; take her to some land where her life would be unmolested; where the shadow of her unhappy past could never reach her. And as he read and re-read her letter, a first suspicion regarding the banker—Mr. Ford—entered his mind.

Had he been deceiving him? Had he really delivered the letter to Eva, which as we know she had only now received? And yet what motive could the man have? Kilmore asked himself. At all events he would soon know, and journeying day and night he hastened home.

He did not stop in town nor telegraph to Eva that he had arrived. He went straight down to Brighton, and having arrived there, drove with a beating heart to the retired house where she had told him she had spent such weary months.

He sprang from his cab and rang the door-bell, which was promptly opened by a respectable-looking waiting-maid. Eva had told him in her letter to ask for Mrs. Scott, as that was the name she had borne in Brighton, and accordingly, in a faltering voice, Kilmore inquired if Mrs. Scott were at home.

"No, sir," answered the waiting-maid, "she left yesterday afternoon."

"Left yesterday afternoon!" repeated Kilmore, utterly astonished. "Where did she go?"

"She did not give us the address, sir, but she said she would write as soon as she reached where she was going."

"And did she leave no letter, no message for me?"

"She left no letters nor messages, sir, for anyone."

Kilmore grew absolutely pale. He stood there staring at the maid and trying to think what could be Eva's motive. She herself had recalled him; she herself had written that if she lived there would soon be a tie between them that would bind them closer. Yet she had gone without a word; gone when she must have known that he was hastening to her side!

"Did she give any motive for going away?" at last he asked.

"Yes, sir; she said one of her relations had met with an accident," replied the maid.

"An accident?" repeated Kilmore blankly. "And did she say anything about the time of her return?"

"She said she was not sure when she would be back, but that she would let us know."

"And you have no idea where she went?"

"She went to London from here, sir, but I don't know where after that."

"It is most extraordinary; she expected me—she invited me to come."

"Well, sir, she was called away quite on a sudden; a letter came for her by the twelve post yesterday, and she began to pack up at once, after going out with a telegram; and she gave the cook and me money to live on, and then she started."

"And did she seem distressed?"

"No, sir, she didn't; she seemed lighter-hearted than I have seen her for long, and she seemed as if she couldn't get quick enough away."

Kilmore naturally could not understand it. There must be some mystery he was thinking. Could she have gone away under some misrepresentation—been lured away? And he naturally thought of George Temple.

"Did anyone come here?" he asked. "Any gentleman?"

"Only Mr. Ford, sir; all the time I have been with missus she had no visitors but Mr. Ford. She lives very quiet, as her husband's away."

"And Mr. Ford came?"

"Yes, very often, sir; mostly at the week ends, on Saturdays and Sundays."

"Can I go in and write a note to your mistress?" asked Kilmore, after a few moments' consideration.

"Yes, sir, if you are a friend of missus, you can," said the waiting-maid, and she showed Kilmore into Eva's little drawing-room.

He stood and looked round as he entered it, and a strange dimness stole over his eyes. What! she had lived here in her loneliness, he was thinking, month after month. His darling—and now he had come to find her gone. Her portrait was standing on the mantel-piece, a duplicate of which he had kissed a hundred times. He had carried it about with him in his wanderings; he knew every line of the fair face. And where was she?

A great anxiety stole into his mind; something must have happened to her he felt almost certain, and his hands trembled as he sat down before the little bamboo writing table in the window, where Eva must have sat when she wrote her last words to him.

On the blotting pad he saw his old name reversed. "Clair, my Clair!" he read. He took up the pen her little hand had held, and silently pressed it to his lips. Somehow he seemed to feel her presence near him. "Clair, my Clair!" she seemed to whisper, and then he remembered what she had written when they parted at Westwold:

"I shall never see you again until my spirit calls you to come, and then if it does you will know I am in some desperate need!"

Was she now in some desperate need? Kilmore asked himself with sinking heart. And where could he find her—where go to her help? He must find her! He looked round and saw the maid watching him with rather an alarmed look on her face.

"I want you to do something for me," he said, and he rose and put two sovereigns in her hand. "I expected to find your mistress here, and I am greatly disappointed that she is not; in fact, I am alarmed, and I will leave a note for her with you, and if you hear from her will you telegraph to me at once? This is my address," and he placed one of his visiting cards in her hand.

The maid courtesied low when she read his name.

"Did you ever hear your mistress mention me?" he asked.

"No, my lord, but she spoke very little," she answered. "Cook and me always thought she was grieving over something she did not talk about."

"And did she seem in good health?"

"Not very, I think, my lord."

"Be sure you telegraph to me when you hear from her, and you shall be handsomely rewarded for your trouble. Now I will write my letter."

And again he sat down to the writing-table.

"My dearest, dearest Eva," he wrote; "I received your letter at Vienna, and started at once to come to you when I did so. I arrived here to-day, and to my bitter disappointment and dismay learnt that you had left Brighton yesterday. How is this, Eva? I am writing this in your house, as your maid tells me you left no address, and I am in great distress and anxiety about you. I entreat you to let me hear from you at once, and I will come to you wherever you are. If you receive this, telegraph to me immediately at Kilmore; and believe me to remain always devotedly yours,

"Kilmore."

He placed this letter in an envelope and sealed it, and entrusted it to the maid, and again and again impressed upon her that if she heard from her mistress she had at once to telegraph to him. He even wrote his address on a telegraph form, and instructed her how to fill it in. Then feeling in a most unhappy state of mind, he determined to return to town and see Mr. Ford.

"He may know something," he thought. "It is very odd why he should go so often to see Eva; the whole thing is a mystery I cannot understand."

His return journey to town was a very miserable one. He had gone to Brighton so full of hope and happiness, and he went back racked with anxiety and fear. He drove direct to the city when he arrived in town, and just as his cab stopped before the banking establishment of Ford & Ford, Mr. James Ford himself was coming out of the entrance. He looked up and saw Kilmore and instantly recognized him, and Kilmore fancied he did not look over-pleased to do so.

"Can I speak to you, Mr. Ford?" said Kilmore.

"Certainly, Lord Kilmore," answered the banker. "Will you return with me to my private room in the bank? You have been abroad, I hear?"

"Yes, for some time."

"What a pleasant change. I have been at the old grind all the winter; but I think I must take a holiday now."

By this time they had reached the banker's private room, and as they entered it Mr. Ford, who did not look as well as usual, Kilmore noticed, closed the door and pointed politely to a chair.

"Won't you sit down, Lord Kilmore?" he said. "And now what can I do for you?"

"I have come to ask you the old question, Mr. Ford," answered Kilmore with agitation. "Can you tell me anything of Miss Eva Moore?"

For a moment the banker hesitated, and a curious change passed over his face.

"A very odd thing has happened," he said at length.

"About Miss Moore?" asked Kilmore quickly.

"About the lady who was Miss Eva Moore at least; but women are unaccountable creatures."

"What has happened?"

"Miss Eva Moore has gone back to her husband, the Rev. George Temple."

"I will never believe it! I do not believe it!" cried Kilmore, and he grew deadly pale.

"It is nevertheless a fact; I have it on the authority of the husband himself."

"Nothing will induce me to believe it," answered Kilmore in extreme agitation. "There is some treachery about this, Mr. Ford; some deceit I mean to discover."

Mr. Ford slightly shrugged his shoulders.

"I cannot account for it, certainly," he said; "yet it is absolutely so."

"But how do you know? How have you heard such an incredible thing?"

"Simply as I told you; from Mr. Temple himself."

"Did he write?"

"No, he telegraphed."

"From where, and when?"

"You must pardon me, Lord Kilmore, but I cannot answer your question."

"But why, Mr. Ford?" said Kilmore with darkling brow and quivering lips.

"Because it would only do harm, not good, for you to interfere between husband and wife."

"This is folly!" cried Kilmore passionately, beginning to pace the floor with uneven steps. "I have a right to know —because Eva in her youth, in her young girlhood, was induced by this man—a man she hates—to commit an act of folly; is her whole life to be thrown away?"

"The law says so, Lord Kilmore."

"I will never believe that she has returned to him; willingly returned to him," continued Kilmore in increasing excitement. "Only three days ago I received a letter recalling me to her side! I went to Brighton to-day, to the address she gave me, and found her gone!"

"So she wrote to you?" said Mr. Ford, and a slight flush rose to his face.

"Yes, she wrote—and, Mr. Ford, I ask you as a gentleman to tell me the truth? In this letter she made no mention of the letter I sent her through you—and yet—but I suppose she received it?"

Mr. Ford's color deepened, and his eyes shifted, but still he continued to answer quietly enough.

"Yes, she certainly received it."

"She did not allude to it in the letter she wrote, but, Mr. Ford, I must find her! I have, I believe, the strongest reason that a man can have. Give me, at least, Mr. Temple's address."

"Lord Kilmore, I cannot," answered Mr. Ford hoarsely, and he turned away his head.

"What motive have you for keeping it a secret? Do not say anything more about it being right or wrong; whether I act rightly or wrongly is nothing to you."

"I will have nothing to do with it," said the banker, still in that hoarse, changed voice.

"Then I believe that you are concerned in the plot—that this is some plot! If you have betrayed this poor girl to this man, Mr. Ford, all I can say is you shall bitterly repent it."

"Do you threaten me, Lord Kilmore?" asked the banker, trying to recover his usual manner.

"Yes, I do! I believe you are deceiving me; I believe Eva has been deceived by some vile plot that you and this Temple have concocted between you, and that it is a lie that she has gone back to him."

"Really, Lord Kilmore, I must request you to leave the room. I am sorry for your disappointment, but I cannot control the vagaries of women."

"Did you tell her I was about to be married?" asked Kilmore fiercely. "Her maid told me that no one went to her house but you, and if you were her informant about my marriage you must have known it was utterly untrue."

"I am not aware that I was her informant."

"Yet she wrote to me that she had heard it!" cried Kilmore passionately. "She did not believe it—thank God for that!"

"Then it is not true?"

"No, certainly not."

"I confess I heard such a rumor, and I may have mentioned it to her, and perhaps this accounts for her returning to Mr. Temple?"

"No! this does not account for it; nothing accounts for it. Mr. Ford, do you positively refuse to give me Mr. Temple's address?"

"I positively refuse, Lord Kilmore."

"Then I shall discover it; I shall set the police to work."

As he spoke these words Kilmore turned and left the banker's room without any salutation, and Mr. Ford frowned as he did so.

"I was a fool to interfere," he was thinking, and as he stood listening to Kilmore's departing footsteps his reflections were far from pleasant ones.

As for Kilmore, he left the bank in a state of mind scarcely to be described. He was convinced now that for some purpose or other which he did not know, Mr. Ford had formerly deceived him. He must have some motive now also for suppressing Temple's address.

First he thought of putting the affair in the hands of the police, but afterward remembered he really had no charge to bring against Temple. He knew nothing of him, in fact.

Then he remembered Mr. Onslow, the clergyman at South Kensington, who had married him to Eva. He would go to him, and from him might find some clue to Temple's present abode.

But of one thing he felt sure; Mr. Ford's story was a lie, and not willingly had Eva returned to her husband's house, if she actually were there.

CHAPTER XLV.

A VAIN APPEAL.

It was the early morning when Eva first roused herself from the heavy sleep brought on by bodily fatigue and weariness; and in a moment, with a swift pang of pain, all that had happened yesterday rushed across her mind.

She sat up and put her hand to her brow, and looked at her strange surroundings. Then she glanced at the little jeweled watch on her wrist—Clair's gift—and saw it was not yet five o'clock. After a few moments she rose and went to the window, and drew up the blind and looked at the outside world.

A strange and dreary scene! Hurstwood House stood in a neglected garden, where tall grass and thistles flourished, and where the walks were overgrown and green. No hand had apparently touched them for years, no footprint fallen on the tangled weeds. It was partly surrounded by an untrimmed tall yew hedge, which added not a little to its gloomy appearance. Beyond the garden a wild track of moorland appeared to stretch, and no house or hamlet was visible from the window where Eva stood.

"What a lonely, desolate spot," she thought with a shudder, and then she looked at the fastenings of the window. It was nailed down like the one downstairs, but the room was so far from the ground that had it not been so to escape by it would have been impossible.

With something between a shiver and a sigh she returned to bed. She lay there full of gloomy thoughts. Lay until eight o'clock, and then she heard a heavy footstep outside the room door and a moment later the key in the lock turned.

The table she had placed against the door, however, obstructed the intruder's entrance. Then came an angry exclamation, a push, and one of the chairs was overturned, and the trunk on it came tumbling to the floor.

Another push, and in the now half-open doorway Mr. Temple appeared.

"What folly is this, Eva?" he said, harshly.

By this time Eva had sprung out of bed, had hidden the knife which had lain under her pillow during the night in the pocket of her dress, and now stood facing the half-open door.

"How absurd!" continued Mr. Temple, pushing the table away with one hand and forcing open the door with the other. "May I ask why you have barricaded yourself in this fashion?"

"There is no bolt to the door inside," answered Eva.

"There is no occasion for any bolt. Please end all this folly, Eva."

She did not speak.

"Well, how have you slept?" he went on, looking at her. "You look pale, but better than you did last night."

"I slept fairly well," replied Eva coldly.

"That is all right. Will you come down to breakfast or have it here?"

"A prisoner has no choice," said Eva, and she turned away and went to the window, and pushed away the blind and looked out on the deserted scene below.

Mr. Temple did not speak for a moment, and then he crossed the room and laid his hand heavily on her shoulder.

"Don't touch me!" cried Eva, shrinking back.

"Listen to me, Eva," said Mr. Temple; "it depends on yourself, on your own conduct, whether you are a prisoner or not. If you will return to your duty, and act as a wife should act, you shall be no prisoner even in spite of the past. But if you continue this perverse conduct then you shall certainly remain under lock and key, and I will take good care to give you no chance of escape."

"How dare you act thus?" said Eva, turning round and facing him.

"There is no daring about it; I have simply brought you to your husband's house and I mean to keep you there. Say nothing more," he continued, raising his hand as Eva was about to speak. "I have told you my resolve, and nothing will move me from it, and your wisest course is to make the best of the situation. But now I will go and see about your breakfast."

"I do not want any."

"Oh, yes you do. It will be ready presently, and if you prefer it here I will bring it up."

Eva made no reply to this, and then Mr. Temple left the room, locking the door behind him, and Eva was once more alone. She bathed her face after he had gone, and smoothed her hair, and then sat wearily down.

"What am I to do? Oh! what am I to do?" she moaned out in her despair. "Is there no rescue for me? If Clair only knew—"

"Oh! Clair, Clair!" she cried out aloud, "come to me, come to me!"

She also at this moment remembered the words of her letter to him when they had parted. "I am in desperate need now," she murmured; "Clair, do you hear me call?"

The key turned again in the door and she started to her feet. It was Mr. Temple, carrying a tray on which was Eva's breakfast.

"You see what an attentive husband I am," he said a little grimly as he placed the tray on the table.

Eva did not speak.

"If you want any more tea, ring," he said; "here is the bell."

Still Eva said nothing.

"Now I will leave you to get my own breakfast," continued Temple, "and afterward I will come up to take you to the sitting-room downstairs if you like to go."

After this he went away, again taking good care to lock Eva in. She was thirsty and she drank some tea, but she did not ring for more, and in about an hour Mr. Temple once more appeared.

"You had better come downstairs now," he said.

Then she made another appeal to him.

"Oh! let me go!" she said piteously; "please don't torment me any more! What good will it do you? If you want my money you can take it—you can take it all—only let me go!"

"And allow you to return and live in sin with Lord Kilmore? No, Eva, I will not let you go. I don't want your money, I want you, and I have got you, and here you shall stay."

She moaned and fell with her head on the bed, and there was a choking sensation of unshed tears in her throat.

"You are cruel—cruel!" she murmured.

"No, I am not cruel," answered Mr. Temple. "I was cruel long ago when I left you, a wayward, untried girl, to the tender mercies of the world. You fell, and I have only myself to blame for it. You irritated me in those days to such a degree that the love and regard for you that I had at one time seemed utterly gone. I told myself we had both made a terrible mistake; that it was no use any longer utterly spoiling two lives. We parted by mutual consent, and let me tell you I had enough trust in you even then to believe that you would never dream of marrying anyone else during my lifetime. Then, as I told you, years and loneliness softened my feelings toward you. I remember one night in Africa, when the moon was shedding its light on the wild and lonely plain lying before me, that I first felt compunctions of conscience concerning you. I had not done my duty to you, an inward voice seemed to tell me, and I listened to that voice. I had bound myself before God's altar to protect and cherish you, and how had I done this? I had allowed you to return to your uncle in India, as I then believed, to enter the anything but strict society of that country, bearing your maiden name. This was neither just to you nor myself. I did not act hastily; after due consideration I determined to return to England, and if I did not find you there to go to India to claim you."

"It was somewhat late in the day," said Eva bitterly, raising her head from the bed.

"Have I not told you that I blame myself? I sinned in leaving you, and allowing you to leave me, and I have been terribly punished for it."

"And what do you think it is to me?" cried Eva passionately. "To me, married to the man I love, whom I shall always love! Make no mistake; nothing can change what has been, nothing will change it! You may keep me here till I die, but when I die I shall still love my Clair!"

"You only make things worse by your folly," said Mr. Temple coldly. "Lord Clair, or Kilmore, or whatever his title, is not your husband, and I am. You shall stay here and live with me as my wife, and as I told you before, you had better make the best of the situation."

Eva impatiently turned away her head.

"It is useless to speak to you," she said.

"On this subject it is useless, so please do not renew it. But you had better come downstairs to the sitting-room, and you will find some books there to help to amuse you."

Eva made no reply to this proposition. It flashed across her mind at this moment—would she have more chance of escape downstairs?

"Are you coming?" asked Mr. Temple, after a moment's pause, "or shall I lock you up here?"

"I will go," said Eva, rising, and she went. He took her hand as if to lead her downstairs, but Eva pulled it away. "I will follow you," she added, and she did, looking curiously around her as she descended the staircase. There was but one flight of stairs, she observed, from the hall to the sitting-room. She glanced over the bannisters and could see the hall door from where she was.

When they got to the landing Mr. Temple stopped and

motioned to Eva to enter the sitting-room first. This she did, and he followed, closing the door after him. Then he placed an easy chair by the fire for her.

"It is a cold, gusty day," he said; "here are some books and a yesterday's paper. The books are not trashy novels which fill the heads of foolish young women with absurd ideas of life and religion. A religious novel I consider absolutely blasphemous, written as they usually are by half-educated women who air their ideas on the Creator and His Laws with the coolest audacity. But here is a book on the mammalia of Africa that I think you will find interesting."

He handed her the book as he spoke, and Eva let it lie unopened on her knee.

"Have you not a to-day's newspaper?" she asked.

She said this with a purpose; she wanted to know what communication he held with the outside world.

"No," he answered, "I have none; and I have no one here to send for one."

Eva said nothing more; she got up listlessly, went to the window, and stood looking out on the deserted garden below. Both the rooms she had been in were evidently at the back of the house, and the cloudy sky above made the whole scene inexpressibly dreary. She sighed heavily, and then went back to the fire, and found that Mr. Temple had seated himself before a writing desk, and was writing industriously. She heard the faint sound of his pen, which never ceased, and saw him turn over page after page of MS. A sort of drowsiness then began to creep over her with the heat of the fire and the stillness. Fainter grew the sound of the pen; her head fell to one side, and presently she was asleep.

After sitting about an hour with bent head at his work without looking up, Mr. Temple did glance in Eva's direction and her attitude made him rise softly and approach her. Then he saw she was sleeping, and something in her drooped head, in her girlish loveliness, touched some almost forgotten chord in his cold heart. A feeling of pity for her awoke there, and he stood looking at her with softened eyes.

"Poor child," he was thinking; "poor misguided child."

He really believed that he was acting rightly to Eva; that he was doing his best to save her soul from eternal damnation. He was a man of narrow creeds and dogmas, with small pity for the faults and failings of those weaker than himself. In their early married days he had sternly tried to bow her will to his own, and thus utterly alienated the affection, or rather the delusion with which she had regarded him before their marriage. She had believed him to be a good man, self-denying, holy, and she had found him a tyrant.

She rebelled, refused to be coerced, and after many bitter quarrels they had agreed to separate and keep their secret marriage a secret still. He stood thinking of this time as he watched her sleeping. Then, suddenly and with a start, Eva awoke, and looking up, saw him standing before her.

"You have been asleep," said Mr. Temple in a more gentle tone than he had yet spoken to her in.

"Yes, half-asleep," said Eva, rubbing her eyes.

"You had better try to go to sleep again," said Mr. Temple with a half-smile.

But no; Eva roused herself up and began opening the pages of the book still lying on a table near her on the mammalia of Africa; and Mr. Temple returned to his writing, and so the weary hours wore on.

CHAPTER XLVI.

TRAPPED.

The day grew worse, and at mid-day it amounted almost to a storm. Fierce gusts of wind swept around the house, and the rain kept dashing against the window-panes. The deaf old woman brought up the early dinner at two o'clock, and Mr. Temple pressed her to eat and drink, but she had no appetite.

She felt bodily ill, and worn out with weakness and depression. After dinner she went upstairs, and Mr. Temple followed her up and locked her in.

"You had better lie down and have a little rest," he said as he quitted the room.

She was so weary that she took his advice; she lay
down on the outside of the bed, after first placing the table
against the door, and in spite of the wind and rain outside
she was soon fast asleep.

About four o'clock a ring at the outer door of the house
awoke her. She started to her feet; she listened intently.

"Had help come?" she was asking herself with a fast-
beating heart.

But no; she heard the door open and shut, but no further sound. It was, in fact, the country postman who had
called, and when Mr. Temple opened the door, as the old
woman in the kitchen had not heard the bell, the postman
delivered a letter into his hand addressed to himself.

He opened it hastily in the hall, and as he did so an
ominous frown contracted his brow. It was from Mr. Ford,
and was very brief.

"Dear Mr. Temple,"—(he read)—"I think it only right
to inform you that the young lord of whom we spoke, called
here to-day, and was most urgent in his inquiries about a
certain lady. It seems that she had written to him when
he was abroad, and he came to England for the purpose of
seeing her, and went to the address in Brighton that you
know of, and found her gone. I told him the lady had returned to her husband, which statement he refused to believe, and he was extremely impertinent to me when I declined to give him your address. He left declaring he would
put the affair in the hands of the police, and I advise you to
be most careful about her guardianship and to allow her to
have no opportunity of correspondence with the young
lord. Excuse me for giving you this hint.
    "And I remain, Rev. Sir,
        "Yours faithfully,
           "J. Ford."

A dusky flush rose to Mr. Temple's dark skin as he read
and re-read this letter, and the softer feelings that he had felt
for Eva during the morning died out suddenly in his
heart.

"She had written to call him back then," he thought bitterly; "but she shall never see him more."

Still this letter disturbed him greatly, and he did not go
near Eva for many hours after it arrived. Then as it grew

dusk he remembered that she had had no tea, and was shut up in a room without a fire on a cold and stormy day. He therefore ordered up tea and supper together, and when the deaf old woman had arranged this meal he went up to seek Eva.

He found her sitting by the window in the semi-darkness watching the storm. Unconsciously his voice was harsher when he spoke to her.

"Tea is ready; you had better come downstairs," he said.

"Very well," answered Eva, and she rose and followed him downstairs.

He poured out some tea for her, which she drank, but he was in a very silent and gloomy mood. He did not speak of Mr. Ford's letter to Eva, but it was rankling in his mind during the whole meal.

Then it grew quite dark; the old woman came into the room, lit the candles, and carried away the tray, and retired to her kitchen downstairs. Mr. Temple sat down to his writing silently, and Eva listlessly took up her book.

By this time it was absolutely blowing a hurricane, and Eva suddenly looked up from her book and addressed Mr. Temple.

"I believe the glass of that window will be blown in," she said. "Are there no shutters?"

"I don't know. I will see," answered Mr. Temple, and he rose and went to the window. "There are shutters," he added, "and I will fasten them."

He was in the act of doing this, the storm outside deadening every noise, when swift as a flash of lightning Eva rose and fled to the room door.

In a moment she had crossed the threshold, in a moment turned the key in the lock outside, and with it in her hand ran hastily downstairs after locking Mr. Temple in!

He looked round as he clasped the bar of the shutter, and saw she was gone. An angry exclamation burst from his lips, he sprang across the room, he reached the door, and found it locked. He had fallen into his own trap; he had always left the key outside, and the lock was a new one, put there for the purpose of guarding Eva. Now he shook the door in vain; he swore, he cursed, but there was no one to hear him.

The deaf old woman was asleep in her kitchen; the

hand-bell was outside, and the bell-wire in the room was broken.

Mr. Temple felt like a wild beast newly caged. He dashed himself against the door; he tried to break it open with the furniture and the poker, but it resisted all his efforts. There he was a prisoner himself, and the woman he had trapped was no doubt escaping from the power which he had so securely reckoned on. A perfect tempest of rage swept over him. This ordinarily cold, sedate man was shaken by a blast of passion and rage which utterly overwhelmed him. He shouted, he cursed, but the howling tempest outside was the only sound which reached his maddened ears.

* * * * * * * *

In the meanwhile Eva had rushed downstairs like a creature flying for life. She reached the hall; in a moment she saw the key was in the lock inside the door, for a small oil lamp was burning on the passage table. She turned the lock easily, opened the door, and the fierce wind and rain rushed in and beat on her face. It took away her breath, and she glanced round to seek some protection from the storm. On a peg of the umbrella stand in the hall a woolen shawl was hanging; a brown, checked shawl, such as are often worn by country women. She caught hold of this, wrapped it round her head, and then ran out into the wild night.

She closed the house door after her as she went, and still grasping the key of the room in which she had locked Mr. Temple, she stood a moment peering round her in the darkness, wondering which way to go. As far as she could see the house stood apparently in a lane, and after a brief hesitation she fled down this as fast as her trembling feet could carry her.

But this roadway was apparently but of short length, and amid the blinding rain and howling wind, Eva soon found herself on a barren tract of moorland.

Not a light was to be seen; in darkness above and around she ran on, on, never for a moment pausing to take breath. She was flying for something dearer than life, flying for shelter anywhere from the man she dreaded more than death.

Suddenly her feet struck on a block of stone, and she stumbled and fell. She arose quickly, but an acute bodily pang ran through her frame as she did so, and a deadly faintness crept over her. But presently it passed off, and again she commenced her wild flight. She knew not how long she ran, or where she went, but she became conscious that her powers were becoming exhausted. Again that sharp pain passed through her; again the cold dew broke out on her brow.

"Oh! God, help me, help me!" she prayed in her anguish, looking up to the darkling sky.

But the wind and the rain swept on, and a great fear came over her. She felt she could scarcely any longer drag on her weary, pain-racked limbs, and that soon she would be forced to lie down on the sodden grass. Again she looked up in wild appeal; again lifted her arms to ask for help; and as she did so—even as her lips opened and her cry went forth to God—a light shone before her; a light from the window of a cottage standing on the edge of the desolate moorland.

The welcome gleam seemed to give her new life. On, on, she went, tottering, swaying, but still creeping nearer to the light. At last she reached the house from which it shone. There was a little railed-in garden in front, and the light came from one of the lower windows. She undid the latch of the garden gate and went up the neat graveled walk. Then she rapped at the knocker on the door, and a few moments later it was opened, and by the passage lamp within Eva saw a grave-faced young man in the dress of a clergyman standing before her.

"For God's sake give me shelter!" she gasped forth.

The young man looked at her with his serious eyes and bowed his head.

"I will give you shelter," he said. "Come in; it is a wild night."

Then Eva entered, and he closed the door behind her and led her into a small room at one side of the passage, in which a lamp was lit and a fire burning.

"Will you sit down? You are terribly wet," he said, looking at her pityingly.

With a moan Eva sat down on the easy chair he had placed for her by the fire as he spoke: a moan wrung from her pale lips by bodily anguish, and the young clergyman thought she was about to faint.

He therefore hastily unlocked a closet and drew out a

bottle containing brandy, and then went to the small sideboard and poured some in a glass with water and handed it to Eva.

"Drink this," he said, "it will revive you," and he held the glass to her quivering lips.

Eva did drink it, and then with a strange, sobbing sigh she looked up at the kind young face bending over her.

"Is there any woman in the house?" she asked in piteous accents.

"Yes, my sister is in the house," answered the clergyman; "she has just gone up to bed; I will bring her to you."

He left the room as he spoke, and a few minutes later a lady some years older than himself returned with him.

The lady then went up to Eva and put her hand on the rough wet shawl, which was still wrapped round her head.

"How wet you are," she said gently; "let me take off this shawl and your shoes and stockings, and get you some dry clothes?"

She removed the shawl from Eva's head as she spoke, and Eva's long beautiful light brown hair became unloosed as she did so and fell in rippling beauty on her shoulders. The lady noticed also the rich silk dress which Eva wore, and which she had traveled from Brighton in, and the small, once daintily embroidered slippers in which her little feet were clad. She pulled these off and the wet silk stockings, and then began chafing Eva's wet feet with some brandy.

"You are quite exhausted," she said pitifully. "Have you walked far? You seem in great pain?"

Eva raised her large dark eyes to the lady's face, and then bent down and whispered a word in her ear, and as she did so the lady slightly started, and a faint flush rose on her cheeks.

"Is this your brother?" then said Eva, looking round at the young clergyman.

"Yes," answered the lady, "this is my brother, the Rev. John Walton, and he is curate of the parish here."

"Can I do anything for you?" asked Mr. Walton, now stepping forward.

"Yes," answered Eva, in a faint, low, but still steady tone. "Will you send three telegrams for me?"

"Most certainly; but I cannot send them to-night, it is too late."

"But you can take them down," said Eva; "I may be too ill to-morrow to dictate them. I want three telegrams sent to one person—the Earl of Kilmore. I am not sure of his address, but I want to call him to my side—he must come at once."

The brother and sister looked at each other as Eva spoke, and then Miss Walton faintly sighed.

"Send one to Kilmore Hall," went on Eva, still steadily, "and another to Brighton, and the third to his club in town. He is sure to get one. How soon can you send them in the morning?"

"I will ride into Peterborough with them early to-morrow," answered the curate. "Will you give me the addresses now, and dictate what you wish telegraphed?"

Upon this Eva gave the three addresses quite plainly, though her twitching face told all the while she was suffering great pain, and then she dictated the words of the telegram.

"Come at once when you get this, Clair; I am lying here in desperate need. The clergyman who is sending this, and who has given me shelter, will telegraph to you where to come to; but do not delay.

"Eva."

"And you wish this sent to Lord Kilmore?" asked Mr. Walton, looking up after he had written down Eva's words.

"I do. I cannot thank you, sir, but give me shelter till he comes," answered Eva, with her eyes fixed on his grave, earnest face.

"You are most welcome to shelter, and to any service I can render you," said the young clergyman. "And my sister will, I am sure, do all she can for you."

"God bless you both," murmured Eva in a broken voice; "I—I—was married to Lord Kilmore—I must see him before I die."

Again the brother and sister exchanged pitying glances, and then Miss Walton spoke in her gentle, yet decided, way.

"My brother will see after your telegrams first thing in

the morning," she said; "and now let me help you up-stairs.   I am sure you would be better if you were in bed."

She raised Eva up from the chair that she was sitting on as she spoke, and Eva moaned as she did so; and then Miss Walton helped to lead her from the room, and the curate returned once more to the work on theology he had been studying when she first rapped at his door; but his attention constantly wandered from his book.

"An extraordinary story," he was thinking, his mind dwelling on the stranger beneath his roof. "A sad history, I fear. She said she was married to this lord—well, it may be so."

About a quarter of an hour passed thus, and then once more Miss Walton entered the room, looking very grave.

"Jack," she said, addressing her brother, "you must go for the doctor at once; the poor thing upstairs is very ill. I fear a baby is coming!"

"Good heavens!" cried the curate, starting to his feet.

"Put on your thick cloak," continued Miss Walton, "and tie a comforter round your neck, for it is a dreadful night. But we must have a doctor; give Dr. Munro this slip of paper. I have written to tell him what is the matter, and you must bring him back with you. I fear it's a very bad business."

"I will go at once," answered the young clergyman. "Poor soul! where can she have come from; she might have died alone on the moor."

"She said she saw your light just when she was about to lie down and die. It is the Hand of God," replied his sister solemnly.

"May He help her," said the curate with equal solemnity, and then he at once made ready to go out and face the storm in search of the village doctor, who lived about a mile distant.

But he was young and active and accustomed to rough weather, and many a sturdy tramp he took across the moorland on his visits of charity and benevolence among the scattered hamlets amongst which he lived.

He had a pleasant face, with grave eyes and large, well-formed features. He was one of those who have chosen the better part, and ever looked heavenward. Once his sister, who was much older than himself, and as a rule used a little gentle authority over his actions, remonstrated with him strongly for attending the death-bed of a man dying of smallpox.

"It is dangerous," she said, "and no use; the poor man is unconscious."

"My dear," answered the curate, "no prayers are useless. Who knows that through his dimmed senses he may yet find some comfort in my words?"

And he went, and the man died with his hand in his, and he took no hurt.

Such was his daily life, and the weary wanderer who had dragged her feet to his door had entered the house of a good man whose hopes and aims were not bounded here.

Soon he was ringing at the village doctor's door, and presently the doctor himself appeared to answer his summons.

"Why, Mr. Walton," he exclaimed in surprise, "whoever expected to see you at this time of night? I hope nothing is wrong with Miss Walton?"

"No, Bessie is all right; but an extraordinary thing has happened, doctor. A poor lady has strayed to our house, and she is very ill—this is the note my sister sent you."

"Come in," said the doctor, and then he put on his glasses in the hall, and read the note. "Ha—hum—I'd better go at once. Miss Bessie is not a woman to be alarmed for nothing. I'll just get on my coat and tell my wife I'm going out, and then we can start."

Half an hour later he was standing by Eva's bedside, and when he saw her he at once agreed to remain at the curate's cottage all night.

"She is very ill," he said briefly, in answer to the young clergyman's inquiries.

And she was very ill during the whole night. Everything that could be done for her was done, Miss Walton and the servant of the house both sitting up with her; but in the early dawn Miss Walton roused her brother, who had at length sunk into a restless sleep.

"Jack, you had better get up," she said, "and ride to Peterborough with those telegrams at once, she's so anxious for them to go. I'm sure I can't help crying," continued the kind woman, her eyes filling with tears; "all night she has had one moan: 'Only let me live till Clair comes; only till he comes.' She has repeated that over and over until it just breaks one's heart to hear her."

The curate needed no second bidding. He rose immediately.

"Is she very ill?" he asked anxiously.

"As ill as ill can be," answered his sister. "It's the exposure in the storm has done it, the doctor says. I'm sure, poor soul, I hope she will live until this young lord she calls her husband comes."

Then, when his sister left him, the curate knelt down and prayed for the suffering woman beneath his roof.

"Oh! turn not Thine Ear away from her cry!" he asked. "Let her once more look on her husband's face!"

After this he left the house, carrying Eva's three telegrams with him, also three urgent ones from himself to Lord Kilmore; at the same time enclosing his address.

"The lady is extremely ill!" he wrote. "Do not delay!"

Then he mounted his horse, and started on his early ride; and just as he did so the sun rose, and he lifted his eyes with a strange, solemn, yearning look to the sky.

CHAPTER XLVII.

AN ANSWERED PRAYER.

Kilmore did go to Mr. Onslow's after his interview with the banker, and found the genial vicar at home. But his brow clouded when he heard the young lord's errand.

"I have seen or heard nothing of Temple for months," he said. "The last time I saw him—" and then Mr. Onslow hesitated.

"Well?" said Kilmore impatiently.

"I fear it will be a painful subject, Lord Kilmore; but he was then starting on a tour abroad, as he had reason to believe that—the unfortunate young lady whom, as you know, he married in her early youth, had quitted England."

"And you told him nothing?"

"Nothing; how far I was justified in such a course I cannot tell, but I never even mentioned her name."

"I expected no less from you, Mr. Onslow."

"And you—have you seen her since she left Westwold?"

"I have not," answered Kilmore truthfully, and then after a few more words he went away.

It was evident Mr. Onslow knew nothing, and there was no reason why he should tell him of Eva's letter to himself, or of her mysterious disappearance. He therefore parted with the vicar, and spent a restless, uneasy night at his club.

But the next morning when he was taking breakfast one of Eva's telegrams, and one from the curate, Mr. Walton, was placed in his hands.

With a half cry he sprang to his feet after he had read them. Eva ill! Eva in terrible need! What could it all mean? he asked himself in desperate haste. But there was not a moment to be lost. He sent a telegram at once to Mr. Walton, telling him he would start by the first train for the north, and at ten o'clock he left King's Cross in such a state of miserable anxiety that he felt the suspense was almost more than he could bear.

The train was a fast one, yet to him it seemed to lag on the way. Would they never reach Peterborough? he kept repeating to himself with his pale writhing lips. What could have happened? How could Eva be at this clergyman's?

Again and again he referred to the telegrams. Moorland Cottage, where she was, Mr. Walton's telegram told him, was five miles from Peterborough. How had she got there?

One after another these questions kept thronging through his distracted brain. He was, in truth, half-mad with misery and anxiety, and when at length he did reach Peterborough his nervousness and agitation were so terrible that people turned their heads to look again at his white quivering face.

He hastily engaged a cab, and bade the man drive at his utmost speed, offering him a heavy reward to do so. But the drive was long to the outlying hamlet he was bound for, and Kilmore's anxiety increased each moment.

At last, however, the cabman drew up and pointed with his whip to a pretty cottage with trellis-work in front, and a neat and well-cared for little garden.

"Do you think that can be the house, sir?" he asked.

"Try," answered Kilmore, hoarsely.

The cabman then drove to the little garden gate, and Kilmore sprang from the cab, and as he did so the door of the cottage opened and a young clergyman came down the garden walk and met Kilmore midway.

"Are you Lord Kilmore?" he asked, gravely.

"Yes," gasped Kilmore. "How is—"

"She is very ill, but a little relieved at present. Come in, my sister will speak to you," answered Mr. Walton feelingly.

With faltering footsteps Kilmore then followed the curate into the house, and as they crossed the threshold the feeble wail of a new-born babe fell on their ears.

"I will bring my sister to you," said Mr. Walton, pointing to the sitting-room. "Will you go in there? She will be with you directly."

Kilmore spoke no word; he felt he could not. He stood in the sitting-room cold, pale and trembling, and a few moments later a middle-aged, pleasant-faced lady entered the room and bowed gravely.

"You are Lord Kilmore, my brother tells me," she said, "and have come to see the poor lady upstairs? A little babe was born before its time some hours ago, and the young mother is, we hope, now somewhat better."

"Thank God! Thank God!" murmured Kilmore with his white lips.

"But it is my duty to tell you she is and has been terribly ill," continued Miss Walton sadly. "She arrived here last night on foot in a storm, in a completely exhausted condition. She has given no explanation where she came from; she has only asked to be spared to see you."

And Miss Walton's eyes grew dim and her lips quivered.

"I cannot understand it," faltered Kilmore hoarsely. "I was abroad and she wrote to me to ask me to go to her at Brighton, and I traveled as quickly as possible to her house there, and found she had left the afternoon before, and given no address. How she came here is an absolute mystery to me."

"Perhaps she will explain it to you. But I must warn you that the slightest agitation may be fatal to her. She knows you are here, and wishes to see you at once, but you must be very careful."

"Yes—may I see her now?" asked Kilmore in a voice broken with emotion.

"Yes; if you will follow me I will take you to her," said Miss Walton, and she led the way up the narrow staircase, and then entered a bed-room on the landing after first putting her finger to her lips to indicate that Kilmore should be silent.

"Stay here till I call you in," she whispered as she entered the room, leaving Kilmore outside. But a moment or two later she reappeared and beckoned to Kilmore to go in, who did so as noiselessly as possible.

The doctor moved from the side of the bed as Kilmore entered the room, and also held up a warning finger.

And on the bed Kilmore saw Eva—saw a white wan face, and wide-open dark eyes, which gladdened as she recognized him.

"Clair," she whispered.

He did not speak; he went up to the bed and kneeled down, and took one of her hands and laid it against his face, and his eyes were dim with tears.

"You must not grieve," said Eva, faintly.

"Hush, hush! my darling," he murmured; "I am with you now! We shall never part again!"

A faint smile passed over her wan lips, but here the doctor interfered.

"Now, my dear young lady," he said, approaching the bed where Kilmore still knelt, "you have seen the gentleman, and I can allow no longer interview at present. You must try to sleep; sleep is absolutely necessary, and I have no doubt the gentleman will remain in the house, and you can see him again a little later."

Kilmore rose, bent over the bed, and kissed her face.

"Try to sleep, darling," he whispered; "try to get well for my sake."

"You will stay?" asked Eva wistfully.

"I will never leave you again," answered Kilmore; and as if content with this promise, Eva smiled and let him go.

He went downstairs and found the curate awaiting him in the sitting-room. Kilmore was greatly moved, and held out a trembling hand to Mr. Walton, who took it sympathetically.

"I do not know how to thank you for your kindness— to my wife," he said with quivering lips.

"Then you are married?" asked the curate.

"We were married more than six months ago," answered Kilmore, and he turned away his head and sat down and covered his face with his hand, remembering at this moment their brief happiness and its bitter close.

The curate spoke to him gently and kindly, and the little clock on the mantelpiece went ticking cheerfully on, but Kilmore never raised his head.

Life or death!   He dare scarcely realize what trembled in the balance.   Nearly two hours passed thus, and the doctor came downstairs and addressed Kilmore.

"My lord," he said, "the poor lady upstairs seems most anxious to see you, and is very restless; she has something she wishes you to know, she says, and perhaps it would be well to have this off her mind."

"Is she—any better?" asked Kilmore with faltering lips.

"She has not turned the corner yet," answered the doctor, "but we must hope for the best.   The child, however, seems likely to live."

The child!   Kilmore had never thought of it in his overwhelming anxiety about Eva.

"Is it a boy?" he asked quickly.

"No, a little girl, very small and fragile; but still I think it will live," replied the doctor.

Kilmore sighed deeply, and then followed the doctor to Eva's room, who looked up and smiled as she saw him enter.

"Clair," she said, feebly holding out her hand, "I have something to tell you, and I want to tell you now."

"Yes, darling," he answered, and again he took her hand and laid it against his lips; "but do not excite yourself, you can tell me some other time.   I will stay with you now; but try to sleep."

"I would rather tell it now," answered Eva, with a little plaintive smile passing over her wan features.   "It is about how I came to be here, Clair—after I wrote to you."

"My dearest one!"

"Did you get my letter, Clair?   The letter in which I asked you to return to me?"

"Yes, at Vienna, and I traveled day and night to come to you, Eva.   It made me very happy, but when I reached Brighton I found you gone."

"Yes, I know.   Clair, look on the toilet table.   I asked Miss Walton to put it there, and you will find an envelope. Yes, that is it," she added as Clair rose and took up an envelope from the table.   "Read the two letters in that, Clair, and then you will understand."

The doctor, who had been looking out of the window during this conversation, so as not to interfere with it, now turned round and approached the bed.

· "Let me give you your medicine," he said, addressing

Eva, "and then I will go downstairs and leave you in charge of Lord Kilmore for a little while."

"Thank you," said Eva gently, and she took the medicine, with her eyes all the while fixed on Kilmore, who had opened the envelope, and was looking at one of the letters. Then, as the doctor left the room, he went back to Eva.

"This is my letter to you, Eva—written long ago?" he said.

"Yes, and I only received it two days ago. Mr. Ford kept it back—he wanted me never to see you more for—his own vile ends. Do you understand, Clair? I never saw that letter until it was sent as a lure to me. Now read the one that came in the same envelope, and at the same time."

Then Kilmore read the letter purporting to be written by a Dr. Page, but in reality written by George Temple, and as he did so, a fierce exclamation, which, however, he instantly suppressed, burst from his lips.

"The scoundrel!" he muttered.

"It was Mr. Ford's revenge," continued Eva, "because— because I rejected his dishonorable advances, and told him I loved you still. Clair, when I got that letter, when I thought of you lying injured, I started at once to go to you. I arrived at Peterborough, and found this Dr. Page, as I supposed, waiting for me at the station with a carriage to convey me to you. I never doubted nor suspected—I went with him to the lonely house where he said you were. Who do you think I found? George Temple!"

"What!"

"George Temple. I had been falsely lured there by your letter, for I knew it was your letter, as none other could have written it but my Clair! Do not look so white. I escaped from that lonely house—escaped in the night—and ran here—I should have died rather than stay there. I—I escaped safely, and crept here—to die with you!"

"Oh! no, no, my Eva!" cried Clair, falling on his knees by the bedside and clasping her hand fast in his; "live for me, my darling—no one shall part us now—and both these men shall rue the day they so basely deceived you."

"It was cruel, was it not? I ran all the night—I nearly died on the moor—but God guided me here, and then the babe was born. Clair, if the little one lives, be kind to her —take her to your mother—if I had only had a mother—"

"Hush, hush, Eva! you break my heart!" cried Kilmore,

utterly overcome. "You have told me, dearest—try to sleep now—the doctor said you must be quiet and try to sleep."

"Yes," said Eva faintly, "but stay with me, Clair."

"I will stay; do not be afraid. I will sit here and watch you, dearest."

"Kiss me then, and I will try to sleep," answered Eva. "I am tired—I will try to sleep."

He bent over her and kissed her lips, and then with a smile Eva closed her eyes, and presently Kilmore knew by her breathing she was asleep. By and by the doctor came in noiselessly and looked at her, and then went out again, and still Eva slept on.

The room was quite still; outside the spring day was dying over the moorland, inside Kilmore sat with the hand of the woman he loved in his, with his heart racked with a great anguish, but still Eva slept on.

It was not until the moon rose over the curate's little cottage that she awoke, and raised her dark eyes to her pale, anxious watcher.

"I am quite happy, Clair," she murmured faintly—"quite happy!"

By this time the doctor and Miss Walton were in the room, and they bent over her, and tried to make her take some restorative; but Eva gently shook her head.

"Try for my sake, Eva," prayed Kilmore, and then she tried, and took it from his hand, and presently once more sank into a placid sleep.

They watched her thus hour after hour.

"It is useless to disturb her," the doctor had whispered in Miss Walton's ear, and so they let her slumber on.

Downstairs the curate was on his knees praying for the departing soul; upstairs Kilmore still sat clasping her hand in his, still looking on her fair face, though all hope had died from his.

But just about midnight again Eva awoke and there was a strange new light in her eyes.

"Look after the child," she said; "let me see the child!"

Miss Walton went out and brought in the tiny sleeping babe, and placed it on the bed by her side.

"Take care of it—for my sake, Clair," whispered Eva, looking up in his face; "and—and forgive—me all."

"There is nothing to forgive, my darling—my darling!" he answered, his voice broken by sobs.

Eva did not speak again for a few minutes, and then through the gathering dimness of death she muttered her last words.

"I am quite happy, Clair—quite happy to die with you."

CHAPTER XLVIII.

GOING BACK.

The scene after Eva had drawn her last fluttering breath was inexpressibly painful. For a moment or two Kilmore did not realize it, but the doctor laid his hand on her wrist, and then said feelingly:

"It is all over, my lord; the poor lady is dead."

"No! no," cried Kilmore frantically, and he caught Eva in his arms and raised her to his breast and pillowed her head there, covering her face with kisses. "Eva, my darling, my darling, look at me again, speak to me—only once, Eva—only once!"

But the still lips made no reply, and the bright head nestled no closer.

"It is no use, my lord," said the doctor, shaking his head, while Miss Walton sobbed aloud.

"Come away now, Lord Kilmore," she wept, laying her hand on his arm in her kindly fashion; "you can do the poor darling no good now, and she had her prayer answered. She prayed always in her anguish to look again on your face—and she died with her hand in yours."

"Leave us alone," said Kilmore hoarsely without lifting his head, after a few moments' silence; "leave me with my darling alone."

And Miss Walton, after a sympathetic glance at the doctor, raised the child in her arms, and the two went out and left Kilmore alone with his dead.

And let us leave them alone. There are moments too terrible almost to be borne, and to Kilmore this was one of them. Moments when it is best no human eye should see the dark anguish and passion of our souls; when reason is overwhelmed, and we cry out in our wild grief words which none should hear. Thus Kilmore wailed and wept by the woman he loved, and it seemed ever afterwards to him that her spirit still lingered near.

*   *   *   *   *   *   *   *

Long he mourned there, but as the night wore on, just before the dawn, the curate entered, and he too knelt down by the bed and prayed, and spoke holy words of comfort and peace.

"My brother, she is asleep," he said, laying his hand on Kilmore's. "Hush, do not disturb her with your grief."

And this idea seemed to have some effect on Kilmore. He rose and tottered to a chair, and sat there in silence. But he would not leave her, and when the new day rose he was still watching by his dead.

And during the sad days that followed he scarcely left her. He sat by her when she lay covered with white flowers; when all her old loveliness seemed to come back to her, and she was beautiful as the fair girl he had first wooed by the gurgling Ayre.

The day after her death another came, too, and asked to look on her face. This was George Temple, who arrived in the morning, a rumor having reached him the night before that a lady had taken refuge there during the storm, and was lying desperately ill.

On the night when Eva had fled from his house he had in vain endeavored to break open the door which she had locked, and of which she had taken away the key. It was not until the deaf old woman in the kitchen roused herself, and began thinking of her bed, that he could make anyone hear him for the violence of the storm.

But as the old woman went upstairs she became conscious that some unusual noise was going on behind the sitting-room door. She stopped to listen.

She had been told when Mr. Temple engaged her that his wife had been out of her mind, and that she had to be constantly watched, and kept under lock and key. Temple inside heard her footfall on the stairs, and renewed his shouts and endeavors to break open the door.

"Turn the key!" he screamed at the top of his voice. "I am locked in."

"The key's gone," answered the old woman.

Again Temple cursed and shouted, and shook the door

in his rage, while the tempest roared and howled outside, but his efforts were all in vain.

Then he bade the old woman go for a locksmith to pick the lock, and she screamed back there was none lived near for miles, and she could not go out on such a night.

He told her to look if his wife were in the house, and the old crone did, and brought back the news he expected to hear.

She was gone, and Temple then knew that Eva must be struggling outside with the storm.

The old woman then went downstairs and brought up a wood-chopper from the kitchen, and began hammering with it at the locked door; but she was feeble, and it was hours before she could make any impression. At last she did, and between them the door was broken in about three o'clock in the morning, and Temple at once rushed out into the wild weather outside to seek for Eva.

He came back about dawn perfectly exhausted, having seen nor heard nothing concerning her. All the next day he sought, also in vain, but late at night he heard a rumor that a lady had taken refuge at the curate's cottage across the moor, and early the next morning he started forth to make inquiries.

He asked to see Mr. Walton, and the grave-faced young curate went to the door to speak to him.

"Did a lady come here," he asked in an agitated voice, "the night before last?"

"Yes," answered the curate slowly; he was wondering who this harsh-faced man, dressed in the garb of his cloth, could be.

"Was she young and fair—is she ill?" asked Temple in an agitated voice.

"She is at rest," said the curate solemnly; "she died last night about midnight."

"Died!" echoed Temple, and he staggered back against the door-post as though he had received a sudden blow.

"Yes, a child was born in the morning, and she never rallied. She had been exposed in the storm, and had evidently come from some distance, and this killed her. We telegraphed by her wish for her husband, Lord Kilmore, and he arrived in time. She died in his arms."

Every word of this speech smote like a sharp sword through the listener's ears. He grew ghastly pale; his harsh features were convulsed. All the past rose in grim array before him as he leaned against the curate's doorpost. The school-girl he had urged into a secret marriage; their unhappy wedded days; their parting, and his long absence.

And the last two days.

The curate's words rang in his ears.

"It killed her! I killed her!" thought the stern conscience of the man, stern even to himself.

For some minutes he did not speak. Then he said hoarsely:

"Can I see her?"

"I think not," answered the curate gravely. "Lord Kilmore is with her, for we can scarcely persuade him to leave her side. It is a terribly sad case; all through her illness she only prayed to live until he came; and I thank God," added the curate reverently, "that her prayer was answered."

Again for a brief space Temple was silent; then, still in that hoarse strained voice, he spoke.

"Tell him—Lord Kilmore," he said, "that I—George Temple—have been here."

And then, without another word, he turned away, and went staggering across the moorland, haunted by the footsteps of the woman he had killed.

An hour later the curate told Kilmore of this strange visitor. And Kilmore started and grew ghastly pale as he listened.

"Did he say any more?" he asked with quivering lips.

"Nothing; only that I was to tell you that George Temple had been here. He seemed deeply agitated."

And Kilmore also said nothing more. He gave a heavy sigh, and then with bent head went back to the room where Eva lay in her strange beauty. He stooped down and kissed her cold hand; through his mind passed a new thought, which he acted on the same afternoon, addressing the following letter to his mother:

"Dear Mother—The day after to-morrow I propose to bring to be laid in the family vault at Kilmore all that is left to me of the woman I loved—of the woman whom I married more than six months ago, so that when my time comes my dust may lie near hers.

23

"A little babe was born to us before its time—a frail, feeble child—but one of her last wishes was that you should be a mother to it, and I pray you, for my sake, do not refuse this; and spare me also at this moment of extreme grief any questions on the tragedy of her life and mine.

"Your son,
"Kilmore."

He dispatched this letter, and when during the evening with extreme delicacy the curate approached the subject of Eva's last resting-place, Kilmore answered:

"She shall sleep where I shall sleep. I mean to take her to Kilmore. Will you go with me, Mr. Walton?"

"Most certainly," answered the curate; "anything that I can do to spare you pain, I will do with all my heart."

The sad details were settled after this, and the following day brought a letter from Lady Kilmore:

"My dearest, dearest Son—Bring home the beloved one you have lost, and the little babe she has left to you. I will be a mother to the child, and I pray that God will comfort and help you in this bitter hour of bereavement and sorrow.

"Ever your deeply attached and loving mother,
"J. Kilmore."

"This is my mother's letter," said Kilmore, after he had read these words with dim eyes, handing the letter to the curate, who then also read it.

"I thank God you have such a mother," answered Mr. Walton.

"She is the best, the dearest," said Kilmore, with faltering tongue; "her own heart was broken by my father's death—she will understand."

Her son's letter had indeed been received by Lady Kilmore with the deepest sympathy and agitation. She had not heard from him since his return to England, and had forwarded poor Eva's telegram and Mr. Walton's to his address at Vienna. Therefore the whole thing came on her as a sudden blow.

She called Annette Gower; she held Kilmore's letter in her trembling hand when Annette entered, and her face was very pale, and her eyes full of tears.

"Annette, read this," she said; "it is so sad, so dreadful!"

Then Annette read Kilmore's miserable words, and her face too grew white, but her trembling lips made no sound.

"It must have been that poor girl," continued Lady Kilmore pitifully. "Oh! poor, poor Clair!"

Still Annette did not speak.

"And the little babe, the child. Oh! I am so glad it is coming to me."

"Yes," answered Annette huskily.

Then Lady Kilmore looked at her niece, and saw by her face how deeply she was moved.

"It is terribly sad, my dear," she said gently; "but he is young—he will get over this early blow—and it will bring him home to us."

Again Annette strove to answer "Yes," with her pallid lips, and then left the room, going to her own, and after locking herself in, broke down into a sudden passion of tears.

"Oh! Clair, poor Clair!" she sobbed, and sat there weeping, thinking of her cousin and of the bitter grief which had come to his young life.

In the meanwhile Lady Kilmore was writing to her son, her heart fluttering at the prospect of once more clasping a little child to her breast.

"Poor little babe," she kept repeating to herself; "poor motherless little babe—but motherless no more."

The thought seemed to give her new interest in life. She wrote again the same evening to her son, impressing on him how the greatest care must be taken of the child, and asking what time it would arrive at the Hall, and inquiring about the nurse, and various other questions.

To this letter Kilmore replied that Miss Walton had kindly consented to bring the babe and its nurse to the Hall.

"I will take my lost one straight to her last home," he added, "and Miss Walton's brother, a young clergyman, will accompany me, and has made every necessary arrangement."

Lady Kilmore understood from this letter that Kilmore wished everything to be conducted as quietly and plainly as possible. And this was so. The bitterness of his grief was too great for outward show.

* * * * * * * *

So when the time came they bore her away from the little cottage by the moor, where she had taken refuge in her bitter need, and carried her back to Kilmore, where her young lover had first looked on her fair face.

George Temple, if he knew, made no sign nor claim, and had indeed left Hurstwood House, a saddened, conscience-stricken man.

The funeral was quite a private one, only two mourners—Kilmore and Mr. Walton—following the woman Kilmore had loved to her quiet resting-place.

He knelt down and kissed the coffin before it was lowered to the grave, whispering some words as he did so that no one living heard. Then he rose with bowed head and turned away, feeling that all that had made life dear to him was now hidden from his sight.

Miss Walton, in the meanwhile, had taken the little babe to the Hall, where Lady Kilmore received it with the tenderest affection. It was asleep in her arms when Kilmore, changed and sorrow-stricken, returned from its young mother's grave.

"My dear, my dear!" cried Lady Kilmore when she saw him, starting to her feet, still with the child in her arms, and going up to him she kissed him fondly, and then showed him the face of the little babe.

"It is a dear little thing, Clair," she said, and tears came into her eyes as she spoke; "thank you for bringing her to me."

"It was her wish," answered Kilmore with faltering tongue; and then he bent down and kissed the little hand of his child.

"I accept the sacred charge," said Lady Kilmore with deep emotion; and not another word was spoken between the mother and son on a subject which Lady Kilmore saw his heart was too sore to endure.

* * * * * * * *

A year passed away: a year with its changes and chances: a quiet year at Kilmore Hall, where the young lord lived with clouded brow all through the revolving months. But when the primroses began again to flower in the dells, and the blue bells decked the woods, and the day that Eva died in last year's springtime was past and gone, Kilmore went up to town on an errand that he had unceasingly cherished in his heart, though he had spoken of it to none.

Not even to his friend Walton, to whom he had by this time presented the living at Kilmore, as the old incumbent had died during the hard winter days. Not to his mother, who loved him so well, nor to his cousin, to whom he was yet dearer still.

He kissed the little child before he went away, and Lady Kilmore noticed when he raised his head after he had done so that his face was paler than its wont. He was going to avenge Eva's wrongs, and there was a stern and settled purpose in his heart.

The banker, Mr. Ford, sat in his private sitting-room that spring day, and there was a frown upon his brow. A letter lay on the escritoire before him, written in a handwriting he hated to see. A letter from Madame de Cimbri, demanding money; money that he hated to give.

"She is harpy," he thought disdainfully; and then somehow—by one of those subtle links that bind our thoughts, his mind wandered to another woman—to a woman lying in her grave, and he sighed uneasily, for Mr. Ford loved not painful memories.

He had heard of Eva's death from Mr. Temple, who had gone to him with hard and bitter words, and lately a correspondence had passed between them regarding the transfer of Eva's fortune, of which Temple claimed as much as the law allowed him, and which he meant to devote to a distant mission in Africa.

Altogether the subject was an unpleasant one to the self-indulgent man, and he tried to put it from his mind. He rose, went to the window, and stood there looking out, but still the thought of the beautiful woman he had so greatly admired pursued him.

A rap came to the room door, and he turned round.

"There is a gentleman wishes to see you, sir," said one of the clerks, who now appeared.

"Show him in," answered Mr. Ford. He was glad to have a visitor; he thought it would divert his mind.

A minute later, pale, stern, and dressed in deep mourning, Kilmore entered the room.

The banker visibly started when he saw him. Then he tried to recover himself.

"Lord Kilmore?" he said, half-nervously.

"Yes," answered Kilmore, whose gray eyes were fixed with a strange concentrated look on his face. "You understand, I suppose, why I am here?"

"Indeed I do not."

"I have come to call you to account for a shameful wrong done to a woman lying in her grave—to which you sent her!"

"Nay, Lord Kilmore—"

"Do not deny it," went on Kilmore sternly, and with gathering passion; "you acted like a cur! You suppressed my letter, and then gave it as a lure to the man she hated! But you shall not escape. I give you your choice: will you cross over to France with me to-night, and let us fight to the death, or take from me now what you so well deserve?"

"I protest against such conduct, Lord Kilmore! I will go on no fool's errand—"

"Then take that! and that! and that!" cried Kilmore, producing, as he spoke, a heavy dog-whip, and springing forward and showering as he spoke, with his strong young hands, stinging cuts on the banker's face and shoulders, who was so completely taken by surprise that he scarcely made any efforts to defend himself. "You cur!" went on Kilmore fiercely, "how dare you do what you did—how dare you?"

Mr. Ford screamed for assistance, he tried to get to the bell, he took up a chair, but all was of no avail. Kilmore did not spare him, but ruthlessly plied his whip, and he finally left Mr. Ford smarting, bleeding, swearing, and vowing all sorts of vengeance on his head.

But Mr. Ford never took any proceedings against him. The affair was hushed up; perhaps the banker's conscience told him his punishment was well deserved.

THE END.

www.ingramcontent.com/pod-product-compliance
Lightning Source LLC
Chambersburg PA
CBHW051127120726
47905CB00005B/1454